ALLEN COUNTY PUBLIC LIBRARY
D0409035

THE PELICAN AND AFTER

The Pelican and After

A Novel About Emotional Disturbance

Tom Wallace Lyons

Prescott, Durrell & Company Richmond 1983

The Pelican and After: A Novel About Emotional Disturbance.
 For information address Prescott, Durrell & Company, 2218 East Grace Street, P.O. Box 393, Richmond, VA 23202

ISBN: 0-9609506-0-5

Library of Congress Cataloging in Publication Data

Lyons, Tom Wallace, 1943-
The pelican and after.

I. Title. II. Title: Emotional disturbance.
PS3562.Y4495P4 1983 813'.54 83-3283
ISBN: 0-9609506-0-5

But no one has the right to take a character in a book and say, this is meant for me. All he may say is, I provided the suggestion for this character.

The Summing Up
—Somerset Maugham

Oh wad some power the giftie gie us
To see oursels as others see us!

"To A Louse"
—Robert Burns

This book is dedicated with gratitude and affection to Bruno Bettelheim and to Barbara. It is also dedicated to my mother. And to Elsie Mills who helped make it possible.

PART I

The Kiss

1

Excerpt from Tony's Diary:

Tessa is a girl at my school who is too far gone to talk and could not get along in regular society. This morning it was thought that she had gotten hold of some Sani-Flush while she was out shopping with her group. She had to be rushed to the clinic. Luckily she only had a few blisters around her lips.

Deirdre thought that the feelings in our group about this might have had to do with all the talk between Ronny and Igor. Igor was by his bed switching some dials on his electrical dream world. He was telling Ronny that Dr. V.'s bowel movement contains highly flammable explosives and how he was checking the strength of these explosions with his dials. Ronny likes to get Igor talking this way. I was tempted to ask what would happen if Dr. V. dropped a cigarette in his toilet. (Dr. V. doesn't smoke.)

Then Ronny and Igor started making sounds to imitate the explosions. And Lewis was by his bed where he kept pounding his chest and shouting, "Friends, Romans, Countrymen!" He was imitating some actors from Julius Caesar he had seen in New York,. Then Mickey and Ralph, the two younger boys, started something. Ralph started playing OH WHAT A MULE WAS CHARLEY at a high pitch on the record player, and Mickey started keeping time by beating on the candy box with a drumstick. At that point Deirdre shouted, "Could we have a little quiet!"

It's later now and Deirdre just said, "And I bet you're taking it all down." She is right.

P.S. It will be nice to get out of this place for Christmas vacation next week and go with my family to Mexico City and Acapulco.

4

Another excerpt:

At supper last night Deirdre said she thought a lot of the acting out in the dorm had to do with the Sani-Flush business. She didn't like the fact that there was very little talk about this amongst my group. Just before supper I had to have my temperature taken and talked about the thermometer as a lollypop. At supper Deirdre also connected this with possible thoughts about the Sani-Flush. Why should I care when I hardly know Tessa? Deirdre did not reason like this. She always sissys me by expecting me to be scared about everything. But this time we got into an interesting talk about an Egyptian Pharoe who starved himself to death so he wouldn't eat food that might be poisoned. (People like to poison kings and pharoes.) Deirdre and I interested each other by talking about and analysing that and things like that, natural things. I told her I thought I might be ready for more natural things on the outside. She just shrugged at that. I guess she thinks I still need to be here. I'm afraid I still need this place too.

* * *

"I can see now that you still need the School. A fourteen-year-old boy just does *not* act this way."

"Exactly what am I doing?" Tony Hastings turned to his mother whose youthful face bore an expression of haggard sadness and exasperation reflected in the tired way she spoke.

"So what am I doing?" Tony persisted.

"Can't you keep your voice down! You have the whole restaurant listening to you!" The dark features of Tony's stepfather were distorted by angry annoyance.

Even though the remark had been addressed to Tony, his mother spoke more softly. "You're making a terrible scene, and there's really no reason for you to be upset. Paul said you could have the fish, and. . ."

"Look, I'm not upset, but this guidebook on Acapulco showed a group of people in a boat, and more than one person was allowed to bring back a sailfish. Now what's the matter with the dopes we've hired to take us out? They say you can only bring back one fish per boat. Now why don't we hire a different boat so that. . . ."

"Tony, I said that if I caught the first fish, I would have it turned loose so if you caught one you could bring it back."

Tony looked at his brother, Paul, two years younger than himself, and then at his mother who said, "I really don't see what the scene's about. *Paul* has decided to be a good sport."

Irritated by the emphasis on his brother's name, Tony turned to Paul: "Don't you want to keep a fish if you catch it so that you can have a good memory of our Christmas holiday here?"

"Look, I said you could be the one to keep the fish," Paul countered. And Tony wondered whether Paul was really making a sacrifice or just making it seem so.

"But why don't we hire a different boat so that both of us can keep a fish and. . . ."

"Look, we've already hired a boat. Can't you get it into your head that it's settled!" Tony felt floored by his stepfather's abruptness, but he would not be silenced.

Instead, he said, "That damn guide book sure is badly written."

"Well, it was written to attract tourists." Paul's mocking logic angered Tony. It was by no means the first time Paul had dropped a stinging remark to which there was no comeback. And Tony thought he might have tried to answer his brother in kind had he not been momentarily indebted to him.

The silence made him feel awkward, so he broke it by saying, "You're right, Paul, the guys who wrote that book are just a bunch of filthy cheats."

"Here we go again." Tony's stepfather spoke tonelessly.

"Well, I'm right, aren't I?" Tony shrugged and looked at his stepfather.

"You're always right."

"Look, if a bunch of bastards write a book full of lies, I've got a right to point it out, don't I?"

"Yes, you have a right." The tone of his mother's voice was unacceptingly tired. Tony gnashed his teeth. "Tony," she said slowly, "it was obviously a mistake for Dr. V. to let you go fishing so soon. . . ."

"That old bastard had no business stopping me in the first place." Tony interrupted.

"Oh well, it's hopeless. You won't even listen."

"Damn!" Tony suddenly rose from the table. He had taken all he could. With some difficulty he controlled his voice. "I'm going for a walk," he said and quickly made his way toward the door of the restaurant.

* * *

Tony walked along the beach. Soon you'll be back at the School, he enunciated silently, and then you won't be free to take walks like this. Soon you won't be able to go out alone. He glanced about his tropical surroundings and inhaled deeply. He hoped this would give him a sense of exhilaration, but he felt nothing. It's not at all what you hoped it would be, is it, he asked himself. But you don't want to leave this place. You feel that you just might be able to find happiness if you stayed here long enough, but you also feel that you're probably just as likely to find it at the School. It's a depressing fact, isn't it, that one place seems to be just as good as another for happiness. Of course you don't know this for a fact since happiness is something you've never found.

Why do you feel cold now on this tropical evening, the kind you've dreamed about for so long? It's not that you're cold, it's that you need something. And Tony remembered a dark brunette with hair done up in a chignon. She had worn a white dress, and he had caught a glimpse of her in one of the plush, dimly lit hotel bars. A smile on rouged lips hinted a tenderness which made Tony say, "Hold me!" Now he felt his arms go round her shoulders—

"Damn! I want to live!" Tony snatched up a shell and dashed it upon the soft sand. "I wanta live! I wanta live! I wanta live!" He was only partially successful in working himself to a fury and, for a few seconds, canceling out the emptiness he felt in his existence.

He began to feel uneasy, and he walked faster. *Oh well, it's hopeless.* His mother's ominous words had not left his mind. He wondered what meaning they really carried.

. . . . "Well, he was making a scene in front of everybody." Tony imagined he was back in Chicago at the School and that his mother was talking to Dr. Vorlichten or, as everybody called him, Dr. V. Then he stopped imagining because he found he was not exactly sure what there was to tell.

Just what've you done? he asked himself. You wanted to play a game with nature in which the fish either would or would not bite your hook. If it bit, you would have a trophy; if it didn't bite, tough luck. Then these bastards who run the boat say that not only do you play against nature, but also you play against the chance that Paul might catch the first fish. You fight against playing by their rules because you want to play by your own. Exactly what's so wrong with that? . . . . "Ah, so Tony vants to run zhe vorld." Tony imagined that his mother had told Dr. V. whatever she had to tell. "Is zat vhat you vant, Tony?" Tony estimated that Dr. V. was only a shade taller than himself, and he felt a moment's fear as he contemplated the man's small eyes which stared right into his own through the powerful lenses of horn-rimmed glasses. "Vell, Tony?" Dr. V. was waiting.

Tony looked straight back into Dr. V's eyes and calmly answered, "If you want to take it that way, I can't stop you." Then, to himself on the beach: "You know you'd never talk that way to Dr. V. And you'd never look back at him like that either. At least you wouldn't unless you were really desperate. Then perhaps you might if you had to have a showdown."

"Tony! I varn you zat I von't take zhe smart answer!" Tony was once again imagining himself at the School.

"You'll take the answer I give you." He maintained his calm. But he winced, almost instinctively, as one of Dr. V.'s hands shot out, smacked one cheek and returned with a sharp backhand across the other. Though Dr. V. was rather stout and somewhat flabby, he was terribly dexterous. A few seconds passed in a maddening silence. "Vell, Tony, vhere do ve stand now?" Dr. V. asked calmly.

"You had no right to hit me!" Tony's whisper would have been plainly audible to anyone on the beach. Dr. V. stared at him without saying anything. He often stared while he thought. And Tony imagined that he was able to look right back into Dr. V.'s eyes without wavering.

"All right, Mrs. Hastings," Dr. V. turned to his mother, "maybe you should just take your vacations vis your husband and your younger son. You can leave Tony vis us."

"Dr. V."

"Yes, Tony?"

"You might as well see about getting me a train ticket. I'm only going to stay here long enough to get my stuff packed, and then I'll leave. I've been told I have that prerogative."

"You vill stay here vis us!"

Tony felt a surge of raging defiance. "You said I didn't have to stay here!" he screamed—his scream only a whisper—and he choked because his throat had gone dry. After that he blinked furiously to keep back imaginary tears. "The police are gonna be damn busy," he continued, "because nothing but force is gonna keep me in this damn place." Then he turned defiantly upon his mother. "I'm getting out of here, and I'm gonna fish the way I want and as much as I want. I'll fish all day if I want. And nobody's gonna lock me up anymore just because they don't like my habits or the things I say. I've done nothing against the law, and I've got a right to get outta here!"

Would Dr. V. keep him if he wanted to go? Tony wondered. "If you don't like it here, you can leave," Deirdre, his chief counselor, had told him it seemed a thousand times. "You can lead a horse to zhe vater, but you can't make him drink," Dr. V. had said on one occasion. And more than once Dr. V. had pointed out that the doors to the School were always open. No, they probably wouldn't keep him if he really insisted on getting out.

Sure you can leave if you want, Tony told himself. They have no way to make you obey those damn girl counselors if they can't tell you to leave when you're not willing to do what you're told. After all, you're fourteen going on fifteen, and you're five feet six and five-eighths of an inch tall. It's not as though those girls can take you by the hand like a baby. If only they couldn't hold it over you that you can leave any time you want. If only you could get out of there! But you can't, damn it. You can't. You know you need the damn place. That's why they can hold the knife at your throat by telling you to leave if you don't like to put up with all their silly restrictions.

It was a Sunday evening, and in exactly one week he would be back at the School. He would probably be lying in bed thinking about this past Christmas vacation and the year to come. He would be lying in bed while Paul would be at the local movie theater in Glenville, Illinois, some three hundred miles south of Chicago. Paul, his younger brother, would be up and dressed at a movie while he was in bed in pajamas! Damned injustice! "Can you ever stop hating it?" Tony asked himself and balked at the proposition.

If it hadn't been for Paul, there would have been no argument about fishing arrangements, and his mother would not have told him he still needed the School. There would have been no argument had Paul not been born, had he not existed. And now it was necessary to thank Paul for giving up his opportunity to bring back a fish. "Kill him!" Tony seethed.

"I'm going to mash you!" Tony imagined that he and Paul were sitting in the restaurant and that Paul had hit him once too often.

Paul had lately made a habit of imitating his facial expressions, and yesterday Paul had reached across the table and landed a light tap on his cheek. "I'm going to do that," he had said, "until you learn to sit with your mouth closed."

"If you don't like the way I sit," Tony had reached into his shirt pocket, "I'll give you half the money Mother gave me for our lunch, and then I'll go eat somewhere else." But that morning his mother had happened to hand Paul the lunch money.

"You'll stay right here," Paul was grinning. "You see, even if you are pretty wacky company, I don't want to eat alone."

The summer before, Paul had started talking about the "wacky school" until he had been told to stop. To any bystander, perhaps even to their parents, "wacky company" might have seemed an innocent enough insult, but not to Tony.

"Paul," he had said, his voice shaking slightly, "if you touch me again, I'll hit you even though we're in a restaurant." He had meant it.

"If we had a fight in here, it wouldn't be particularly bad for me, but it might be for you." Tony was sure Paul's warning had been a subtle allusion to the possibility that at the School they would not approve of his getting into a fight.

"Don't worry," Tony had warned, "if I beat you up because you hit me, nobody at the School is going to be too upset about it." He was only half sure he was right.

At that point Paul had given him the money with the parting injunction, "I've had all I can take of *your* type for one day."

"I'm going to mash you!" Tony quickened his pace on the beach, and his left arm moved as he imagined that he rose from his chair and landed a smashing blow in his brother's face. Seconds later he and his brother had come together. Tony's hands closed, and his arms swung rhythmically as he pretended to pump his fists into his brother's stomach. Paul doubled over and sank down on his hands and knees. Now, with all his strength, Tony let him have it openhanded on his arched back. Hurting, Paul straightened out. Tony took two handfuls of his brother's hair, and with them he pushed his face into the floor. He pushed hard, feeling the dull thud of Paul's head hitting repeatedly on the floor. "Kill him! Kill him . . . . Kill him!" he breathed the words, and they seemed to have a sweet taste. Then suddenly Tony's pace slackened and his arms ceased their rhythmic movement. "Granny," he said, "I'm sorry."

He now imagined himself on the farm in Kentucky—in a house which overlooked the Ohio River from its isolated perch on top of a hill. It had to be a summer scene because Granny was lying in her bed on the closed porch. Her filmy pink nightgown lay slack over a small, weightless body. Its folds fluttered slightly in the breeze created by an air conditioner which kept the porch very cool. Granny found summer heat unbearable. She was sad now, and Tony felt her eyes on him, loving eyes which gazed out of an emaciated face. "I'm sorry, Granny, but it seems that I just can't help the way I feel." Tony looked at her tenderly.

"I know," she answered quietly. "Brothers always fight. But you're the older. So I think you should try a little harder to be friendly. Then I'm sure Paul will do the same. You know he's really very fond of you."

"But . . . ." Tony thought a moment and suddenly found he had nothing to say. His grandmother's words, ". . . . he's really very fond of you," had momentarily checked his anger. He wondered whether Granny was right. She had said this to him on many occasions when he and Paul had quarreled. However, Tony felt Paul's actions hardly bore her out.

After yesterday's lunch, Tony did not want to be friendly with his brother. Perhaps Granny would sympathize with his feelings if he could tell her what Paul had said. But her mind was no longer geared to the present; she was always talking about the past. Some effort on the part of them both would be necessary were he to spell out the malicious implications behind "wacky company." And, even if all could be explained, it would not be a good idea. Granny would worry, and that would be bad for her because she was so weak.

"Go on," Tony imagined that she was still talking to him, "try for Granny's sake." Her voice was very soft, and Tony felt the pleading encouragement in her fragile face.

"I'll try," he whispered, and he bent over and kissed her on the cheek near her lips. And, as she returned his kiss, he saw the tiny perpendicular wrinkles form on either side of the middle of her upper lip. This caused a sudden quickening of his heart, and he stood still on the sand.

You really care how she feels, don't you, he said to himself. She's the only person in the world you would have made such a commitment to. Of course, as a commitment, it really wasn't much. It didn't stop you from defending yourself from Paul, and it didn't force you to do anything except be a bit nice when Paul was decent. Was that a real commitment to make to Granny, then? Was that what Granny wanted? What did she actually want you to do? What *can* you do? You can't go into that with her in detail. You can't be a Christ and turn the other cheek. It would simply be impossible for you to live that way, and Granny would hardly expect that of you. Tony concluded that his imagined promise, "I'll try," was the best that he could have honestly made.

How long was Granny going to live? Tony had always thought she was weak, but now she was weaker than she had ever been. How would he feel when she died? "Come give Granny one last kiss." Tony imagined that Granny's whisper was soft and calm as she lay in the large four-poster bed in her bedroom upstairs. She was extending her arms to him for the last time.

Tony resumed his slow walk down the deserted beach. He remembered the first time he had imagined this scene one evening four years before while playing jacks on the dormitory floor. Deirdre had sat down beside him and asked why he looked so sad. With some difficulty, he had pretended to be perplexed by her question. Sensing that he did not want to talk, Deirdre let him be. A few minutes later he had gotten up, taken his jacks and put them on his bed. Then, with a forced smile, he had quietly walked across the dorm and into the bathroom where he locked himself in one of the two toilet stalls. There he tried to control his jerked breathing while he let the tears slowly squeeze out from beneath his eyelids. The bathroom was empty, and he hoped nobody would hear him. Or, if he were heard, he hoped that his breathing would be attributed to other functions. "You can't bear it if she dies. You can't bear it, you can't bear it, you can't bear it." The words formed at the back of his mouth in swift accompaniment to the slow movement of his tears. "She means so much to you." He made himself silently articulate the words in order to stop his crying. "If you hadn't been able to go out to the farm with her before you came here, life would probably have been a lot more miserable for you."

Now Tony had to admit that he was left cold by the once so painful scene of Granny's dying. Why? The guilt-plaguing question incessantly tormented him. Suddenly he hummed an old melody while the words sang themselves in his mind: "We will sing one song for my old Kentucky home, for my old Kentucky home far away." Why did you hum that, he asked himself. Are you trying to feel sentimental or something? That song, he shook his head slowly, dramatically. It's in the very roots of your life, isn't it? It's been with you longer than your memory. That beautiful song goes back to the days before you went to the School when you were eight. You were so close to her then when you went out to the farm with her, and she told you all those stories, and you played records together, and there were the dogs, and—and what else did you do? Tony was disappointed to realize that he could not remember many other things, but in a single evening only so much could be done. You were so close to her then, he repeated.

Tony glanced over toward the docks lined with fishing yachts which varied greatly in size and price for a day's fishing excursion. He strolled out on one of the piers and came unexpectedly upon two gigantic sharks; hulking cadavers, of fearsome aspect, even with their cartilaginous frames sloppily sprawled over hard wood. He poked one of them and felt tantalizingly uncomfortable. It was intriguing to be so close to danger, yet so safe from it.

This feeling of paradox made Tony recall an eventful evening, some two years past, when he had first come to realize the turning point in his feeling about his grandmother. That evening Tony's group was watching a television program on the Amazon jungles in which there were authentic films on inter-tribal warfare. "I didn't know they were going to have this," Deirdre said when the films were shown. Tony waited until the program was over to avoid any danger of having it turned off. Then he and a couple of other boys expressed to Deirdre their extreme satisfaction with all they had seen.

But he was by no means satisfied that night as he lay in bed. He was engaged in a titanic struggle to come to terms with an idea: savage violence in the hidden depths of a distant jungle. That was a way of life. There was also his way—a civilized environment whose special conditions spelled absolute protection. For a long time he had intellectually known that the civilized and savage life existed in one world. But he had always felt that the world in which he lived was in no way part of that other. It was as though violence belonged to another sphere of existence as did the exciting events of distant history about which he often read. It was the idea of those two worlds, existing in one, with which he was trying to come to terms.

Tony yearned for the adventure in that other world and, because he had to be chief in every thing he cared about, he suddenly felt it necessary to become an authority on life in the Amazon. He was in a state of feverish excitement.

"Now, if you could read two books about that stuff each week for a year," he spoke silently while he squinted in concentration, "two books each week," he repeated, "what would you have? You would have quite an extensive knowledge on the subject. So how much money could you get each year to buy the books? You could probably get about thirty books for a library of your own." But thirty wasn't enough, so Tony quickly refigured. "No, you could probably come by about seventy," he concluded without really feeling sure he could come by thirty. All this had gone through his mind several times with very little variation while he checked and rechecked new possibilities. But none were forthcoming, so he only derived the ambiguous pleasure of feverish anticipation.

"And meanwhile," he continued, "you could toughen up for the jungles by starting yourself on a new program of push-ups and chin-ups, and. . . ."

And, for seemingly no reason, it flashed through his mind that he would not cry if Granny died. What! Life without Granny bearable! Tony imagined that Deirdre had just informed him that Dr. V. had received a call reporting Granny's sudden death. And, lying in bed, he tried to visualize his life as it would be without her. Not only was it bearable, it was hardly changed! You don't love her, Tony silently damned himself, and he called over to Deirdre who was lying stretched out on several chairs beside the group table.

"What's the matter, Tony?" Deirdre asked as she sat up.

"I want a chance to talk to you tomorrow."

"All right, but you should get some sleep, young man."

"I guess you're right." Tony violated his habit of disagreeing on such matters because he wanted her to leave him alone. Deirdre lay down again, and Tony recommenced his thinking.

Why the sudden change? He had never before felt he could bear to part from Granny. But as he thought the matter over, he realized he had a lot less to do with her now than before entering the School. Why did you stop going out to the farm as often as you used to, he asked himself, thinking back to visits home to Kentucky before his stepfather had moved the family to Glenville. You just didn't enjoy doing things on the farm so much. Also, Granny was so weak that you always had to be careful, and you were happier staying in town with Mother and playing with other kids.

But you still enjoy doing things with Granny, even though it's not the way it used to be, Tony told himself as he turned over in his bed. And he wondered why the revelation of his flown love had flashed into his mind five minutes before while he was thinking about the Amazon jungles.

Even now, as he ambled off the pier, Tony was not sure he could answer that question. He simply realized that Granny in no way figured in his ambitions about the Amazons or in his ambitions concerning a lot of other things. He knew that long ago the Old Kentucky Home had, in a sense, slipped far away . . . .

. . . . "So you felt she meant your whole life to you and you suddenly found that you could live without her. What's the problem?" Deirdre had asked Tony after that turbulent night.

"But do you love a person if you don't feel you'll miss her if she dies?" Tony had asked in his turn, and Deirdre had shrugged. . . . "There's nothing that would make Granny sadder than to think her death would make you unable to go on living a good life," his mother had once told him. He remembered that this had added a note of frightened desperation to his melancholy anticipations because he did not know what he would do were Granny to actually die. . . .

You're more considerate of Granny than you were before, since you don't have the saintly love to boost your damn conscience, he told himself, scuffing at the sand. And perhaps the best would be never to have that saintly love return. *"You don't love Granny."* He countered these thoughts with an indictment that seared into his conscience, but not very deeply because his conscience had hardened.

You feel pretty low about yourself, Tony decided unemotionally. The anxiety he had caused his mother, his feeling that he did not deserve such a lavish Christmas trip, his inability to love, had all come together in his mind.

Traffic sounds caused Tony to glance up at several cars racing along the nearby road. An old thought hit him, a thought often brought on by speeding cars: you could be dead in seconds. The ease to end everything, to plunge head first into the fender of a speeding car! In seconds no more life, and better never to have lived at all. The familiar impulse carried a familiar guilt. You're not suicidal, Tony quickly tried to reassure himself.

Not that this particular evening had been so bad; others had been worse. But Tony had dreamed of a happy vacation only to find that Mexico provided no more happiness than any other environment. So why continue to live? Why stay at the School? "Of course the School's already helped you a lot," Tony conceded silently, "but you're still no better off alive than dead, and once you were able to love." Now, not only was he unable to love his grandmother, he also felt her frailty so intensely that he was every once in a while visited by an urge to try to smash it, to strike it out of existence. This frightened him, and he wanted desperately not to think about it.

Another car rushed by. "Just stand here in the sand," Tony commanded himself against an impulse which he felt might force him to take a step toward the highway. "Oh help, you're not suicidal, are you?" He became panicky. "Hell, you're gonna stay alive for the rest of your life just in case things get better." It was a decision he had made on previous occasions. But he was not secure in his argument.

In order to get his mind off suicide, Tony remembered that Paul was the cause of his evening's troubles, and he imagined himself, clad in princely garb, standing on the rampart of some ancient castle. Beyond, his view of the surrounding domain was blocked by Paul who stood, arms crossed and feet apart, his regal colors flapping in the wind. *Kill him!* Tony's hand tightened into a fist, and he raised his arm, pretending to clutch a dagger. He drew his arm back and struck with all his strength, burying the knife hilt-deep between his brother's shoulder blades.

"Who are you killing now?" Tony had not heard Paul come up behind him. "It couldn't be your dear brother by any chance, could it?" Paul gave Tony an annoyingly boisterous slap on the back.

"What's this about killing?" Tony faked perplexity.

"This!" And Paul gnashed his teeth as he thrust his arm backward in animated imitation. Tony had no answer. "Well, anyway," Paul continued, "I want to talk to you about something."

"What?"

"Why do you care so much about bringing back a fish?" Paul asked.

"Wouldn't you like to bring one back?"

"I suppose I'd sort of like to, but I don't actually care that much."

"Well, thanks a lot for the fish," Tony shrugged. He had finally gotten Paul to say what he wanted to hear. Now Paul couldn't claim any serious debt for having made a great sacrifice.

"Of course, there's a price for everything," Paul grinned. "That'll cost you one dollar." He held out his hand.

"Here you go." Tony pulled his wallet from his pocket and took out a bill. This was too good to be true. From here on, Paul had absolutely no claim upon him.

"No, I was joking, I don't want any money. I just wondered if you were willing to pay up."

"C'mon, take it," Tony urged, "take it."

"No, that's all right," Paul shook his head. "You don't owe me anything." Tony put his money away. "But I'm curious why you want to bring back a fish so much. Just what would you do with it?"

"If I get a sailfish, I'll cut its sword off and mount it on a plaque. If I catch a shark, I'll take out several of its teeth."

"Would they let you have those things at the School?"

"Dr. V. said I could have a stuffed fish on my wall, but he just might think it scary if I only put up parts of the fish. I don't know. I'd like to have the whole fish stuffed, but it costs too damn much."

"Look, you say you want to go deep sea fishing because you think you'll find it exciting to fight with a big fish on your line. What's so wrong if you just catch the fish and let him go?"

"It's like this," Tony thought a moment. "I just don't feel the sport would be complete if I let the fish go. I like to have something to show for what I do. I mean, if I have a big fight with a fish, I feel it all goes for nothing if I catch him and then just throw him away. Also, during those dull, cold winters at the School, it's nice to have something to look at that reminds you of better times."

They walked briefly in silence, then started back in the other direction. "Paul," Tony's voice became softer, "do you think Mother was right in what she said about my needing the School?"

"I don't know," Paul said thoughtfully. "Most boys your age just don't ask their parents to spend thirty dollars to get another boat. But then that doesn't make it bad, does it?"

"I never said we should hire another boat. I said we should try to find a different boat that offered decent fishing terms, but Dad must have thought it was too late or something."

"Remember before supper you said that if all boats were like ours, then we should hire two boats."

"Oh, that's right," Tony nodded. He had never thought either suggestion would be taken seriously. But heated discussion of both alternatives had finally impelled his mother to say to Paul, "I know that the fish is less important to you than it is to Tony. If you catch the first one, do you think you could please have it turned loose so that if Tony catches one he can bring it back?" Tony had thought all along that the argument would culminate in this request from his mother. And better that than to personally beg a favor from Paul! But best of all would have been to hire a different boat and avoid all questions of a favor.

"Of course," Paul was saying, "I can't see anything terribly wrong in asking Mother to spend more money on an extra fishing boat. I think we can afford it."

Tony had often wondered whether he benefited by having Paul in the family. That Paul could see eye to eye with him on this matter was an extremely positive point in his favor.

"You're absolutely right," Tony agreed. "Mother tells us that she and Dad spent nearly fifteen hundred on this vacation, and then she gets upset because I ask her to spend thirty or forty dollars on a boat. And, *I mean,* I only ask her. I don't twist her arm. Does that mean I should be institutionalized?"

"No, it doesn't," Paul shook his head, "but there's one thing I want to know. Do you still think you're emotionally disturbed?"

"Well, if you asked Dr. V., I'm almost sure he'd say absolutely yes, even though he said that I would never go to an insane asylum. But I don't think in terms of being disturbed or not disturbed. I guess I'm disturbed, but either way, I feel there are certain things about myself which I need to improve. And I can't think of a better setting than the School for this improvement. So I go there. It's as simple as that."

2

As they walked together, Tony gloried in the one-to-one affinity that had arisen between himself and his brother as a result of their conversation. Thoughts raced through his mind, and he recalled an entry in his diary made at the end of his seven-week summer visit. On September eleventh he had written:

> *Tonight is my last night at home for awhile. Tomorrow I go back to the School. I go there because I am not as happy as I could be. The School offers me the opportunity to help myself to a better life in this world. I have been going there for six years. If I hadn't gone there or to some place like that I would have had to have been withdrawn from the public. Now with the exception of school work and emotions I am as well off as any other boy my age.*

Tony remembered that he had stopped at this point to turn on a T.V. western and raid the refrigerator, two freedoms he did not enjoy at the School. Afterwards he had continued:

> *I will be sad to leave my mother when I go back. Also, some of the ways the School is run, I despise. Then in other ways I like it very much, and I know I must go back there.*
>
> *If I was always as happy as I am when Dad sings and I play my accordion and Mother watches and talks to us I would be so much better off than I am. This I have never done very much before tonight. This was a suggestion of Mother's. So we went and routed him out of a Stag magazine which Mother calls trash. However, Dad is a college professor of Political Science, and he found some good literature in it. So I come further in proving that these men's magazines are good.*

I guess my main reason for going back to the School is solitude. Unlike tonight, it usually follows me everywhere. It follows me when I play in the basement gym with Paul and in the dormitory where I am so solitary at the School. I guess that is mainly why I need to go back to the School.

Solitude was something Tony wrote about freely. But his guilt over love was too sensitive for commitment to paper or for discussion outside the School. This guilt had been evoked, prior to Acapulco, in early December when his grandmother suffered a stroke. At first it looked as if the trip to Acapulco had to be canceled. But an astonishingly rapid recovery had caused his grandmother to insist that the plans not be altered.

After hearing about the stroke from Dr. V., Tony had spent the week hating himself for feeling he did not care about his grandmother's fate. His dislike for himself and the School fed on one another. In his memory, dislike for both were epitomized by an experience one Saturday afternoon in the gym, a get-together of the three boys' and three girls' dormitory groups, about forty children in all.

It was hot, perhaps because the gym was overheated, perhaps because the game was dragging, or was it the feeling, real or imagined, that seemed to emanate from the din of young male and female voices which sounded unpleasantly loud and discordant on this particular afternoon?

Tony heard one counselor say to another, "Look, this really isn't going too well. We'd better stop it soon."

"You're right," the other counselor agreed, "It's around that time of the year." Tony knew she was alluding to the impending Christmas visits, a time when the staff was always on the lookout for feelings. Attitudes of staff members often rubbed off on their charges so that assumed feelings, as well as real ones, became material for a tense atmosphere.

"Hey, c'mon, let's spread this circle out!" "Yeah! Move it back!" "C'mon, let's give the people inside more room!" Several annoyed voices rose above the din, and all those on the outside took two or more steps backward. Then the tension lessened as people found they had more space.

Almost all those who had started inside the circle had had their shins or calves hit by the dodge ball and had been compelled by the rules of the game to join the crowd on the outside. Ronny, Ted and a few girls were the only ones who still remained within. Tony watched as Ronny and Ted skipped around the circle and crossed it intermittently, shaking hands whenever they met. Since the game consisted of nearly forty boys and girls, varying greatly in age and athletic ability, Ronny and Ted had to play this way to make the game exciting.

Tony stepped inside the circle to retrieve the dodge ball which rolled languidly in his direction. "Hey Tony!" Ronny shouted gleefully as he made his way toward Tony at a slow galloping skip, his feet and arms flailing in a deliberately ridiculous manner. Tony felt a twitch of irritation at the ludicrous movement of Ronny's wiry body, a body just a little shorter than Tony's, but more compactly proportioned, and endowed with a coordination Tony envied.

"Wanta talk about something?" Ronny scratched through his short, closely cropped brown hair as he danced up and down about ten feet in front of Tony. Tony shrugged in an effort to appear disgustedly bored. He was angered by the teasing smile that lit up Ronny's boyish face, by what he thought was going to be his inability to get Ronny with the ball. For the moment Tony found his dorm-mate repulsive and wanted him to sense this.

Tony's hands tightened around the orange ball. As he bent forward, squinting his concentration on Ronny's feet, he suddenly sent the ball rolling at a surprise angle. His attempt was way off mark. Ronny raised his foot leisurely and watched the ball roll past him into the circle. Then he turned to Tony and knitted his brow. "What were you aiming at?" he asked.

"Scoot!" Tony gestured angrily, despising himself for lack of sportsmanship, and Ronny made off in another direction. When defeated, Tony could only take so much bragging, and Ronny was forever bragging about any number of things, often about the horses he had galloped as a boy in Arizona. He talked endlessly about horses, the West, his dream of becoming a cowboy, a dream for which he always dressed in cowboy jeans, jacket, and shirt. This and his constant word barrage seemed to constitute a rugged shell of resistance to any staff effort to help him become part of the School, to relieve him of his loneliness.

Tony watched Ronny as he dodged still another ball rolled at him. "Hey Ronny!" Ronny turned to Ted who had come skipping up behind him, and they clasped hands. Tony reckoned that Ronny must have clasped Ted's hand some fifteen times since the two had started in the circle. It seemed to Tony that Ted was the only one in the School toward whom Ronny showed any real desire for friendship, a desire which he could only express through a handshake.

Ted lived in the oldest boy's group, the Blacksmiths, down the hall from the Eagles where Tony and Ronny lived. He was tall, and he had the good looks of a youthful cowboy hero. There was a certain open manliness about him, and Tony felt Ronny was drawn to it just as he was. He felt Ted was one of the only boys at the School who could be truly warm, whose warmth could penetrate the loneliness of others. Like Ronny, Ted also loved the West. He loved to watch TV westerns and dress up in cowboy clothes. And Ronny had often said he liked the way Ted was able to stand up to Dr. V. and yell at him, which he often did. Tony knew that neither he nor Ronny had this courage, and he shared Ronny's admiration.

"Haaay!" Shouts erupted around the circle. Ted had been surprised by a hit on the calf. "Hey, Ted!" Ronny yelled ecstatically, then, "Excuse me, excuse me, excuse me, excuse me," as he skipped through a cluster of girls.

"Oh stop it, Ronny." A couple of girls were annoyed.

"Ted!" Ronny clasped Ted's hand. Ted smiled in playful sheepishness at Ronny as they shook up and down. "Congratulations, old boy! They finally got you!" Ronny slapped Ted on the shoulder. Congratulations was a joke, a form of camaraderie, another means by which the older boys made the game more fun.

"Hey, that's enough," one of the counselors protested the hand-pumping, and Ronny and Ted let go of each other. You were supposed to keep your hands to yourself at the school. Such demonstrations were often considered phony and nasty by the counselors.

"O.K., Ronny. This one's for *you!*" Ted snatched up the dodge ball and Ronny jumped back. Several of the girls crowded behind Ronny to be near Ted whom they all liked. There was a moment's quiet while Ted held onto the ball. Tony could hardly see the two boys because the girls blocked his vision. But he heard the ball hit the floor and saw several people jump; then a shocked cry from Ted's side of the circle.

Tony watched as people broke from the circle and began to crowd around the area where Ronny stood. "Please stand back!" a counselor shouted, and the crowd cleared allowing Tony to see Alice, her shoulders hunched forward, while she pressed both her hands over her right eye. "Here, try to move your hands," her counselor spoke soothingly while Ronny and Ted watched; Ted with an air of concern, and Ronny with an expression Tony was unable to decipher.

"Ronny bumped Alice with his elbow." The story quickly got around, and Tony's first thought was that Ronny almost certainly had it coming from Dr. V. who did not know the meaning of the word "accident." If Ronny had not hit Alice deliberately, he hit her because of feelings he had not faced. Either that, or Dr. V. might say something about his behavior to explain what had happened.

Tony felt a slight momentary exultation that Ronny's athletic capers had finally landed him in trouble. But even while carrying an element of horror movie excitement, anticipating Dr. V. was not very pleasant, and Tony found himself wishing nothing had happened. He resented the School where an accident was never an accident. Also, it was too bad that whatever Ronny had tried to achieve with Ted had come to a bitter end, even if the shallow handshaking were merely a vain effort.

"All right, will the Eagles please go over with Laura." Irma's loud voice interrupted Tony's thoughts. One of the senior counselors, Irma had planned the dodge ball game, and now she wanted each group to leave separately to avoid congestion on the way to the dormitory building which was right across from the school building which housed the gym.

"Tony, we're going now," Laura tapped him on the shoulder.

"O.K.," Tony nodded as he looked into Laura's blue eyes. Laura had a lot of blonde hair, some strands of which draped over a full bosom packaged in the softness of a blue sweater. At twenty-four, Laura just missed being beautiful due to a slightly rough sculpting around her mouth. This had deceived Tony who had not thought of her as particularly attractive at first. Then he had found himself wanting her to come over to his bed and take him into her arms, something that had not happened——yet.

All the Eagles were quiet as they descended the school building steps. Laura's face was serious; the group was anxious. In all likelihood, Dr. V. would make his rounds shortly after three, in about fifteen or twenty minutes.

Out in the side yard, the cold air made Tony's bowels churn uneasily. He walked his middle and index fingers over the bricks on a part of the wall that jutted from the school builidng. He pretended his fingers were the legs of a man being marched to execution deep in the recesses of a large prison somewhere in a small alien country. Surrounding this country, there was another country to which the man belonged but from which he was now totally isolated.

For a moment, Tony thought about the Midway, a stretch of grass and trees that ran in front of the school. From where he stood, he could not see the Midway, but out there on the Midway were people who knew nothing about Dr. V.'s anger, who had never heard about hidden feelings and accidents that weren't accidents. Tony envied these people, but he also felt that they missed out on something basic to life though he was unable to say just what. Nor did he try. He simply allowed himself to be momentarily impressed by the paradox of two worlds, so close yet so different.

Up in the dormitory, Tony sat on his bed and watched Ronny and Laura. Ronny was sitting on his bed, and Laura had pulled a chair over from the group table.

"Have you tried to think about why you did that?" she asked softly.

"Yes," he answered. "I jumped up and my elbow went out. I didn't *see* her."

"Why didn't you?"

"I don't know, I couldn't. I just didn't see her. She was out of range of my eyes."

"You have perfectly fine eyes, Ronny. You could have seen her if you'd wanted to." Tony wished Laura would throw her arms around Ronny rather than show what he felt to be a prescribed concern. After all, whatever Dr. V. was going to do, Laura was probably ready to stand by and watch. After eight months at the school, Laura seemed to know the counselor line too well, a line Deirdre probably wouldn't have used.

The Eagles waited in different ways. Lewis had his bed next to Tony's. He was a short, extremely thin, quiet boy. Now he waited by occupying himself with the effort to be quiet. A cup of water had been on his dresser: he had quietly taken it into the bathroom, emptied it, washed it, then refilled it. But time hung ominously, and he became self-conscious just sitting on his bed. So he repeated his activity, making sure to get rid of any germ that might have remained in his cup.

Harry sat on his bed, which was on the other side of the dresser he and Lewis shared. He was reading a sports magazine, but his serious expression was hardly on a par with the seriousness of his literature. Curly haired, Harry was thin and tall for his age. Tony wished that he and Harry could be alone together so he could confide in him about the way he felt. There would be nothing wrong with communicating the same to Dr. V. or any other staff member, but Harry would be more likely to sympathize. As equals, living at the School, they often talked about life there with a mutual concern and curiosity they could not have shared with any of the staff.

Igor was sitting small, hunched up on his bed. He was turning a knob on a cardboard electrical device attached to the wall above his pillow. His bed lay just beyond Harry's, but parallel to the wall. All around his area, he had constructed a complexity of cardboard, tape, and wire, which composed his electrical dream world.

Ronny's bed extended from the wall just beyond the dresser which he shared with Tony. The dresser was at the foot of Tony's bed. Mickey and Ralph, who were some six years younger than the other boys, had their beds across the dormitory on the other side of the group table. They played quietly with their soldiers, only partially tuned in to what was going on. They were usually noisier.

Tony decided to relieve himself. He was not sure what was going to happen, but he wanted to be comfortable. Also, he could not be absolutely certain that Dr. V.'s anger would not, for some reason, be turned on him. Dr. V. had not made him piss in his pants since he was eleven, but he did not feel tough enough to consider the possibility part of his past. Better be prepared.

As he walked down the dormitory past Harry's bed, Harry looked up. For an instant their locked eyes communicated.

"Tony," Igor whispered to him as he came out of the bathroom.

"What?" Tony asked very softly.

"Do you s-s-see this switch?" he asked in a whispered stutter. He was turning a tiny knob on a box attached to his bed. Tony thought it was either a radio or some kind of switchboard. It had a lot of knobs on it. Then, even more softly, Igor asked, "Do you know what it's for?"

"No." Tony's voice was barely audible.

Igor became a bit more bold. "Th-this switch," he said, "is to turn down the voltage power in that robot so that when he comes in here, Ronny won't get into too much trouble."

"Look Igor," Tony said sympathetically, "if he were really a robot, you would have turned him off long ago."

"No, y-you can't do that," Igor smiled. "That would ruin his batteries, and we don't want to kill him." Tony enjoyed a small laugh. Igor usually bored him. But he was delighted with an imagination that tried to reduce Dr. V. to a mere product of mechanics. He also knew Igor had just tried to express an awakening interest in the troubles faced by one of his group.

At that moment Deirdre came in on three o'clock duty. For snacks she had a large bunch of green grapes on a paper plate. "Hi," she smiled at Tony, and he was momentarily relieved from his tension by her warmth. All the boys went over to the table since they were supposed to get together and plan a group activity. But the older boys were in no mood to plan.

Grapes were an excellent snack. Time would tick away while you picked one grape after another. Laura drew Deirdre aside, and they whispered for a few seconds. Tony thought he heard Laura say something about Dr. V. Deirdre nodded. Then Laura looked at her watch and hurried out. Tony wondered whether there was a reason for her hurry, or whether she wanted to avoid what might happen.

He heard the door by the stairs open and slowly click shut. Dr. V. spoke to someone, his voice sounding grim. Afterward there was the slow, rhythmic squeak of well-kept shoes drawing near the dormitory.

Deirdre patted Igor on the back, and Dr. V. appeared in the doorway. He wore an ominous expression, something between disgust and anger. Tony watched Dr. V. advance toward Ronny whose chair was on the side of the table that faced the door. Dr. V. stopped and stood over Ronny without saying anything. He seemed thoughtful. "One thousand, two thousand, three thousand. . . ." Tony counted silently, hoping not to reach five thousand, hoping to set a numerical limit to unbearable tension.

"Since ven do ve hit people in zhe eye?" The question that broke the silence was soft and menacing.

"I didn't *mean* to," Ronny's voice was a subdued, protesting whine. Tony winced as Dr. V's left hand caught Ronny on one side of the face, then returned with a swift backhand across the other. SMACK! SMACK! SMACK! SMACK! SMACK! Dr. V.'s left hand moved quickly, methodically back and forth across Ronny's face. Then: SMACK! SMACK! SMACK! SMACK! with both hands on the back of the head as Ronny ducked forward. Dr. V. grabbed a small tuft of his hair and shook. And with both hands he caught Ronny by the shirt and hauled him halfway out of his chair.

"Vhy did you hit her in zhe eye!"

Tony realised that he felt helplessly, humbly subdued before Dr. V.'s thundering anger.

"It was an accident," Ronny's voice was distinctly tearful.

Dr. V. stepped back; he watched Ronny while the latter sniffled once or twice. Suddenly he extended his hands, palms up, in grandiose gesticulation. "I didn't mean to! It vas an accident!" he shrilled mockingly. This made him appear less frightening. In his more normal, but still menacing voice, he asked, "Does zat make it feel any better?" Ronny shook his head. "All right, zhen, remember zat ven you have accidents, I vill have zem also. Is zat clear?"

"Yes," Ronny nodded.

"Vell, it had better be. So vhat are you doing?" Dr. V. turned to look at Igor who had crept over to his bed. Tony wondered whether Igor had gone to turn the switch down some more.

"H-h-h-h-h," Igor stuttered, "h-, I was," and then very softly, "just fixing something."

"Vell, come over to zhe table. I vant to talk to you." Igor obeyed.

"Ronny," Dr. V. went on, "Just vhat ver you doing before you hit Alice? I hear zat you vent to shake hands vis somebody."

"I went to shake hands with Ted and congratulate him because he had just been gotten out with the ball."

"You vill not make friends doing zat!"

"Uh uh," Ronny shook his head in agreement.

"All you ever do is antagonize! You know zat, don't you?" Ronny's head moved in a barely perceptible nod. "So vhy do you congratulate?"

"Oh, a lot of us do it." Ronny's voice was very small.

"Is zis only Ronny?" Dr. V. looked around the group. Nobody spoke, and his eyes lighted on Tony.

"It's done by a lot of us older boys," Tony said softly, including himself. Now he felt silly because the handshaking was rather ridiculous even though it had not seemed so in the gym. He wanted to tell Dr. V. that congratulations and other forms of foolery were only necessary because the staff made the older boys play with the girls and the youngsters, but he did not dare.

"Ve are going to *stop* zis congratulating!" Then Dr. V. turned to Deirdre. "You see, Deir-de-ra," her name was heavily syllabified with the Austrian accent, "zhese boys have nossing better to do zan to dream up vays to be nasty to vone anozer." He looked at her for a few moments, then turned to Ronny. "Ronny," his voice was no longer angry, "if you vould stop constantly trying to show off to people, and to constantly yak at zem, you vould probably not find yourself in so much trouble. And you, Igor," he turned again to Igor, "vhat ver you fixing?"

"Oh, something," Igor said in an undertone.

"Vhy don't you fix yourself!" Then more calmly, "You can fix machines all your life in zhe nuthouse. But you don't have all your life to fix yourself here. And you too, Ronny. Do you sink zhey vill tolerate you out zhere zhe vay you act?" Dr. V. gestured toward the Midway outside the School. Ronny shrugged unhappily. "Vell, I can tell you zhey von't." Tony wondered whether or not Dr. V. was serious about Ronny. "And you, young man"—Tony found himself in the line of fire—"you have made progress. You von't go to zhe nuthouse." As if I didn't know, Tony said to himself. "But you know somesing, my dear boy?" Dr. V. paused. "You may never have a real friend in zhe vorld. Now tell me, is zhere anyone you really like?"

Tony thought a moment. Finally he said, "Deirdre sometimes," but he was not sure he was being entirely truthful.

"Deirdre sometimes," Dr. V. repeated. "Oh, zat vill get you far."

Now, as he walked along the beach with his brother, Tony felt he had gotten far indeed—away from Dr. V., the School, the fear, but only temporarily.

"Tony," Paul broke into his brother's revery, "who do you love most in the world?"

"Oh, let's not get into that," Tony shrugged, brushing off the question.

"Why not? It's not such a difficult question."

"We can talk later. I want to go into town."

"Don't you think it's kind of late?"

"No, it's only 11:30."

"Well, I think I'd better go on back to get a dose of shut-eye, and I'm supposed to tell you, orders from Mommy-quarters: you're supposed to be in by twelve-thirty. So don't fight World War II out here all night. And," Paul suddenly grinned, "don't go looking for what I think you're looking for without a rubber."

"Don't worry," Tony grinned back. Then he started up one of the small side streets. Paul had guessed what was on his mind. He had heard from a boy in the hotel that there were plenty of whores in Acapulco, but so far Tony was not sure he'd recognize opportunity in the flesh. His main problem, he thought, was that he did not know where to look for them. He had only an inkling that perhaps they could be found on the shabby side of town and that sometimes they were in bars.

Last summer, a friend named Eddy had told him this when they were spending a day together on the farm at Granny's. Eddy had claimed to know this from a pal who had also told him that in New York there was this shady district where a lot of nutty people hung out. The area featured a big building with a large Christmas tree all done up in red lights during the Christmas season. Above the entrance, a small sign with red neon letters -H-O-A-R-H-O-U-S-E- advertised its purpose.

"Well, I don't doubt the Christmas tree, but the spelling's another matter," his stepfather had smiled as he referred Tony to a dictionary.

"But isn't there more than one way to spell a single word?" Tony had suggested, knowing the futility of his hope, never having really believed Eddy's story.

"Oh, don't you wish it," his stepfather had laughed, "but you're not going to New York any time soon, so why grind the ax?"

"Well, where *can* you find whores?"

"I'm afraid I can't answer that one."

"Are there places where they can be found?"

"Well, in the gangster movies, they're often huddled up at a bar, and I think I may have seen one or two patrolling street corners, but don't you go panting up to every woman you see waiting for a bus."

"I wonder . . ."

"Don't push it. You've got plenty of time." Tony's mother of course agreed with her husband, to whom she had been married for three years and, in Tony's mind, the whores had become as distant as gangster movie-land, the Amazon jungles, and his future manhood.

Tony emerged from the side street into a larger one where there were some bars. Tony loved coke. He realized he was thirsty. He stepped into a dingy bar and seated himself at a small wooden table. After his first drink, he ordered another. He sipped it slowly and his mind wandered back to the School.

He imagined it was after the holidays and that he was talking to Laura. "Can you give me one good reason why we can't see *West Side Story?*" he asked.

"Yes, it's a rather disturbing movie. Now, is there any reason why you keep looking in the direction of your bed?"

Tony looked back at Laura—at her breasts on which he wanted to lay his head. Perhaps, though he hoped not, he also found something attractive about the overly cautious care that she and other women at the School bestowed upon him. "Oh, my eyes just sort of wander every now and then to that fish on my wall," he answered.

"Why?"

"Well, whenever I get a bit digusted with this School's silly restrictions, I just like to look over there and remind myself that at least during part of the year I'm not treated like a baby."

Of course that's not the real reason you want the fish. It's not to show them you're a man, Tony argued a question that had plagued him. He tried to imagine how he would feel about mounting a fish or part of one were he not going back to the School. He wondered if the whole affair would not suddenly lose its significance. But hadn't he told Paul the truth when he said he would lose satisfaction with the sport of fighting and landing a fish if he did not keep at least some small part of it?

"One only proves zat he is a boy if he sinks he can look like a man because he lands a big fish," Dr. V. had told him shortly before the holidays. Tony had agreed emphatically. He had nothing against trying to prove himself, but even women could land a fish in one of the tourist boats.

Again he imagined he was talking to Laura. "How did you catch that fish?" she asked him while a couple of the other boys listened. "From what I've heard," her face wore an expression of counselor-type concern, "it must have been a pretty frightening experience."

"It wasn't particularly frightening," Tony shook his head. "You see, I saw this big fish floating around in the water. So I found this small log on the shore," .... and now he imagined that, club in hand, he was walking waist deep in the steamy slime of swamp water. A dangerously large fish was floating just an inch or two beneath the surface. Suddenly it flexed its tail and made straight for him. Tony raised his club, aimed very carefully, and landed a smashing blow on its head. This was the kind of adventure he had dreamed about—to fight a savage fish on his own daring terms, not to struggle with a sailfish from the protection of a tourist boat. Were he really to prove himself, that was how he would go about it. He imagined that the fish rolled over and that he brought his club down viciously again and again on its upturned body. And suddenly there was a slight stirring in his loins. That bothered him. Wasn't it unhealthy? Well, he could talk about it back at the School. "You do need that damn School," he told himself. Meanwhile, there was nothing wrong with wanting to go fishing. It certainly had other attractions.

Tony was discontented. It was twelve, and his mother wanted him in the hotel at twelve-thirty. But the evening just could not end now. If only something more would happen—something to satisfy, to at least momentarily supplant the thousand conflicts, guilt-ridden worries, and unconsummated aspirations upon whose tempestuous crests he had ridden since the beginning of supper.

In the bar he had kept a constant lookout for whores, but he did not think he had seen any. He had already paid for his cokes, so he stepped out onto the corner of the fairly crowded street and carefully scanned the surrounding area. And then he thought he saw her, just a block away, mysteriously shaded in the lamplit shadows of a practically deserted intersection. She paced slowly back and forth, her head cocked at an expectant angle and, in her right hand, she held a folded umbrella balanced against her shoulder. He thought she looked his way and smiled. Perhaps she was waiting for a bus or a taxi, but it wouldn't hurt to walk quietly past her. Now Tony could feel his heart pounding, and he was shaking slightly. There was a nervous sensation in his stomach. As he approached her, he noted that her body curves were well outlined beneath a tight black skirt and a grey sweater. Her black hair fell down around a somewhat haggard face with too much makeup. A purse swung from her left shoulder.

Tony thought this was just the way a whore should look even though he had seen women very much like her who led a more protected life. Of course you can't go with her even if she is a whore because Dr. V. says you can't come back to the School if you behave like a delinquent, Tony reminded himself. Besides, you don't have a rubber, and you don't want to produce a baby. Anyway, she's not too good-looking.

She smiled at him. He nodded, smiled, then suffered the depressed sinking expectation as she let him walk past her. "Ssssst!" she suddenly hissed, and Tony felt the tip of her umbrella between his shoulder blades. "Adonde vas?" her voice rasped.

"What?" Tony turned around startled. He did not know a word of Spanish.

"For the fucking?" she grabbed his arm, pulling him close.

"Just take this, Honey." Tony bent forward and touched her partly open mouth with his closed lips; then freed himself and made off in the direction of his hotel.

"So what, you kissed a whore," he whispered roughly as he made his way through the streets. "Big man kissed a whore," he mocked himself joyfully, amazed that he could have even thought about suicide in a world so full of possibility. And his body quivered in tremulous ecstasy as he breathed hard through his teeth. He had never thought he would actually see a whore in Acapulco although he had imagined it many times. Oh, this did put him beyond the School. Some of his dorm mates didn't even know what whores were. Of course you kissed her because it was supposed to feel nice even though it didn't, he reminded himself. "Look, I know what women can be like," he imagined he was talking suavely to Laura.

Then he tried to tell himself he was no different from what he had been two hours before. But he felt he had transcended his protective world into that other world of adventure inhabited by those savages he had seen on television. Savages! Whores! Sharks!

They were all part of this other world, or so he felt. But he knew he was still the Tony he had always been. "Give up that fish," he pleaded with himself. "Let Paul have the fish if he catches it first. Be a sport!" And he visualized himself as a smiling, handsomely masculine hero with a laughing contempt for all those securities both emotional and physical to which the ordinary man had to cling. It was as though he were suddenly freed from everything. Freed from Paul whose caustic comments could do nothing to him now, and freed from all guilt including that which questioned his capacity for love. Now he would be his own god in his own world living by his own laws. Then for a moment he thought he could be something that was perhaps even better: a man who could simply be happy without keeping his fish.

He did not know why, but in this bliss that had come over him, Tony felt sure he was at least momentarily endowed with a strange freedom. Yes, he felt like a man as he walked along the winding street and looked at his tall shadow looming in front of him on the lighted pavement. "Give up that fish!" he pleaded. But something was holding him back. He tried desperately to cling to his new manhood which seemed just within reach. Then suddenly he stopped. You are what you are, he told himself. You've got to keep your fish even if Paul catches one first. He knew that he had to because, in his heart, the only thing he felt capable of changing was the arrangement made at supper. He was not the smiling hero. He was Tony Hastings.

3

"You can't count on fisherman's luck," Tony shrugged off his and Paul's failure to catch anything.

"Well, I think it's a good sign you can take it that way," his mother smiled.

"I never minded taking chances against nature. But with Paul. . . ." Another argument to a draw, this one before it had a chance to get under way.

An hour later, Tony, his mother, and Paul were riding donkeys single file behind a guide who was leading them to an inland lake for a boat ride. This was the result of Mrs. Hastings' effort to arrange a tour into "some real jungle," or at least to "truly primitive country."

When in very broken English, along with the aid of Mrs. Hastings' pidgin Spanish, the guide conveyed his non-association with any travel bureau, Tony happily said, "Then you're an adventurer! Just what we need."

A surprised but cheerful smile spread across the guide's plump face. "Si, si," he nodded vaguely. And Tony noted with pleasure that they were beyond sight and sound of cars, highways, and telegraph poles. He surveyed the surrounding countryside which abounded with low tropical plant life plus a liberal scattering of palm and other trees. The only signs of human life were occasional mud-thatched roof huts amid small patches of corn. It was four-thirty, and the sun was pleasingly warm rather than hot. It was very peaceful.

During six hours of sleep, Tony had kept his nocturnal episode to himself. Better, he thought, not to spill it out like an excited little boy. Then at breakfast he had managed to attach it as trivial confirmation to a couple of general statements about prostitution. Since then it had not left his mother's mind, and Tony and Paul had talked about it all day. Only the fishing had occasionally distracted them.

"Hey Tony," a mischievous smile spread across Paul's face, "any idea what you might do tonight? Remember, it's your last night here."

"Well, if it wasn't for that bald bastard back at the School, I'd have quite a night in store for me."

"What does he care if you fuck or not?"

"Paul," Mrs. Hastings said, "would you please not use that word when I'm present."

"But Mother, don't you think Tony's old enough to fuck if he wants to?"

"No," their mother gave a sigh of forbearance, "I don't think Tony's at all ready to go to bed with a woman."

"Why not?" Tony challenged. "What don't I know? You've been briefing me about prophylactics for the past two years so I won't have any bad accidents before I get married. Now, do you think I'm going to let all that knowledge lie around useless until I'm twenty-one, or something?"

"I think that might be a good idea," his mother said calmly. "Now tell me, what exactly did Dr. V. say when he talked to you about this?"

"Oh, he has the same ideas you have about my not being ready and all that. But it seems to me his main point was that if I wanted to be a delinquent, I needn't bother coming back to the School. And I asked him if he meant by delinquent that sex was against the law for unmarried guys, and he said that usually the people who did it were a lot older than me. Then I told him about some boys my age outside the School who I thought had done it. And he asked me why I thought they'd done it, and I told him it was because they'd told me they had." Tony paused to breathe, then continued, "So he said," Tony imitated Dr. V.'s accent, "vell, can't you tell zem zat you've done it too?"

Mrs. Hastings gave a short laugh. "That's excellent advice," she said.

"I like the last part, too," Tony agreed. For a few moments they rode on in the silence of the tropical afternoon.

Then his mother asked, "Didn't you talk to Deirdre about this?"

"Oh yes," Tony nodded. "She was really stupid about the whole thing."

"What do you mean?"

"Well, I was telling her that I didn't like the way she came into the bathroom when I was taking a bath. So she started asking me all this stuff about my feelings and what bothered me as though my desire for privacy was rather strange for a guy my age. So I told her I never wanted to undress in front of a women unless I was going to bed with her. Then, for a little while, Deirdre and I just talked about this with her just repeating that I wasn't ready for a woman yet."

"Well," his mother said, "she's also right."

"But there's something fishy," Paul said.

"What?" his mother asked.

"Well, you know, if there are laws against people going to bed together, aren't there also laws against boys undressing in front of girls after the boys reach a certain age?"

Mrs. Hastings shook her head. "I can assure you," she said, "that Dr. V. is acting well within the law. He says in his books that he wants the child to become more relaxed about his body, and. . . ."

"I'm not a child," Tony interrupted hotly.

"I know you're not, but. . . ." But Tony did not want to listen to her repeat the kind of explanations she had given on previous occasions, so he interrupted her again by bringing up a subject that had run through his mind lately.

"You know," he said, "it mightn't be delinquent for boys my age to go to bed with women down here in Mexico since that whore seemed to think I was old enough."

"Tony," his mother cut in, "you really *are* unsophisticated if you think that woman was bending over backwards to obey the law."

"Well, I've just had the feeling that it's not against the law even without her."

"Tony," Paul said thoughtfully, "I'm afraid that your idea about not being a delinquent wouldn't help you anyway."

"Why not?"

"Well, look, if you kill somebody in Mexico, do you think they'll let you loose in Chicago?"

"No, but there's a difference," Tony protested.

"That's certainly true," his mother agreed. "But Tony, for a boy who wants so much to go to bed with a woman, you're awfully modest."

"Well, when two people get undressed together to go to bed, the degradation is at least mutual," he said with a trace of bitterness.

"Tony," his mother gasped, "is that what sex is to you—an act of degradation?"

"Well, in a partial way, yes," Tony answered. "I mean that's by no means all of it."

"Certainly *not.*"

Tony had a feeling his mother was worried. "Well, you know," he went on, "Dr. V. told me and some of the other boys that sex would mean something totally different to us when we were older. He may be right, but I certainly don't agree with him that a boy's too big for his britches because he wants to go after it at my age."

"El lago!" The guide pointed ahead. It looked as though the country was half submerged in smooth, dark water. "Bonito, no?"

"Everything looks so wild!" Tony said excitedly.

The guide turned his donkey onto a side path which seemed to lead more directly toward the lake. In the distance, half hidden by a couple of corn patches, there stood a small thatched-roof house. Several naked boys could be seen running around. The guide said a few words to Mrs. Hastings who turned and told Tony and Paul that the man who owned the house was the one who was going to take them in his boat.

A mischievous smile broke unevenly across the guide's placid face. "Muy prolifico, no?" he said with his eyes on Mrs. Hastings.

She turned to Tony and Paul. "The guide says that the man who owns the house is very prolific. Did you see all the children?"

"What does prolific mean?" Paul asked.

"It means he has a lot of children."

"He really ought to use birth control," Tony said softly.

"Yes," his mother nodded, "but let's not go into that again. You know they don't use it down here. And perhaps the less said about it now, the better. You don't know who might understand you."

Moments later they drew up to the house which lay only about thirty yards from the lake. The boys had been called inside, and within could be heard the scolding whispers of a woman. Then the boys, aged somewhere between two and seven, reappeared in jeans. Behind them, in the doorway, there appeared a hefty woman with long pigtails. She had a shawl draped over her back in which a sleeping baby was wrapped. She wore a white blouse, and a long, colorful skirt hung down to her bare ankles and brown feet.

"You see, she's dressed the boys for company," Mrs. Hastings smiled.

"Yes," Tony forced himself to give a tiny laugh. Though he did not know why, his mother's observation about the boys embarrassed him slightly.

Then the woman looked inside the dark house. "Chico," she whispered, "Chico."

A barefoot man, still squeezing sleep out of his eyes, appeared beside her. He wore dirty brown cotton trousers, a faded green shirt, and a worn, short-brimmed hat. He looked at the guide, and they spoke rapidly together for a couple of minutes.

"Mother," Tony whispered, "is that man's name Chico?"

"I think so," his mother answered.

"But doesn't that mean boy?"

"Shh! Don't say that here." Then quietly, "It does." But Chico seemed to be an ironical name for this man. Even while he yawned sleepily, there was something in the solid sculpturing of his face, in the trim neatness of his greying mustache, that aroused in Tony an intuitive respect.

After speaking to Chico, the guide turned and spoke to Mrs. Hastings. Then again he spoke to Chico, and finally it was agreed that Chico would take them on a two-hour boat ride for an American peso—one dollar. Tony was sure, however, that his mother would pay more at the end. The agreement reached, they all dismounted.

They gave their donkeys to Chico who took them off to pasture in a small grassy area nearby. While Chico was gone, Mrs. Hastings smiled at the children who stared back at her in goggle-eyed curiosity. One of them finally broke and smiled, and the others soon followed suit. Mrs. Hastings also smiled at the woman, and Tony knew she hoped the woman would show her the baby sleeping in her shawl. But the woman only nodded and smiled shyly. Tony did not see how his mother could be so fond of the children. He thought the donkeys were far more lovable and wondered if there weren't something wrong with that.

He looked at his mother who remained absorbed in the children. She was trying to make conversation. Then two of the boys took her hands and led her in no particular direction. Paul followed.

Tony glanced down at a small, green lizard that was making its way in his direction. He wondered whether or not it was dangerous and thought perhaps he should crush it. But he knew such an act would worry his mother because she would think he was trying to gratify his desire to kill things. She had first seen signs of this in his early childhood, and maybe she was right. He wondered what it would be like to feel the small reptilian body break beneath the pressure of his foot. Also, it was always fascinating to bring about the passage from conceivable life in this world to unknown death.

Tony knew the word *peligroso* meant dangerous because he had seen it on a movie billboard the day before and had asked his stepfather for a translation. He looked at the guide who was leaning comfortably against a small tree. His head nodding, the guide stared tranquilly at his pot belly. Tony touched his arm, and he looked up and smiled. "Peligroso?" Tony asked, eyeing the lizard which had now drawn near them.

"Nah," the guide deprecated wearily, "no es peligroso." The guide gazed at the lizard for a second and then pressed it into the soft mud with the sole of his shoe. After that he settled back against the tree and lost himself in sleepy oblivion.

Tony stared at the lizard partially embedded in the mud. The guide had not even put his weight on it. Its outward form was not noticeably altered, and every now and then it flexed its tail just a little bit. It was not yet dead. Tony wondered whether it would be able to crawl away if it were freed from the mud in which it was sealed.

No, most probably it would never move again but would lie there and die after several hours of agony. But since it was going to die, since it was not going to offend whatever it offended by innocent crawling, there was no reason for the guide to extinguish its life. The proposition of a lizard's suffering would be totally out of place in his mind. Cut off from what could have been a meaningful life on its terms, the lizard might as well retch in reptilian agony, for obviously nothing about the reptile could ever affect the guide.

Probably the lizard was unable to move because a good number of its vital organs were irreparably damaged. Probably it would never be able to excrete properly. Probably its breathing was terribly hampered. Perhaps even its reproductive faculties had been totally destroyed. Its mouth opened spasmodically to emit a faintly reddish fluid, and Tony wondered how much pain a reptile could actually feel. Perhaps it was crying in reptilian fashion. Tony imagined the pitifully agonized screams of a child coming from its open mouth while tears dropped profusely from its reptilian eyes.

Something much deeper than disgust simmered unpleasantly in his stomach so that he had to tighten the muscles there. It boiled over into the more private recesses of his being where he could no longer fortify himself by muscular hardening. Ravishingly it surged into his lions. Then ever so ticklishly it invaded his penis so that he had to thrust his left hand into his pocket in order to hide a partial erection. The sensation was exquisite, but Tony was glad when it quickly faded. Pervert, he damned himself silently.

When Tony had mastered himself, he immediately stooped down, scooping the lizard from the mud, and tossed it onto some hard ground and stamped its head to a pulp with the heel of his shoe. He could not let an animal suffer. The guide saw what he did and regarded him with an expression of total contempt. Or absolute amusement? Tony could not tell which. Then the guide broke into a loud, incredulous laugh which bewildered Tony.

Suddenly the guide came toward Tony, threw an arm over his

shoulder and hugged him tightly. Tony forced himself to smile while he tried tactfully to break loose. But the man's hold was strong, and he thought he felt the man's lips rubbing just behind his right ear. However, he wasn't sure, and just when he was about to do something violent, though he did not know what, the guide set him free.

Chico had come back from pasturing the donkeys, and Paul and his mother were returning with the children. Tony noticed a look of alarm on his mother's face; he was almost sure Chico's return had caused the guide to release him. It seemed that during his absence something decent had begun to decay.

"Tony, what did you add to your list of victims?" Paul asked as they made their way toward the boat.

"What were you killing?" his mother asked, a troubled expression on her face. When he told her what he had done and why he had done it, he knew that she was deeply pained, deeply disgusted. "Listen," she said, and her voice was not normal. "I don't want either of you boys to get off alone with that guide. Is that clear?"

"Why not?" Tony asked. "What would he do?"

"Shh, not where they can hear us. I'll explain it in the hotel."

It was a beautiful boat ride. For an hour and a half the boat cruised among plant-tangled islets. Birds in flight were darkly etched against an amber sunset. Tony sat facing Chico. His mother and Paul were behind him, and the guide slouched drowsily in the back of the boat.

They talked occasionally. While the guide's head nodded, Mrs. Hastings got Chico to agree to accompany them and the guide back to the stable. Tony whispered that there was no need for this, that he could handle that pot-bellied guide, and if things really got bad, Paul could give him a hand. But he was not sure the guide would be so easy to handle. His mother whispered back that Chico's presence would simply make her "feel better," that she did not really think the guide would do anything. And deep down Tony was glad of this arrangement, because Chico's calm presence protected him from the sick loathing the guide had aroused.

Chico told them little bits about his life. He had never consulted a doctor about his health which had always been excellent. Twice, however, he had called a doctor to his house: once when a child had been stung by a scorpion; another time for a child bitten by a rattlesnake.

Suddenly he motioned for everyone to be quiet. "Mi amigo," his voice slurred cheerfully as he slowly poled his boat toward a large pelican perched on the crest of a limb that protruded diagonally out of the water. The pelican was almost beautiful, striking its regal pose of ridiculous yet dignified majesty. A smile of delighted wonder spread across Mrs. Hastings' face. Tony felt himself charged by a shock of wistful ecstasy. Slowly the pelican's wings began to move, and it rose into the air and landed a second later on the prow of the boat beside Chico. Chico picked up two small fish which had lain half submerged in a puddle on the bottom of his boat, and he dropped these into the pelican's large pouch. The pelican tossed its head and gulped as the fish passed through its long throat. Then its wings hunched a couple of times and whipped the air rapidly so that cool water sprayed both boat and passengers. Finally, it stood motionless and cocked its head. For a split instant the large bird and Tony locked eyes.

Had he dared, Tony would have reached out for the bird as its wings once again began to move, slowly lifting it into the air. Tony did not understand what had happened. But it was something beautiful. Thrilling! He watched the pelican become a dark speck against the deepening twilight, and felt that he had a new friend; that in this fleeting contact he had transcended everything mean, even his reaction to the guide's cruelty to the lizard.

A short while later Chico was telling them he had no real hope for any improvements in his living conditions during his lifetime. He said that Mexico needed more brave men like Pancho Villa and Zapata to lead the people in new revolutions.

"But he's man enough to do it," Tony protested to his mother.

"How?" Paul asked cynically.

"Well, if he wanted to, he could kill us here and get our money to buy weapons. Or he could get his men together and systematically disarm the police, take a few wealthy tourists for ransom, and take over Acapulco. Then he would be on his way." Tony had become inspired.

"Do you have to suggest these things out here?" his mother whispered.

Tony felt embarrassed. His gaffe ill became a true adventurer. "But I thought he didn't speak English," he whispered back to his mother.

"Shh, you never know," his mother admonished. Tony let the matter drop. He looked up at Chico. Suddenly Chico picked up his machete. He had his eyes fixed intently on Mrs. Hastings. Before anyone had time to think, his arm snaked out and the blade flashed dangerously near her head. A scorpion fell from her hair to the floor of the boat. His blade flashed again, killing the scorpion.

The twilight thickened. It was time to turn back, and Tony realized that his trip and all his hopes for adventure had come to an end.

4

Tony sipped a coke in the dim light of the hotel bar. He looked across the bar at the long, wide mirror and tried to adjust his tie. Now that it was his last night in Acapulco, he wished he had more time. He knew how he wanted to live now: always in a suit, always in softly carpeted bars, always in an exciting world.

Better this luxury in the tropics, the lure to adventure, than the fear of Dr. V. who wouldn't let an accident be an accident. Better to live free than under indictment for not being able to love. With last night's erotic promise beckoning, Tony wanted to become a delinquent, to give up worry about love and solitude, the problems he felt made him need the School.

Then he saw Marta reflected in the bar mirror. She was a tall, finely shaped, beautiful woman with long black hair. Earlier that evening Tony had met her through his mother who had made her acquaintance while he was fishing. Marta claimed to be taking a vacation from her family, and Tony had the impression that his mother thought Marta was promiscuous.

"Oh, look who I find." Marta thrilled Tony with her accent as she approached the bar.

"Sit down." He tried to sound suave. She sat on a stool beside him and smiled warmly. Tony could not help smiling back, almost laughing, but his heart was pounding. His mother had said she thought Marta was living a rather lonely life, but he seriously questioned this.

"What do you say?" Marta was still smiling.

"Oh, I have nothing to say," Tony answered and suddenly felt embarrassed.

She smiled at him for another unbearable moment. Then he remembered. "Can I buy you a drink?"

"No," she laughed adoringly, "I buy my own drink. Who taught you to be such a gentlemen?"

"Gentlemen aren't the only type of men that'll buy you a drink." Before he finished, Tony wished he'd said nothing.

Marta burst out laughing. "Where do you learn such things? If you were my boy, I would spank you for that."

"If I was your boy, I'd have an incurable Oedipus complex."

Marta laughed, taking in Tony's quip.

"A tequila," she said to the barman, then to Tony, "Just how do you know this kind of thing?"

"Oh, Mother and Dad are always talking about the old doc from Vienna. I suppose you know who I mean."

"I have an idea," Marta spoke after a moment's amused contemplation of Tony. "Why don't you tell me your life story? *You* ought to have a very interesting life to tell about."

The School flashed before Tony's mind. He did not want Marta to know about it. "I have a better idea," he answered. "*You* tell me about *your* life. I'll bet some interesting things have happened to you."

"O.K., I tell you about my life," Marta said. "I don't know. It seems when you tell about your life, you should only tell about something that is very important to you. It is the important thing that is really a part of you, no?"

"Absolutely," Tony nodded.

"Well, when I was a girl of about twenty-one, I was walking to my house one day, and I saw this handsome man standing near a truck. I said to myself, this is the man I am going to marry. It was just like that; I had fallen in love, you know."

"Sure," Tony nodded encouragingly.

"So I go up and tell him I'm in love with him. I was very brave to declare my love like that, no? Maybe too brave?"

"The world needs brave people."

"O.K., so he tells me he works for this truck company, then

soon we become engaged. Well, you should have heard my father! He thought I had no business to go with a truck driver, and we argued all the time. You think I was a bad girl?"

"Hell, no. A girl's got a right to go with whoever she wants to."

"Well, it turned out that this man was taking some bad kind of drug, so he was put in one of these institutions. So I went to see him, and he looked just terrible. Well, he broke down and cried, and I tell you I just can't stand to see a man cry. Do you think a man should cry?"

"Sure," Tony answered knowledgeably. He enjoyed being asked for his opinion. "I think even a man should let himself cry when he feels very sad about something. But I sure don't like to cry about any physical type of pain."

"You *poet.*" Marta put her hand on his back, and a feeling of tender warmth charged his whole being. "Well, I go and hold his hand because I don't want him to know how I feel. And a little later I leave. Then I call the institution and find that he's died. So," she sighed as though she were bored, "I don't think I want another man after that. Then I marry my present husband, and I'm always taking vacations. Now what do you say?"

"I don't know," Tony shook his head. "You sound romantically inclined."

'Hmm." Marta pondered his answer for a moment. "Are you romantic?"

"I like to think so."

"Well, you know what I think?"

"What?"

"I think you're a big bambino!" With her right arm Marta drew Tony from his stool close to her. For a moment he allowed his head to rest against her shoulder just above her breast where he experienced a mingling sensation of glowing tenderness and smooth, fragrant skin. He also felt slightly frightened, slightly embarrassed. She released him, and he got up.

"It's ten-thirty," he said, "and Mother has the idea that I should get some sleep for tomorrow."

"Well, your mother is right. So why don't you kiss me good-bye?"

Where, Tony wondered. Then he bent down and kissed her ivory-smooth shoulder next to the spot where the skin cupped by her collarbone.

* * *

Marta at the bar where he wanted to be; Deirdre at the School: Tony lay in bed, torn between two women. It was beautiful the way Marta allowed herself to love on sight. But Deirdre would ask, "How the heck can you love a person just by looking at him?" Certainly there was something deeper about Deirdre than Marta.

Marta hated to see a man cry, but Deirdre would think it perfectly all right if he expressed what she called "genuine feeling." At twenty-six, Deirdre was pretty in the sense that she was not plain, but she was neither beautiful nor seductive like Marta. Deirdre, the School: the two were interchangeable. "Marta, I want to stay with you." Tony hugged his pillow. But he felt he had to return to everyday living, to pursuit of genuine feeling.

Once he had loved his mother as deeply as his grandmother, but shortly after the T.V. show about the Amazon, he had found he no longer cared about her either. At that time he had been very close to Deirdre and John, his teacher. Now he did not think he needed anybody. Why did love seem almost silly? He remembered telling Deirdre he planned to confess his lack of love to his family. "What's to tell?" Deidre had asked, and Tony had kept his feelings secret. "Maybe you don't want to be close to people," Deirdre had said on another occasion.

Now he wondered if he should live like his biological father, Ram Matthews, a movie director. His mother had told him she thought Ram's life was lonely: a Cadillac in Hollywood, a rapid exchange of mistresses. But, Tony thought, he never suffers loss. Tony began to imagine himself driving a luxurious Cadillac over a gigantic streamlined bridge. A woman like Marta sat close beside him. The sun had just set, and the balmy evening was bathed in a soft purple-neon haze.

The purple color reminded Tony of a silk curtain, shining over a lighted movie screen, which he had seen when he was eight. It was his last night with his mother, for he was to enter the School the following day. Dr. V. had told him it would be quite a while before he would see his mother after that, and she was taking him to a movie, which he had picked, in order to raise his spirits. Clinging to his mother in a state of sadness, numbed by fatique, Tony let his tear-stung eyes imbibe the softness of the purple curtain.

Suddenly his senses were jarred by a blast of violent music and a screeching war cry. The curtain was jerked back, and Tony's heart fluttered as a savage Indian chief, leading a horde of mounted warrriors, charged into his world of momentary peace. The movie title and cast flashed onto the screen while the Indians surrounded and massacred a wagon train. Another blast of music, bloodcurdling screams of triumph, and the Indians were off.

At that point the chief wheeled out of the horde and started down a canyon. Tony thought it was his savage scream that had broken the precious silence, and there was something frightening about his expression. Then the camera descended to a log cabin. A woman swept the cabin porch. "She looks like you," Tony whispered to his mother.

"A little bit," his mother agreed.

"She can't get killed, can she?"

"We'll see."

The woman picked up a bucket and stepped off the porch. "Oh no," Tony groaned. "Shouldn't she know to stay near the house?" This was too much. Now he could hear approaching hoof beats. The woman stopped by the well and waited expectantly. "Why can't she run?" Tony squeezed his mother's arm. "This is dreadful," he whispered.

The quiet was deadly; no sound except for the hoof beats while the woman stood waiting. Then a piercingly sinister crescendo of music, and the woman screamed. "Oh, no!" Tony gasped. And suddenly he froze, horror-stricken and speechless. The Indian shouted something Tony did not understand, but somehow his savage Hollywood guttural had been a perfect mimic of Dr. V.'s Austrian accent.

The Indian charged onto the scene, and the woman ran a few steps and fell. The Indian swung off his horse, glared toward the audience as he whipped out his knife and— "I've been waiting for this!" The camera cut to the cabin, and there stood the hero, big in the open doorway. His face was too handsome to be fierce, but he looked plenty mad and not a bit afraid. He too pulled out a knife and stepped off the porch.

"Oh, I bet I'll be as big as that man some day," Tony giggled in hysterical ecstasy as the antagonists began to circle while the woman watched, terrified, clinging to one of the porch posts. "I wish I could fight like that man," Tony whispered. "This is almost my favorite movie." The two adversaries had come together, and moments later they were rolling in the dust. Then the hero lost his knife, and the woman screamed as the Indian thrust.

Oh my god, what would I do then, Tony wondered, and watched in glee as the hero kicked his assailant against the well, snatched his knife, and sprang to his feet. For the last time the Indian glared fiercely at the audience as he slowly picked himself up and sank back upon the well, panting, snarling, poised with his knife. Suddenly he lurched forward. For a few moments, he and the hero grappled in fast and deadly struggle. Then they came apart, and the Indian stumbled backward, the hero's knife protruding from his stomach.

Tony's mother sucked her breath through her teeth.

"Gosh, Mother," Tony gasped blissfully, "could you get me a knife like that for when I come home next? I would be very careful with it and would only use it to defend the family from robbers."

Now he imagined himself tough as he was soft as he drove with his mistress in the purple evening, his life like his father's. There was a slight breeze in his room, and he filled his lungs with clean fresh air. As he exhaled he felt the exhilaration that had eluded him the night before on the beach. What a life! He felt quietly happy at the mere contemplation. But there was also a subterranean fear. It had to do with death looming always in the future. And Tony realized he needed something more powerful than a soft neon beam to search out whatever he wanted from life.

Still, why go back to the School? Wasn't it there he'd lost his ability to love? But was the School to blame? In any case, certain things could happen only at the School, and once again he thought of the afternoon on which Ronny had hit Alice in the eye.

"Seven different boys in seven different worlds." Deirdre looked around the table after Dr. V. had walked out. "It must be very lonely." A moment's pause. Then tremulously, "It's your lives." Tony thought she spoke with what she called genuine feeling. It made him uneasy, dissatisfied with himself. "Is there ever a kind word among you?" Deirdre asked sadly. And Tony suddenly wanted to tell her why Igor had turned the switch on his wall, why Ronny had shaken hands with Ted, how he and Harry had often confided in one another. But these things were difficult to explain. He could not be sure about Ronny and Igor, and he thought Harry might not want him to betray their confidences. Deirdre's voice became more severe: "As Dr. V. said, the way you sometimes treat each other is *absolutely despicable.*"

Now, along with self-disgust, Tony felt a disgust for Deirdre, Dr. V., the entire School. He looked at all the boys, first at Ronny, and happily noted that Deirdre had not reached him. Ronny's distance was for once appropriate. Then he looked at Mickey and Ralph who whispered and occasionally giggled. What Deirdre had said did not yet apply to them. There was Lewis listening quietly, as quietly as he could. Igor's spare frame seemed to be shaking slightly. He kept pinching his cheek, trying to feel his jawbone, trying to release his feeling through touching activity. He was unhappy, and he wished he could do something about himself so that what Deirdre was saying would not apply to him. He also wished to be back in his mechanical world, playing with the fixtures around his bed. Harry sat quietly, his sadly serious expression somehow seeming too appropriate for the moment. If only you could feel the way he looks as if he's feeling, Tony thought.

"It's too bad," Tony broke the silence, "that we can't make friends like we make a cake. It would really be something if we could have recipes for each kind of friend, like mother, father, schoolmate, mistress, you know? I mean, there's just no real way to make them that you can know how to follow."

For a moment Deirdre looked searchingly at Tony the way she

often did. "Gee, you can be a phony." There was unconcealed disgust in her voice.

"What I said is true," Tony spoke defensively. But Deirdre only looked at him. "I guess you don't think I do much about having friends when I haven't told anybody about my grandmother."

"You said it, I didn't."

"I guess I'm just not as concerned as I should be, and I don't see what the others can do if I tell them."

"Tony, can I ask you what this is?" Harry ventured.

"My grandmother had a stroke, and it's possible that she'll die. Actually, I wasn't keeping it a secret. I just didn't see any point in telling it."

"Tony, I'm sorry that happened." Tony wished his heart could contain the sincerity of Harry's words.

"Well, thanks, but I really don't see how there's any way you can be concerned, and besides she is probably going to pull through."

"Tony, " Harry said sympathetically, "I'm afraid I can't be too concerned, but sometimes I wish I could be."

"Harry, I'm glad you said that. It makes me feel less alone."

Despite his disgust with the School, Tony still warmed to the memory of that moment with Harry. As he stretched in his bed, he realized he almost looked forward to going back. But not only because of that conversation at the table. It had more to do with the wind that blew outside in the tropical night. The sound made Tony think of snow melting in Chicago when early spring winds blew soothingly along the Midway over the campus, creating the thrilling stir of expectation, reawakening a thousand dreams both vague and unfulfilled. Tony was not disappointed with the trip to Acapulco, but none of his dreams, his yearnings, had been satisfied. A sudden gust of nostalgia fanned his senses with a memory from the preceding summer.

Dr. V. had come into the dormitory while Tony was telling Deirdre he thought her a sissy for not letting him find out what it was like to stay up all night. Dr. V. had told him to cut the smart talk, get a book and read in the playroom till the next morning.

At five o'clock in the morning, Tony was nearing the book's

climax. He was a very slow reader, and he had tried to make the book last. He looked up and saw that the morning had turned a dark and mystically peaceful gray. The air was alive with the discordant chirping of hundreds of birds. Tony got up to look out the window into the side yard. This is wonderful, he thought. If only it could stay this way for eternity.

Then he returned to his chair and resumed his reading. The scene described in his book was also set during the hours of dawn. Suddenly Tony found that he desperately wanted to sleep. He had to struggle merely to keep his eyes open. He forced himself to look at the page, to run his eyes over the words. Then the setting in his book swam into his fatigued mind. He could see the Amazon jungles, darkly mysterious in the grey dawn, and he could hear the harsh, rhythmic chirping of hundreds of birds. It lasted only a moment. Later, a breeze from the window filled him with an exquisite tension of expectation: expectation of what Dr. V. might say to him the following day, and of the mystery of hidden jungles; of a pretty counselor who filled him with desire whenever he looked at her, and of his yearnings for exotic jungle love.

Now, in Acapulco, listening to the wind, Tony yearned for the School, for the vision to which retrospect had given a new allure. He was gripped by a fusion between the dawn at the School and the Amazon dawn in his book.

Tony clutched his pillow and hugged himself against it. "Marta," he murmured, "hold me! Hold the big bambino!" Marta seemed to be very kind, ever so kind for a woman who did not want to love deeply. Wasn't her life a good and meaningful one? You want to fuck her, Tony thought. What would it really be like, he wondered.

Then he dreamed. He and Marta were riding alone together in a small horse-drawn carriage. They were riding somewhere—where no one would follow them, where they would be alone forever. Marta had her arm around him, extended across his shoulders, and they both held the reins of the horses. Tony's head rested comfortably below her shoulder, just above her breast. The atmosphere was dark, a mystical grey dawn. Hundreds of birds could be heard, and a warm, purple haze seemed to envelop the lanterns on the front of the carriage. Tony looked down, and there, nestled against his feet, sat the pelican. Once again it cocked its eye at him, and he reached down to touch it.

5

"Daisy!" Tony spread his arms as the tiny Shetland sheep dog flew toward him. Daisy leapt, Tony caught her, then held her at a distance to keep her from painting his face with her salivating tongue. Now, with Daisy, all was frenetic struggle: to wag her tail, to lick, to show love with every inch of her nervous body. Tony watched this a moment, then gathered her in his arms. Immediately she quieted, only once thrusting her head upward in an effort to lick his cheek.

Looking at the small animal, Tony shuddered with a rush of tenderness. He pressed her against the flesh around his left nipple. "Daisy's my baby," he said lovingly. He worried that this tenderness derived from a female element in himself, but it seemed so natural he thought perhaps he should accept it.

With Daisy in his arms, Tony mounted the back stoop to the Hastings house in Glenville, Illinois. He let the dog ahead of him into the kitchen where Paul was sitting at a table and their mother was washing dishes. Daisy ran over to the table to lap up some fallen crumbs. When Paul glanced down at her, she looked up and wagged her tail. "Why did you bring her in now?" Paul asked.

"I thought you said a few minutes ago that she should be fed soon." Tony knew he had bungled into Paul's trap.

"Did I say she should be fed *now?*"

"I went and got her because I wanted to."

"You went and got her because you thought it was time to *feed* her. Do you want to *kill* her?"

"Paul, you know he doesn't want to kill her," their mother said as she started out of the kitchen. I'll be right back", she added. "I'm going to get the mail."

"We're only supposed to feed her at certain times." Paul zeroed into Tony as the door closed behind Mrs. Hastings.

"I thought you'd forgotten to feed her this morning, or you wouldn't've talked about feeding her like you did just a few minutes ago." Tony knew Paul was trying to make him seem a fool, totally unworthy to share in ownership of Daisy.

"Listen, Tony." Paul bent down and lifted Daisy into his arms. "I want to get something straight."

"What."

"You own the back half of this dog while I own the front half."

"I know you care about her more than I do because I'm not at home with her all the time. But, just because you're at home—that doesn't give you any more right to her than I have—unless you think you can profit off my being at the School."

"The point is I can take care of her—which seems to be something you just can't do." Tony felt his brother's gaze, a gaze that probed for vulnerability. Since their return from Acapulco, two days before, Paul had insisted that Tony help care for Daisy. This had involved nightly feeding during which Paul presided with a viciously critical attitude, alluding to the wacky school and Tony's need for it. Tony would not have tolerated this had he not considered Daisy's care a serious responsibility because her health was indeed fragile.

Paul looked away from Tony as Mrs. Hastings re-entered the kitchen and returned to the sink. "I think there's something you should understand, Tony," Paul grinned. Tony felt the tension knot.

"What?" he asked.

"I just wouldn't be low enough to profit off the fact that I have a *WACKY* brother."

Tony controlled a spasm of rage. "Paul," he said in a mock bored manner, "I'll hold Daisy while you get the ax."

"What do you mean?" Tony's mother looked up from a dish she was drying.

"It was Paul's idea, not mine. He wants to divide her up, me getting the back half, him getting the front. So I said to go get the ax in the garage. I don't mind as long as she doesn't suffer." Tony hoped the suffering clause would serve to assert partial decency.

"I bet you wouldn't care if she *was* killed." Hostility was written in Paul's face.

"I couldn't care less."

"Oh, c'mon, Tony," his mother protested.

"See, Daisy? He hates you." Paul looked down at the dog in his lap. "Now you hate him, don't you?"

Tony was not without self-disgust for what he had said, but hadn't Paul asked for it? "I guess it's kind of rough to share such a nice dog with a guy like me," he leered.

"I ought to break this bottle over your head." Paul had grabbed an empty coke bottle, his voice shaking with hate. Tony tensed, slightly frightened. It was always that way when close to a fight with Paul. He did not like to tangle with his brother who could fight with the rage of a cornered beast.

"Try it," he challenged, but their mother had taken all she could.

"Paul, put the bottle down," she ordered.

Paul obeyed, but looked at Tony. "I bet you feel lucky that Mother's protecting you."

"That's right. Otherwise, in about fifteen minutes from now, I'd have the big job of scraping your remains off the floor."

"Could *both* of you *please* stop it?" Mrs. Hastings pleaded as she made her way around the oblong table to the stool on the other side where she placed herself between her two sons. Her voice was tired. "Paul, I wish you would stop needling Tony. You know he goes back to the School the day after tomorrow." Tony was sorry his mother had appealed to Paul's sympathy. Then she turned to him. "Tony," she asked, "do you know the story of King Solomon and the two women with the baby?"

"That's the one where one woman wants the baby divided in half so he gives it to the other?"

"That's right."

Tony flushed with embarrassment as he tried to keep from laughing at himself. Then he let himself smile. "Just think," he said, "history would have been repeated if Paul had offered to give me Daisy."

There was a moment's silence. Then Paul snickered. "Tony," he asked, "where do they keep the girls at your school? Or do they put you all together?"

"No," Tony answered, "the girls have three dormitories on the first floor, and the boys have three on the second." Tony wanted Paul to understand clearly that the sexes were not mixed.

"I don't see why the boys and girls aren't put on the same floor." Paul continued his snicker.

"Well, they aren't."

"But if you're already undressing in front of those girl counselors, what difference does it make?"

"Maybe you've got a point there. But I *don't* undress in front of the counselors."

"But what do you do with them in the dorm?"

"I manage," Tony answered, wishing Paul would drop the subject now.

"How?"

"Well, it's easy. With Deirdre I just undress behind a pair of trousers, and with Laura I go into a toilet stall."

"But, with Deirdre, can you really call that privacy?"

"Paul!" Their mother cut in, but she was also listening intently.

"I get what's necessary." Tony defended himself.

"But why the hell do you do one way with one counselor and another with the other?"

"Deirdre won't let me go into the stalls when she's on duty, but I guess she doesn't care what I do with Laura because Laura's newer and younger."

"Didn't Deirdre used to let you go into the stalls?"

"Yes, but her policy seems to change whenever she wants to find out what my feelings are, and that's damned annoying."

"Boy, I'd like to get into that dormitory of yours just to see what things are like there," Paul leered.

"Well, I'm afraid that's impossible since family members are only allowed on the front side of the fire doors."

"What's the front side?"

"Where they have Dr. V.'s office, the staff room, and counselors' rooms. We're usually up there only when we're getting into trouble with Dr. V. or going out on visits."

"Visits?"

"You know, to see the family."

"How do you feel about not being able to have Mother or anyone else back there?"

"Well, I sort of feel shut off in a separate world, but there are advantages; like I don't have to put up with you back there."

"Why Tony!" Paul brought his hand to his cheek in mock indignation.

"Tony has a point," their mother spoke up. "When he was nine, he told me it would be hard for a boy to say, 'I hate my mother,' if he always had to worry about her coming into the dormitory when he said it. And Dr. V. says. . . ."

"I know what Dr. V. says," Paul interrupted. "He wants the kid to feel safe from his family. But that doesn't stop *you* from wanting to see what goes on back there, does it?"

"No, it doesn't. About once every month, except when Tony's at home, I dream that somehow by accident I've gotten lost in one of the passageways and find myself behind those fire doors. Then usually I see Tony with a group of children having a good time. I guess that dream is something of a wish fulfillment."

"Mmm." Tony did not know what to say. He was angry at Paul and consequently in no mood to express affection.

"Boy, they really charge you for a place they won't even let you look at." Paul looked at his mother. "How much is it, anyway?"

"Now it costs five thousand dollars a year."

"Hear that, Tony? Five thousand just for one guy. You're going to have the whole family broke before long."

"No, he's *not,*" their mother countered. "Fortunately we can afford it. Besides, it's not so much when you consider that psychoanalytic sessions can sometimes run up to fifty dollars an hour, and I've never seen psychoanalysis do as much for anybody as the School has for Tony." Tony was glad his mother had spoken up. The subject of finances made Tony uneasy and he thought Paul knew this.

"But aren't there a lot better things you can do with that money?" Paul did not let up. "I don't think that stuff's really worthwhile when so many people need to be fed and educated. They shouldn't all be held back just for a few sick people."

Tony looked at Paul's calm face. He felt outraged by his brother's intimation that he was a parasite not worthy of cure. But he had no comeback since he was not sure he disagreed. In his mind's eye, he saw himself pull two handfuls of his brother's hair as he pushed his head face-forward into one of the lighted gas burners on the stove.

"Well, I think psychology's very necessary," Mrs. Hastings answered Paul after a moment's thought, "and I feel strongly that help should be available to more people."

"But five thousand's so much money. I know you think Tony's very intelligent, but why not spend that money on some kind of genius or at least on somebody who isn't wacky? That kind of person could really reach the sky."

"Well, I feel I owe it to Tony because I'm his mother, and besides, a great many of his problems are my fault. They have to do with things that happened when I was married to Ram, and. . . ."

"Yes, Mother," Paul deprecated, "you've told me how Ram used to try to make him act like a twelve-year-old when he was only three, and how you were so tense because Ram picked on you all the time. Maybe your tenseness was hard on Tony and maybe you should have left Ram a lot sooner. But did that really cause it all?"

"Well, there was a lot more—."

"O.K., O.K., I didn't make it sound as bad as it was, but a lot of boys went through more than Tony and didn't come out like him. So don't you think it's just your bad luck to have a son with all these problems?"

"He had his problems for a reason."

"But why *Tony* and not somebody else?" Paul stabbed, and Tony had an answer.

"I'll tell you," he spoke slowly. "If you're one kind of person and are hit with one kind of problem, you can be hurt by it even though it wouldn't necessarily hurt most other people. But then other people might be hurt by things that wouldn't hurt you."

"But aren't some people just hurt more easily than others?" Paul interrupted.

"Maybe yes, and maybe no. But that also goes for physical health. In other words, you can't say why a whole block of kids gets a kind of polio that only gives them a cough and keeps them in bed for a couple of days. Then, after they've all gotten it, somebody else gets it in such a way that he waddles around like a duck for seven or eight years." Tony was alluding to the polio his brother had contracted when he was two years old. It had caused him to walk in a slightly unsteady manner until he was nine.

No one spoke for a few seconds. Then Paul snatched a wet dish rag from the sink and threw without taking careful aim. Tony did not even have to duck. It missed him by a foot. Tony's voice was steady: "Even a guy with polio could do better than that." Their mother leapt up instinctively.

"Don't worry, Tony," Paul warned, "I'll get you when Mother's not around." Tony smiled.

"Paul," his mother said severely, "No threatening!"

"Hey Paul!" The call from the back yard came from Herbert, one of Paul's friends.

"Go see what he wants," Mrs. Hastings suggested, glad of the interruption. Paul got up and walked around the table, past Tony who watched him carefully. He opened the door and went out on the stoop. Tony and his mother just looked at each other. There was nothing to say. Poking his head in the door, Paul said he and Herbert were going over to the woods near Highway 11. After that he picked up Daisy and put her on the stoop. "Call her," he said to Herbert. Herbert called and Daisy obeyed. Without warning, Paul darted back into the kitchen, spat at Tony, then dashed out the door and across the back yard.

Tony followed him only as far as the stoop. "Take Daisy with you if you want," he shouted, trying to imitate the defiant scream of a movie hero, "but remember to leave my half in the garage!"

Tony returned to the kitchen. "This really distresses me," his mother said as she sat down again, and Tony worried that she might cry. "I'm especially sorry this all had to happen when you're about to go back to Chicago. But you really shouldn't have tried to make Paul feel badly about his polio."

"Well, he wasn't exactly trying to make me feel good about going to the School."

"You're right. I shouldn't take sides, and some of the things he said were certainly intended to hurt. I'm sorry I let him go on with those questions. But I think you got him very angry when you suggested chopping Daisy in half. He's really so fond of that dog."

"He had it coming after those cracks he's been making about the way I feed her."

"Tony, I'm not taking sides," his mother repeated. "I just wanted you to know."

Tony was bothered by his mother's distress. He felt it had to do with whatever she considered his disturbance. "I'm sorry," he shook his head sympathetically, "but don't you think Paul is somewhat disturbed too? I mean he's really been going after me."

"I know, but he's been tested by psychologists."

"You mean with stuff like those ink blobs where they can decide you're sick because you see Peter Rabbit when they want you to see Bugs Bunny? I guess just because Paul's made the right guesses, nobody thinks he's disturbed." Tony felt angry.

"Tony, you know Dr. V. did not base his opinions about you just on those ink blot tests."

"Well, I wish he'd look at Paul."

"I suppose it's unfair," his mother conceded, "but when you talked about chopping Daisy in half, I couldn't help being reminded of how you first told me, 'I'm interested in killing,' and how you just sat for hours crushing ants."

"Yes, I remember that. You'd been reading to me about the queen poisoning Snow White, and I got very fascinated with the change from life to death."

"I certainly shouldn't have read you that book, but Ram insisted—even though it scared you. Then remember when we were fishing in Florida, the only interest you took in fishing was to kill every fish we caught."

"Yes, I really liked using that knife." Tony felt an urgent need to irritate his mother. After having been needled about his disturbance, he did not like hearing about his past.

"I don't think that's funny," his mother said tonelessly.

"Hell," Tony became merrily bitter, "you worried about my

killing little ants and fish while Dr. V. thinks I had the mind of a murderer."

"Good heavens!" His mother was startled. "When did he tell you a thing like that?"

"After I overheard you talking to Dad about how, before I went to the School, I supposedly tried to castrate Dr. Carter. Dr. V. just wanted to talk to me about that to see if I was upset, and he said I might have committed murder if I hadn't had some of my problems solved while I was young."

"God, I really thought you and Paul were asleep. I never intended you to hear that at any time in your life."

"Actually, I don't remember ever trying to castrate Dr. Carter. Just what did I do?"

"You used to. . . ." His mother's expression became one of distaste as she searched for words she did not want to find. Then she made a clawing gesture, her hands turned up. "You used to just grab at him. . . . between his legs, session after session."

"I don't remember that, but I do remember his telling me not to worry, that I couldn't hurt him, no matter how hard I tried, and that I shouldn't be afraid to try. So I guess I thought I was just playing. Hell, I was only six. But you never thought I was really dangerous. After all, you did let me carry around that sword I found in the attic."

"Yes, I thought I could trust you not to do anything dangerous, but I just didn't know how sick you were. That's what Dr. Carter wanted to get across when he told me about your trying to castrate him. He said you scared the daylights out of him that morning you ran into his office brandishing what he called 'that terribly lethal weapon,' and announced you were King Arthur."

"I guess he must have crossed his legs in fright," Tony laughed naturally as he tried to joke away embarrassment.

"No, he told me his idea was to get that sword firmly lodged in a piece of wood at the work bench."

"Oh, now I see why he always wanted to play King Arthur and Excalibur. I still remember that," Tony continued his humor. "Say, just what did you do about that sword after you talked to Dr. Carter? It was my property, you know."

"I bought it from you for five dollars. Then you really terrified me when you rammed that old lady with your tricycle and when you punched that baby in the park."

"It's funny, I don't remember those specific things. But I sure remember a lot of other things I used to do, like the way I used to beat on Paul all the time. Are you sure I didn't hit that old lady by accident?"

"That was no more an accident than your butting old ladies and everybody else in the stomach when I tried to enter you in that school in Topeka. You were so uncontrollable there they didn't think you could be helped."

"But remember, you were told not to restrain me and that I was supposed to be allowed to act freely. But what exactly am I supposed to have been diagnosed for?"

"Childhood schizophrenia, if there is such a thing."

"Well," Tony suddenly giggled, "a lot of that's over now and if I want to chop Daisy in half, I can assure you it's for no other reason than to get at Paul."

"That really consoles me." Tony detected a quiver in his mother's voice, and he realized he had gone too far.

The telephone rang. "Mother, I'm sorry." Tony got up to go to her.

His mother answered the phone. "Hello? Oh, hello, Doris. . . . wait one moment." Then, looking up, "Tony, why don't you go play? I have to talk to Mrs. Humphrey."

"Mother, look I'm sorry."

"That's all right. Go on." But Tony did not feel it was all right as he descended the basement steps, cursing Mrs. Humphrey who could keep his mother talking interminably.

For about fifteen minutes Tony pounded the punching bag, showing, he thought to himself, unusually bad form. Then he got his BB gun and set up one of the tiny cylindrical ammo cases for a target. Standing at about fifteen feet, he fired a shot and missed. Usually he was able to hit. Nothing seemed to be going right, so he went into a small padded room called the gym which his stepfather had set up for exercise. He flopped down on the matting and found he was uncomfortable. Then he got up and started pacing around.

You really feel bad about that last thing you said to Mother, Tony decided. That's why you feel so rotten now. So the best thing would be to go say you didn't mean it. But did you mean it? Of course you wouldn't want to chop Daisy in half, but you'd sure like to make Paul suffer.

Suddenly Tony imagined that John, his teacher, was with him in the gym. John was a big man, handsome as a movie hero. Now his calm smile seemed to express a conviction that there existed no problem whose end was not in sight. "I just don't know what to do," Tony spoke to John. "I mean, Paul really got me mad."

"So what did you do?"

"I said some nasty things that got him mad right back and upset Mother. But he really provoked it."

"Maybe he did, maybe he didn't. But how did you feel when you said those things?"

"Not too good."

"Well, that's what concerns me, not what your brother did."

"I don't know what else I could have done."

"C'mon, don't give me that. You're a pretty smart boy. You could have thought of something if you'd wanted to."

"But what?"

"Why don't you tell me?" And Tony had to stop imagining. Until a short while ago, he had been very close to John, but now he was often uncomfortable when they were together. He was not sure why except that he felt unequal to his teacher. Tony knew there were answers other than the ones he had given Paul. In John's book there were always answers, and it was quite possible to enjoy everyday life under practically all circumstances. John preferred books to movies, and would rather spend vacations in Chicago with his family than go cavorting halfway around the world. But if he went around the world, he would also manage to have a good time. John's philosophy was by no means unique, but John was unique in that he was a living example of it.

Tony was fatigued by this philosophy, by the man whose qualities he wanted to assume, but suddenly he had an answer to John's question: Why don't you tell me?

"I've thought of something."

"Go ahead."

"I really think it might be a good idea if I give Daisy all to Paul."

"So, let's hear a little more about this."

"Well, he really loves her, and she just doesn't mean that much to me. I mean, I just don't see her that often."

"O.K. So you give him the dog. Now what's that supposed to do?"

"Well, I don't know. It's sort of as if now I'm standing between him and something he really loves."

"How do you do that?"

"Well, I don't really. But maybe he'd just like to feel that she's all his."

"That's possible."

"You see," Tony continued, "he really does own her emotionally, and maybe he would like to own her legally, and perhaps it would be nicer if I did let him have her. Also, it would probably make Mother happy."

"Well, Tony," John became matter of fact, "I have no idea whether this would help your mother and brother. . . ."

"You mean you don't really feel I stand in his way?" Tony asked.

"I don't see what you stand in the way of." Tony was glad to have John say that. Somehow it put him in a better light. "No," he had John continue, "I can't see that this is going to necessarily help your brother, but I *can* see from the things you say and from your general attitude that it might help you a little. So maybe you should give it some consideration."

Tony was not sure he should go through with the idea. Certainly not immediately. Paul could interpret it then as a form of capitulation. But it was worth consideration, he decided, as he made his way out of the gym and on toward the steps. Now was the time to talk to his mother about it. If nothing else, it would probably make her feel better. And if she agreed, he would probably go through with it.

"Tony! Where are you!"

"Yeah!" Tony was surprised to hear Herbert calling from the kitchen above him.

"Hey, Tony, Daisy's been hit!" Tony bolted up the basement steps.

"Let's get Mother!" he shouted as he charged through the kitchen door, Herbert behind him, then up the stairs and down the hallway to his mother's room.

"Hey Mother!" Tony's shout brought her to the door. "Daisy's been hit!" While his mother ran and snatched a pillow from her bed and her purse from her chair, Tony rapped loudly on the door to the study, then remembered that his stepfather had gone to a college faculty meeting.

"Where is she?" Mrs. Hastings asked in a frightened voice as she, Tony, then Herbert, hurried back along the narrow hall.

"I left 'em out on Highway 11," Herbert gasped.

"Good God!" Mrs. Hastings was shocked. "I hope he has sense enough to move her off the road. What do you mean hit? By a gun or a car?"

"By a car," his words came now in gasps and tears. "Paul was trying to speak to her, but he couldn't get her to do anything. I ran all the way back here."

"Did you see what happened?" Mrs. Hastings asked.

"No, some kids found us in the woods, and told us she was lying out by the highway."

Mrs. Hastings pulled out of the driveway and turned down Wilmington Road which led out of Glenville proper into some hilly country. Nobody had anything to say. Tony found himself feeling totally unemotional except for the fact that he was tense. He did not want to confront Paul retching in an agony of which he was incapable. He sensed that, if Daisy did not respond when Paul spoke to her, then she was dead.

They turned off on Highway 11, which was very narrow at this point, winding through woods. "Now where's Paul?" Mrs. Hastings asked Herbert.

"Over there," Herbert answered, pointing to a side of the road, but he was no longer there.

"Oh dear, I hope he's not in an ambulance somewhere," Mrs. Hastings said tonelessly. She turned the car around, and they started back.

"There he is!" Herbert shouted. They had missed him the first time. He had gone off on a small side road, half lying, half sitting, concentrated over a tiny bundle. Mrs. Hastings pulled the car over and they all got out.

Paul was crying uncontrollably. Daisy lay quietly in all her beauty. There was no alteration in the way she looked except that she was totally still. Mrs. Hastings dropped down beside Paul and tried to put her arm around him but he brushed her off. "Oh Paul, I'm so terribly sorry," her voice was very sad. "Let's take her to Dr. Kinkaid's immediately just in case there's a chance."

"Ah-h-h. . . . she's dead!" Paul managed to scream between spasms of breathing. Tony ran to get the pillow from the car. Now he noted, a little bit surprised and somewhat gratified, that he too was capable of crying. He took the pillow back and gently laid it down beside Daisy. His mother broke down into a series of painful sobs as she carefully lifted the small, ethereal body and placed it on the pillow. A drop of blood spilled out of Daisy's nose and a crimson spot stained the smooth, white linen. Her tail seemed to move, but ever so slightly. Was it the wind? Or was it a last effort to communicate a love that she lavished so happily upon the family?

In the car Paul kept petting the face which still had not lost its loving expression. "Daisy looks like she still loves me," he cried, and a few more drops of blood spilled out of her nose. When he saw that, he burst into fresh tears. On the way to Dr. Kinkaid's, only Paul spoke, uttering words to Daisy amidst his sobs.

In minutes they were at Dr. Kinkaid's. Tony jumped out of the car and went around to the back where the office was located. "Dr. Kinkaid!" he called and rapped on the door. Dr. Kinkaid appeared just in time to open the door for the others. Mrs. Hastings carried Daisy on the pillow. Now Daisy was perfectly still. Even her tail was still.

"Put her there," Dr. Kinkaid said softly, indicating a stretcher table by the medicine cabinets. With his left hand Dr. Kinkaid felt around her right shoulder, and with calm, professional detachment he partially lifted her little body, then let it drop slack.

"I'm very sorry," he said, "but I suppose you must already know she's dead." Paul was no longer crying. Now only his breathing was occasionally racked. He went around to the other side of the table, and in an almost detached manner, began to compose the corpse, to straighten out the legs, to smooth the already smooth hair, and to wipe the blood from around her nose and mouth with his own handkerchief. Then, once again, he broke into agonized sobs.

Herbert reached out to pet her. “Don’t you touch her,” Paul snarled, “or I’ll break your little head open.” Tony felt a twinge of something between fear and rage light up in his stomach.

“Paul,” his mother said compassionately, “don’t act as if it were Herbert’s fault. He came to get me as fast as he could.”

“Well, it wasn’t fast enough,” Paul said bitterly.

“Daisy died the instant the car hit her.” Dr. Kinkaid spoke with finality.

“Will you bury her?” Paul asked him.

“Yes, certainly,” Dr. Kinkaid answered. Paul lifted Daisy’s head slightly to straighten out her ears, and more blood poured out of her mouth and nose.

“I didn’t know that blood flowed after you were dead,” Mrs. Hastings sobbed. Paul bent down and kissed Daisy’s closed eye. Then again his crying broke out while he kept tenderly stroking her fur over and over again. Mrs. Hastings turned to Tony and Herbert. “I think you boys had better go now,” she said. Tony felt as though she were disposing of him, as though no part of him could ever be equal to Paul’s sincere grief.

“O.K.,” he nodded to his mother, and he and Herbert left Dr. Kinkaid’s office.

When he got home, Tony knocked to see if his stepfather were in so he could tell him the news. But he was still out. Then he went to his and Paul’s room and threw himself face down on his bed. A second later, he leapt up to see if the lock on the door worked. It did not. So he went and locked himself in the bathroom. It was a large bathroom, and there was space for his feverish pacing which lasted for about a minute.

Then he rallied his emotions; the aching sting behind his eyes throbbed to a crescendo, causing his lips to curl and his eyes to squint. He sat down on the edge of the tub. His whole body heaved as the tears squeezed out, and his breathing became jerked. He was sorry to lose Daisy, but he had also been made sad by Paul's hysterical crying, by his mother's grief and as he cried he thought about his grandmother, and about the possibility of her dying. "I'm going to miss you," he said so softly that he himself could hardly hear it.

Sad though he was, Tony knew his grief was in no way comparable to Paul's. He did not even have to cry if he did not want to. He comprehended his grief. It was nothing great, but because he hadn't really felt anything similar for a long time, he wanted to have it out now. Nobody else, however, should see it.

About fifteen minutes went by. When Tony rose from the tub, he found that even if his grief were spurious, it gave him a sense of contact with people that he had not felt for a long time. He soaped around his eyes at the sink and then rinsed with water. After that he combed his hair and so, to his satisfaction eradicated the last trace of sorrow.

Tony wondered what it would be like when he faced Paul again. How would Paul take to him? He went back into their bedroom. In order to keep himself busy while he waited for the rest of the family to come home, he began to pack. He heard the sound of a car, and he looked out into the early twilight and saw the Plymouth pull into the driveway. He continued to pack, working slowly and scrupulously at the job. This was not his habit, and it would please his stepfather to see that he had a neat suitcase. Tony became conscious of the fact that he suddenly wanted to please.

He heard the kitchen door shut, and then his mother's footsteps as she moved toward the living room. The kitchen door opened again, and Tony heard Paul's steps on the back stairs. He was surprised to find he was frightened, his emotions closely akin to those experienced while waiting for Dr. V. to deal with Ronny. It was often said at the School that people were afraid of Dr. V. because they felt guilty about something. Tony had never been able to decide whether that was true. But he thought perhaps now he was afraid of his brother because Paul's grief made him feel some dislike toward himself.

Then Paul was in the doorway. In his hands he held the ax from the garage. He stood quietly, looking at Tony with open hate. Tony could not bring himself to believe his brother would do anything, but he felt the dull sensation of his heavily pounding heart. Paul suddenly flexed his arms, and Tony jumped. Paul's giggle nearly broke into a bitter sob. "Afraid, isn't he?" he sneered. Then mockingly,"Well, don't worry, I'm not gonna hurt the big brat." Paul let the head of the ax fall on the floor, but he held its handle in his right hand. "I'm gonna give the brat this ax so he can go and get his half of Daisy over at Dr. Kinkaid's." And with all his strength he hurled the handle forward so that it hit the floor two feet from Tony. Tony jumped again. Then the sound of running footsteps.

"What do you mean threatening him with that ax!" Mrs. Hastings burst upon Paul. And then his mother and brother were grappling and, without knowing what he was doing, Tony found himself between them. Somehow he managed to push Paul in one direction, and he caught his mother by the shoulders.

"Wait a minute! Let me explain!" he pleaded with his mother. "Paul wasn't threatening to hurt me! *He wasn't!*" Tony was not quite sure how to explain what had happened, but Paul had not threatened him. All three just stood there silently, each looking at the other.

"Tony," his mother said slowly, "go get that ax and get it out of here." She got some keys from her pocketbook. "Take that ax and lock it in the garage, and if Paul should dare to stop you, I want you to drop the ax and give him the thrashing of his life. I just *can't* have this." She was in tears. "I just can't have this," she repeated confusedly.

Tony walked into the room, picked up the ax, then went back out into the hall. In order to avoid passing Paul, he walked down the hall toward the front of the house and went out the front door. He felt good all over. He had enabled his mother to turn to him in a moment of family crisis. Now did she think Paul was disturbed? "You must feel pretty good about yourself." He imagined that John was smiling at him. "You really had a lot to contend with there."

Tony put the ax in the garage and locked the door. He was feeling a bliss somewhat less intense than, but akin to what he had felt in Acapulco after kissing the whore. Once again he felt himself endowed with a new manhood he could not quite grasp. The twilight was a dark gold, and as he paused by the garage, Tony breathed in the cold air. Somehow it seemed that this was weather both for deep joy and deep grief.

Today you tried to do right, he told himself, and felt proud. For one happy moment he felt that everything in his life would turn out all right. "Dear God, I thank thee," he said reverently and was embarrassed by his impulse toward a belief he often ridiculed. But he felt the need to direct his thanks toward something more pervasive, more powerful, than mere circumstance.

PART II

The School

6

Tony woke up gradually on the Sunday he was to go back to the School. The morning had dawned gray. Something bothered him. He felt unjustly abused, as though he had been attacked or punished for a reason he could not determine. Somehow it all harked back to Deirdre's rather unpredictable anger, to rules Tony did not always understand. When she really screamed, she was frightening, though much less so than Dr. V., and at this moment her anger seemed almost palpable. Then his mind cleared, and he realized he had been dreaming. This made him feel better.

Locking the bathroom door and draping his clothes over a chair, Tony prepared for a ritual which would last more than an hour. Its sole purpose was to get clean enough to be able to avoid baths at the school for three, maybe four days, during which he would not have to worry about Deirdre seeing him in the tub. He turned the faucets for his bath water.

He imagined he was a warrior preparing for battle. Before the contest, he had to be absolutely purified, thoroughly cleansed. What a contrast between this state and the filth in which he would return after a long, grim struggle! First he brushed his teeth very carefully, then he shaved, using his stepfather's razor to eliminate minute traces of fuzz on his upper lip. He was going to get very clean indeed. He slipped off his pajamas, got into the tub and turned off the water. He began by meticulously washing between the toes on his right foot and from there he continued to work around the arch and the instep. Yes, it was an art to get clean, an art of perfection. He progressed from his feet to his shins, on upward.

He washed his genitals with scrupulous care, working up a heavy lather. These were the parts he most needed to tend since the opportunity to clean them would not present itself often enough at the School. There he would have to sit constantly hunched in the tub to protect himself in case Deirdre walked into the bathroom.

The washing caused a stirring in the lower regions of his body and, moments later, he was not washing, but massaging. Now he was no longer the soldier being anointed for battle. Instead, he was the sacrificial victim of an ancient cult, lying on the altar of a grand temple while the indifferent hand of a voluptuous priestess rendered the life-giving sap of his being up to a sacred deity.

But before he could die on the altar, before the all-enveloping climax, the priestess became Deirdre while he lay in the tub at the School. With this gesture of total surrender, he would succumb to whatever childhood she wanted for him, to that state of his being in which she found it suitable to deny him the privacy he felt should be due any boy his age. And he imagined she looked at him with that calm expression that was often typical of her as she went about her duties in the dormitory. Then he became the lizard suffering agonies beneath the detached, ruthless ministrations of the guide. He tried to push this out of his mind and visualized himself having intercourse with Marta. But that was hard to imagine while he lay on his back and massaged with his hand. Marta, the guide, the priestess, Deirdre, Marta, their images unfolding as he groped rhythmically, always toward something more consummate until tumultuous climax swept all in its wake.

* * *

Tony and his mother hailed a taxi at the Sixty-third Street station in Chicago. Mrs. Hastings gave the School's address to the driver, and soon the taxi was traveling through street after street lined with apartments and small shops. Now Tony wished he could talk to his mother and not waste precious seconds. He searched for something he might want to tell her before they were parted, but could find nothing.

"I wish I could know exactly when I'll see you again." He broke the silence. "I hope you and Granny will be able to come and see me on my birthday the way you always do." There was a pause. "Maybe I can come home for a few days in the spring as usual."

"Well, honey, you know I hope so too so long as Dr. V. thinks it all right."

Tony's teeth chattered. Anxiety ground in his guts. Memories of how he had felt as a child suddenly became vivid. Then it had been so painful to part from his mother that he had usually cried for a long time. Now he was much closer to his childhood than he had been for a long time. But he was afraid that, once settled into the School, he would no longer feel this way. You'll always remember how you feel now, he promised himself.

Then the taxi turned a corner, and there was the School. The front hallway behind the orange door was lighted, and Tony could see into Dr. V.'s office. Dr. V. was at his desk, and Tony noticed the light shining on the top of his bald head. "Was there anything we were supposed to talk about?" Tony quickly asked his mother.

"No, I can't think of anything." Then Mrs. Hastings opened the door and got out. The driver helped Tony get his bags off the front seat while his mother went up to ring the doorbell. Tony looked at the muscular black man in his worn leather jacket. *His* teeth didn't chatter. He looks more comfortable in that old jacket than you are, Tony thought. And suddenly he imagined the ideal life to be that of a taxi driver patrolling the streets at night, driving from place to place, free from specific destination, from Dr. V.

"You make it, buddy?" The driver's base voice had a soothing effect on Tony who felt he was talking to a strong man with a warm personality. It was a relief to talk to this man just before his confrontation with Dr. V. which he anticipated with both anxiety and eagerness.

Tony bent down and grabbed the two bags. "Sure!" he answered the driver, then, "thanks." This was probably the last thing he was going to say for awhile to anybody outside the School except on shopping excursions or when he talked to his accordion teacher. He was truly glad about the accordion lessons.

Dr. V. opened the door just as Tony mounted the last step to the entrance. "Vell, *hello,* Tony. Hello, Mrs. Hastings." Tony and his mother returned the salutation while Dr. V. held the door ajar. "Can you manage zat?" Dr. V. asked as Tony heaved past him with his luggage, following his mother.

"Sure," Tony smiled. He already felt warmed by Dr. V.'s greeting.

"So how did it go?" Dr. V. addressed Tony and his mother.

"It went very well," Tony answered, deciding on the spur of the moment that he was not stretching the frustrating truth.

"It was very nice," Mrs. Hastings chimed in.

"Vell, you know," Dr. V. was smiling, "it vasn't so long ago zat zhe only place I had to chase zis young man vas to his dormitory. Now I have to chase him all over Mexico."

"A good place to be chased." Tony's smile was no longer forced. It was even a bit defiant.

"Vhat? Speak up."

"A good place to be chased," Tony said more loudly.

"I see." Dr. V. paused, then turned to Mrs. Hastings, "So is zhere anysing you vish to tell me?"

"Uh, no, nothing in particular." Tony's mother seemed slightly put off guard by the question.

"Zhen Tony, I guess it is time to say good-bye to your mozer," Dr. V. suggested softly.

"I'm afraid so," Tony assented, holding back a sigh. And the old aching welled up behind his eyes. The pang was greater than anything he had felt just days before when Daisy had been killed. As he and his mother put their arms around each other, something tightened in his throat, and he forced his tongue down against the glands in the bottom of his mouth while his eyebrows went up in a spasmodic effort to waylay the tears. "Well, it shouldn't be long," he whispered while he and his mother held onto each other. His utterance was meant as much for Dr. V. as for his mother.

"Now try to put your mind on what needs to get done," his

mother advised, "and try to relax and have a good time at the School." The hell! Tony screamed defiantly in his mind.

Mrs. Hastings put her hand into Dr. V.'s, then turned to leave. Before she got out the door, Tony hugged her once again. But the pang of sadness was already departing. Now his feelings were overtaken by an apprehensive eagerness to once again confront life at the School.

"Well, here's Deirdre." Dr. V.'s hand fell gently on Tony's shoulder as they turned away from the door. Deirdre was standing on the stairs that led down to the vestibule.

"Hi!" Tony greeted Deirdre.

"Hi," Deirdre answered. She was smiling warmly.

"So before you and Deirdre go upstairs, I vant to hear vhat you did vhile I vas chasing you around zat savage country." Dr. V. looked intently at Tony for a second, and then at Deirdre.

Only one item registered in Tony's mind: "I found a whore." He spoke with casual affectation.

"Vhat!"

"Well, I mean I only kissed her," he was quick to explain.

"Zhere, I knew ve could trust him," Dr. V. smiled at Deirdre. Deirdre was still smiling, only now her lips were pursed ever so slightly as if to say, I knew the kind of mischief you'd try to get into. Or perhaps she was anticipating how, if, and when Tony planned to break this bit of news to his group. For a second Tony and Deirdre locked eyes. Then they burst out laughing.

The laughter quickly subsided, and Tony turned to Dr. V. "I can promise you right now that if all whores look like she did, you can trust me forever."

"Vell, I don't know," Dr. V. mused. "In any case, don't make any promises at your age." A moment's silence. "So how did zhe fishing go?"

"Oh, that went a little rough," Tony answered and started to tell about all that had happened the night before the fishing trip. Better that than paint a pretty picture of the events and face the possibility of answering to Dr. V. after his mother had written a report of details. Also, Tony prided himself on telling the truth.

Dr. V. stopped him. "Did you bring me back a big fish?" he asked. "You know, I vanted vone to hang in my office so zat ven zhe chancellor from zhe University comes to see me, he can sink I am a real big fisherman."

Oh well, there're other ways to impress people like him," Tony answered. "And I'm afraid I didn't catch anything."

"So, vere you disappointed?"

"No, you can never count on a fish to bite."

"Now *zat* is vhat I vanted to hear. Vell, maybe zhis year you go after zhe fish razer zan vait for it to come to you. And zhen you vill get it. And you have already shown us quite a few signs you are ready to do zat. . . Vell, I guess you can go vis Deirdre."

"Yes, I guess so," Tony grabbed his two bags, heaved them off the floor and started up the stairs.

"Here, let me take one." Deirdre reached out for Tony's suitcase.

"No, that's all right," Tony insisted.

"Oh come on, those bags are heavy." Deirdre was also insistent.

"Zat's all right. Tony's a strong boy," Dr. V. called over his shoulder as he turned toward his office. Tony and Deirdre stopped before passing through the fire doors so that Tony could rest a moment. He did not know why he was slightly tense now that he was alone with Deirdre. But he was not surprised since there was often quite a bit of tension between them, and he wondered whether his feeling was centered at least in part around what he had thought about in the tub. He wanted to be more at ease, so he took Deirdre's hand. "Dar'dra," he said softly. His voice was very special, an affectionate childlike drawl. It was a voice he never wanted his mother or Paul to hear him use with Deirdre. Never!

Deirdre gave his hand an affectionate squeeze and looked at him intently. Her lips pursed, and then she said with genuine feeling, "Well, it's good to have you back."

"Dar'dra," Tony repeated as he freed his hand from hers and clumsily dropped his arms around her neck. He leaned on her and in his special voice, speaking whimsically through partially closed teeth, he said, "Tony's getting kind of hefty, isn't he?"

"Uh huh," Deirdre replied, and Tony released her—before the rhythmically turbulent sensations below his belt could lead to visible manifestation.

With Tony back, the Eagles were fully reunited at snack time. Laura was in for the occasion, and Deirdre had gotten ice cream and cake which she served on multi-colored paper plates set on a fancy paper table cloth. The plates and cloth reminded Tony of a children's birthday party. But he was in no mood to resent the childish atmosphere. He wanted to feel that the coming year was going to be better than past years, that it would not be filled with solitude.

Because of the way he was momentarily feeling, Tony did not mind talking to Mickey. Blond-haired, blue-eyed Mickey had the esthetically cute face one might expect to see in a Golden Book or a children's movie. Mickey was seven and rather childish even for his age. Usually Tony would not speak to him, but not having seen him for awhile, he felt differently.

"So what did the pelican do when he landed in your boat?" Mickey asked, all attention, as Tony gave a censored story of his adventures in Acapulco.

"He just winked at me and took off."

"Gee." Mickey was impressed.

"Did you see any scorpions down there?" Ralph asked. A year older than Mickey, Ralph was very mature for his age. He and Tony often had wonderful talks about exploration in distant jungles.

"Yes, I did see one," Tony answered. He wasn't certain Deirdre would approve, but feeling he had the atmosphere under control, he told about the scorpion which had fallen from the tree into his mother's hair.

"Did it kill her?" Mickey asked eagerly, and Tony noted Laura's typical new-counselor expression of animated concern. He enjoyed this; but Deirdre's non-committal stare made him uneasy.

"No, I wouldn't be telling you like this if the scorpion had done anything. The man who took us out in the boat got rid of it with his machete."

Tony thought he had told enough, and he was glad when Ronny suddenly asked him, "Did you see *West Side Story?*"

"You didn't think I'd miss that, did you?" Tony answered, looking over at Laura with a slight feeling of triumph.

"Yeah, I saw it too," Ronny answered.

"So did I," Lewis spoke up.

"What about you, Dar'dra?" Tony turned to her teasingly, "Did you see it?"

"Nope," Deirdre shook her head.

"Ohhh! It's too bad you missed it. It's *really* good," Lewis broke out enthusiastically as he turned toward Deirdre. She did not react.

"Hey, Laura," Harry grinned, "did you see it?" And before she could answer—

"Did you?" some of the others asked eagerly.

"Is this the third degree?" Laura smiled.

"She saw it!" Ralph's voice was one of knowing accusation.

"Did you find it disturbing?" Tony's lips curved involuntarily upward.

"Yes, Tony, for you it must have been disturbing." Laura became sure of herself. She looked Tony full in the face. His mouth opened in surprise. Something in Laura's attitude made him want to throw himself into her arms. Then he heard the squeak of Dr. V.'s shoes and looked up.

"Yes, Tony," Dr. V. had just entered the dormitory, "don't you sink you got zhe answer you asked for?"

"I guess so," Tony answered softly.

"Now," Dr. V. said thoughtfully, "you can see zat she's going to take good care of you." He stood facing Tony from the other side of the table.

"I guess so," Tony repeated in an intentionally disinterested tone. He did not want to openly defy Dr. V., but he wanted him to know he did not appreciate being cared for by a girl counselor who thought him not ready to see *West Side Story.*

"Vell, doesn't zat make you happy?"

"I don't need to be taken care of." Tony's voice belied the boldness of his assertion.

"Zhe *hell* you don't." Dr. V.'s voice became ominously unpleasant. He seemed disgusted. Tony did not dare look directly at him for fear of meeting him eye to eye. He tightened his stomach muscles in an effort to strangle the tension created by the awkward silence. 'Vhat are you at zhe School for?" Dr. V. asked.

"To get rid of my solitude."

"And to get help from ozers—yes?"

"Yes."

Dr. V. looked at Tony a few more seconds. Then he shrugged, extending his hands. "Look, Tony," he was pleasant now, "isn't it nice somebody vants to take care of you?"

"Should I want somebody to tell me I shouldn't see *West Side Story?*" Tony was proud of his stance.

"No, Tony," Dr. V. shook his head. "No." He shook his head again. "Now man to man, Tony, between zhe two of us, I sink it vas all right for you to see zat movie vhile on your visit."

"What do you mean? I couldn't see it at the School."

"On visits you are supposed to try out new sings, and I don't sink zhe movie was any problem for you." Tony glanced at Laura and thought he detected an expression of confusion. "Do you understand me?"

"I think so," he nodded at Dr. V. He felt he had an intuitive understanding, but he was not sure.

"But I vorry," Dr. V. continued, "ven you spurn zhe care zat somebody at zhe school vants to give you. Now you are almost fifteen. Is zat correct?"

"Yes."

"So you are right on your way to become a young man; I hope a fine young man. But Tony, a man does not outgrow zhe sings he basically needs. Razer, he grows up to learn to get zhose sings."

"But *what* exactly should I get?"

"I sought I had no longer to lead you like a boy. Some sings a man has to find for himself. Not everysing can be explained, you know."

Tony thought he knew.

7

On Monday the Eagles finished breakfast at 8:40—fifteen minutes before school. Then Deirdre took them into the playroom where they joined the Kangaroos, the youngest boys' dormitory group. "Hi Tony! I'm in love wif you!" Little Freddy ran at Tony, his arms open. He was wearing an apron.

"Hi Freddy, why don't you take that apron off?" Tony suggested, conscientiously employing a voice that sounded a masculine contrast to Freddy's. He extended his hand in greeting.

"Awight, I take it off," Freddy assented sweetly. They shook hands, and Freddy smiled up at Tony, showing his large yellow teeth. His round freckled face had an unhealthy pallor. He was eleven, but his height was that of an eight year old.

"You like me?" he asked.

"Yes, I like you, but without an apron." Freddy often visited Tony while he played his accordion, and Tony thought Freddy had singled him out from among the older boys as a friend.

"There, no more *apron,*" Freddy said animatedly after he removed it.

"Good," Tony smiled.

"Well, for heaven's sake, look who he listens to." It was Minney, the Kangaroos' counselor, a plain woman with freckles and brown hair. She was leading Kevin, a small, slightly built boy who kept his head forward. "I've been trying to get him to take that darn apron off for two days," she continued, "and you come back from a visit, and he does it for you just like that."

"Well, maybe he wants to be nice to me after I've been away for awhile." Tony and Minney both laughed.

"Ha!" Freddy smiled widely as though he were in on the laughter.

"Hey Kevin," Minney bent down and looked into Kevin's face, "don't you want to say 'hi' to Tony now that he's back? C'mon, look up at me."

Kevin looked up seemingly distracted. "Hi Tony, yes sir," he muttered, then giggled, and once more his head went forward. He had never uttered a full sentence.

"Hi Kevin." Again Tony used the manly voice, maintaining contrast between himself and the small boy.

Then Deirdre told the Eagles to get their coats and start out into the side yard. "I go wif Tony." Freddy grabbed Tony's hand and looked at Minney.

"No, Freddy, I'm going with my group now," Tony shook his head. He did not want Freddy tagging after him.

"That's right, Freddy," Minney nodded.

"I wanta go wif Tony." Freddy was about to cry. Tony knew Freddy could cry about almost anything.

"I'll see you, Freddy." He freed his hand.

The only others in the side yard were the Lambs, a girls' group, "Izh Tony." Tony found himself face to face with Tanya, a Polish refugee his own age who had been at the School almost as long as he had. She talked with a thick accent and could not carry on a sensible conversation.

"Hello, Tanya," Tony said pleasantly. She was giving him her typical mischievous smile, and Tony could not prevent the grin that spread across his face. He wondered whether she was about to attack him the way she sometimes did. Secretly he hoped she would since he wanted to see whether he could control her as easily as men controlled women in the movies. It irked him that he had never been able to. "What's Tony doing?" she giggled.

"Oh, just wandering around, waiting for school." Tony turned away from Tanya before his hopes could be realized. He thought he should not provoke her.

Also, something else was on his mind. There was a change in his schedule of sessions with Deirdre, and he could not remember whether she meant to change Monday or Thursday. Feelings were in everything at the School, and if you didn't remember something, there was a reason. Tony found the question important since he did not want to interrupt anyone else's session. Sessions were absolutely sacrosanct. Tony remembered Dr. V.'s terrible anger at Ted, punctuated by countless slaps, after Ted had accidentally thrown a ball through a window where his counselor was beginning sessions with a new child. Probably Dr. V. saw a great deal of significance in Ted's throwing a ball through that particular window, but how explain why the old screen guard had suddenly broken?

"Boo," Deirdre spoke affectionately as she came up behind Tony and put her hands on his shoulder.

"Boo," Tony answered softly. "Listen, one thing we didn't straighten out about our session change—I see you on Wednesday afternoon, but do I skip Monday or Thursday?"

"Didn't I tell you Monday?"

"I'm not sure. I may have forgotten."

"Was there something you wanted to see me about today?"

"No, I just wasn't sure which day it was." Tony and Deirdre looked at each other, and Deirdre gave one of those smiles which said "there's more to it than that." But Tony did not think so. Nevertheless, he capitulated and grinned back unable to help himself when he looked Deirdre in the face.

"Hey, there's John." Tony saw him in the doorway to the school building.

John opened the door as he saw Tony approach. "Hi John." Tony made himself smile. He was disappointed at being less eager to see John than he had anticipated. They shook hands as Tony stepped inside. Tony felt gratified that John let him in the building since children weren't allowed entry before school. "So how are you?" he asked conversationally, feeling at a loss for words.

"Ohhh," John shrugged contentedly, "same as usual."

"Hmm!" Tony grunted with forced animation.

"Hmm what?" John looked into Tony's face with the warm, searching smile that was so familiar. Tony quailed beneath a warmth he felt he did not deserve. Hmm what, he asked himself and couldn't find anything to say, feeling shy with a man he had known for six years.

"How did it go?" John broke the awkward silence.

"Oh, it had its ups and downs," Tony answered philosophically, imitating John's style of talk as though that would bring back the days when he and John had been closer together.

"Hey Tony," John asked gently, "what's the matter?"

"What do you mean?" Tony balked at a question he did not want to answer.

"What do you think I mean?"

"You tell me," Tony smiled. John just looked at him.

"Oops, it's nine." John glanced at his watch and opened the door for Tony to join the groups assembling outside.

Seconds later John stepped out on the stoop and announced that for ten-thirty recess all classrooms would meet to play dodge ball in the gym. Contemplating John's pleasant expression, Tony was reminded of a certain morning about a year previous. . . .

Now he could see John squatting easily, forearms resting over his knees, as he smiled down at Mark who lay on the classroom floor in a drugged stupor. "C'mon," his voice slurred softly as he looked into Mark's half closed eyes.

"Doewanto," Mark muttered sleepily, barely moving his lips. Under sedation, his adolescent face was calm and mature, unlike its usual appearance when his cheeks were puffed with food or liquid, his fluid-stained mouth puckered to spit.

"C'mon, Mark," John repeated.

"Doewanto," Mark reiterated the jammed phrase he used so often. It was the closest he ever came to saying anything on his own. Usually, when spoken to, he only repeated three or four of the words used by the person who spoke to him. His talk had hardly changed during his four years at the School.

"I sink you vill have to carry him," Dr. V. said.

"Ernie," John glanced at one of his colleagues, signaling him to lend a hand. Then John took Mark by the shoulders while Ernie took his feet. Together they carried him out.

For the rest of that morning, Deirdre took over John's class. At noon, just before lunch, Dr. V. called all the classes into the playroom. There he announced that Mark had been placed in a mental institution.

"Could there be something wrong with Mark's brain?" one of the older boys asked. Dr. V. acknowledged that the possibility could not be ruled out but that tests indicated no organic damage.

A few days before, for reasons unknown, Mark had become practically uncontrollable. He had run out of the building several times and around the block to a small food store from which he snatched various items. Though the temperature was barely above zero, he had often gone without some of his clothing, and once he had tried to leave naked. He had been put on drugs in the hope that he would sleep off whatever bothered him, but that had not worked. When the drugs wore off, he was wild as ever. So Dr. V. and the staff had come to the conclusion that they could do nothing for him. . . .

"So, we're all back," John said as he took hold of Igor's spare shoulders with his strong hands and glanced around at Lewis, Harry, then Tony. Tony met his eyes. Then John broke into a wide, happy smile, and Tony returned it, feeling sheepish as he always did during this kind of exchange. John's smile seemed to say that despite their brief talk before school, things were generally all right.

Then John glanced behind the small circle of desks at Estelle who knelt on a three-piece couch alongside the wall. Hunched on her shins, Estelle stared into space. She seemed to be thinking, but she never spoke. She raised herself up and began to rock rhythmically from one knee to the other. Once, when Tony had seen her do that, a girl had told him she was masturbating. Tony wondered whether it was true. He hated Estelle because she urinated by the couch where he took his accordion lessons and because she had torn up a drawing on which he had worked very hard.

"Well, I guess we better see what's doing with the arithmetic," John suggested after the class had indulged in several minutes' idle talk. Tony got his book with its "6th Grade" written on the cover. "How're we doing?" John came over and squatted by his desk. He looked at the page Tony had worked on just before the holidays. "Here, why don't you do these?" He indicated a batch of problems with his red pencil. "They ought to be a good review."

As he began his arithmetic, Tony remembered the many times John had told him that in any situation, "You get out of it what you're willing to put into it." Certainly John had put a great deal into his efforts to help Mark.

There were the hours spent at Mark's desk trying to teach him simple things. John would ask, "Where's your nose?" and Mark would point to his own nose. Then the questions continued with Mark pointing to the different parts: "Your ears?" "Your eyes?" "Your mouth?" "Your legs?" and "Where is your penis?" Everyone, except Mark and John, would laugh at the last question. John alway kept a straight face which Tony thought a sign of real maturity. At best, he was never able to refrain from a smile.

There were also the lunches during which Tony tried to make sure he never sat near Mark. Mark always spat up his food and made sickening messes on his plate. He also smeared bits of spit-up food on John's shirt, but John never got mad. Asked how he could stand it, he simply said, "Food's never been known to hurt anybody." When the laundry became too much for his wife, John got himself a lab coat. Then his only problem was to be quick enough to keep Mark from getting something in his trim hair. But this never unnerved him.

During recess, John had tried to teach Mark to jump rope. Mark would be taking jump-like steps back and forth from one foot to the other. "Uh! uh, uh, uh! uh, uh, uh!" The sounds came over and over from deep in his throat while his head and body pitched back and forth, the movement punctuated by an emphatic up and down motion of hands and forearms.

John's voice had been full of enthusiasm as Mark pitched backward and forward: "Well, you look like you're in a good mood to do some jumping." He took Mark by the arm and lead him to the pavement between the school and dormitory buildings. As he had often done, Tony turned the rope while John caught Mark beneath the armpits and jumped up with him. They cleared the ground by a few inches as the rope made a slow revolution over their heads and hit the pavement with a lethargic thwack. Though Mark was very thin, he was quite tall and heavily boned so that he weighed about one hundred forty pounds, some fifty pounds less than John. "Hey," John puffed, "can you get that rope moving a little faster?"

"Should we really?" Tony asked.

"Of course! Between the two of us we ought to be able to get up and down fast enough."

And then there had been a certain afternoon which seemed to epitomize all that had been beautiful in Tony's relationship with John. John had been reading to the class for an hour. Listening with uninterrupted interest, Tony had lain forward on his desk, head on his hands, knees on his chair. Now he did not feel like devoting the next half hour to free reading on his own, and this he told John. "So can I work with Mark?" he asked.

"What do you mean, *work*?" John asked in an affectionately scornful tone. For months Tony and Mark had been pounding nails into an old, clumsy looking block of wood. First Mark hammered in a nail while Tony held onto the block. Then Mark held on while Tony hammered. Lately Tony had suggested to Mark that they follow a pattern in their pounding: triangle, circle, square, etc. But Mark wanted nothing to do with that. Now, because of John's question, Tony thought it might be appropriate for them to do something different since they usually hammered during free time after Tony's arithmetic.

"I think maybe Mark and I should try some writing," Tony suggested to John. "As *we* know, that can be *work*." Tony could not help smiling as he referred to the agony-ridden hours during which John had tried to help him develop correct, somewhat legible script. Lately John had been trying to teach Mark to write his name.

"O.K.," John assented, "but the name only." And that made Tony proud because he felt John was treating him like a responsible person.

Moments later, Tony was seated on the floor by Mark. He had a pencil and a stack of paper. "Here Mark, let's write your name." Mark put his hand over Tony's, and Tony started to guide the pencil over the paper. Then suddenly, before Tony was halfway through shaping the letter M, Mark forced his hand to scribble a circle.

"Don't you want to write your name?" Tony looked up at him.

"Doewanto."

"I know how you feel. I had a terrible time learning to write, and I don't think John's recovered from it yet."

"Don't listen to him, Mark. He wasn't any harder than you," John laughed from his desk. Then he gave Tony a friendly, confident wink.

"Here we go." Tony took another sheet of paper. The second trial ended in failure identical to the first. By the time Tony embarked on the sixth effort, both he and Mark were struggling in earnest, really wrestling over the pencil. Tony knew John was watching, and he felt gratified that John respected what he was doing to the point he did not enforce the School's regulations against physical struggle. Then he noticed Mark was smiling. "Oh, you think it's funny."

"Doe-wan-to-write your *name*," Mark giggled shrilly. He always talked about himself in the second person.

"Oh, come on, just once."

"Doe-*wan*-to." Mark made throaty giggling noises while he pressed his elbows against his stomach and rubbed his face against the backs of his hands.

"Look, Mark," Tony panted laughingly, "you've had your way six times out of zero. Now I'm going to have my way if I have to write your name once myself so we can have something to copy from." Tony didn't invite Mark to join his seventh attempt. Abruptly, Tony turned away when Mark tried to interrupt his efforts. Then Mark reached out and mussed up his hair. Tony quickly dropped the pencil and went for his comb. Mark grabbed the pencil, snatched the paper, and reduced the name to a scribble.

"He sure knows how to get your goat," John laughed, alluding to the efforts Tony's vanity compelled him to lavish on his hair which was carefully combed into an elaborate wave and plastered into place by half a bottle of lotion. "Well," John beamed at Mark, "I can't see giving you an A for name writing, but psychology just might be another story. So if you'd learn to write, we could eventually proceed to more interesting subjects." Tony looked at Mark and noticed that he continued to smile. Then the thought flashed through his mind that his fun had been somewhat inhibited.

"Hey, John," he got up, "you think you could get me a crayon? I don't think Mark and I should use a sharp pencil while we're having this trouble with name writing."

"Here you go." John came up with a crayon and gave it to Tony.

"Thanks." As Tony turned back to Mark, John caught him by the arm, and once again he faced his teacher. "Listen," John said. "I like to see that kind of responsibility."

"You mean about the crayon?"

"Yes."

"Good." Tony felt himself flush. "I like it that you think that," he said awkwardly as he smiled at John. He felt very warm; warm toward John, toward Mark, and more generally toward the world. For the moment, he was free of solitude.

But for Tony the day's climax came during the evening when Mark paid their friendship a tribute which drove even John's compliment into the background.

Tony was lying in the tub. The door between the tub and the dormitory was halfway closed. "Hey Tony," Harry was grinning excitedly as he came through the doorway.

"What's up?" Tony asked.

"Mark was just here to see you. Anyway, I think that's what he was here for."

"What do you mean?" Tony suddenly sat up in the tub.

"Well, he was saying he wanted to see 'boy's bed,' and we figured he meant you. So we showed him your bed and told him you were in the tub. . . ."

"Where is he now?"

"Oh, he went back to his dorm."

Five minutes later, Tony was in pajamas and robe visiting Mark in his dormitory. For the next hour, he and Mark pounded nails into an old block of wood.

Now, sitting at his classroom desk, Tony recalled the time when

Mark had become his dorm-mate in the Eagles for the year before he left the School. Tony had felt only relief at Mark's departure which ended certain limitations on group activities and the necessity to store possessions that would otherwise have been destroyed. He had lost interest in the things he did with Mark, and their activities had all but ceased, even though Tony knew that for a while he had actually cared about Mark. But now, as with all other people, his feeling for Mark had declined.

Tony regretted the passage of their friendship as he regretted the fading of all his other feelings of closeness. This he had told John, and John had said, "Well, I guess you didn't want to put any more into it."

"But I couldn't help it. I just didn't feel like it."

"So?" John's noncommittal "So?" had left Tony with a sense of guilt. So what? So you only get what you work for. Yes, maybe that was right. So are you going to spend your life moving mountains you don't want to move? Tony asked himself. He wondered whether John's joy of living, his great maturity, did not derive from a mountain-moving will. Could he ever be like John? He felt stifled, shackled, by the thought of trying.

He solved his arithmetic problems mechanically while thoughts and memories of the past crowded his mind. Almost unconsciously he tapped the floor with his right heel in rhythmic accompaniment to his emotions.

"Hey Tony, could you please stop that?" It was Billy who sat on his left. Billy was a few months younger than Tony and terribly fat.

"You mean my tapping?"

"You know what I'm talking about."

Before the holidays, Tony had cultivated the habit of whistling softly at his desk. This had bothered Billy, but nobody else. "I don't see why I should stop for Billy," Tony had argued with John more than once. Now, however, he wanted to get the new year off to a good start.

"I'm sorry," he said, but he could not keep his lips from stretching into a smile as he confronted Billy's serious expression. Billy had a wide face, a thick head, and a thin colorless crew cut.

"No really, we ought to make this year a good one." He tried to turn his smile into encouragement.

"Yeah, Tony, that's what you always say," Billy accused.

"Look, it won't hurt to try." Tony was taking much more from Billy than usual because, in John's words, he wanted to feel good about himself.

"You two at it already?" John was exuberantly cynical as he rose from Igor's desk and approached Billy and Tony.

"I was just tapping my heel. I didn't intend anything," Tony explained confusedly.

"All done so soon?" John bent over Tony who had absentmindedly closed his arithmetic book.

"No, the problems need to be checked." Tony took the book and pulled apart the pages indented together by frequent pencil jabs. Glancing at the answer sheet, John checked the problems one by one. X X X X X X X X . . . His pencil left a nasty trail. Arithmetic had turned against him, and Tony felt the familiar sense of frustrated rage.

"You seem off to quite a start," John commented.

Ordinarily, Tony would have jabbed the page with his pencil. But, wanting to postpone falling back into his old ways, he simply said, "Guess I'd better pay more attention."

"Is something the matter?"

"No, I've just got to be more careful. I do intend to make this year a better one, whether you believe it or not."

"Why shouldn't I believe it?"

"Oh, I don't know. I'm just not sure I can do it, but I can try."

"That's the spirit." John patted Tony on the back, then went over to Harry who had raised his hand.

As Tony began to correct his problems, he glanced up at Billy with whom he had lived for five years until the dorm change. Tony felt that Billy had been put into the Blacksmiths, instead of himself, because he had been at the School longer. Often Billy played with younger children like Mickey and Ralph, and Tony doubted that living in an older group would, as Dr. V. had phrased it, help Billy grow up. Tony hated Billy for what he was and for his privileges. He also hated his arithmetic, and Billy was fun to tease when the work became frustrating. Because of Mickey and Ralph in the dorm, John's room was the only place where Tony felt he could, as he put it in a self-excusing way, "kick up a little fun like any guy my age." Often he could not resist it.

But he wanted somehow to achieve with John whatever they had had together in the days when he had pounded nails with Mark. Of course, he acknowledged, those days also had their ups and downs. But nostalgia made it hard to believe. Still, why not make this new year as good as the nostalgic past? Tony glanced at his arithmetic page, at the sharp X's staring impudently up at him, and it was no longer easy to think he would soon come to feel good about himself.

8

"Hey, let's have that ball!"

"C'mon, pass it around."

"Keep the ball moving." John's order momentarily dominated the coarse din of voices in the gym as the dodge ball passed in quick arcs over the crowded circle. First to Tony, then to John, then to Ronny who, after hesitating, threw it to Ted; then from Ted back to Tony who saw Harry strutting toward him. "Ted," Tony whispered, indicating Harry with a jerk of his head. He tossed the ball to Ted who returned it immediately. Then Tony sent it spinning. Harry jumped, and the ball sped under his feet.

Tony suddenly noticed that John was looking out across the gym. His eyes followed John's, and he saw Anna leading Freddy toward the circle. Freddy tried to hang back. "Now you heard what Dr. V. said." Anna's voice was soft. Then with the soothing conviction of a nursery school teacher: "We both think you're quite ready to play dodge ball with the others."

"I don't want to play." Freddy was almost in tears.

"C'mon, Freddy." Anna sounded as though she might get angry. Anna was a short woman. She wore a grey skirt that fitted tightly over large hips, and her wide triangular face was set against thickly curled grey hair. "C'mon now," she repeated.

"No," Freddy began to sob.

And Tony remembered children teasing him, threatening to kill him at age three when his mother and father made him stay outside in order to become brave, to learn to get along.

"Freddy, you're holding things up." John's tone was crisp.

"No," Freddy protested.

John took Freddy by the hand. "I don't want to," Freddy cried and sat down. John caught him under the arms, lifted him up and carried him inside the circle.

"O.K., we're going to jump together." He put Freddy on the floor and held on to him. Lewis sent the ball rolling, and John whisked his charge up high as the ball sped by them. For a couple of minutes John continued to hoist Freddy off the floor whenever the ball came close. "You're on your own," John said as he set Freddy on his feet and took his place in the ring.

"No," Freddy whined as he started to leave the circle.

John stepped into his path and looked at him sternly. "Alice," he held out his hands for the ball which Alice threw to him. "Tony," John winked at Tony and sent him the ball. Tony felt a wistful burst of joy and pride. This was a continuation of what he had started with Mark.

"O.K., Freddy." Tony looked at Freddy and noted with satisfaction that he was smiling. "Not so close," he cautioned playfully as Freddy approached him. Freddy stopped about three feet away. With an emphatic nod and a jab toward the floor with his index finger, he stood his ground.

Tony bent over, heaving back and forth with the ball in an effort to be playful, to tease and confuse, yet not do so too much. He wanted to play just right, like when he and Mark had pounded nails together.

All eyes now on him, Tony gloried in assumed admiration, until he heard one of the girls shout, "Throw the ball, already!"

Tony's concentration and the pressure he now felt caused him to overlook factors of chance and angle. He felt a twinge of fear when the ball he threw hit the floor on a short hop, and bounced into Freddy's spread-leg jump. The ball hit him square in the crotch.

"Hey! Hey! Hey!" John started toward them.

"God, I'm sorry!" Tony whispered his shock as he looked into Freddy's face, hoping he would not cry, hoping there had been no real impact between the lightweight ball and Freddy's scrotum.

Certainly the throw had been hard, but not dangerously so. Freddy's lips began to twitch. Then, as John and Anna approached him, his mouth opened and he broke into a soft, high-pitched sob. "Are you all right?" Tony asked helplessly. He caught John's eyes and read anger in the rock stern expression. Anna also looked at him as she and John squatted beside Freddy. Anna's expression was noncommittal, but it made Tony feel awful. How many times had he been trusted with charge of her class while she ran an errand? Tony read her demeanor as accusation that he had broken her faith.

But it was an *accident,* he told himself, wishing Anna would scream at him so he could be angry back. He watched her gather Freddy into her arms. Freddy was really crying now, the tempo having increased as he flung his arms around her neck.

"I'm sorry. I didn't gauge the distance to the floor right, and the ball slipped too fast over my fingers." Tony stumbled into an explanation. John said nothing, and Tony quailed beneath his gaze. "It was an accident," he repeated. He realized he was not only beneath John's scrutiny, but also that of the School, and he struggled to retain a trace of dignity.

John turned to Freddy who already was wiping his tears. Anna had just put him down and was standing over him. "I'm sorry, Freddy." Tony found it difficult to control his shaking voice. He realized that, independently of the School, he felt quite badly about what he had done. Freddy was so helpless, so easily hurt.

"I'm awight." Freddy's soft response seemed directed both to Tony and John. At just that moment the circle began to break, and Tony noticed that Ernie was back from staff meeting. Recess was over.

"Can I see you?" Ernie signaled for John to follow him into his classroom which was just off the gym. As he watched John follow Ernie, Tony noted that his heart was pounding. And he imagined Dr. V.'s face darkening with anger at the account of his hitting Freddy in the crotch. Watching the others file out, he wondered whether John would think he was running away if he left now to get out of his gym shoes so as to be ready for social studies.

"And why are you suddenly so interested in your social studies?" John might ask.

"The truth is I'm not, but I thought I might as well change my gym shoes." Satisfied with his answer, Tony followed the others. While changing his shoes by his locker right outside John's room, Tony noticed Anna and Freddy standing over him. He regretted not being on his feet where he could take whatever they had to say with more dignity than the floor afforded.

"Freddy has something to tell you." Anna used her serious nursery school teacher voice. "All right, Freddy, now tell Tony what you told me."

Tony watched Freddy with interest. The hint of a smile was discernible on his pursed lips. "I bery *mad* at you." Freddy gave a single emphatic nod and then a broad, grotesque smile.

"All right, Freddy, you've told him how you feel." Anna put her hand on Freddy's shoulder and steered him toward the other end of the hall. "You don't smile at people when you're mad at them," she instructed.

Tony looked around, as he finished tying his shoes, and noticed Ted who had just emerged from the lavatory. Ted was watching Anna and Freddy, his head cocked at an angle. "So Freddy told you his feelings," he said. "Some day somebody's going to push that fake smile of his right down his little throat."

Warmed by Ted's sympathy, Tony ventured to ask, "Do you think I hurt Freddy?" He did not try to conceal the fear in his voice as he rose to his feet and placed his gym shoes in his locker.

"I don't know," Ted shrugged. "That kid turns the tears on and off like a faucet. But why did you throw that way?"

"I didn't gauge the distance to the floor right."

"You've gotta watch that."

"Yeah," Tony nodded and turned toward his classroom. Suddenly he felt Ted's hand on his arm. The grip was warm and strong so that for a moment his loneliness and fear were smothered. Ted wheeled Tony around, placed his hands on Tony's shoulders.

"Ya know, this place gets on my nerves sometimes," Ted raised his voice. Tony wondered how he had ever suffered from solitude with a person like Ted at hand. They had often complained about the School to one another, but Tony felt it required a carefree manliness for Ted to say his bit when it was highly possible that trouble with Dr. V. was imminent, and when Anna could hear him while she helped Freddy out of his gym shoes.

"Two, four, six." John glanced around moments later at the circle of desks, then over at Estelle who had resumed her perch on the couch. "Listen," he said, "I've got to go see Dr. V., so why don't you boys get out your social studies. Then, if you have any questions, I'll be back shortly." On his way out, John gave Estelle a bar of clay.

After he shut the door, there was absolute silence. Why doesn't he take me along, Tony wondered. John had only referred him to Dr. V. on rare occasions. Then he had usually taken him over to Dr. V.'s office where things were settled quickly. For a moment Tony and Harry caught each other's gaze, and Tony wondered if Harry was trying to show some sympathy.

Time was ten after eleven. Session in twenty minutes, Tony thought. He tried to derive comfort from the fact that, if anything were to happen, it could be all over by session. But once, after Tony had socked Billy, John had not spoken to Dr. V. until lunch.

Heavy footsteps sounded in the hallway, and Tony felt a constriction in his throat. Was John alone? Was Dr. V. with him? Be brave, he commanded himself, meaning he should act with as much dignity as he sensibly could. He wanted to feel he had courage. But when the door opened, it was only John. He checked Tony's, Harry's, Billy's and Igor's reading assignments, then went over to Estelle.

So maybe you're not in trouble after all, Tony decided, remembering how Ernie had drawn John aside, perhaps to give him a message from Dr. V. But was Anna telling? Was Dr. V. waiting to settle everything at lunch? To simply ask John about his situation would be self-accusation, or so Tony felt. At the School, worrying about trouble with Dr. V. was often thought to signify feelings of guilt.

"I was trying to play just right, not too hard or too easy." Tony imagined an explanation of what had happened. He balked at explaining the feelings that had dominated him since just before school, and now he wondered how much they had fanned his feverish concern about how to treat delicate Freddy.

"Tony, there's a reason why you hit him where you did." Deirdre's probing eyes filled the blank in Tony's mind as he anticipated a session where the subject would have to be broached since failure to do so might not look good.

"I didn't *aim* there. How could I have known just how he'd jump up?"

"Oh, I see. It was all his fault. Listen, Tony, things can't go on this way. There's got to be some changes." Perhaps change would be spelled by a ruling that he could no longer undress behind bits of clothing. Tony did not like his choices. Not to broach the subject at all could imply failure to face up to things while the alternative implied feelings of guilt.

At eleven-thirty Tony was relieved to rise from his desk and leave the classroom. He still had no idea how to explain things to Deirdre, but he almost enjoyed what he thought would be a challenge to his verbal dexterity. Out in the hall he waited for a moment to see if Deirdre would appear. Then, because he was not supposed to loiter, he went into his session room and shut the door. Moments later he heard Deirdre's familiar footsteps, the jingle of her tiny keychain bell.

Suddenly Tony realized Deirdre was talking to someone. Mickey! Only then did he remember the change of schedule. For a wild moment he glanced at the windows, but they were protected by screen guards. No time for anything! Deirdre and Mickey were right outside.

Tony opened the door and stepped into the hallway. "Gosh, what are you doing here?" Mickey smiled in surprise.

"I got the times mixed up," Tony gasped. "I'm *sorry!*"

"You get back to your classroom right now, young man," Deirdre said with vehement severity.

Back at his desk, Tony was hardly able to run his eyes over the words in his reading assignment. He had hoped to escape punishment for hurting Freddy. Now he was sure he'd had it.

"You were looking for trouble," Deirdre would say when it was all over, and who could deny it seemed that way? From time to time, Tony felt John's eyes on him. Did John know why he had left the classroom? When he stopped at his desk for a perfunctory work check, he acted as though nothing unusual had happened.

Only his comment, "You're rather slow today," seemed to suggest it might be beneficial to discuss the reason why work was not progressing normally.

Dr. V. did not turn up for lunch, but Tony knew he'd probably make his usual dormitory rounds after school. By two-thirty, as he sat over free reading, Tony was no longer frightened, only somewhat tense, except during moments of apprehension when he conjured up the reality of the trouble he expected. Soon, he thought, you'll really be frightened. He wondered if, during the final hours before execution, a criminal sometimes failed to register the enormity of imminent death.

Though he felt relatively calm, his thoughts kept turning to Dr. V. "Don't give me zhe excuse zat vhat you did vas an accident." He imagined Dr. V.'s expression as ominous as his voice.

"When I act deliberately, I act deliberately. And when I do something by accident, it's an *accident.*" Tony gloried momentarily in a dream of defiance.

A repellent horror flickered inside him. Yes, the things done today were accidental, but could he honestly, with requisite courage, be so unequivocal? He had just sensed something akin to what had seized him in Acapulco. Now he remembered vividly his compulsion to take a single step toward suicide, a compulsion similar to an occasional urge to smash his grandmother's withering frailty.

At times Tony felt driven by a will that was certainly part of him, sprung from within himself, but separate from the will with which he directed all phases of his conscious life. This other will drove him toward acts he abhorred. He felt it was a will against himself, that he was its captive, its puppet.

When younger, he had sometimes hurt people because he wanted to, though he had never inflicted real injury. But this will frightened him because it impelled him toward acts he did not want to commit. So far he had mastered it, but he feared that it might someday master him. It attacked only occasionally, sometimes seeped into his muscles until he felt it was in his very fingertips. For a moment, just as he defied Dr. V., this will had flared from within, though toward no specific object. Often it directed him to acts of violence which could classify him as dangerous in a way he had never been. Sometimes it made him silently shout certain words or phrases of an excruciatingly embarrassing nature.

And even now, Tony felt hot, blushing dampness on his face as he recalled an incident in Kentucky during a visit to some of his mother's and grandmother's close friends and relatives. Before this visit, his mother had told him she wished he would try to make a good impression in a circle where it was common knowledge that he was under treatment for a severe emotional disturbance. She had also pointed out that some of these friends had known him earlier when his behavior was less than sterling.

He remembered thinking his impression fine indeed as he engaged in animated conversation with two young girls. One was attractive, and she smiled at him pleasantly. The rest of the crowd consisted of older people who seemed to enjoy talking to him. Tony was certain his behavior would cause these people to be astonished that he still needed treatment.

But while he cut his impression, he felt less than comfortable even though he was having fun. The word, which had come slowly to his mind, soon became more insistent: Penis, Peni*ss,* Peni*sss*—Penis, *Peniss,* Peni*sss*—like a rising tide, this word, this will, seeped into the muscles of his mouth, his tongue, so that he was forced into careful concentration on all he uttered. While he played the suave sophisticate, uninvited pictures of his sessions with Deirdre invaded his mind. He squirmed as he thought about the way she sometimes held him on her lap like a baby. This was the Tony he did not want people to know, the Tony he wished did not exist.

"Are you afraid to say the word 'penis' to me?" Deirdre had asked him during a recent session. As with undressing, he had become inhibited about using that word in front of her. He did not understand all the reasons, but because the word was used so freely and frequently at the School, he tried to assume the desired image of a fully grown, normal outsider by not using it. As he chatted politely with the two girls, he realized he would hardly mind death itself as much as a freak turn of events by which the girls could become acquainted with the question Deirdre had asked him.

He made the girls laugh a couple of times and became more relaxed. Then he glanced at the elderly woman who carried a tray of peanuts from which he had already helped himself several times. When she passed him, he tapped her on the shoulder and spoke in a conscientiously suave, polite tone.

"Please, may I trouble you for just one more penis? *Penis!* I mean peanut," he groped helplessly. He had spoken softly, but felt everyone had heard. The ensuing silence was for Tony painful testimony to the impression he was making. Moments later, his mother said it was time for them to go.

In the car, his mother had assured him that their departure had nothing to do with his blunder. She had even tried to heal his ego by describing blunders she and other members of the family had made, but none seemed to match his.

Tony could remember no other occasion when he had been so dominated by this will against himself. Now he reasoned that it had not even dominated him at the party since what his mother called a Freudian slip had not been consciously made.

You're free from it right now, Tony said to himself, not entirely sure what he meant by "it." Nor was there any way to predict when "it" would strike. Tony did not remember being attacked by this will while he carried around the sword he had found on the farm. To this day he did not think his mother had been wrong to let him have the sword, and he often joked about it with Deirdre, enjoying her emphatic expressions of shock that, with all his "angry feelings," his mother had allowed him to handle such a weapon.

Recently during snacks, however, Deirdre had let him cut bologna with a butcher knife. Tony had gloried in the trust but thought of all the mistakes he could make to abruptly change her mind: if he left the knife on the table; let someone else use it; pointed it at somebody while cutting the bologna; cut himself by accident. He had suddenly become aware that with a single wilful movement, he could cause people to worry about his "angry feelings" for the rest of his life.

The will to literally slash the fragile trust, to disburden himself of the fragility, invaded his mind, his hands. But toward what action? To stab somebody? No, his will had not been that specific. Do they have an inkling of this thing in you? Tony wondered about Deirdre, John, Dr. V.

He had a boundless, unreasoning confidence in these people, and in all they had done for him. But what to tell about the will? How to tell it? You'll just make yourself seem like a murderer when you're absolutely not going to do anything, he decided. And hell! Righteousness returned to Tony Hastings. If Deirdre, John or Dr. V. wondered about his will against himself, why only probe for it after an accident?

What happened was an accident, nothing but an accident, Tony told himself as he and the others crossed over to the dormitory building at three. But could he honestly tell Dr. V. that *all* his actions would be either accidental *or* deliberate? The question sank Tony into a guilt-ridden gloom. But is Dr. V. supposed to be some kind of confession booth you tell everything to just because you accidentally hit somebody with the dodge ball or burst in on a session? Tony flashed back to the righteous courage he thought he would soon need.

On his dormitory floor he stopped in the hall and drank from the fountain. Now his ears were keenly alerted to sounds of voices, footsteps, the opening of doors. He waited by the fountain a moment, not wanting to go into his dormitory where he would have to confront Deirdre. Also, he was afraid Mickey would embarrass him with a few comments.

During snacks Deirdre said nothing to Tony except when she asked if he wanted a doughnut, so he was unable to divine her attitude. He just sat waiting and listening for Dr. V. who was likely to appear any minute. "Hey Tony," Mickey grinned.

"What?" Tony noticed Deirdre looking at them, but to his surprise, that did not make him uncomfortable. He decided anxiety had inured him. Mickey seemed to notice Deirdre's gaze also, for he glanced at her.

Then he looked again at Tony and said, "That was pretty funny your turning up in my session, wasn't it?" At that moment Tony heard the grating of the fire doors. Dr. V.! Shock passed at the sound of a lively jingling keychain bell, a woman's light footsteps.

"I'm sorry, I got the time goofed up." Tony was surprised his answer came so easily.

"Deirdre says I should be mad at you, but that's all right." Mickey was still smiling. The fire doors grated again.

"I see." Tony tried to hide any jubilation he might have enjoyed at Deirdre's expense. His voice was very low so Dr. V. would not pick up the conversation—but once more a light, quick footstep, a false alarm.

Deirdre looked at her watch. "Listen," she said, "there's something we should talk over before we leave for swimming. Henry's going to be coming here again to teach woodshop and we can work with him from four to five on Wednesdays, if you want to." Silence followed her announcement.

Last fall the Eagles had taken woodshop for a short while, and Deirdre had decided it should be discontinued because of the group's apathy. "There's no point in taking up Henry's time," she had told them crossly. Tony knew Deirdre wanted him to use his hands, to see that he had good hands and, in John's words, feel good about himself. But he disliked woodshop.

Now nobody cared to answer Deirdre. Tony felt that he definitely should not be the first to speak since it would not do anything for his predicament to have Dr. V. catch him in an argument.

"I don't think I want to go to woodshop," Harry finally ventured, a touch of solemnity in his voice.

"What about you, Igor?" Deirdre first asked Igor, then went around the table, finishing with Tony.

"I don't think so." Tony's voice was barely audible. All answers except Igor's had been negative.

"I guess that settles that." Deirdre did not seem annoyed, and Tony felt a trace of guilt for rejecting what he considered part of the School's effort to help him. But would it be right for him to engage in an activity for which he had neither use nor desire?

"Well, I think I'll go to my room and get my coat." Deirdre rose from the table. "And then we can start over for swimming." Tony realized that within a few minutes the group would be clear of the School, of Dr. V., unless he showed up promptly.

Dr. V. appeared neither in the afternoon nor at supper. After supper, as he lay on his bed, Tony decided nothing was likely to happen. Certainly Deirdre wasn't angry since she had drawn up alongside him in the pool and asked pleasantly if there had been something he wanted to talk to her about that morning. Also, at the School, one was not usually kept waiting for punishment.

The door to the stairway opened, and there were heavy footsteps. Once again the fear. But it was John, and Tony was surprised since John was usually at home in the evening. "Deirdre," John said, "can I take Tony now?" Deirdre nodded.

"Want to come with me?" he asked, looking down at Tony.

"Sure," Tony answered, wondering where John wanted to take him. To Dr. V.?

Their destination was the woodshop in the school building. "I thought we could work on this house together." John picked up a small toy house from one of the work benches. Tony remembered having spotted the house while in charge of Anna's class shortly before Christmas vacation. He had told John there were loose nails in the house and that it was badly splintered.

Now he ceased to anticipate trouble with Dr. V. John would hardly be so friendly if he had a complaint to lodge. The way John was treating him ran so contrary to expectation that Tony was moved to a profound sense of gratitude.

"Why don't you get a hammer and some nails?" John suggested as he unlocked a cabinet that contained glue and paints. Tony knew John did not really need him. He felt he was being given another chance at the opportunity he had turned down that afternoon. You're not meant for this kind of work, he thought, as he selected nails and hammer, then went to join John at the work bench. John had a cumbersome looking jar of glue and some paper, and he was assembling variously sized chips that had broken off the house.

"Ready?" Tony smiled. He noticed a smile on John's face like the one under which he had cringed that morning.

"Yes, I suppose," John nodded. For a moment Tony thought of the morning recess, of how he had tried to throw the ball just right, as though that would have enabled him to capture something out of his past with John. He resolved that he would, to use John's words, "put a lot into" the work laid out before him. He was not sure what his resolution would accomplish, but he hoped it would put him close to whatever he admired in his teacher. Perhaps that would erase the discomfort that was mixed with his gratitude.

"Here, these are small enough to glue on." John picked up some small chips.

"That's right. A nail would split them open." Tony tried to sound knowledgeable.

"How do you think we can apply the glue without getting the house sticky?" Tony felt from the way John looked at him that he was more interested in how the question would be answered than in the answer.

"Why don't we use a small paintbrush?" Tony became resourceful. When John looked doubtful, he suggested a wet paper towel with which the glue could be dabbed on by finger. He was not sure why he wanted the towel to be wet, but it had something to do with the way the glue looked so dense and dry.

"Maybe this'll work." John picked up a stiff piece of paper and folded it until it was tightly pleated. "Here, try it out." He dipped one end of the strip into the glue, then gave it to Tony. He made another strip for himself.

At first Tony felt uncomfortable, but the feeling quickly faded as he and John worked together, gluing small chips, nailing larger ones, and fixing the roof and chimney. Random conversation almost led him to forget his discomfort. After he finished nailing a large chip, he noticed that the heads on some of the nails protruded. "Someone could get scratched on these," he said, hoping to make an original statement about the repairs.

"We'll fix that." John's tone indicated he had already spotted the problem. "We're going to do some countersinking," he continued. "You know what that is?"

"No."

"Take your hammer." John took a nail and placed its point on the head of one of the nails embedded in the house. "Now you give this nail a few taps, and that'll drive the one on the bottom out of sight. Pretty good trick, isn't it?"

"Yes, it is," Tony nodded. He gave a couple of taps with the hammer, then stopped. He feared that he would miss and hit John's fingers. "Listen," he said, "you'd better let me hold onto the nail because I don't want to hit you."

"Go on, I'm not afraid of you. You'll do all right."

Cautiously, Tony hit the nail three more times. The head of the first nail buried, they moved to another one. Suddenly Tony was aware he had been invaded by his abhorrent will against himself. He felt it strongly, felt it in all the muscles of the arm holding the hammer. He felt a compulsion to deal a smashing blow to John's fingers, to ruin John's confidence in him, to destroy and be free from whatever he and John had worked to achieve during the past half hour, during the past six years, and to be free from whatever they had not achieved. Carefully Tony countersank the remaining nails.

"Well, I guess that does it," John sighed contentedly.

"Hell, I'm just not very gifted at his kind of work." Tony wanted John to say something to the contrary.

"Who says you're not?" John challenged.

"Well, you seem to know so much more than I do."

"So you can learn."

"But don't some people just have less ability than others for this kind of work?"

"Some people have a harder time learning than others, but they can learn if they want to." Tony noticed John looking beyond him toward the doorway, and his eyes followed John's. Dr. V.!

"Vell, I'm certainly surprised to see you two down here," Dr. V. commented.

"That's mutual," John answered.

"I see. Vell, I came to check zhe lists in zhe cabinets to find out if our new supplies have been ordered."

"I dropped the list off in the office this afternoon."

"You did? Zat's good. Zhen I don't have to vorry. So vhat are you two doing here? Let Tony tell me."

"We came to fix this house," Tony answered. "It was badly chipped and splintered."

"Oh, I see."

"It belongs to Anna's class," John added. "Tony told me it was in a rather dangerous state of repair just before Christmas."

"Vell, zat's good. Didn't you tell me somesing else about Tony helping vone of zhe kids vis zheir arismetic?"

"You mean Hank?" John asked. "I believe Anna told you Tony had found that Hank was having trouble with his multiplication because he didn't know his tables."

"Yes, now I remember. Zat vas very good, vasn't it?"

"I think so." There was a hint of pride in John's voice.

"You have really come a long vay." Dr. V.'s gaze shifted to Tony. "I like to see you assume zis kind of responsibility."

"Thanks," Tony muttered.

"No, I really mean it." A moment's silence. "Vell, I have an appointment," Dr. V. said abruptly as he looked at his watch. "So good night." He turned from the doorway and left.

Tony felt good for the rest of the evening. He felt good when at seven-thirty Deirdre took the group down to the kitchen to bake chocolate chip cookies for snacks. There he did more than his share of the work, and he mediated a quarrel between Mickey and Ralph, both successfully and quickly, for which he received Deirdre's praise. He talked with Lewis and Igor more than he usually did, and he felt good about that too.

But Tony did not feel entirely good. He thought of Marta and the whore in Acapulco. There was no room, at the moment, for that way of life. And the dearth made him feel incomplete. Now he re-lived and improvised on the experiences he had had with John and Mark, and in Anna's classroom. But there was something lacking in this whirlwind satisfaction, and in a flash of insight he told himself, "All you're imagining with John and the School is a thousand happy endings to all your problems."

9

Tony had started a push-up regimen in order to strengthen his muscles for future Amazon adventures. One evening after supper Harry joined him at his practice, and they kept count for each other until Laura's attention was caught by their competitive attitude, and she ordered them to stop. Now, seated on the floor with their counselor, Tony and Harry were trying to persuade her to revoke her prohibition.

"Tony," Laura was saying, "could you please tell me what you told Dr. V. the night you got back from your visit?"

"You mean about getting rid of my solitude?"

"What do you think?"

"Well, knowing you counselors, you probably think I'm very lonely with Harry when we do these things together."

"Are you?"

"I don't know. Not everything you do with a person has to be an act of making friends. Hell, if I had Harry visit me in Glenville, we'd do a lot of things you counselors would disapprove of, but that wouldn't stop us being friends."

"What would you do in Glenville?"

"Well, first there'd be certain things we'd want to find out. Right, Harry?"

"Right," Harry leered mischievously.

"Like what?" Laura asked.

"Like we'd first want to see who could wrestle best. That's something we've been wondering about for years," Tony answered. "C'mon, Laura, you know that's how most kids outside the School play. Even if it's not the best way, you can't expect us to be some kind of saint that doesn't even exist."

"Just what kind of authority are *you* on kids outside the School?"

Suddenly Tony was angry. "You think you keep us cooped up in here so much we don't know what goes on, huh? Well, you know we *are* let outside and sometimes we enjoy ourselves like that time last summer out at Red Cloud."

"Red Cloud?"

"You know, that dude ranch in Colorado where Mother took me and Paul."

"What happened?"

"Well those kids came out with their switchblades. You know what those are, don't you?"

"What *is* this?" Tony could tell by Laura's concern that she was duly impressed. It made him happy.

"Oh yeah, I remember *that*." There was a faint smile on Harry's face.

"Well," Tony began, "these two kids came out to Red Cloud Ranch for a couple of days. Anyway, I went with some other kids into their room, and they had their switchblades out. And we had a big discussion, with me leading it, about how we'd use those knives to defend ourselves. Then we had mock knife fights, keeping the knives closed."

"Is that the way you always play?" Tony thought he detected a hint of sadness in Laura's voice, and he wondered whether it would be appropriate to grab her hand.

"Why can't you just face the fact that men are men and sometimes like to play around with knives?" he pleaded in the tone that he might have whispered, "Hold me! Hold me in your arms!"

Laura just looked at him without answering. Then she asked, "Why are knives so important to you? You mention them constantly."

"With a knife you can cut somebody down to size," Tony answered bitterly.

"What do you mean by that?"

"Well, if a person's bigger or stronger than you, and you fight him with knives rather than hand to hand, you have a better chance of winning since size won't make so much of a difference."

"Why is it necessary to fight at all?"

"It's necessary to be able to."

"Why?"

"Well, it's hard to explain exactly. But take what happened to me out at Red Cloud. . . ." and Tony avoided Harry's and Laura's eyes. "I was down at the corral horsing around with this ranch-hand named Dirk. . . ." Detail by detail he recounted what had happened at the ranch.

"Hey, you can't even run fast." Dirk had caught him by the shirt and brought him to a jolting stop. "Now I thought you said if I let you get away, you could outrun me."

"I guess I was wrong," Tony panted between giggles as he struggled to keep away from a small pile of manure where Dirk had threatened to drag him, could easily drag him if he wanted. . .

Dirk let him go. "Hey, Tony, you mind lettin' me in on somethin'?"

"Guess not." Tony pushed his shirt back into his pants and looked around the corral at a couple of wranglers who were idling on top of the fence, and at the pretty girl from the kitchen who sat between them. He also glanced over at Paul who had been watching them intently from his perch on the gate. "What do you want to know?"

Dirk looked at him appraisingly, curiously. "*How* can you be so weak?" he asked.

"What do you mean?"

"Why, you can't *fight* worth a damn, and I bet you couldn't even race my grandmother."

"I bet I can take Paul as easily as you took me," Tony challenged. "And Paul's closer to my age than I am to yours."

"Let's just see about that." Then Dirk waved to Paul, "Hey, c'mon down." Tony watched as his brother jumped down and advanced toward him. Without warning, Paul hurled himself forward, gnashing his teeth the way he did when he was angry.

Tony was thrown by the impact of his body; he felt Paul's arms clamp savagely around his neck. And he found himself struggling beneath his brother in the dust, unsure whether Paul was merely trying to pin him or really hurt him. Never had he known his brother to wrestle so ferociously.

"Get'm Paul! Get'm Paul! Get'm Paul!" Dirk, the other wranglers, and the girl screamed their frenzied ecstasy. With both hands, Tony caught at the collar of his brother's shirt. His eyes squeezed shut, he clenched his teeth and pulled, until his brother's face was very near his own. "One!" Dirk shouted joyfully, and Tony knew that everybody would consider him beaten by his little brother if he were still down after the count of three. "Two!" Dirk yelled, and the others yelled with him. Spurred by terror of humiliation, Tony heaved with his whole body and, in an explosion of excruciating effort, he hurled his brother into the dust beside him. "Three!" they shouted, but it was too late. Then Paul launched another furious attack, and again he heard the chorus of shouts . . .

"It took me a few minutes to finally pin him and he's so much younger than me." Tony looked up at Harry and Laura, hoping Harry would say something on his behalf.

"Well, if somebody jumps you the way your brother did and gets you off guard—hell, it would probably take anybody a few minutes." Tony was glad to have Laura hear Harry's opinion.

"Why did you let yourself get into that kind of situation?" Laura asked.

"Well, it just kind of cropped up. There I was just messing around. And then, suddenly, I found myself kind of on the spot when the guy said I was so weak."

"Why were you roughhousing with that man?"

"Just for fun." But roughhousing was not considered fun at the School.

"Those people out at the ranch were *nasty*." Tony thought he detected disgust in Laura's tone.

"Hell, why shouldn't they encourage my brother? It's nice to see a kid be able to take on somebody older and bigger than him. What do you want—everyone to be like counselors?" Tony wanted to appear a good sport, to reject the School idea that things were nasty when not so intended. But inside he liked what Laura had said. Why had everyone shouted, "Get'm Paul! Get'm Paul!" Didn't they know it hurt to be beaten by one's younger brother? "Of course it hurts," he added, "when someone smaller than you can take you on, so I want to do push-ups and learn to handle knives so I won't be one of those guys who can be taken. I don't want to just rot like a protected weakling in this School."

"Tony, do you think Dr. V.'s a strong man?" Laura asked.

"No, I *don't* think Dr. V's a strong man," Tony shook his head, wondering how many times counselors had asked him that question. "I think he's a rotten physical specimen. You know, I've never seen him in anything but a neat suit, like he's always ready for Sunday-school or something. But you don't have to bother to tell him that."

"Why shouldn't I?"

"I know you counselors tell him everything, and he's been hearing about himself for years, long before I came to the School."

Mickey and Ralph suddenly broke into a fight over a piece of candy, and Laura had to intervene. Tony was relieved from the burden of his push-up regimen, but he realized he had not received an explanation for its curtailment. An hour later he joined Laura outside at the hallway kitchenette where she was making fudge for snacks.

"Boo," he said as he drew up beside her. "Can I dip my finger in for a lick?" His finger poised over the fudge, he spoke teasingly, affectionately, the way he often talked to Deirdre.

"It's too hot," Laura answered.

"I'll dip my finger in real quickly."

"No," she said. Tony felt tempted to take her hand.

"Look, I really don't see what's so wrong with those push-ups," he recommenced his old vein.

"Tony, I don't like to see you drive yourself. Now you can talk to Dr. V. if you think I'm wrong."

Tony winced at arbitrary authority; then he had a new angle. "Hey, Laura," he smiled, "supposing we went down to Dr. V., and I told him I didn't think you should stop us from doing push-ups, and he said I was all wrong and started smacking me back and forth across the face, and pulling my hair, and knocking me around with his fist, and shouting 'Vhy don't you listen to your counselor! Vhy don't you listen to your counselor?'—would you feel sorry for me?"

"Why should he do all those things to you?"

"I don't know," Tony shrugged. He felt Laura's question evasive, but she couldn't be expected to commit herself to feelings that implied disapproval of Dr. V.

"Tony," Laura said after a moment, "are you so sure you're in such control of things around you that you don't occasionally need other people to tell you what you should or shouldn't do?" Tony thought of the will which had made him want to hit John's fingers with the hammer. Did he need control? Did Laura's question derive from some staff intuition about his problem?

"I don't see how anyone's bossing me around can help me," he finally answered, then ducked over to the fountain for a sip of water.

"You're thirsty," Laura observed.

Tony knew she did not really think that was the case. "Water's good for you," he countered with a comment he realized was meaningless. "You need it after you do push-ups," he suddenly added, once again on safe ground. "Hell, why can't we do those push-ups? They're good exercise."

"Tony, I've said all I have to say."

"You mean I have to go see Dr. V. now?" Tony asked.

"Do you want to go?"

"No, I'd better not. Hell, if we went down there, he'd probably beat the crap out of me and leave me groveling at your feet on the floor."

"Tony, do you believe that?" Laura looked at him.

"Oh, I don't really think he'd do anything," Tony laughed. "But supposing he did. Suppose he left me all black and blue, groveling at your feet, and went back into his office after telling me to apologize to you. Then, if I apologized and begged you to forgive me, would you pick me up?" Barely had the question escaped his mouth before Tony wished he had not asked it.

"What is this?" Laura turned and looked Tony full in the face.

Tony hoped she had not registered the implication that he would like her to pick him up, to hold him in her arms.

"Oh, I was just curious," he answered.

Laura continued to look steadily at him. "What do you want me to do when I pick you up?" she asked.

"Well, I'd rather have you raise me off the floor than leave me lying there," Tony evaded. "Hey, Ronny!" He turned to refuge as Ronny came out of the dormitory.

"Yeah?"

"Has Hounds Dog been put away in his kennel tonight?"

"Snap! Snap! Reep! Tear! . . . . ooh! He's reely getting you." Ronny combined for imitation the accents of Dr. V. and a former Swedish counselor.

"Oof!" Tony caught at his own arm, then at his leg. "Pleeze, Hounds Dog," he pleaded in a voice very much like Ronny's.

"Zhere, you reely get it ven you talk zat vay!"

"I guess you just don't put Hounds Dog into kennels."

"Zat's right!" Ronny nodded for emphasis, and Tony nodded with him. "Oooooh," their mouths formed into long o's as they looked into each other's eyes and nodded into each other's faces as though something very significant had passed between them. "Zat's right!" they repeated, continuing to look at each other the way Dr. V. and the counselors looked at them when something significant was being said.

Laura was perplexed. "What is this about Hounds Dog?"

"Don't you know who Hounds Dog is?" Tony and Ronny turned on her. "You mean you haven't heard about him?"

"I've heard you two mention him, but that's all I know."

"Well, you see," Tony explained, "Hounds Dog's a cross breed between Elvis Presley and Dr. V." Tony and Ronny snickered.

"How can anything be crossed between two men?"

"Vell, eet's all a razer oreeginal seetuation," Tony answered. "You see, vone morning Ronny vas seenging to me, 'You ain't nosing but zhe Hounds Dog, just a cryin' all zhe time.' So I told heem vhat I sought of zhe Hounds Dog, and I've been getting eet ever seence. You see, I alvays provoke zhe poor Hounds Dog." Tony began to employ a counselor-type voice. "And if you provoke, you take zhe consequences," he concluded with a remark often made by counselors.

"Zat's right," Ronny agreed as he and Tony nodded at each other. "You know how many Tonys zhere are left now?"

"About seventy?"

"No! Seexty-nine!" Every now and then Ronny announced that Tony had succumbed to one of Hounds Dog's attacks. At the outset, Tony had existed one hundred fold.

"Hey, vhat happens after all zhe Tonys are gone?"

"Zhen zhere are no more Tonys." Ronny shook his head. "Oooooh," they laughed into each other's faces. Tony had no idea what had developed between himself and Ronny with the advent of Hounds Dog. Once, after being snapped at several times, he had asked Ronny, "Vhere do *you* come eento all zis?"

"Ooh!" Ronny had raised his eyebrows, and they had nodded at each other in imitation of a significant interchange of understood feelings.

"So vhere *do* you come in?" Tony had repeated in vain, for Ronny was to yield nothing more than a brief nod, leaving Tony with a touch of loneliness. For a few seconds neither he, Ronny, nor Laura had anything to say. "Well," Tony shrugged, "I guess I'd better keep that lousy cur off my back."

"Snap! Snap! Snap! Reep! Now he's reely hurting you."

"Oh pleeze, Hounds Dog! I deedn't mean zat!"

"Zat's too bad! Zees time you've reely had it!"

"C-c'mon, Ronny—I mean Hounds Dog."

"Ooooooh!" They were both startled by Tony's slip, and their mouths formed long o's which strained to break into smiles as they nodded at each other. At such moments Tony felt closer to Ronny than during any other interaction.

"You know you two are saying some pretty nasty things to each other," Laura cut in.

Tony was thoughtful for a moment, not at all surprised by Laura's attitude. Counselors often considered various types of interchange to be nasty when they were not so intended, but he was unable to see anything particularly unpleasant in what he and Ronny were doing. "God, aren't we nasty," he agreed mockingly.

"God, aren't you a fresh little boy," Laura retorted.

Tony thrilled at her unexpected denunciation. "Aren't I though," he mocked her once again.

"All right, young man, I don't want you out here with me anymore." Laura sounded fed up. "You can go on back into the dormitory."

"Oh, I wanted to stay out here with you," Tony protested in a teasing tone.

"You *heard* what I said."

"Oh c'mon, please." Tony looked pleadingly over his shoulder. "Please!" he begged. "Please please please. . . ."

Please! Please! Please! Please, he begged softly later that night as he wrapped his arms around his pillow. Please, Laura, I just want you to hold me. I won't be fresh with you anymore. Please just let me be your baby.

For a moment he lay still, tightly embracing his pillow, while he thought about this longing to be held. It embarrassed him; he did not want people to know about it. At least he did not want people to know how he felt toward Laura. But after a certain night last summer at Red Cloud Ranch, he had begun to accept his feelings.

That night one of the wranglers had taken Tony and some of the other boys into the hills for a twenty-four hour camping trip. Though it was to have been an all-male outing, another wrangler had brought some girls for a brief visit, good looking girls in their twenties who worked in the kitchen. Tony soon found himself by the fire with a popcorn popper, and he suddenly noticed that three or four boys his age were on their sleeping bags, each cuddled up with a girl. And he wondered whether his solitude had something to do with his being harnessed to the popcorn popper.

Later he had approached one of the boys for information concerning preliminaries necessary to land a girl on a sleeping bag. The boy was a junior ranch hand who spoke with a southern accent. "Ah, that was nothin'," he had answered carelessly. "We was jus' messin' around."

You want some of that messin' around too, Tony told himself, while his arms tightened around his pillow.

10

Tony wrote in his diary:

> *Tomorrow or sometime soon I will have to make my birthday list. Always around Christmas or my birthday I try to get something real expensive and nice. I want it to fill a gap in my life. It is as though I had a chunk taken out of my life. Perhaps it is my solitude that causes that gap, for I never use people to fill it. I try to acquire instruments with which I can have fun without people. This is quite important to me, and I have given it some thought. I want a set of Gibbon's Rome and Prescott's books on Mexico and Peru. With these books I will have quite a bit to do and read.*

To do and read: Tony imagined himself pouring avidly over the intrigue and lore of past civilizations, vanishing into a world of his own when he was angry at Deirdre, at the School. Recently he had seen Gibbon's and Prescott's handsomely bound works in a nearby bookstore, and he thrilled at the thought of having them adorn the shelf at the end of his bed.

He saw himself older as a reporter accompanying an expedition through South American jungles in search of a lost city. With knowledge derived from Prescott and others, he would be able to make casual statements about the city's history and the legends surrounding it. Over evening drinks, beneath mosquito netting, he'd drop offhand remarks, comparing various historical similarities between the ancient Roman and American civilizations.

More immediately, he could mouth brilliant comments at the group table with Laura listening. Of course, you really want those books for the knowledge, Tony told himself and believed it.

His mother had told him it was appalling that he did not know the names of certain artists. So Tony added in his diary:

> *In order to become cultured, I will ask for an art book with artists whose names I don't know.*

He had never been moved by a good painting and wondered if he ever would be. He felt the gap in his life could be partly filled if he became a well-rounded man.

Tony wrote his birthday letter to his mother on a Wednesday evening, the same evening Dr. V. left for a trip to New York from which he was due back Monday. Deirdre read the letter and ruled out Prescott and Gibbon, telling Tony they were too advanced for him.

Unfazed, Tony asked if he could get a telescope with a camera attached to it. How wonderful to take pictures of things far away! Perhaps of headhunters from a safe vantage point when he got to South America. But Deirdre squelched that aspiration, saying he was neither old nor experienced enough to handle such equipment. A tape recorder was his next idea. What fun to record Dr. V., the group, various T.V. shows, then play them back. But Deirdre also considered the tape recorder too advanced.

Dancing lessons were his final suggestion. When not working as a reporter, Tony planned to become a night club man with his accordion, so the dancing had to fit in at some point. But the accordion was already one connection outside the School, and Deirdre told him no dancing lessons unless he wanted to stop seeing his accordion teacher.

Frustrated and feverishly angry, Tony paced around and around the group table. "Hey Tony, smile!" Mickey poised a small rubber camera in front of him.

"Good heavens, while he's so mad at me?" Deirdre laughed, and Tony ducked out into the hall. He did not think Deirdre had laughed to hurt him, but simply, without malice, at his situation. Still he wanted to get away. But the hall, a drink from the fountain, offered only temporary seclusion, for one was not supposed to loiter.

The School allowed no privacy for anger at a counselor's rules to be quietly nursed. Tony had felt this keenly two weeks before when he had gone upstairs ahead of the group. Even though he was at times permitted to go about the building by himself, the group was supposed to stay together, but he had failed to realize the group was not behind him. "Don't be a disgusting liar," Deirdre had almost snarled when he explained this, and in the ensuing argument she had told him he could leave if he didn't like the way things were run at the School. But Tony was not about to leave. He even felt it cowardly to do so while he needed to improve himself. So at times the anger had to bottle up.

Saturday evening the Eagles were joined at supper by Ed, a young psychiatrist who seemed always on the verge of a smile. Ed poured himself some water. Deirdre took his glass, emptied it into the pitcher, poured the water again and gave it back to him. Startled at Deirdre's action, Tony wondered what Ed thought about Deirdre's enforcement of her new rule that only counselors pour drinks at mealtimes. Tony chafed beneath this restriction, which he found inconvenient and degrading, but he sympathized to some extent with Deirdre's worry about how very much he and the others drank.

Harry poured himself a glass of milk, and Deirdre enforcing the new rule took his glass for a while. Harry protested that his mistake was the result of established habit, but Deirdre did not buy that, so he said, "I'm going to watch every little thing you do."

"All right, Harry," Deirdre promised, "you'll do just that." Tony glanced at Ed and thought his expression indicated amused curiosity. Did he, an adult, fail to understand Deirdre's attitude? Perhaps. And Tony decided that Deirdre would probably bring Ed to her point of view in the staff room, the sanctuary where he thought counselor opinion was more or less molded.

In spite of the pitcher incident, which did not really concern him, Tony truly enjoyed himself in a talk with Ralph about exploration in the Amazons. When the Eagles rose from the table, his mind was in the tropics. He started out at the head of the group, then on up the stairs without noticing he was not with his group.

When he reached the top of the stairs, Tony realized no one was behind him. "Shit!" he whispered to himself. "Deirdre's going to yell at you." As he descended the stairs, Tony felt slightly frightened, the way he did with Dr. V., only to a much lesser degree. He tried to take comfort from the fact that Dr. V. was out of town and could not be attracted by Deirdre's yelling, but that was no great relief.

He entered the locker room through the doorway to the stairs just as Deidre came out of the playroom, the group and Ed behind her.

"Where were you off to?" Deirdre asked.

"I was up the stairs. I thought everyone was following me until I looked around."

"You deserve a slap in the face!"

Tony winced, embarrassed in Ed's presence. "After my talk with Ralph about the Amazon, I was sort of dreaming off, and I didn't know that nobody was following me," Tony answered, hoping Deirdre would understand about "dreaming off" which often explained why a person didn't "know what was going on around him." His explanation was the truth.

"You know what you were doing." Deirdre's voice was a toneless accusation. This was one of her favorite phrases, and there was no logical rebuttal to it.

"Deirdre," Tony said evenly, "I did not mean to do what I did, but I hate your silly rules, so maybe I did it because of angry feelings that I haven't faced." Tony seriously doubted this, but it was fun to throw the School at Deirdre. And who could know for sure what unfaced feelings undergirded one's actions? He thought he had her speechless while she gave him one of her long, searching looks. He averted his eyes and wondered whether she knew he did not take what he had said very seriously.

"Why don't you leave him alone!" Ralph suddenly turned on Deirdre. "Tony's a big boy and doesn't need a counselor by him all the time."

"Thanks, Ralph," Tony said. "I can handle my own problems." Tony gloried in Ralph's adulation, but only for an instant.

"How dare you thank him?" Deirdre's voice bordered on outrage, and Tony suddenly felt small inside. It was wrong to encourage Ralph to say what he had said, to exploit Ralph's crying need for his friendship. But it hurt to reject him without an assertion of thanks.

"Well, I told him to keep out," Tony protested helplessly.

"Tony Hastings," Deirdre said softly, "you and I both know what you were up to, and I don't like it one bit."

"Tony, I'm going to help you whenever I want to." Ralph was loyally defiant.

"No, you won't," Tony countered.

"Oh yes I will."

"No, absolutely not."

"You mean you don't want me to?"

"That's right."

"Then I'll hate your guts!" Ralph screamed.

"That's all right with me," Tony shot back, embittered by Ralph's transformation. Tony usually resented Ralph because he misbehaved with Mickey. But occasionally they had good experiences together, like at supper. Tony felt that solitude would not be a problem if he could have such experiences more often with boys his own age. Meanwhile he needed Ralph's companionship and admiration.

"Well, I have to leave you boys now," Ed spoke up. And Tony wondered whether his need was visible to Ed as he nodded good night to him.

The Eagles went up to their dormitory. "All right, Harry, get a chair," Deirdre ordered.

"What's this?" Harry wanted to know.

"You're going to sit and watch everything I do."

"What *is* this?" Harry seemed outraged.

"Too many empty things have been said around here lately." Deirdre paused for emphasis, wanting the group to hear. Then, to Harry, "Now you're going to sit on a chair and watch me just the way you said you would at supper."

"I won't." Harry shook his head.

"Harry," Deirdre warned, "I don't want to see you make a liar out of yourself."

"I'm not going to watch you."

"All right, then get out of the dorm."

Harry complied.

Sprawled on his bed, Tony ground his teeth as he watched Harry shut the dormitory door. Deirdre doesn't care a bit about his or your pride, he said silently. Then, squirming uncomfortably: You're fourteen going on fifteen, and you're being treated like a dirty criminal who's not even trusted alone in a building. You're treated like a three-year-old.

Last week Deirdre had allowed him to go by himself to get a book he had left in his downstairs locker. And last Sunday she had sent him up ahead of her with the evening's snacks from the kitchen. She's not afraid to let you loose, Tony told himself over and over. No, there was no reason for the group to keep so tightly together except that was how Deirdre wanted it. "We've got to stick together," she had told them because of the feelings she thought they all had about Dr. V.'s going out of town. What do you mean—stick together? We're *stuck.* Tony had almost spoken out loud.

She needs to be obeyed, Tony continued his silent monologue. That woman just needs to be obeyed, he repeated in a tone of finality. And now the dormitory atmosphere was dominated by the playful laughter of that same woman as she tried to coax Ralph to undress for a bath. Ralph was resisting her for all he was worth, repeatedly calling her every obscene name he knew. He was angry at being interrupted while writing a letter. He often wrote foreign dignitaries, presumably about political questions, but Tony imagined that Ralph was simply trying to reach out, the way he had done at the bottom of the stairs. "I want to finish writing to Haile Selassie, you bitch," he protested.

"I haven't seen you play with your motor boat in awhile," Deirdre countered.

You once treated her that way, Tony remembered. However, it was at least a year since he had even called her a name, and now he found himself shocked by Ralph's vicious rejection of her kindness. Even though he thought it unlikely, he felt apprehensive that Ralph might go too far, and he marveled at what seemed to be a persistent effort to do so. Well, he shouldn't have to take a bath now, Tony concluded, satisfied with this explanation of Ralph's behavior.

The behavior certainly did not bother Deirdre. She was all smiles with Ralph and not at all affected by the fact that, within the half hour, she had screamed at a fourteen-year-old boy who had accidentally gone up the stairs by himself. Of course, when she was fourteen, she never had to go through anything like this, Tony thought bitterly.

Moments later, exiled Harry opened the door. "Can I come in now?" he asked. Deirdre had just carried Ralph into the bathroom, and she was getting his pajamas from under his pillow.

"You can come in if you'll do what you said you'd do," she replied.

"O.K., I guess that's better than wasting my evening out here." Harry tried to sound bored, but Tony knew his pride was hurt. He wondered if Deirdre realized this as she went back into the bathroom, apparently unmindful of Harry who sat down in a chair and began to watch her. She probably didn't care; she probably felt Harry had brought his troubles on himself and should take the consequences. Pride was an issue Deirdre worried little about.

Deirdre did not relieve Harry from his forced vigil until she had cleaned up around Ralph's bed and the group table. Then she began to get Mickey undressed. She talked and laughed with him as she picked him up and carried him into the bathroom. Yes, Tony thought bitterly, she could rule out birthday gifts, television shows, not allow him out of her sight, trample on his dignity by walking into the bathroom while he took a bath, and this for no other reason than to fill a cup of water. And through it all she could remain happy. For a moment Tony thought of the potbellied guide lounging against a tree while a helpless lizard retched in reptillian agony at his feet.

But she too can be hurt—when you don't obey her, Tony enunciated silently. Yes, he concluded, she needs to be obeyed. And he saw himself, Harry and the others, victims of this need. Many years ago his mother had told him it was because of his parents that he was disturbed, and Tony thought people at the School were supposed to be above whatever faults created disturbance.

Was Deirdre? For a moment he thought not, but he listened to her laughter while she played with Mickey and Ralph, and he chafed inwardly at his inability to form an untroubled opinion one way or the other. Of course, if Deirdre did have such faults, if she herself had emotional problems, Dr. V. had not noticed them, so they would probably never be noticed. There was nothing he could do, nothing, nothing, nothing—Tony felt helpless anger while he listened to her laughter.

Again he remembered that she too could be made angry. "You deserve a slap in the face!" she had screamed. The memory soothed him.

He stretched comfortably. Dr. V. was out of town. That meant he could have Deirdre screaming at him without immediate risk of trouble. Nor was trouble likely so long as he was not guilty of actual or threatened disobedience. Yes, get her as mad at you as you are at her tonight; it will do you good. You need to see her mad. He listened as Deirdre emerged from the bathroom.

"When you're ready to get out, just call me," he heard her say.

"O.K.," Mickey called from the bathroom. Then light footsteps, and the jingling of the bell on her keychain as she drew near.

"When are we going to do something about that dresser?" Tony knew Deirdre was talking to Lewis who monopolized the top of the dresser which he shared with Harry.

"I just fixed it," Lewis answered, and they argued quietly for a moment. Tony knew Deirdre was in the right, but was it fair that she and other counselors had so much space in their private rooms?

"All right, Lewis," Deirdre concluded abruptly, "either you get to your dresser in the next few minutes, or I'll have to remove some of your things in which case you won't see them for awhile."

Tony heard Lewis rise obediently from his bed, and he grimaced at an inward spasm of anger. He listened to the jingle of the bell on Deirdre's keychain, to footsteps walking past him, light and firm footsteps of someone confidently able to exact obedience but personally unoppressed by any authority. Deirdre went out into the hall, and Tony heard her open and shut the door to the locked closet, probably to put something away. Yes, it would certainly feel good to take her down a peg. Once again the footsteps, but this time they stopped by his bed, and Tony felt a gentle hand on his shoulder.

"Dar'dra," he said softly, tenderly. He didn't know what to say. It was disconcerting to have an evening's anger swept away in a moment.

"Is something the matter, Tony? You don't look too happy over here." Deirdre's voice showed concern as she squatted beside him. He wondered whether or not he should persist in his decision to make her angry even though his heart was no longer in the idea. It was wrong to be won over by a moment's affection, but it was also wrong to go against natural feeling. "So is something the matter?" Deirdre persisted.

"What does Dar'dra think's the matter?" Tony hedged. Rather than antagonize, rather than become embarrassed by the fruitlessness of his complaints, he would try the impossible: to get Deirdre to see that he was angry at her need to be obeyed.

"If something's the matter, why can't you just tell me?" Deirdre asked. They looked at each other, and Tony felt the muscles below each cheek forcing his lips into a smile. He had no idea why, but this often happened when he and Deirdre looked at one another, when he tried to impress her with his anger. It was embarrassing.

This time, however, he allowed himself to break into a laugh. "Why does Dar'dra think something's the matter?" He tried to feign hilarious incredulity, implying that Deirdre had her own reasons for such an idea. But Deirdre seemed unaware of any implication. The two simply continued to look at each other, and the silence made Tony uneasy.

"Dar'dra knows what's the matter." There was a slight hint of accusation in his affectionate drawl.

"Oh?" Deirdre's intonation left a silence that had to be filled with an answer.

"Tony doesn't like to always have to worry about whether the group's behind him when he goes up and down the stairs." And, to another uncomfortable silence, he added stiffly, "Dar'dra heard what Tony said."

Deirdre shrugged. "You know the alternatives." It was unnecessary to repeat that if he did not like the way things were run at the school, he could leave.

"But Tony's afraid that he still needs to stay at the School if he wants to have a good life, and he wants to be happy while he's here." Tony stretched and yawned while he spoke, trying to dignify his helpless protest with a pretense of boredom.

"Look, Tony," Deirdre extended her hands. "This school is an *institution,* and things are going to be the way they are whether you like it or not. Now do you want to stew all evening?"

"If things can be different in the Blacksmiths, why can't they be different down here?"

"Because they can't." Tony had all but discarded his intention to throw Deirdre into a rage, but now he'd had all he was going to take. "You see, we're all out to get you," Deirdre smiled playfully. "Don't you know that's what we always plan in staff meeting, how to make life miserable for Tony Hastings?"

Tony was unable to suppress his laughter, a frustrating laughter that forced its way out of him. But he turned it to his own purposes. He took Deirdre's hand and pressed it against his chest. "Oh yes, Dar'dra's just so mean," he laughed. "But just what could poor Dar'dra do if Tony decided to disobey her? Poor Dar'dra's not very strong after all." He increased the pressure of his grip. Deirdre pulled at her hand, and Tony quickly let go, not wanting her to think, or be able to infer, that he was trying to be rough with her. Once again she just looked at him. "Really there's nothing you could do—you know what I mean?" Tony propped himself up on his elbow. His tone of voice was cheerful, but he had dropped the affectionate drawl.

"Are you looking for trouble?" Deirdre asked without emotion as she rose to her feet.

"No, but there'd be nothing you could do if I was," Tony stabbed.

"Tony, that's enough of that." Deirdre sounded as though she meant it.

"How do you know it's enough?" Tony shot back.

"Because I said so." Deirdre leveled her eyes into Tony's to make her point.

"So that's how you think it goes," Tony sneered. "Well, maybe

I've had enough of a few things around here, too. Maybe it's time to make a few changes in the way things are run—"

"Look, Tony Hastings! If you want a change, just stop your threatening and get the hell out!"

"I wasn't threatening anybody." Tony smiled a little, feeling slightly frightened.

"Don't you lie to me! You know darn well what you're up to!" And Tony knew it was time to be careful. "Why don't you just get off the high horse! I'm tired of seeing you put yourself above everybody in this group!"

Tony looked at Ronny who sat on his bed, his vacant stare noncommittal; at Lewis puttering at his dresser; at Harry whose expression seemed sympathetic; at Igor who pinched uncomfortably at his cheek. He turned back to Deirdre and said, "I'm not putting myself above any of the older boys. I think we should all have more privileges."

"Dammit, then leave! You can get the hell out! But you're not going to stay around here just to threaten! You can either take things as they are at the School or go some place else! *Is* that understood?"

"Um," Tony nodded, then countered his submissive assent with a partial shrug.

"You think you're so damn smart! Don't you?"

Tony wondered whether Deirdre was reacting to his gesture or to himself in general.

"Just a hundred and twenty-five I.Q.," he dared venture.

Deirdre gave Tony one of her long looks, and Tony snickered. "You think you're going to pull something while Dr. V.'s out of town?" Deirdre's question was filled with warning.

"I'm not going to do anything," Tony assured for the sake of his safety. "You don't have to be afraid," he added as an edge to submissiveness.

"All right! Then I don't want any more . . .!" And the storm broke. She did not want any more threatening, had had enough of his snotty attitude, did not like what he was trying to pull. . . . "And if his royal highness doesn't like the way things are run here . . ."

"I can leave," Tony found himself repeating automatically at intervals, but with a half-shrug and a cynical half-smile. He had gotten all he wanted, perhaps more.

They were interrupted by several knocks at the dormitory door. "Who is it?" Deirdre looked over her shoulder. The door opened: it was Eunice, the Blacksmiths' counselor. "Deirdre, can I see you?" she asked. Both her voice and expression were in marked contrast to her usually cheerful demeanor. Deirdre stepped out into the hall and closed the door. Has something happened, Tony wondered.

When Deirdre returned, she said, "I'd like everybody's attention, please." In the quiet she announced, "Dr. V. wants us all down in the playroom. We're to be down there in five minutes."

"Hey, what's this?" "Is Dr. V. here?" "What does he want?" "What's going on?" The shock erupted in a burst of questions.

"Dr. V. will explain everything," Deirdre answered calmly. Then, to Mickey and Ralph, who were peeking out of the bathroom, "O.K., you two, let's get into your pajamas."

"Why don't we sit together?" Tony suggested to Harry. It was practically the only thing he said during the next few minutes. He was a little embarrassed by his proposal, but he suddenly wanted to be near somebody with whom he had often stood against the School.

Then, to himself, when they started down the stairs: Somebody's dead. It had to be that, or at least something very serious, to make Dr. V. cut short one of his trips away from School.

The other groups were already seated by the time the Eagles got to the playroom, but Dr. V. was not yet there. The Blacksmiths occupied the chairs that lined the walls, so the Eagles joined the girls groups and the Kangaroos who were seated in front of them on the floor. "What is this?" "I wonder why he's back so soon!" "What does he want to see us about?" The whispers of shock circulated among the younger childen while the older ones were more or less quiet.

"Are all the kids in here?" Irma's firm voice rose above the din.

The counselors answered separately for their groups and Irma closed the door to the playroom, hoping to create a more settled atmosphere.

"Irma, what's happening?" Some of the younger children were a-buzz with hushed questions.

"Dr. V. will be down here in a minute," Irma tried to reassure them. The fire doors grated; then there was a heavy jingling of keys and instantaneous quiet as Dr. V. opened the door and entered the playroom.

Dr. V. walked over to a table where he stopped and faced the School. Tony could not remember having seen him so fiercely grim. He wished he were someplace else, far away from the School and Dr. V., far from all possibility of repercussion for his effort to provoke Deirdre.

"Ve are all here?" Dr. V. looked questioningly at Irma as he settled back on the table, raising his right leg so his thigh rested on the top.

"Yes, everybody's down here," Irma answered.

Dr. V. looked thoughtfully toward the floor for a moment, then he raised his head. "I don't know how many of you have heard," he began slowly, "but zis morning Ted left zhe School grounds by himself to go and buy a suit downtown at Carsons. Since zhen, ve have had no sign of him. Zhe last time ve saw him vas at ten o'clock. . . ."

At Carsons there was a certain Mr. Schaeffer who was very popular with the Blacksmiths, and Ted had stated his intention to have Mr. Schaeffer help him select a suit. After that, Ted was to get himself some lunch, then go to a movie. He had not been expected back at the school before three o'clock.

Dr. V. paused a moment and looked down again, and Tony wondered what the movie had been, for he knew the Blacksmiths had a much freer choice of movies than the Eagles. Should you really be thinking about that now? His question bothered him. Then—why shouldn't you? A sudden rush of justifying hatred took in all he had felt that evening.

Dr. V. raised his eyes and they accidentally met Tony's. Tony looked away, and Dr. V. continued, "At first nobody got upset ven

Ted failed to show up because ve all feel zat Ted is quite able to look out for himself. But by five o'clock. . . ."

By five o'clock, when there was still no sign of Ted, Eunice had phoned Carsons and contacted Mr. Schaeffer who told her he had not seen Ted that morning or that afternoon. When he realized that Ted was missing from the School, Mr. Schaeffer asked for a description of his clothing. Then, after making a diligent check among his co-workers, he had phoned the School and told Eunice that, so far as was known, Ted had never shown up at Carsons. Eunice called the police and informed them Ted had been missing since ten that morning. She gave them his stated destination. But of course it was impossible to say whether he had gone downtown at all, or even to the train station.

The question of greatest concern was whether Ted was missing by his own choice or for some other reason. It was hardly a secret that Ted was not very happy at the School, and he had recently discussed the possibility of leaving. But nobody had expected him to run off, especially since he had neither family nor other connections outside the School. In any case, arrangements had been made to have someone near a phone throughout the night, and now there was nothing to do but wait for news or for Ted to reappear.

"In zhe meantime," Dr. V. concluded, "ve can only hope zat, vherever Ted is, he is safe." Dr. V. paused a moment, then said, "Vell, I'm glad I got back here at zis time. Of course, I had not planned to come back until Monday, but fortunately my business vas terminated sooner zan expected." Another pause, and then, "I really don't know vhat more I can tell you. So if zhere are any questions. . . ." At that moment, the door was opened by Eunice.

"Dr. V." She had barely spoken before Dr. V. was up from the table. He followed her into the hall where their voices were too low to be heard as their footsteps receded down the cloak room toward the fire doors.

Now the playroom was as intensely quiet as when Dr. V. had first entered it. But the quiet no longer had anything to do with Dr. V. Instead it was the quiet of fear, the anticipation of dreadful news. A large fraction of a minute passed, then a couple of whispers were heard. "Shhh," the whisperers were admonished, for somehow it seemed wrong to break the established silence. Irma glanced down at her watch, and then she looked up. Tony thought she was wondering whether something could be done so the kids would not have to sit and wait. A few more whispers broke out, and soon there were signs of restlessness.

The fire doors opened and shut; again absolute quiet while everybody listened.

"Ted's O.K," Eunice said as soon as she entered the playroom. She was smiling. Immediately the accumulated tension was released in a jumble of sighs and exclamations. "It seems as if Ted just took off." The playroom became quiet as Eunice answered the clamor of questions. "Dr. V.'s talking to the police on the phone," she added, "and he'll be able to tell you everything in a few minutes."

A moment later, Dr. V. opened the door. He was smiling, and he seemed relieved. "Vell," he said, "I suppose Eunice has told you Ted is safe." He walked over to the table where he settled into his former position.

Once more he looked down toward the floor, then up again. "For quite some time Ted has not been happy vis his life at zhe School." Dr. V.'s tone was somber, and he no longer smiled. "Of course, you all know zat zhe doors here are open, but . . . ." But since Ted had not told anyone his intentions, it had been necessary to call the police because nobody knew whether something had happened to him. The facts were that Ted had decided to run away, and he had gotten some fifty miles outside of Chicago where he had been picked up by the police. John was now driving out to get him, and the two were due back later that night.

"So I am sorry zat Ted had to run off visout telling us," Dr. V. concluded. "He had no more zan a few dollars in his pocket, and I don't know vhat he planned to do vis himself. He boasted on zhe phone about how he had managed to get by visout spending most of his money, but still zat is no vay to get out of here." A pause. "Vell, Ted might have had a reason for zhe vay he left." Dr. V. suddenly smiled. "Maybe he really expected to come back all along." Tony thought he detected a hint of triumph in Dr. V.'s voice and expression. "You see," Dr. V. continued, "zhe police vere not even looking for him zat far out of Chicago. Razzer he looked for zhem. Zhey picked him up about a half hour ago out on a turnpike vhere he had his thumb out just like a regular hitch-hiker."

Dr. V. shrugged and continued to smile, "Vell, I vas glad Ted vants to come back, but it was terribly dangerous for him to be hitchhiking out on zat turnpike." Tony felt that Dr. V. was gloating even while he admonished. "He could have very easily been hurt." Dr. V.'s smile faded while he paused for emphasis. He looked down at his watch, then slowly scanned those who sat before him. "So are zhere questions?" he asked.

"Dr. V." It was Mike, a tall, wiry boy of eighteen from the Blacksmith's dormitory.

"Yes, Mike." Dr. V. shifted his position on the table.

"How do you know Ted was trying to thumb down a police car?" Mike's voice was absolutely calm, and to Tony's ears it sounded fearlessly defiant. At that moment Tony felt very close to Mike, and he wished he could join him in a stand against Dr. V.

"Look, Mike," Dr. V. extended a hand, "Ted vaited for zhe police vis his thumb out."

"Have you ever tried to thumb down a car on a turnpike at night?" Mike calmly challenged.

"Oh, I do it all zhe time." Dr. V.'s answer sparked a few uneasy laughs. Tony was one of those who laughed, and afterwards he looked at the floor in order to avoid Dr. V.'s gaze, but he was not at all sure whether he cared if Dr. V. saw him. "So vhat are you driving at?" Dr. V.'s eyes remained on Mike.

"Well," Mike replied, "I was hitchhiking out on a turnpike last New Year's, and with the cars coming out of the dark, I couldn't tell whether one of them was a police car or not. Now maybe I was just too drunk to see straight. But hell, I was afraid I would get picked up."

"Vell, zhey should have picked you up! Did you vant to kill yourself?"

"Look, I'd been in a bar where I'd busted this guy's face because he was bothering me, and I had to get out because the guy had friends there." Tony became ecstatic.

"What does it matter who can beat who in a fight?" John had

asked him scornfully just a few days before. Now Tony felt with profound conviction that it would always matter deeply; that John had a maturity beyond his reach.

"Yes, Mike," Dr. V. said after a few moments hesitation, "you're a fine example to zhe younger kids here!" Dr. V. looked down, and for a moment his and Tony's eyes met. Smiling just a little, Tony returned his gaze for an instant, then looked away.

"Dr. V., I'm not trying to set an example for anybody," Mike countered, "and I don't intend to answer to you for what I did at home." Tony felt an ecstasy of triumphant rage as Mike held Dr. V.'s silent gaze. "Now how do you know Ted wasn't trying to thumb down a regular car?" Mike persisted.

"Mike, Ted told me over zhe phone zat he vanted to come back. He *insisted* on zat because I asked him twice." It was Mike's turn to be silent. "You know zat neizer you nor Ted has to stay here! Ve can manage quite gracefully visout zhe two of you!" For a moment Dr. V. glared fixedly at Mike. "So are zhere ozzer questions?" His gaze shifted abruptly as he scanned the whole School. There were no other questions, so he suggested that the groups leave singly for their dormitories.

Up in their dormitory the Eagles automatically gathered around the table for the inevitable feelings. Tony remained aloof while others expressed surprise at what Ted had done. Discussion eventually progressed to Ted's thumbing down a police car and the conclusion that he had "very mixed feelings" about running off.

"And he must have also had mixed feelings about coming back," Tony added, and was grateful that the others immediately agreed with him. He glanced with muted triumph at Deirdre.

"Listen," Deirdre said after a moment, "these mixed feelings certainly don't belong to Ted alone."

"Well, naturally they don't," Tony agreed. "Hell, this School's a hospital, and nobody likes to stay around a hospital, but you have to stay in order to save your life."

"What do some of the rest of you think?" Deirdre turned to the others, and that made Tony wish she had screamed at him. He hated her for being so unimpressed. At the same time, he became somewhat sad. What he felt to be her rejection of him, his feelings, caused him to miss her.

After a moment, Tony had the satisfaction of hearing Harry and Ronny express feelings similar to his. Then Deirdre had Lewis accompany her to the kitchenette for snacks. They returned with a pitcher of milk, coffee cake, and paper cups. Deirdre began to pour the milk which Lewis passed around with the cake.

"Here's one for Tony," Deirdre said, handing Lewis a cup.

"Hey, you know I don't drink milk," Tony protested. His stomach rejected the white liquid.

"Why don't you try a little sip?" Lewis smiled. "It certainly won't be as bad as some of the things you'll have to drink when you go exploring the Amazon."

Tony was touched by Lewis' unusually aggressive friendliness, but it also made him shy because he was not used to it. "Oh, I'll take coke with me," he smiled back.

"And if you spill the coke, the head hunters will only have milk for you." Tony thrilled at Lewis' spark of humor, and the laughs let out by Mickey and Ralph were as much surprise as amusement.

"You know," Tony smiled wryly. "You're right." He felt the familiar welling behind his eyes, the unadmittable craving for Deirdre's sympathy, as he said, "The head hunters will probably tell me that if I don't like the milk, I can just get the hell out of the Amazon."

"What's the matter, Tony?" Deirdre asked before Lewis had time to say anything.

Finding himself without a direct answer, Tony said, "I think it's terrible the way Ted had to come crawling back here—I mean, if he's only coming back because he left with hardly any money and no place to go to."

"Maybe there's a reason Ted left the way he did." For a moment Tony and Deirdre looked at each other, then their smiles broke simultaneously.

"But Ted could have stayed out longer since he hadn't spent

most of his money when he said he wanted to come back," Tony added. And Deirdre laughed at Tony's effort to give Ted the benefit of all possible doubt. Tony could not help laughing with her, even though it embarrassed him somewhat.

"Any new ideas with the milk?" Deirdre turned to Lewis.

"Yes, Deirdre," Lewis raised his eyebrows and nodded, "I have an idea: it's called dunking." Lewis broke off a piece of his coffee cake and dipped it into his milk. "Now behold," he ordered, and he took a small, dainty bite out of the soggy morsel which he chewed with ceremonial emphasis; then he swallowed it. "Now certainly that's not too much milk for anyone," he said to Tony while everybody smiled. "You can even pretend it's water," he added. "You drink plenty of that, Tony."

"Tch," Tony wrinkled his nose. "Cake in water—I could *never* take that." Then, afraid that Lewis would feel rebuffed, he tried to joke. He glanced at Ronny and smiled. Then, to Lewis, "We should really have a couple of bowls in here for the milk. You know for who, don't you?"

"Ummm." Lewis' forehead wrinkled in mock thought. "Could this be for a certain eminence whom I believe I've heard two people discuss?"

"Zat's right." Tony replied. "Ve need vone bowl for *Meester* Hounds Dog and anozzer bowl for *Meesus* Hounds Dog."

"Oh, this eminence is married?" Lewis seemed astonished.

"Yes, now zhere's also a *Meesus*," Tony nodded emphatically, suddenly wanting to include Lewis in the game he played with Ronny.

"Good heavens," Deirdre broke in laughingly, "is it going to be the three of you?"

"Oh, Dar'dra, we could make it the more the merrier," Tony answered. "First there's the three of us, then there's Meester and *Meesus*. . . ." He stopped mid-sentence and turned to Ronny. "Actually, eesn't zhere more zhan vone *Meesus* Hounds Dog?" he asked.

"Snap, snap! Snap, snap! Reep! Tear! Ooh, you're really getting eet now!"

"Oh please, Hounds Dog! Oh Meester Hounds Dog!" Tony's hands snatched at himself in various places.

"Eet von't do any good to talk to Meester Hounds Dog," Ronny shook his head, and Tony continued to get snapped.

"Poor Tony," Ralph smiled.

"He's really getting it," Mickey grinned.

"Oof! Ouch!" Tony continued to grab at himself. "Vhy shooldn't I talk to Meester Hounds Dog!"

"Because eet's Meesus Hounds Dog zat's snapping at you!" Ronny burst out laughing, and everyone laughed, Deirdre included. "Ooh, hoo, hoo, hooo!" Tony and Ronny laughed significantly into each other's faces, their mouths forming round o's.

"Why, Dar'dra's laughing!" Tony became affectionately exultant as he leaped from his chair. "Now Dar'dra shouldn't be laughing," he muttered through his teeth as he clasped her forearms and gently nudged the side of his face against hers.

Deirdre patted his cheek tenderly. "Oh Tony, what am I going to do with you?" she asked softly as Tony rose up.

"Vell, you might see about getting him to bed." Tony and Deirdre looked around to see Dr. V. who had just entered the dormitory through the partially open door. "It's getting late, you know." Dr. V. glanced at his watch as he approached the table.

"I guess it's about that time," Deirdre agreed.

"So how is life here treating you?" Dr. V. put a hand on Tony's shoulder.

"At times, fine," Tony's pride kept him reserved in his concession.

"Vell, at least at times." Dr. V.'s grip tightened affectionately.

11

A few days before his birthday, Tony dragged himself out of bed and got a pair of slacks and undershorts from his dresser. Then he took the slacks he was currently wearing from his chair on which they hung and placed them with his undershorts on his bed. After that, he covered his crotch with the slacks from his drawer and began to peel off his pajama pants.

"Tony, enough of that," Deirdre spoke from the table.

"What do you mean?" Tony asked in alarm.

"You heard me."

Holding the slacks in place, Tony quickly pulled his pajamas up, then put the slacks he had used for cover back into his drawer. After a moment's fidgeting, he turned to Deirdre and asked, "What's the matter with what I was doing?"

"The way you change your clothes is ridiculous," Deirdre answered.

"It's for privacy," Tony protested.

"For someone so set on privacy, you certainly find a conspicuous way to shed your pajamas." Deirdre's eyes shifted from Tony to Harry who had also begun to change behind a pair of slacks. The boys exchanged glances; no use to argue with Deirdre that she had ruled out the toilet stalls. Then Deirdre left the dormitory on an errand, and Tony and Harry quickly changed.

All morning Tony worried about what he would do since Deirdre did not always leave the dormitory. His anxiety showed, and after the morning recess, John asked him if something were wrong. He told John what was bothering him, and they began to talk about it while Billy and Harry listened.

"So what if a girl counselor sees you naked?" John asked. "You know, you didn't always have these inhibitions."

"You can say that again," Billy piped up. "Tony, remember how you used to stick your penis out even when the girls were around, and—"

"Yes, I did some pretty bad things," Tony turned directly to Billy, "And a lot of you kids had quite a bit to say about it. But we also talked about a fat little pile of blubber lying naked on its bed so everybody could see its microscopic little—"

"Tony, do you want to talk or not?" John cut in.

Tony looked beyond John to Harry. Harry was smiling. Then, to John, "Why don't you speak to Billy? Why should I take that kind of thing from him?"

"Why are you so bothered by what he said?"

"I might have dishonored myself when I was a kid. But he's hardly anyone to remind me of it." Tony glanced scornfully at Billy.

"Just how did you dishonor yourself?" John asked.

For a moment Tony was silent, unable to answer John's question. Then, suddenly, "If it's no dishonor to be seen naked," and his voice grew angry, "Why is it that us kids never see you counselors and teachers naked?"

"How would you feel if you did?"

"I did once, and the world certainly didn't come to an end."

"Oh?" John's forehead knitted in surprise.

"Don't you remember how when I was nine I went to get Nora who was night counselor because I was scared of the dark? You remember what I saw then, don't you? I mean, I talked about it enough." Tony tried to give an impression of sophisticated amusement at his former childish fascination.

"Isn't that the time you went to get her and she was lying in bed asleep with her nightgown up?" Billy asked eagerly.

"That's right," Tony grinned.

"And how did you feel?" John's eyes were on Tony.

"Well, I was surprised, but really, John, don't you think it's dishonorable for a guy to be seen naked by a girl if he's not gonna screw her?"

"Why's it dishonorable?"

"If it isn't dishonorable," Tony challenged, "then why are we supposed to change in the bathroom whenever a girl visits the dormitory?"

"Wouldn't you feel uncomfortable if you didn't?"

"Why should I feel any more uncomfortable with half-developed adolescent girls than with fully developed girl counselors who're at their peak of sexiness?"

"But your counselor's in the dorm to take care of you."

"At eight or nine years old, fine. But not after eleven, not with every girl from the University who comes to observe our group for a day or two, then leaves. I have this friend outside the School. Well, I talked to him privately about the way things are done here, and he was *shocked.* He wondered why I didn't revolt, and I told him I was too big to be controlled and that I would just be thrown out if I did."

John shrugged. "Too bad this fellow is so set against the idea that some people take care of others."

"You're a fine one to talk." Tony's eyebrows went up. "You won't even use the same washrooms as us. Whenever *you* need to take a leak, you have to go all the way to the basement rather than just use the bathroom that's right here by us."

"You'll find that in most schools the adults have separate toilet facilities."

"I've been in plenty of washrooms where adult men use the same urinals as boys! But I bet I'll never live to see the day you change in front of a girl counselor or a girl counselor changing in front of *us.*"

"You probably won't," John agreed.

"Why not?"

"We're adults."

Suddenly Estelle began breaking her crayons and throwing them about. They were forced to end their discussion. Tony glanced at the clock and saw it was fifteen minutes to session. He thought Deirdre might give him more latitude if he would discuss his feelings, especially "your feelings about your body," something counselors were always wanting to discuss with the children. But he had nothing to tell her. He began to wonder if the privacy problem would ever lead to a showdown with Dr. V. A while ago he had written in his diary:

> *Privacy is the only thing for which I am determined to fight Dr. V. if I have the courage at all. In almost all other things I am always as mild as a lamb with him because I am so afraid of him when he's mad.*

Tony thought he and Harry were alone in their desire for privacy, alone except for Igor who seemed to be adopting their ways. At one time he'd been all alone. Nearing puberty, he had found he did not like to be naked in front of female counselors when angry at them. At eleven years old, upon returning from his Christmas visit, he had undressed in a toilet stall for the first time. That evening he had felt somewhat resentful toward the School, and from his feeling derived a desire to keep a certain distance. John had said counselors were supposed to take care of him, and Tony felt a need to set limits on that care.

But was privacy really worth the trouble, the anxiety? Tony remembered his mother had said his following the School's ways wouldn't cause him to be looked down on by people on the outside. So why not quit the whole privacy kick and end all worry? Inspiration struck. What would happen? What would he lose? As he rose for session, Tony felt giddily, drunkenly blissful at the rushing possibility of infinite release. Yes, the possibility was beautiful, but the real thing? He wondered.

Moments later, Tony seated himself on the couch in his session room and invited Deirdre to join him. But as usual, she pulled up a chair. Tony knew this was because he had demonstrated too much affection when they sat together. "Dar'dra, Tony's been thinking about this morning." Tony looked at her, wondering what to say next—wondering whether to give up his privacy kick, but seriously doubting he should.

"Tony," Deirdre said, "Dr. V. wants to know if you'd like to spend your birthday out at your grandmother's. You'd go on Friday and come back Monday."

"That would be great." Tony felt a spark of happiness. "Will Mother be there too, or is it just Granny?"

"Your mother's there now."

"How come?"

"She's been helping your grandmother out."

"Is there any special reason?"

"Your grandmother's an old woman and sometimes needs help."

"But why now? Has something happened?"

"Tony, do you think we'd keep information from you?"

"No," he laughed.

"Well, there's one thing Dr. V. wants to know," Deirdre continued. "He wonders if you'd mind traveling to Kentucky by yourself."

"God, no." Tony was emphatic. "That's much better than having poor Mother come all the way up here the way she always has. Will I be flying?"

"No, the planes are on strike, so you'll have to take the train. The train leaves tomorrow morning at five after nine, and you'll be on your own most of the day."

"That's fine," Tony assured her once again. It would be exciting to travel alone for the first time. He had not been on his own since the Christmas holidays. "I'm surprised you think I'm ready to do this," he said to Deirdre. "I mean, here I can go all the way to Kentucky on a train by myself, but at the School I can't even go around the block alone."

"Tony, we have no reason to believe you can't handle yourself on a train."

"I see," Tony nodded. In other words, he was all right for a soft-carpet atmosphere, but not for the city streets where there was always the small possibility of trouble. "Deirdre," Tony broke a momentary silence, "it's because of that homosexual, isn't it, that you suddenly became afraid to let us go out alone?" Tony was sure it was that. Last year Deirdre had begun to let the older boys go by themselves into the neighborhood. But early in the fall something had happened at Ryan's Woods, a small forest preserve . . . .

Deirdre, Laura, the Eagles: all were looking down at a hideous smidgen of something that vaguely resembled a baby bird. It lay screeching in the middle of the path. "Gosh, what's that?" Tony gasped.

"It's a baby bat," Deirdre replied.

"Should it be lying out here?"

"I don't know."

"Can I go see the game warden? It said on the map that his place is by the parking lot."

"Yes, you can go, if you want to. We'll wait right here."

Tony ran off, proud and happy that Deirdre saw fit to let him carry out this mission alone. It showed she was developing some sense, and he was glad she hadn't treated him like a baby in front of Laura. He sprinted over a couple of paths, then down beneath an underpass. There were several houses and a parking lot on the other side. "Excuse me, sir," Tony called to a small blond man who was getting out of a cream-colored, open convertible, "can you please tell me which of these houses belongs to the warden?"

"I believe that one." The man pointed; then Tony noticed a sign by the house saying: "Warden, Office at Back of House.

When Tony returned, the man was pacing back and forth. "What did you want to see the warden for?" he asked.

"Oh, I'm with a group, and we found this baby bat on one of the pathways, so I went to ask the warden if anything could be done for it."

"What did he say?"

"Just to leave it to fend for itself." Tony tried to answer succinctly because children from the School were not supposed to associate with people they didn't know.

"You know, you're a very nice boy. I wish there were more like you—with your sense of responsibility." The man sounded sincere.

"Thanks." Tony enjoyed the compliment.

"How old are you?" the man asked as they approached the underpass.

"Fourteen."

"Fourteen? Say, you're pretty big for fourteen."

"Thanks." Tony expressed polite surprise at a compliment he sensed was false.

"Tell me, where did you leave your group?"

"Down beyond this underpass, then in the woods a bit."

"Hey, why don't you let me drive you there?" the man suggested as Tony began to descend into the underpass.

This man was friendly, but perhaps too interested in him, and now that he had offered the ride, Tony was sure he was up to something. "Thanks," he answered, looking back at the man, "but I can walk back, and I don't think any roads lead to where my group is waiting."

"Oh, c'mon, let me take you," the man persisted, "I know the way."

"That's all right, I can make it, but thanks a lot anyway," Tony called back over his shoulder.

"Hey boy?" the man called after a few seconds.

"What?" Tony looked around.

"Come here a minute."

"No, I've really got to get going." Tony turned and ran, and as soon as he found his group, he told Deirdre about the man.

Since childhood, Tony had been cautioned not to go off with adult strangers, but nobody had told him what to fear. So he was left to his imagination when he speculated to Deirdre about the man's intentions. He had been haunted by newspaper accounts of Chicago's famous Triple Murder, and he often wondered what lead to the strangulation of three boys his age whose naked bodies left no clue as to the motive for their murder. Could the blond-haired man have been the Triple Murderer? He had teased Deirdre about this possibility, and from that time, neither he nor any of the others were allowed out on their own.

Now, in this session, Tony tried to get Deirdre to tell him why his and the group's privileges had been so sharply curtailed just after the Ryan's Woods incident. As usual, Deirdre wanted him to figure out the reasons for himself, but he had no intention of trying to guess since that would lead nowhere.

"There's one thing that puzzles me." Tony looked at Deirdre. "I know that that man at Ryan's Woods was probably a homosexual. Probably all he wanted to do was screw my ass, or whatever they do, and then send me on my way. It's very unlikely he would have killed me, but I thought about that all the same because I didn't even know what homosexuals were. And I wouldn't know now except for the fact that that guide tried to play around with me in Acapulco and Mother told me all about homosexuals and about how some of them try to get young boys to go off with them. Now I wonder how come you didn't explain all this to me. I mean, it would have saved me a lot of wondering." When Deirdre said nothing, Tony repeated his question. "So why didn't you explain it all?"

"Why do you think?"

"You probably thought I had enough worries without your adding any."

"See, you knew it all along."

"I thought that was it, but it really doesn't make sense. I mean, why are you so afraid of creating worries? If you'd told me the man was homosexual, and I'd been frightened, wouldn't that have been something to explore?"

"You'll explore anything you want to explore."

"Then why are you so concerned to have me explore my feelings about my need for privacy?"

"Who said I was concerned if you're not?"

"Well then, even though you may not be over-concerned, isn't it true that you don't want me to have privacy as long as I don't explore my feelings around it?" Deirdre did not answer. "If I really went into the feelings," Tony persisted, "would you care if I undressed in private or not?"

With a surprised smile, Deirdre asked, "Are you trying to make some kind of a deal?"

Tony cringed inwardly, embarrassed by his blunder. He knew full well that counselors did not bargain, and now his efforts to probe his feelings would probably not be free of suspicion. He also felt guilty for having never really tried to understand his desire for privacy, but just what was there to understand? Perhaps it would be best simply to yield to his inspiration and give up the privacy kick. That would rid him of at least half, if not practically all, the tension-ridden situations he confronted at the School.

But deep down he felt he could not, perhaps should not. He did not feel able to defend his need for privacy, but Deirdre had never told him why he should not have it. Now he felt intuitively that, if he did not insist on it, he would become able to give up anything simply by denying it a place in his heart.

"Tony," Deirdre suddenly asked, "why don't you take baths when Laura's on?"

Tony was shocked into realizing he had never really intended to fully give up his privacy. "I don't like to," he answered Deirdre softly. "I'm sure I don't understand all my feelings in this area, and perhaps I should try harder." He became penitent. "But I just couldn't stand sitting in the tub in front of her." Deirdre's sudden mention of Laura made him wonder whether a total assault upon his privacy were not underway.

"Tony, what's the matter?"

"I just can't stand the idea of taking baths in front of Laura."

"Well, you act as though something's being expected of you that's not being expected at all."

Tony was relieved. Gratitude itself now motivated him to talk, to explore. "I don't know what it is." He shook his head. "But I just wouldn't feel right being in the tub in front of her. I mean, with you it's not so bad, because at least I knew you when I was a kid."

"Why does that make a difference?"

"Well, out at Red Cloud I kissed a couple of girls who were Laura's age, and I just couldn't imagine undressing or bathing in front of them." Tony wondered if Deirdre had any inkling as to how much he wanted to lie in Laura's arms.

"Tony," Deirdre asked, "who ever suggested you undress or bathe in front of anybody? Who pays attention? You know, you can always ask a counselor to leave you alone when you want to undress."

"But I don't feel that's privacy—I mean, with her still in the dormitory —" Tony found himself fumbling for words, not sure what to say to counter Deirdre's brand of logic. Then finally he added, "I don't think a man should undress even in the same room with a woman unless he's having sex with her. Then it's mutual."

"Tony, what do you think people feel when they have sex?"

He thought a moment, then said, "I feel that all people are naturally modest or embarrassed about sex and that when two people have it, the pleasure is sort of in chucking modesty." That was how it had been with the guide and the lizard. When his sexuality had been unable to resist revulsion, it had risen with it. "Is that what you think sex is?" he asked Deirdre. As he expected, she did not answer. "I don't know," he went on, "this might all have something to do with my need for privacy, but I just don't understand it." He noticed she was looking at him intently. "But it's also just that it's so much different here from outside. . . ." Deirdre's eyes ceased to focus: that angle did not interest her.

He looked up at the clock which read five to twelve. Deirdre's eyes followed his. "It's time," she said.

"Dar'dra, things are sometimes hard to figure out."

"You can't figure everything out at once," she agreed, and Tony hoped she felt that at least he had tried to understand himself and that for this reason she would not press her campaign against his privacy.

"Well, Dar'dra, Tony's going now."

"I'll see you this afternoon," she nodded, and Tony returned to the classroom where he got John's permission to go wash up for lunch. Out in the hall he saw Irma with a group of visitors, and he remembered Dr. V.'s announcing that he and some of the counselors would be taking several groups around at noon. Tony quickly went to the washroom since he knew Dr. V. would not want him to hang around the visitors.

He did not consider his session a success. But he felt himself up against a stone wall at every attempt to understand his reasons for not wanting to undress in front of a woman. Maybe there is no basic reason except for your desire to be treated like other boys your age, he thought, but why is it so important to be treated like them? His inability to answer this question made it hard to discuss the problem with Deirdre, or to imagine what he'd say to Dr. V. in the event of a showdown.

"All right, Dr. V., why is it so important to you that I undress in front of these counselors?" Tony found his answer as he stepped into one of the toilet stalls and locked the door. His bladder was uncomfortably full, so he jerked his zipper down, then urinated long and hard. Finished, he pulled at the zipper only to find it had caught on his underpants and had detached from the grooves on its right side.

Frantically he tried to reset the zipper and to detach it from his underpants, but he was unable to do a thing. He looked at his watch which read three minutes to twelve, then resumed his efforts. Of all days for such an accident! On any other day Deirdre could have taken him over to the dormitory building, and he could have prevented her from seeing his genitals by changing behind a pair of slacks. But now there was her new ruling. And it was not unlikely that some significance would be read into his having torn his zipper while visitors were being taken around. "Ah, so you vant to show your penis to zhe visitors." Dr. V.'s menacing face rose before Tony's eyes. He looked again at his watch. Two minutes to twelve! No more time to waste; time now to see about changing in the dormitory and to face whatever there was to face.

You'll need your coat to go across, Tony remembered, and got it from his locker. Now at least he was not exposed; now he could walk around with dignity. He listened for a second to Deirdre who was cleaning up the session room, then went into his classroom and told John, "I have a slight emergency—my zipper's broken."

John studied him a moment. "What zipper?" he asked.

"The zipper to my pants."

"How did that happen?"

"Well, I had to go badly, so I yanked my zipper open, and now it only zips up and down on one side, and it's caught on my underpants."

"Is Deirdre still in the session room?" John asked.

"I think so."

"Let's see if she can't take you." John rose from his chair beside Billy's desk. "Wait here," he added as he went out of the room.

"Gosh," Billy whispered, "I'd hate to have that happen to me while Dr. V.'s taking visitors around."

"You're not the only one." Tony spoke uneasily. He looked at Harry who shook his head sympathetically. Tony took a step toward Harry's desk, wanting to say something, but not sure what. "Better wish me luck." He tried to sound like a movie hero. Of all his adventures around undressing, this would probably be his most perilous, and now he tried to derive comfort from having been in other hazardous situations.

"Good luck." Harry extended his hands helplessly just as John opened the door.

"O.K., Tony, Deirdre will take you over," John said, and Tony went out to meet Deirdre in the hallway.

"Ready?" she asked.

"Uh huh," Tony nodded. He was unable to discern in her expression any indication about how she viewed his accident. He looked at his watch which now read noon, exactly the time Dr. V. had said he would be taking the visitors through the dormitories.

"How did this happen?" Deirdre asked as they mounted the steps at the end of the hall.

"Oh, I don't know," Tony shrugged in an effort to sound casual. "I had to go really bad, so I yanked the zipper down, and then I found it was broken."

"What was the matter?" Deirdre asked. She pushed open the door to the school building, and Tony held it ajar as she went through.

"I don't know," he replied. "It could have had something to do with the difficult things we talked about in session." Certainly it *could* have, but Tony was unable to see any connection. He merely hoped his answer would satisfy Deirdre.

"Tony, what's the matter?" Deirdre persisted as she looked at him.

"I'm tense about going to change when there're visitors over there."

"So why did you tear your zipper today?"

"Hell, I don't know why. I'm no seamstress."

"You're certainly not." Deirdre shook her head in agreement as they reached the door to the dormitory building. "You're not a seamstress," she added, "you're a boy . . ." She got out her keys and unlocked the door. ". . . a boy who's had plenty of experience at zipping up pants." She spoke loudly enough for anyone on the stairs to hear, or so Tony felt, and he noted happily that the stairway seemed empty. It was time for the classrooms to start coming over to lunch and, hopefully, Dr. V. planned to keep the visitors off the stairs during the next ten minutes. Tony pulled the door shut behind them and prayed silently that within five minutes he would be safe and happy at lunch after having managed to change without Deirdre seeing his genitals.

As he mounted the first flight of stairs, he heard the chatter of adults on the second floor. The visitors! And he would have to pass them on his way to the dormitory. Then he heard Dr. V.'s voice amidst the chatter. At the top landing, he stepped aside and Deirdre opened the door. Try to appear polite, Tony commanded himself as he followed her through the door. For an instant Dr. V. noticed only Deirdre while he stood talking to eight or nine men and women. He was smiling, then the smile vanished. "Vhat are you doing here?"

"My pants tore, and I came over to change them."

"Your pants tore? How did zat happen?"

Tony felt this was a perfectly reasonable question, but he was not sure how to answer it. "His zipper broke," Deirdre spoke for him, and Tony felt himself flush beneath the gaze of the visitors.

"Oh, I see. Vell, go and change." Dr. V. turned and led the visitors to the stairway.

Once in the dormitory Deirdre sat down at the table. Tony went to his dresser, opened the top drawer, fidgeted a few moments, absolutely unable to think of any means to change in private. He glanced at Deirdre and noticed that she had picked up a book. As good as her word, she was paying him no attention whatsoever. And once again it occurred to him that life would be much easier if he would just give up his privacy kick. Why care? Now his mind groped for the bliss of liberation it had formerly conjured, and he was able to work himself to some degree of detachment as he took out a new pair of slacks and underpants. But no, perhaps it was wrong to become detached, to give up everything he cherished, to give up life itself.

Nevertheless, the detachment could serve a purpose. Calmly he grasped at the one solution left. If Deirdre did not like the conspicuous way he changed his clothes, she needn't see a thing. Tony went into the bathroom, and despite his supposed detachment, he felt a sense of relief as soon as he entered the toilet stall and locked the door. So Deirdre was letting him go back to the stalls once again. Then she had merely objected to the silliness of his changing behind a pair of slacks. Well, she was right! The stalls were much better.

He pulled on his new pair of pants and stood for a minute, reluctant to face Deirdre. When he opened the door and walked out, she was arranging some things on the group table. "Do you want me to take those pants down to the sewing room?" She looked up, and Tony felt a slight sense of guilt, as though he were getting off easily for someone who had not probed his feelings.

"Sure, thanks, you can take them down."

12

After seven-thirty, the night before his trip to Kentucky, Tony lay on his bed trying to read. He was so bored that he was about to fall asleep.

"Hey, Tony."

"What?" Tony looked up at Igor who had approached his bed armed with a checker board.

"Do you want to play checkers?"

"No, thank you."

"Gosh, y'you didn't want to play last night either."

"And I don't want to play tonight." Tony was annoyed by Igor's stuttering, at Igor's request which made him angry at himself for not taking an opportunity to fight his solitude. Tony and Igor spent most evenings on their beds, and Tony knew Igor was trying to break a lonely habit, but he doubted it could be accomplished with checkers. Nevertheless, guilt-ridden irritation began to fan his anger about something Deirdre had said at supper when the older boys had sat as a group, leaving Mickey and Ralph by themselves at one corner of the table. "You boys probably want to talk together, and that's understandable," Deirdre had commented, "but if you don't include them and they start each other up, it's you who have to sit through it."

Just what do we owe these boys that we should have to put up with them? Tony imagined he was voicing an outrage he always felt when forced into compromise for people he did not consider to have any claim on him.

Why don't you try to do something with somebody, Tony challenged himself, but realized he just didn't feel like it. He did not want to read either. Things had been going badly in the classroom, and in John's words, he didn't feel good about himself. That morning he had taken Harry's pencil and hidden it which annoyed Harry. Tony envied Harry's academic prowess, and he wondered if his feeling of friendship for him would survive his jealousy. Hell, you almost wish you didn't exist. He got up and stretched long and tall, his arms straining toward the ceiling. He stood facing the door so he did not see Deirdre come up behind him. "Boo," she said, and he felt her hands gently clasp him below his arms.

"Dar'dra." He clamped his hands over hers and swayed back and forth for a moment. Then he pulled her hands forward and let his head fall back on her shoulder. How had she known to come just when he needed her? Tony turned around so that they stood only a few inches apart. And between his two hands, Tony clutched one of Deirdre's hands close to his chest.

"So how you be?" Deirdre asked.

"O.K., except I think I'm going to die of boredom."

"Listen, Tony, I haven't once seen you try to play with that electrical set. Has it been sitting in your drawer all this time?"

"Yes, Dar'dra, it's still there." After the Christmas holidays, he had wanted to put the set—a gift to him from the School—away in his closet; but Deirdre had insisted he keep it among his more immediate possessions, and Tony had a vague hunch she would be annoyed if he didn't.

"Why don't you try to build something tonight?" Deirdre suggested.

To his surprise, Tony thought her suggestion a good one. "It might be worth a try," he answered lackadaisically. Moments later he was at the group table looking at a direction booklet which he found hard to understand because he always had a difficult time following instructions. Beside him on the table lay the electrical set.

Then, as he was about to decide to put his set away, Igor joined him. Pinching at his cheek, Igor dropped into a chair and began to look at the various devices in the open box. "Hey, Tony, y'you know, w'we could make a kind of telegraph set with this," he said.

"How?" Tony asked. Then, silently to himself: You don't really want to do this, do you, so you shouldn't encourage Igor to explain anything.

"Y'you can build it with this." Igor pointed to a tiny platform with its various hookups for wires, batteries and light bulbs. "W'we could put lights on this and then connect it to something on my bed, and you'd b'be able to turn the light on at my bed, and I could turn it on at yours. And that way we could beep signals to each other."

"I don't think there's enough wire for that in my set," Tony protested, hoping to put an end to the project. "I only have about five or six feet."

"Oh, that's O.K. I've got plenty in the locked closet." Igor had picked up Tony's direction booklet. "Let's just see wh'what we can do," he added as he looked back at the page and pinched at his cheek. Tony had felt all along that his excuse would probably be useless.

"If you're just doing this for his benefit, you might as well not do it at all," Tony imagined that Deirdre had spoken to him. And perhaps she was right since nothing genuine would likely transpire between himself and Igor if his heart were not in what they did together. Tony looked at Igor as he sat hunched over the book. He said to himself: Perhaps Igor's just interested in your set and not in you.

"Y'you know, w'we haven't done something like this together in a *long* time." Igor looked up as though he had just read Tony's thoughts. "As a matter of fact, I don't think we *ever* have."

"What are you two cooking up?" Deirdre asked. Igor explained, and she appeared enthusiastic.

"I'm not sure this is for me," Tony said.

"Oh, go on," Deirdre encouraged.

"C'c'mon, we've *never* done something like this before," Igor backed her. And inside himself Tony knew it was for his own benefit that he was going to build with Igor. Yes, it would hurt to turn Igor down; it would hurt so much that he had to carry through for his own sake. And suddenly Tony realized he was not in for a solitary evening.

"Well, Igor, if we're going to set up this telegraph thing, what're we going to use for your end of the set?"

"Oh, that's no problem," Igor smiled as he rose from the table and went over to his bed. Deirdre smiled at Tony while Igor turned various dials and switches on the mechanical panoply that surrounded his area. He turned with a small cardboard box on which there were several flashlight bulbs and batteries, three or four dials and switches, and a tangled intricacy of wire. He also had a cigar box that contained some of his supplies. "Here, this'll do for me." And then he laughed, "It's practically all assembled sort of as though I had it *made* for this. Deirdre, c'can you get me my wire and the wire cutters from the locked closet?"

Tony noted that Igor was stuttering less than usual, that in his own element he seemed quite secure. There could be no turning back now. Deirdre brought the wire and wire cutter, then went to run Mickey's bath. Igor began again to pour over Tony's direction booklet, after which he looked up. "Why don't you start getting some of that stuff out of your box?" Tony detached the platform, the wires and other items from the cardboard frame.

Igor took a quick look at the equipment in his cigar box, then proceeded to examine the switches and wires on the unit he had detached from his bed. He picked up Tony's platform and compared the two devices. "L'let's see," he said softly, "w'we'll need to cut some wire for your set." Tony picked up the cutter and his spool of wire.

"Here, no, use mine." Igor held up his spool which had a great deal more wire on it.

"Why not use mine for my part of the set?" Tony protested because of the School's ruling that personal possessions be kept separate.

"M'mine's a better wire. Yours mightn't last too long, and we want this thing to last as long as we're at the School, don't we?"

"Yes, maybe it should." Tony was moved by what Igor said, yet uncomfortable about the commitment it implied. He picked up Igor's wire. "So how much of this should I cut?"

"Let's see." Igor glanced at Tony's directions, then at his plastic platform. "I think you'll need to cut two ten inch pieces of wire, and I'll tell you what for in a minute."

And Igor told him that along with almost everything else he needed to know. With a screwdriver and a pair of pliers from his cigar box, Igor tinkered with the wires and switches on his own device while, every minute or so, he leaned over to study the directions in Tony's book and the work Tony was doing. He always had something to say, and it was Igor, not the directions, which guided Tony in his work. Igor's explanations became rapid and feverish; "W'we've got to make time b'before Deirdre brings in snacks," he explained hoarsely.

Igor gave Tony a direction, one that would not have been difficult to understand had Tony not had what he called a mental block to following directions. Igor had to repeat himself three times. "Oh, come on," he became heated the third time around. And Tony's mouth opened in surprise as he looked up at Igor. Was Igor merely working with him because of his interest in mechanics and nothing else? "Oh, God, d'did I hurt your feelings?" Igor's face and voice were a single expression of concern. "I'it's just that we've never had anything like this together, a'and I really want to have it with you."

"Well, we can do it." Tony tried to sound reassuring.

"B'but time's gone so fast," Igor protested. "It's almost eight-thirty, a'and I'm afraid we can't get it done before snacks, and that we won't have it tonight."

"I think Dar'dra will give us time." Tony looked over at Deirdre who was with Lewis by his bed.

"You two don't have to rush that," Deirdre assured them.

"W'well, I'm sorry if I hurt your feelings."

"Oh, that's O.K.," Tony said emphatically, "you didn't." So, to the tune of Igor's directions, they continued to work on their separate devices. Tony had never before liked to follow the lead of another person, but tonight it was a new and pleasant experience to assume a subordinate role while Igor directed their work with the self-possession of one accustomed to having others depend on him.

"Y'you have those wires connected wrong." Igor pointed into Tony's platform with his screwdriver.

"Oh, I'm sorry, but the book. . . ."Tony indicated a diagram.

"W'we've got to do it differently for our purposes," Igor answered without even looking at the open booklet.

"Oh, that's great." Tony sensed the incongruity of his words, of how they must have sounded, but he knew they were congruous with his feelings, with his desire to have Igor continue his lead. Igor did not seem to notice what Tony had said. He calmly instructed him on how the wiring should be done.

Tony looked down at Igor's spare frame, hunched over the work, vibrant with energy. The idea of abandoning the project invaded his mind, and he felt an inward revulsion as he thought of the pain he could cause Igor. He bit down on his tongue and concentrated on his work in an effort to chase the idea from his mind. Then he said, "We're really having a cool time, aren't we?"

"We sure are," Igor agreed happily, and they continued to work and talk steadily for another hour. "My gosh!" Igor gasped, "Do you realize it's almost nine-thirty? And w'we haven't even gotten our pajamas on." Usually snacks were before nine with all the Eagles ready and in their pajamas.

"Well," Tony smiled, "Deirdre's probably holding up snacks because she thinks it's about time we got off our beds."

"You bet!" Igor agreed emphatically.

"Do you think you could see about getting your pajamas on in the next few minutes?" Deirdre asked as she stopped by the table to see their progress. "How's the work coming?"

Tony and Igor assured her they had just about finished. Then Igor connected his and Tony's devices with a piece of wire. "Boy, this is neat," Tony said as he looked down at the jumbled complexity of wires that laced the underside of his plastic platform. He derived a true satisfaction from having assembled those wires and from feeling he understood what he had assembled, for Igor had carefully explained every step of their procedure.

Igor pressed a switch on his box, and a tiny flashlight bulb lit up on Tony's platform. He released the switch and the light went off. "See if the same thing happens when you press the switch on yours." Tony pressed his switch and Igor's bulb flashed. "Well, we have a telegraph set of sorts," Igor remarked contentedly.

"Gosh, we ought to build other things like this." Tony voiced his momentary enthusiasm.

"Uh, anytime you want to do something like this again, all you have to do is tell me," Igor said.

"Now all we have to do is get the wire hooked up between our beds after we're in pajamas," Tony said happily.

Moments later he got his pajamas and took them into the bathroom. He changed and then noticed Igor entering the other stall as he emerged from his own.

Back in the dormitory Tony came face to face with Deirdre. His clothes in his hands, he felt uncomfortable. "How soon do you think you and Igor will be finished?" Deirdre asked pleasantly.

"Oh, Dar'dra," Tony stretched. "I don't know. We've just got the sets working, and now all we have to do is get them hooked up. But don't worry. I was talking it over with Igor, and we agreed that you'd agree with us that it was about time we got off our beds. That's right, isn't it, Dar'dra?" Tony took her by the hand and squeezed.

"You two are a couple of schemers," she smiled as she returned the squeeze.

After getting into his pajamas, Igor returned to his bed, switched a few dials and restored his box to its old place in the electrical panoply. Then he helped Tony attach his plastic platform to the head of his bed. The ladder was brought in, beds and dressers were moved, and Tony and Igor, along with Harry and Lewis, taped the connecting wire to the wall.

"You going to need anything else?" Harry asked Tony.

"I don't think so unless you want to lend a pencil."

"You want something to poke with?" Harry grinned. "Is that the idea?" And Tony found himself fending with his arm to keep Harry's jabbing fingers away from his ribs. They both laughed as they closed into a wrestling hold with Deirdre looking on. But she didn't say anything. To Tony there was nothing more beautiful than a counselor who could rise to the occasion of a wonderful experience, the type for which he felt the School was made. Such a counselor saw no need for petty enforcement of the School's regulations. Deirdre continued to look on while she went about cleaning the group table for snacks. Then Tony and Harry came apart. "We'd better stop before we scare poor Dar'dra," Tony laughed.

"I guess so," Harry agreed.

"You see, that way she can see that we *know* when to stop," Tony added. At the School, when somebody knew when to stop, he did not have to be watched so carefully by a counselor.

Soon the wire ran from Igor's box, up along the wall, and over Harry's and Lewis' beds and dresser. Deirdre went out to make fried eggs for snacks, and Tony mounted the ladder to tape the wire above the door.

"Tony." He heard Deirdre's voice as she came toward the dormitory.

He jumped down from the ladder and stepped into the hall. "What's up?" he asked and noticed that Deirdre was leading Mickey who looked despondent.

"Could you find something for him to do?" Deirdre asked. "He doesn't think you older boys can find any work for him."

"Well, most of the time we're up on ladders and moving dressers."

"Just find him a little something." Deirdre smiled confidently at Tony.

"Oh." Tony seemed suddenly to remember something. "There's some stuff still to be done for our project. C'mon, Mickey." Enjoying Deirdre's confidence in him, Tony took Mickey into the dormitory and tore several strips from a roll of masking tape. "Now why don't you get some crayons and color these with different colors?" Tony suggested. "Then we can put them up over the tape on the wall and it'll look better." He recalled imagining himself asking Deirdre "Just what do we owe these boys?" and now this question seemed totally out of harmony with the way he felt.

At ten o'clock, Tony and Igor had everything hooked up and tested. Now their project worked wonderfully, and construction was beautified by Mickey's multicolored tape. Because of his contribution, Mickey had been allowed to press the switch on Tony's platform several times. The signals he had sent to Igor's bed had been answered, and now Mickey sat with his head resting against Tony's shoulder while Tony read the night story. The other Eagles sat around the table and listened while they gorged on fried eggs. Deirdre was at the kitchenette, preparing second and third helpings, but no more than three because the group had to go to bed sometime. And to get her point across, she had turned the lights out. Tony was reading by flashlight.

The feeling of Mickey's head against his shoulder made Tony uncomfortable. He was not sure why, but he felt it would be terribly callous, out of context with the way he was feeling, to ask Mickey to sit up. He also felt his mood of friendliness was fleeting, that it would soon leave him. And he wished he could hold onto it, wished that the kindness, which Mickey now took for granted, would stay with him. But he knew it wouldn't, that even now he wanted to break away from Mickey.

Then suddenly he felt a repellent impulse against himself creeping into his muscles, directing him to start beating Mickey's head with the flashlight, to totally eradicate Mickey's trust in his friendliness. Why couldn't this impulse, this will, leave him alone on this kind of night? Tony forced himself to read with more concentrated animation. One of the characters in the book had a German accent, and Tony read, imitating Dr. V. to perfection. He had once practiced this imitation quite a bit, but had ceased abruptly after Dr. V. had told him he was like a little boy putting on daddy's clothes.

"Gosh, you're good at that. You almost scared me." Mickey sat up and looked at Tony. All the Eagles laughed happily together, and Tony forgot about his will.

"Vhat's going on here?"

Neither Tony nor any of the other Eagles had seen Dr. V. enter through the partially opened door. "Oh, it comes out of the book," Tony quickly answered.

"Vhat comes out of zhe book? I vant to know vhat you're all doing up?" Tony and Igor told him. And like Mickey, Dr. V. got to send a few signals on the set.

By ten forty-five the Eagles were in bed and on their way to sleep. Tony and Igor had continued to beep signals to each other until Lewis asked if they could please continue in the morning.

Lewis' request was much more polite than usual for his drowsy state. Suddenly Tony remembered that he had not brushed his teeth.

He got up and did this, then went and stood by the window which looked out over the Midway. The warm, friendly atmosphere of the dormitory became even cozier when contrasted with the cold glow of an illuminated snowdrift that lay beneath a street light. It was a cold early March. For a moment Tony imagined a community in which all the people lived in a gigantic bed where, as one big happy group, they cuddled together beneath luxurious piles of quilts and blankets while blizzards blew outside. He had imagined this at other times, and now he thought he would pretend he was in such a community as soon as he snuggled down under his covers.

"Hey, Tony."

"What's up?" Tony turned to Igor whom he had not heard behind him.

"Guess what we're going to do tonight."

"What?"

"W'we're going to go sailing off in a nice cozy blimp that's all lined inside with a whole lot of warm blankets, a'and we're going to take Deirdre and the rest of the group. W'we'll be going just as soon as I get the gas ready."

Tony nodded. It was almost the same as his own idea. But he wondered whether all of Igor's achievements at the School would become part of his fantasy world rather than the real. He thought about this a moment.

"Hey, Tony, aren't you interested?"

Tony realized he had turned back to the window and left Igor standing behind him. "Yes," he answered, "I'm interested, but I have a couple of things to think over, so I'll beep you two flashes for good night as soon as I get in bed. And you do the same. O.K.?"

"All right," Igor agreed and returned to his bed.

Moments later Tony was snuggling down under his covers. He beeped his warm contact of friendliness into the night. "Good night, Igor," he said silently, and his own light beeped in return.

13

Tony heaved the suitcase onto the rack above his seat, a comfortable swivel seat which faced a window in one of the first class coaches. "Want to put this up?" Deirdre asked as she handed Tony his overcoat. It was 9 a.m., five minutes until the train's scheduled departure for Louisville. Tony put his coat by his suitcase. Then he cast a quick glance at the coach's interior, at the thickly carpeted floor, the mahogany colored walls, the green window curtains, and a small line of passengers coming down the aisle.

"This is nice," he said, "but why don't I go in a regular car? I mean, it would be a lot cheaper."

"Why do you think?"

"I don't know." Tony avoided Deirdre's eyes. "It's not as though these seats really separate you that much from others." Deirdre just looked at Tony, her closed mouth expression indicating nonacceptance of what he had said. "Actually, it's quite a bit more separated than in a regular train car," Tony conceded, feeling foolish and slightly hurt. "Anyway, I don't intend to talk to anybody."

He was glad to turn away from Deirdre and pick up his accordion case. Then suddenly he had the feeling someone was staring at his back, and as he heaved the case onto the rack, he looked through the window. The lighting in the train and the station's semi-darkness enabled him to see the small line of passengers reflected in the glass as they passed through the coach. One of them, a short man, seemed to be casting a backward glance in his direction. Tony was unable to get a distinct impression of him because the glass reflection was too distorted. He pushed his accordion into place, and when he looked around, the man had disappeared.

It seemed to Tony as though Deirdre's eyes had also followed the line of passengers, and he was tempted to ask her if she thought somebody had been looking at him. But he was afraid she would think he was anxious about traveling alone. So, instead, he simply said, "Well, I guess I'm all set." Deirdre nodded, and to fill a momentary silence, Tony said, "I hope I continue to be able to make trips by myself."

"That depends on how this trip goes."

"If nothing out of the normal comes up, how will you be able to determine that?"

"By the way you act."

"So how would I be acting to indicate the idea wasn't too hot?"

"The way you're acting now."

"What do you mean?" A faint smile began to play on Deirdre's lips, and that forced Tony to smile. "Dar'dra," he whispered, trying to relax, to appear at ease.

Deirdre looked at her watch. "Well," she said, "if the planes are still on strike, I'll meet you at the 63rd Street Station on Monday night at eight-thirty."

"O.K.," Tony nodded, "and I'll call you if I get a plane reservation."

"Fine," Deirdre smiled, making Tony feel she had confidence in him.

"Well, I'll see you soon," Tony said, and he and Deirdre hugged briefly.

Tony felt an agreeably uneasy churning in his bowels as the train pulled out of the station. He liked his plush surroundings and the fact that he was going to be far from anyone he knew. He tried to read but couldn't concentrate, a problem from which he often suffered. By noon he had only read a few pages, having been unable to relax and enjoy his autonomy.

He rose to his feet. Time for a good steak in a swanky diner. Deirdre had given him money for this. When he got the steak, it was so hard to cut that he almost pushed it off his plate once or twice. His jaws ached with the effort to chew into its leathery texture, and large doses of ketchup and salt failed to evoke any flavor other than their own mixed spiciness.

Tony returned to his comfortable seat, the steak weighing heavily on his stomach. He slumbered fitfully, then suddenly sat up. He had just dreamed something frightening connected with the man whose indistinct reflection he had seen in the train window. He glanced around the coach to assure himself he was not alone.

He looked at his watch and saw that it was two o'clock. Already half the trip over! Already nearing Louisville, nearing the farm. He began to wonder what he would do over the weekend, and he thought he might ask his mother if he could have Eddy spend the day with him. Usually their days together started in the hayloft in the barn, situated on a hill across from the house. There they exchanged stories and jokes, all dealing with sex, and sometimes they staged mock battles, loads of fun when you could fall down in the hay without getting hurt. He had not seen Eddy since the summer when, in the hayloft, he had asked, "Eddy, have you ever fucked a girl?"

"Is a pig's ass pork?" Eddy had evaded roughly, confirming an impression that this was not a question one guy was supposed to ask another. Living outside the School, Eddy was bound to know such etiquette. Then later Eddy had said, "I once tried to screw a girl."

A few days after this talk, Tony's mother had remarked, "Eddy's more sophisticated than you," and this comment had fanned an already recognized envy.

"I've read forty books," Eddy had announced to Granny three or four years ago.

"Why, that's marvelous," Granny had said admiringly. "Maybe you can get Tony to read some more." Eddy's father was rather poor, and Granny was paying Eddy's tuition at a prep school that planned to recommend him to Harvard. Tony thought Granny cared very deeply about his friend. "Tony's very lucky to have a companion like Eddy," he had heard her say on more than one occasion. And on still another: "Tony, I'd like to see you make a good impression at the party tonight. Try to behave like Eddy. He always talks softly and listens politely to people even when they bore him."

Last summer Granny had given Tony a fancy erector set, a gift he did not appreciate. "Boy, you don't know how lucky you are," Eddy gasped when he saw the set, and he immediately began to construct a motor vehicle. At the end of what Tony considered a boring day, after Eddy phoned his mother to come and get him, Granny asked the boys to sweep the front porch.

"Now, Tony," Granny admonished, "don't let Eddy do all the work like he did on the car." Tony made a conscientious effort to sweep as well as Eddy, but Eddy displayed a knack for getting his broom under chairs and into corners. Then Tony's eyes lighted on a slim green insect that looked like a grasshopper. "Eddy," Tony spoke with vicious indignation as he raised his broom, "I think this little bastard's asking for mercy." There was something strangely prayerful about the insect's statue-like pose.

"Tony!" Granny appeared just as Tony jabbed with his broom, smashing the insect against one of the porch posts. On the verge of tears, Granny told Tony he had destroyed a praying mantis. The praying mantis had done nothing but sit quietly on the porch all summer, bothering nobody, but earning the right to his perch by eating thousands of insects. "And you come along and kill him!" Tony almost thought Granny was going to slap him. "Why can't you build like Eddy? Why do you have to destroy?"

Minutes later, when Eddy's mother came to get him, Tony took off to the woods. "Dear Granny," he imagined himself composing a note as he paced rapidly along a narrow footpath, "I'm terribly sorry about what I did, but the next time you adopt an insect, could you please put your name on it? I'm not as wonderful as Eddy who never does such things. . . ." He stopped: Last Christmas Eddy had told him how he had killed a rabbit, then chopped it open so its intestines spilled out over the mud. What would Granny think of that? Probably not too much.

Hell, Eddy just breathes right. That's all, he just breathes right. He can do anything, Tony was saying over and over an hour later as he sat in the front yard with Jacky, a beautiful black and white mongrel sheep dog Granny had picked up as a stray. Jacky was afraid of men, probably because a man had mistreated her, and it had taken quite a while for Granny to guide Tony toward winning her affection. But now he had it, and it was beautiful to stare into her deep, sad eyes. She looked up at him lovingly as he caressed the back of her neck. She would never be part of his human quarrels; he could always turn to her. For a moment Tony thought it would be nice to take her far away with him, far from Eddy who did everything right, from Granny whom he constantly hurt without even wanting to.

Then he saw Granny coming toward him, and he no longer felt like licking his wounds. He did not want to act bitter in front of her, to have her feel badly on his account. So he playfully rolled Jacky on her back and began to rub her belly.

"I'm sorry I got so cross." Granny's voice was soft and conciliating.

"That was all my fault." Tony defended his grandmother as he helped her to sit down.

"No, I should have told you about the little bug."

"Hell, you know I'm rotten through and through." Tony wanted to hear his grandmother contradict him.

"Now don't talk that way. You know it makes me sad."

Tony glanced out the train window without really seeing anything. It was always so easy to make her sad, he thought as he remembered an afternoon down in the woods on the farm when Mr. Jones, a tenant farmer, was setting up a tent which Granny had given him for his sixth birthday. Seated in a small folding chair on a knoll, Granny was reading to Mr. Jones from a direction sheet. Tony was standing by the chair, but he was looking at his mother and at Paul, whom she held on her lap. Paul began pulling at a loose branch hanging from a log. "Paul!" Tony shouted angrily, "leave that alone. It's mine! Granny said that the tent is mine, and so is the hill we're building it on!"

"Tony?"

"Yes, Granny?"

"Can *I* have that branch?"

"Of course, if you want it."

"All right then, the branch is mine, and I'm giving it to Paul."

"Here, Paul," Tony said graciously as he reached down and tore the branch off the log, "Granny wants to give you this."

Tony thought he had handled the situation quite satisfactorily. But that evening Granny said to him, "Tonikins, you made me very sad this afternoon."

"How?"

"Well, you know there's really no need for you to be so selfish with your brother who just thinks the world of you. And you couldn't have cared one bit about that little branch."

"Well, he got the branch. So let's not be sad anymore."

"I would have liked to see you give it to him without my having to ask you to."

The next day Tony got a saw from the barn, and laboriously cut a large limb off a dead log. Because it was cumbersome and heavy, he asked Mr. Jones to carry it to the house for him so Paul would have it when he was outside that afternoon.

But Tony did not feel that Granny was fully satisfied by his ostentatiously generous comeback. His gesture made her happy, but she had asked him, "Did you really get that branch for your brother?" Another memory, some two years past, caused Tony to squirm in his seat. "Well, maybe some day, if I keep watching from heaven, I'll see you two finally come together." Granny had burst into tears after one of his verbal battles with Paul had culminated in an actual fight.

From the branch to now, there hasn't been much change, has there? Tony thought unhappily. In this fight, he had cut Paul's lip, and it was one of the few times he had seen his grandmother cry, but he felt he had hurt her many times through his constant quarreling with Paul and other people and through his taste for violence and killing. Occasionally he had gotten her furious.

"Want your ball? Speak!" The scene was Granny's room, and Tony was holding the ball for Jacky, waiting for her to bark before he bounced it on the floor. "Speak!" Tony repeated excitedly as Granny had instructed while she lay propped up on pillows in her four-poster bed. Jacky emitted a series of loud, piercing barks.

"Goddammit! Can't you see I'm trying to place a call!" Tony's head jerked around to Granny who had the phone in her hand.

"I'm sorry, I didn't know," Tony gasped as he quickly threw the ball to Jacky. Whenever Granny screamed at him, Tony was hurt, frightened and angry; hurt because Granny was angry at him, frightened through fear of hurting Granny, and angry because he was hurt and frightened. But all vanished moments later when she told him she was sorry she had been so cross. She had a natural temper whose flames were fanned by exhaustion, a temper that usually subsided as quickly as it flared . . . except when he quarrelled with Paul.

If only she would not care so much, Tony had wished a thousand times, but she had always cared and would continue to care as long as she lived. She's suffered so much for you. Tony thought of his grandmother's fragile body driven to exhaustion by years of sickness and the pain he had caused her, and he sank into a dull, somber mood of self-dislike.

Against this feeling, various dialogues began to impose themselves in his mind as he relived the experience he'd had last summer, telling his grandmother about Eddy and the rabbit. After hearing his account, Granny had simply said, "Well, you ought to try to teach Eddy more about conservation. You see, his people are very ignorant about such things, and they just don't know that if they go on killing the way they do, there soon won't be any little animals left."

"I told him I thought what he did was neat." Tony hung his head. "Actually, I wouldn't want to kill a rabbit."

"Well, I'm very proud that you can tell the truth," Granny said. "Now I know you like to sound tough when you're with Eddy, and I know it's sometimes hard to tell our friends things they don't like to hear. But can't you tell Eddy what you really think? He would certainly continue to like you. . . "

And a few days later, while playfully grappling in the hayloft: "Hey, Eddy, I have been wanting to tell you something about conservation."

"Well, I don't want to hear about conservation." And Tony had forced Eddy back against a bale of hay and delivered what amounted to a quick, incoherent, and futile lecture. But the pleasure of telling Granny about it that evening had made it worthwhile.

"Well, Tonikins, all we can do is try, and I'm very proud of you."

Now as he sat in the train, Tony still cherished the memory of the happiness he had sensed in his grandmother's voice. You don't always hurt her. You often make her happy. Tony had worked himself into a glow of joy, and he harnessed that joy into an old fantasy in which he tried to assuage his guilt for not loving his grandmother.

"Here, Granny, I've got everything set up for you, and the path's all made."

"But Tonikins, you know I can't get down that long path."

"But I've got this wheelchair for you, and I'm almost sure you'd see deer one of these evenings." The two-acre yard in front of the house was bounded by a fence wrapped in a lush growth of honeysuckle. Beyond this fence, the ground sloped into a woods about a hundred feet below. Deer were often seen feeding at the edge of these woods, and Tony imagined he had dug a niche out of the hill for Granny's wheelchair. Granny could sit there and watch the deer which he would lure with a salt lick. He knew she would love this, and he thought he might put his fantasy into action if Granny were still alive in the summer.

So Tony continued to imagine various dialogues in which he tried to convince his grandmother that his project was safe. "Listen, Granny," he fancied himself saying, as he wheeled her along the path, "as soon as I've parked you on the hill, I'll go back and get you some coffee."

"Why, Tonikins, that is very thoughtful of you." He gloried in his grandmother's appreciation. Then, on the way back for the coffee, a faint wind began to stir, the sky suddenly darkened, and Tony wondered whether it would soon rain, whether he should return for Granny before it was too late. But he wanted to carry through with his plan and get the coffee. Then a repellent vision, mercilessly intrusive and irrepressible, interrupted his tender fantasy:

He saw himself up in the house; it was raining, and he remembered he had left Granny outside in her wheelchair. She could never get up to the house alone; she would die shivering in the cold. Tony squirmed in his seat and set his teeth in an effort to beat out this picture, to settle into his earlier happiness, but instead his mind ran a gamut of abortive means he would use to save his grandmother.

First to get to her, he imagined himself yanking at the front door to the house—it was often stuck. The door sprang free, and he kicked open the screen door, bounded across the front porch, heaved over the railing and dashed into the yard. Then suddenly he stopped, transfixed by indecision, while he shivered in pounding rain that drenched him to the bone. He was torn between conflicting impulses, one to get his grandmother as fast as possible, the other to hurry back to the house and get a blanket to keep her warm.

"Oh Granny, I'm sorry!" Tony left his indecision, imagining now that he had a blanket and that he was by the wheelchair, looking into his grandmother's haggard face in the vain hope of a communication, for though her head was raised, her eyes were shut. She sat forward in the chair, her hands pressed against the arms in a shaking effort to rise.

How to lift her, how to wrap her in the blanket—Tony's mind dwelt for a moment on these dilemmas. Then he imagined he had wrapped her from head to foot, that he had her in his arms where she lay limp in approaching death. As he started up toward the house, he suddenly realized she could not breathe inside the blanket, and he felt an impulse to let her smother, to personally extinguish his battle to save her. But better yet, just to leave her in the wheelchair, simply unwrap her and set her down, to run away, never to see her again. This inspiration brought a measure of comfort.

Of course, you don't really feel all this, Tony tried to laugh at his fantasy. Hell, Granny needs you, and you want to have fun with her this weekend. Now, as many times before, he wondered whether his horrifying impulses could ever dominate him.

He tried to imagine he was with Granny, to imagine what would happen if he were alone with her, standing over her in her bedroom. This situation was a likely one because he almost always joined her after supper to talk to her, to play his accordion, to play with Jacky.

Now he saw her standing next to him in her pink nightgown, probably looking for something, perhaps one of the medicines she had forgotten to put with the others in the shoe box she always kept at her bedside. As he gazed at her, he could feel her fathomless love for him and the countless agonies she had suffered on his account; he could also feel her years of cumulative illness. And he felt deeply the fragility of her whole being, her health, her life, hanging by a weak thread.

He looked at the upper part of her back, at the shoulder blades where the spine curved forward. And the impulse kept coming, sometimes accompanied by a subtle gust of dread in his chest and behind his eyes where it caused a stinging premonition of tears. The impulse, the will that was part of him yet against him, a part he could not control, could only try to repress, kept erupting in his chest, then coursing through his arm and hand, urging him to land a vibrating open-handed blow between his grandmother's shoulder blades. He brought his hand up to strike, actually raising it from the arm of his chair. . . .

"Why, Tonikins, what—?"

"Just grabbing at a mosquito." An insane excuse for the time of year! He had raised his hand to strike and felt his character damned and exposed by the gesture.

How do you know you won't do something tonight? You *don't* know. Hell, he retched inwardly, you're no better than a murderer because at least you know about it; you could *tell* somebody and do something about it. But no, you just let it pile up inside you, and pile up, and pile up, and pile up, he continued his condemnation, not at all sure what he meant by "it," which he used to sum up his will against himself and his fear of the things it might make him do. You've just let it pile up, he repeated to himself, and it's dangerous. It's actually dangerous. His realization was devastating.

And, in a moment's miserable inspiration, he decided he simply had to tell his problem. Better to tell it than act it, he thought, though the difference was not comforting since he felt that to tell would be a virtual declaration, and hence a decision, that he was something less than a sane citizen.

"Is something troubling you, my boy?" Tony heard a man's whimsical voice behind him and felt a hand on his shoulder. So his anxiety was visible: he panicked and decided there was no longer any point in trying to hide it.

"Yes." He rose from his seat, feeling that if he were going to tell, it did not matter whom he told. And he turned to face a short, slight man with a light complexion.

"You can tell me what's bothering you," the man offered while the hand on Tony's shoulder gave a slight squeeze.

"Nothing's really bothering me." Tony suddenly became incredulous, feeling he had never really been ready to tell a thing. He was not sure, but he thought this was the man whose reflection he had seen in the window. Yes, and there was something familiar about him. The man in Ryan's Woods? Tony did not look long enough to confirm an impression which he gravely doubted.

"Excuse me." Tony forced a smile as he pushed the warm hand off his shoulder, stepped into the aisle and ran to the end of the train car. The man was right behind him. He barged through the heavy curtains at the entrance to the men's lounge, traversed the lounge in a single step, pushed open the door to the toilet stall, kicked it shut, and hit the lock into place. He could hear the man enter the lounge, heard him approach the door.

Why doesn't he say something, Tony wondered during a few seconds of absolute quiet. Would it be safe to open the door? Tony found it tantalizing to feel so close to a possibly dangerous person, yet absolutely safe from him.

But he's not dangerous. He's not the man from Ryan's Woods. Tony was caught off guard by a rush of doubt. Hell, he wants to help you. You know how you must have looked when he came over. And he wondered if the man's hand on his shoulder had not merely been his effort to reassure. He remembered John's once holding Mark by the shoulders while Mark retched with a hidden agony.

Then, suddenly, Tony could hear footsteps and voices. "What you doin', man?" The angry voice of the porter.

"I didn't do anything to him."

Tony heard the blond man's voice almost crack.

"Ah'm gonna turn you in if you don' git off this train at the next stop!" But the porter didn't understand; it wasn't the man's fault. Or was it? Tony emerged from the toilet stall just as the man hurried out of the lounge.

"You all right, young fella?" the porter asked. He was a large, imposing man. "A lady said she seen this guy chase you in here."

"Yes, I'm all right," Tony nodded. But maybe the lady had mistaken the man's intention; the thought was oppressive—the idea that the man could be in trouble when he had not meant any harm. "What do you think he was after?" Tony asked.

"You know somethin'?" The porter shook his head, not even listening to Tony. "You're the second young fella that man's picked on. An' you weren't doin' nothin', but nothin'. That lady says you was jus' sittin' calm an' peaceful-like, mindin' your own business, an' that man, he come along . . . ." The porter continued to shake his head, leaving the sentence suspended.

Tony had never felt such blissful relief. But he masked it and calmly asked, "Do you think the man was drunk?" A delayed impression caused him to wonder if there had been liquor on the man's breath.

"Didn' you smell 'im?" the porter asked incredulously. "Man, he was roarin'! Ah'm jus' gonna hafta pop him one upside-the-head if he tries somethin' again."

Minutes later, Tony was back in his seat, all poise and politeness. He had graciously thanked the lady who had called the porter, and now he relaxed, still feeling joyous relief that he had not drawn the man to himself with his problem. Nevertheless, he was shocked at what he had almost confessed.

But just because you might have an accident doesn't mean you shouldn't go riding in a car. It was suddenly easy to reason this way now that he was more at ease. And it's so damned unlikely that anything will happen that it just isn't worth telling people about this problem of yours and forcing them to change their whole opinion of you to one that would just not be right as far as you know. And think of the unhappiness it would cause people like Mother and Granny who care so much about you.

14

Saturday was Tony's birthday, and, as he knew from glancing at the newspaper, it was also the execution date for a man named Lem Gitler. Lem Gitler had shot six men and raped and stabbed two women on a three-day murder spree. Tony knew this man's short life had begun in an underworld environment that had steered him to an early bisexual gigolo career from which he had ascended to part-time occupations of pimp, night club bouncer, and narcotics smuggler. Suddenly, for no explicable reason, Lem Gitler had capped his small-time notoriety with a once-in-a-decade atrocity. On and off, Tony thought about the fact that somewhere a man was being forcibly put to death. "Is it now?" he kept wondering, fascinated with temporal proximity to a violence as distant from his own life as Amazon headhunters.

Aside from this preoccupation, the day was generally depressing. After Deirdre's rulings, Tony had not expected any birthday presents that would help fill the gap in his life. But this did not stop him from being disappointed in the gifts he received. Granny's doctor had paid an early morning visit and told her to rest until supper. Tony's mother also had to spend much of the day resting because she had a headache.

At six Eddy called and dropped a bombshell, claiming to have spent the previous night with a girl. By supper his mother and Granny felt well enough to come down to celebrate the birthday. Julia, the maid, had baked a cake; they all sang "Happy Birthday," and Tony blew out the candles with a single puff. Immediately he asked them if they believed what Eddy had told him, and they both answered affirmatively.

Granny went on to say she was very disappointed in Eddy. His grades were slipping, and he was slowly adopting the behavior patterns of his family's background, not those of the college-bound milieu in which she hoped to educate him. All this put a damper on Tony's envy. But he wondered whether boys from his own family's background had experienced more than his grandmother suspected. As he listened to her, he felt more strongly than ever that, even if he couldn't have intercourse soon, he should at least learn more about the less protected side of life. Granny paused after enumerating Eddy's reversals, then added, "Well, I'm certainly proud of you, and that's what's important to me."

"Well, I'm glad I can make you happy," Tony smiled flatly. Yes, he thought, with the help of the School he would probably get to college. The question was when. His arithmetic problems had lately shown a malicious tendency to turn out wrong. And he wondered what his grandmother would think if she knew how he was constantly stabbing his arithmetic book, constantly teasing helpless Billy, his only classroom pleasure being a sadistic one. "It's pretty frightening that a boy going on fifteen has to act this way," Tony had said to John in mock counselor seriousness. John often asked how he felt about himself, whether he had anything he was truly proud of, and Tony always had an answer. "Yes, my accordion."

Your accordion's probably the only thing you really care about. Tony looked at his grandmother, feeling she meant less to him. He wondered if she would survive the knowledge of such a fact. She looked the way she had always looked, only somewhat thinner, somewhat weaker. Now there was a certain faintness in her manner which did not smother her vitality, but which gave Tony a new distinct feeling that she did not have long to live.

Supper over, Mrs. Hastings helped her mother into her nightgown and into bed, then told Tony he could go up with his accordion. When he got to his grandmother's bedroom, she was listening to the news. He placed a chair in front of her bed, his usual perch for accordion concerts, and he sat down in time for the newscast of Lem Gitler's execution. This was followed by an angry editorial against capital punishment. The speaker stated that in the final hours, Lem Gitler had become increasingly nervous and had been unable to consume his last meal. His uneasiness had slowly turned to abject fear, and he had fainted while being strapped into the electric chair.

"I think that's just awful." Granny switched off the radio. "I only wish we could be a little more civilized."

"Hell, the man didn't get half what he gave to eight other people." Even as he said it, Tony wished he had not mouthed a moment's belligerence deriving from the frustration of the last two days.

"Well, I'm sorry to hear you express such an attitude," Granny said sadly. "Don't you think a boy with your intelligence and other fine qualities should be more interested in understanding people than punishing them?"

"But what about those people he killed? He had absolutely no reason, and it's just totally wrong."

"Tony, there are always reasons for things that happen. And I hope you'll become the kind of person who's interested in finding these reasons. There are already enough people who want to punish."

"But those people he killed didn't have a chance. Don't you feel a sort of rage about that?"

"Well, I try not to get angry at a person I can't understand, and I can't even begin to imagine what must have been troubling that poor man. Now aren't you just as mystified as I am?"

"Yes." Tony's answer was perfunctory. What had just dawned on him was devastating. He had wondered how Lem Gitler could have been motivated to embark on his senseless spree. Tony knew only one emotion that could impel a man in such a direction.

"Tony, is something the matter?"

"Oh, no, nothing at all." Tony forced himself to smile. "Excuse me one moment." He rose from his chair. "I have to go to the bathroom." Seconds later, Tony locked the bathroom door. Yesterday, on the train, he had concluded that the potential danger of his perverse will was probably no greater than the possibility of an automobile accident.

But where did it lead Lem Gitler? He had nothing to gain by it and didn't do it until he was thirty. You might also do it then. Anyway, you're probably the only one who understands him. Tony felt miserably obliged to communicate this understanding, if not for his own sake, at least to shed light to prevent future murders by others with his and Lem Gitler's affliction.

He turned on the cold water and let it run. Then he cupped his hands and splashed it over his feverish face. Where does the rape come in? he wondered. No, he didn't understand Lem Gitler's raping and stabbing two women, a sexual act toward which his own will had never impelled him. And didn't his own impulses come too quickly for the premeditation evidenced in Lem Gitler's use of weapons?

Tony reached for a towel and dried his face. He realized he had only wanted to do things on the spot—Granny standing before him, John in the wood shop, Mickey's head on his shoulder.

No, you can't explain Lem Gitler at all. Human emotion had revealed itself as a gigantic phenomenon, much too grand to be more than dimly comprehended by the deep yet terribly limited reaches of his own personal feelings.

Now you're going to play your accordion for Granny, and you're going to take real good care of her and make her real happy, Tony spoke to himself exuberantly, trying to hold onto his sudden sense of ecstatic relief. But something was obtruding, and then his will erupted with a new and terrifying force, deep within his chest, but without flowing into his arms and hands, not directing him against any particular person. Tony dropped his pants and sat down on the toilet, trying to make a non-existent need to defecate his reason for staying locked in the bathroom. In the wake of the onslaught, he reflected on how he had been all but free from this kind of worry while with his grandmother. He had hardly thought about it, but when he had, absence of premonition had made him uneasy, as though a natural part of himself were missing.

Locked up and alone, he thought it would be all right to give focus to his will, to let it dominate him. Once again he tried to imagine himself standing over his grandmother, to feel the will seeping into his arm, into his hand, but somehow the feeling did not come naturally. The onslaught had passed. Oh well, he decided, you might as well strap yourself safely behind your accordion, forget the damn thing, and try to have a good time like you usually do. He let himself out of the bathroom.

"Your monster certainly looks heavy," Granny commented as Tony slipped into his accordion.

"Hardly weighs anything at all," he smiled, panting slightly. "Shall I start with 'My Old Kentucky Home'?"

"Why that would be just fine," Granny nodded, and Tony began to play and immediately forgot his worry. A while later, after he had played a medley of old favorites suggested by Granny, he put his accordion aside and sat on the floor to play with Jacky.

"Give it to me," he said teasingly as he tried to pry the ball out of Jacky's mouth. The dog lay on her back, her front paws folded while she pushed her shoulders against the floor to keep her balance. "Isn't it cute the way she has her paws?"

"Yes, Jacky's always cute," Granny agreed, "but play with her gently now. She's tired."

"Oh sure; I'm not really playing hard."

The phone rang, and Granny reached over her medicine box and radio on the bedside table to answer it. "Hello . . . oh, Eva." A moment's pause, then she looked at her watch. "Good gracious, it's ten o'clock. Why yes, Eva, I'll send Tony down immediately." After replacing the receiver she said, "Well, Tonikins, it's time for you to go on down to the cabin."

"The time certainly flew, didn't it?" Tony smiled. "I was supposed to be down there by nine-thirty."

"Well the time always flies when I have you with me."

Tony stood up, pulling the ball from Jacky's mouth as he did so, and Jacky jumped to her feet. He threw the ball before Jacky had a chance to bark, and she sprang after it. Then he stepped over to Granny's bed.

"Now give me a kiss if you're not too old," Granny held out her arms.

"You know I'll *never* be too old for that," Tony said. He could feel brittle bones beneath the lacy nightgown as he embraced his grandmother, and he felt a subtle but quickening touch of nostalgia. First there was the familiar crease of perpendicular lines as her mouth pursed for a kiss; and just before they kissed, he felt a strangely familiar nick as the left rim of her glasses frame touched him above the corner of his right eyebrow. He realized this nick had been part of his life farther back than he could remember.

Tony went down to the cabin right below the house where his mother was staying so she could have a life apart from the nurses who were occasionally needed. Tonight, as on many other evenings, Tony had at first really enjoyed talking to his grandmother, trying to carry out her suggestions for old songs which they cherished, and asking her if she thought he was playing them right. Then in the middle of one of their favorites, he had become conscious of the fun he was having, and consciousness had destroyed his sense of involvement. Afterwards, he had not become bored, but awareness had taken its toll. It would be nice if you could really have fun at something, Tony thought, hoping he and his mother would have an enjoyable talk the way they often did.

His mother asked if he were still writing in his diary. Tony said he was. Their talk progressed to a discussion of Anne Frank, and then to the concentration camps. He told his mother that if he were a concentration camp prisoner, he would not refuse an order to operate the gas ovens if such refusal would mean his death.

"Oh, you'd just be such a *slime*." Tony had never heard his mother speak this way.

"But Mother," he protested, "that's just like killing yourself, not to save your life in such a situation."

"Is your life that much more important than somebody else's?"

"No, absolutely not." Tony stated his true belief.

"Well, I'm glad to hear that." There was something Tony did not like in his mother's tone. She had always put such a high premium on him, his life.

"But," Tony went on, "even if I'm not worth more than other

people, I don't see why I shouldn't kill a person to save my life if that person's going to die anyway. And it wouldn't even really be my fault. It would be the fault of the Nazi who made me do it."

"Oh no," his mother shook her head. "If you killed someone to save your precious skin, *you'd* be the one to blame. You'd be just as much to blame as if you did it for any other reason. *Believe* me, you would."

Tony wondered whether his mother would continue to love him if he became a "slime." Until now he had considered his mother's love impervious to any crime he could commit.

"Tony," his mother continued, "you know that those who collaborated with the Nazis in these executions were the ones who got it worst in the end, don't you?"

"No, I didn't know that."

"Yes, they were the ones selected by the sadists to be tortured since they were detested more than any of the other prisoners."

"Well, in that case it wouldn't be a good idea to kill in order to save yourself. But I still don't see anything morally wrong with it."

"I know, and that distresses me."

"Just give me a logical reason why you shouldn't kill a person to save yourself if he's gonna die anyway," Tony pleaded. "I wish I could see it all your way. I really do."

"Well, I don't see why you can't."

"Maybe if I learn to love more, I'll just see things differently," Tony suggested, wondering if his mother had guessed how little he loved.

"Yes, I suppose I can trust they'll help you with that at the School. Well, I'm exhausted, so let's go to bed."

Sleep was the last thing Tony wanted at the moment. "Mother," he said, "I think I'll take a walk around the farm. I'm just not tired."

"Well, don't stay out too late."

Outside there was a contrast of white against dark. It was dark beneath the trees, but the thin snow was a soft white.

You feel pretty badly about yourself, don't you? He felt there was something evil in his thinking, though logically it seemed infallible. Why, he wondered, was he so split in thinking from his mother who loved so deeply? Actually you have no real basis to think that love has anything to do with this, he told himself.

What would Dr. V. think of his stand, he wondered, remembering that Dr. V. had suffered in concentration camps. "I may be a beast and even think like a beast," Tony imagined himself confronting Dr. V., "but at least I *tried* to think right."

But just what are you, Tony wondered unhappily. The glorious sense of self-righteousness he used to defy Dr. V. was marred by the thought of his destructive will.

He wandered up onto the turnaround behind the hundred-year-old plantation style house where Granny had lived for so many years with his grandfather, Anthony. Anthony had died before Tony was born, and Tony knew from his mother that Granny still cried about him. In that house Granny had raised his mother, two uncles, and several generations of dogs. Tony remembered living on the farm as a small child. Then, Granny had helped his mother raise him, and afterwards there had been the many nights spent with her. As he looked at the house, he remembered once having told a counselor how deeply his grandmother had loved each of the dogs she had owned. "And what about people?" the counselor had asked in her typical counselor-like way.

"She loves people much more, but she loves the dogs, too." He had felt his answer was truthful. Now, as he gazed at the house, he thought of his grandmother sleeping with the peace of mind that comes from having devoted oneself to others, with the peace born of feeling loved. And *still* you don't love her, Tony murmured. Just think if she knew what was in your mind. He did not want to think. Instead, he recalled the previous hour when he had really been having a good time with his grandmother, of how he had become conscious of the pleasure, and how consciousness had spoiled it all.

What a fall, he thought, wishing he could feel his sense of loss, but unable to feel a thing. Well, c'mon now, you really don't expect yourself to care, do you? He became cynical. Hell, all you've still got to care about is your accordion. And he wondered if he even cared about that:

"All right, Tony, zis is zhe end of zhe accordion and zhe lessons," Tony silently imitated Dr. V. as he tried to imagine how he would actually feel if his lessons were in fact terminated. A few moments' thought, then: You feel nothing. Nothing about everything, even the accordion. You're nothing but a corpse.

And Tony suddenly saw his existence as a series of repetitious futilities. He was sure there would always be a gap in his life and that he would never be rid of his solitude. Now he remembered stringing the wires with Igor as more of an arduous than a pleasant affair. Arduously he had fought his will to strike Mickey with the flashlight, to strike John's fingers with the hammer, to strike and break away. But from what, he wondered. You'll never break away from your will, he thought. To break away! To break away! It had become a basic urge. He wanted to break away from himself, from whatever caused him to get a sexual thrill out of a lizard's suffering, from whatever might have prevented him from understanding why he shouldn't kill a doomed person to save his own life.

In the distance, he heard the engine of a heavy truck on Highway 42. He glanced over toward the barn on the hill opposite the house. The barn was practically hidden by a fence and trees. Beyond the barn were hills and fields bordered by dense woods that ran up to the highway. The woods beside the highway were pitch black. Nothing was easier than to conceal oneself from an oncoming car. Then, when the car drew close, there was just enough time to plunge forward into its headlights.

As in Acapulco, Tony was shocked to realize how easily he could end all his troubles. A simple walk toward the highway, a swift exertion, then nothing. Why not? The damning question seared his mind, and he felt the impulse simmer in his being. Oh God, what are you, he challenged himself, feeling that at any minute the impulse might dominate him. You're not suicidal, he protested, panicky at the very possibility that everything in his life amounted to so little. You should tell somebody, he thought, but he was repelled at the idea that others should see him as what he feared himself to be. Why should you tell? He could find no logical answer to his question, only a deep unreasoned sense of guilt at the idea that, by saying nothing, he might deceive people as to his true nature.

He looked down at the path he had made in the snow as he paced back and forth over the turnaround. He realized he had been pacing for quite a while. Now he could feel the impulse urging him toward a single suicidal gesture, a mere step outside his trampled orbit. He thought how simply he could end all worry about being suicidal, how easily he could snuff out his will, his whole life which had become a burden. But there's sex, he reminded himself of fruits not yet tasted. And there flashed through his mind his aching wish to have Laura take him in her arms, Marta's smoothly scented skin cupping like ivory at the shoulder blades, her enchanting smile and eyes that made him weak inside.

At the same time he heard a car racing along the highway and felt overwhelmed by the beckoning of a single, final act. Absurd that a Marta or a Laura, remote possibilities, could justify a life both agonizing and meaningless! Life's just not worth it.

"Coward," he whispered scathingly, aghast at the idea that he was like a soldier frightened of battle. Or even worse, he wondered if he were simply too conventional, too bound by social norms to commit the highly unacceptable act.

In defiance, he embraced momentary decision, stepped outside his small orbit, then recoiled instantly. "You ought to tell Mother," he whispered. But just what to tell, explain? "That was a stupid thing to do," Tony admonished himself, "especially when you're not absolutely sure life's not worth it." He started over toward the barn just to be walking somewhere other than inside his little orbit. Why do you want to be dead, he asked himself. It's just that you want to be free from everything. You want to be free like on the night when you kissed the whore.

His eyes lighted on the white silo as he mounted the hill opposite the turnaround. That would be another way to die: to climb the rungs leading to the top of the silo, then dive to earth. "You have a one-track mind, don't you," Tony whispered, his eyes fixed on the half-open sliding door. Beyond it was ominously dark.

Darkness had always frightened him, especially the black of partially opened doorways. But, he now reasoned, whatever's in there can't do anymore than kill you. And since you don't care about life or anything, you shouldn't be afraid to go inside.

He contemplated the darkness. There's nothing alive in there, he told himself, for he knew the two old work horses had died, and no cattle were being raised. Since he no longer cared about his life, Tony hoped he could at last assume a devil-may-care courage that would bestow heroic dignity as compensation for his loss of feeling and inability to love.

You *are* afraid, he derided himself, feeling his heart pound. Swiftly he stepped inside and slipped the door shut behind him. In the total darkness only his pounding heart had to be acknowledged, plus a vague premonition of tears somewhere behind his eyes. He tried to take his bearings. He knew a tractor stood down near the other end of the barn. And to his right and left there were doors to empty stables and storage rooms.

Suddenly he sensed the presence of something else. Then he heard a distinct sound, something moving right above him in the hayloft.

"Ahhhhh." A non-human whisper.

Tony gasped, taking air through his vocal chords, and he felt the tears well up. "Help! Help! Help!" his terror erupted.

"Ahhhhh."

Tony moved in the darkness until his hand grabbed at what he thought was an ax handle. "Come an' get me, an' I'll *kill* ya, ya sonofabitch!" he screamed as he snatched up the ax and crouched behind it. His fear harnessed into ecstatic defiance, he clutched the handle with all his strength, clutched with a sense of savage security and waited, gritting his teeth in the still darkness. There was more movement in the hayloft, and he jerked compulsively. "C'mon," he whispered through his teeth. The movement seemed to recede toward the tractor. Suddenly there was a scratching sound against the wall, then a heavy thud, and Tony knew that whatever had been in the hayloft was now with him on the floor of the barn.

"Ahhhhh," the sound came again as Tony jumped back against

the door, crouched behind his weapon. Whatever had dropped from the hayloft was now advancing toward him, and instinct prodded Tony to remember the light switch on the wall to his left. He groped frantically for the switch with his left hand while he gripped the ax with his right. Then his fingers connected with the switch, and he flipped on the light. He saw a large, ugly tomcat advancing toward him. "Ahhhhh." Apparently the cat had lost its voice; it could only emit an unnatural sound. Tony flexed the ax and the cat ran under the tractor. "Damn you sonofabitch, you oughtn't scare me like that," he said as he replaced the ax.

His heart was racing. So you *can* still feel, Tony told himself as he stepped out of the barn. You can still feel great fear. How come you didn't think of this before?

Suddenly Tony thought he had something to live for: a life centered around the one emotion he could feel intensely. Yes, life could still be exciting if it were centered around fear, fear like that he had felt in the barn, fear converted to delirious savagery behind the sharp blade of an ax. He had already planned a life of adventure in the Amazon. Now he visualized this adventure as a heightened experience, a dangerous flirtation with the unknown, with death. And there could also be room for that cruelly exquisite feeling that had invaded his loins when he saw the guide step on the lizard.

But you'd lose your fear just like your love, Tony thought. And once again the hopelessness, the doubt about whether life was worthwhile. You might as well hang around this earth for another seventy years just in case something good happens. Was the answer that simple? Tony was surprised he had not already thought of it. Now that suicide was out of the question, there was really nothing to tell anyone. Well, you've got no actual idea just what your life's going to be, Tony yawned. He was getting tired.

Minutes later, he found a temporary solution to his dissatisfaction with life. Washed and in pajamas, he stood over his bed in the room next to his mother's. There was something beautifully, warmly inviting in the color contrast between the thick, brightly patched quilt and the starched white of the sheets and pillowcase. Sleep could be such a wonderful escape from everything, and was much, much more delectable than the head-smashing fender of a speeding car, the heavy tires, the frozen highway.

As he eased himself into bed, he wondered why he had never seriously considered sleep before. Since he had only slept a few hours the previous night, it was wonderful to burrow into a soft mattress, to feel the weight of heavy covers. "Hold me, Laura, hold me!" He hugged the copious pillow and sank his head into it.

15

On the Friday afternoon following Tony's trip to Kentucky, the Eagles went shopping on Sixty-first Street instead of Fifty-fifth because on the previous excursion they had been set upon by a group of boys they referred to as the "Hewds," a street gang. The fracas had barely started when a patrol car pulled up to the curb, and the Hewds had quickly scattered.

Deirdre reported the incident to Dr. V., and he had explained to the Eagles that Fifty-Fifth was becoming a difficult street because a number of buildings there were being torn down to make room for the expanding University. But, he added, "Sometimes your attitudes just invite people to slug you." Then, in order to let the trouble blow over, he suggested that the Eagles not go back to Fifty-fifth the following Friday.

So Tony found himself looking at a paperback shelf in a drugstore on Sixty-first Street. He had saved several allowances for a hardbound historical novel in a Fifty-fifth Street bookstore, but since another allowance would be forthcoming, the anticipated purchase was not going to be hampered if he now put out forty cents for a paperback selection.

The Lem Gitler Story: Tony's heart gave a slight throb as his eyes lighted on the title and a photograph of the protagonist. He picked up the book, looked at the blurb on the back, then glanced over several of the pages. As he did so, he remembered his resolve to become more knowledgeable about the less protected side of life. And now Tony decided he definitely wanted *The Lem Gitler*

Story whose blurb promised an exciting narrative along with a lurid and detailed picture of a world so unlike his own. The only problem was Deirdre. He was not at all sure she would tolerate this book even though she was much more liberal about reading matter than about TV and movies. He took the book from its stand, and holding it up to Deirdre, he said, "Tony's going to get this book."

"Forty cents just to annoy me?" Deirdre smiled, and Tony made his purchase, knowing that with her present interpretation of his motives, she was not going to give him any trouble.

The following afternoon, when the group was getting ready to go to the Woodlawn Library, Laura happened to notice *The Lem Gitler Story* on Tony's bed. She told him she did not think he should be reading it.

"But it's all right with Deirdre," Tony countered.

"Well, I'm not Deirdre," Laura answered, and Tony knew Laura was coming of age as a counselor.

"I know you're not Deirdre," Tony decided to tease her, "but don't you have a great deal of respect for her opinions since she's been here for such a long time?"

"And just what did Deirdre say about the book?"

"Well, actually, all she said was that I was getting it just to annoy her."

"Oh, I see."

"Well, she knew I was going to get it, and she didn't say anything against it."

"Have you shown the book to Dr. V.?" Laura asked, and Tony became uneasy. He was glad Dr. V. had already made afternoon rounds.

"I don't need Dr. V.'s approval for everything I read." He feigned self-assurance to avoid a direct answer.

"I don't think you'd get his approval," Laura said, and Tony hoped he would not have to try.

Already disliking the book, Laura became particularly piqued when she found that Tony was taking it to read at the library. "With all the fine books they have, do you have to bring *that?*" she asked as the group walked slowly down the street.

"Well, I want to read it," Tony argued.

"Then read it," Laura shrugged, and afterwards Tony found she was not interested in talking to him. She seemed resigned to his reading, and this made him suppose she was not going to talk to Dr. V. about it. Nevertheless, for the rest of the walk, Tony imagined various confrontations with Dr. V. in which he defended his reading matter with both courage and persuasive conviction.

During most of the afternoon at the library, Tony read *The Lem Gitler Story,* but his mind stayed on Laura and her attitude about what he was doing. Toward the end of the afternoon, he noticed her surveying a row of books on a shelf close to where he was sitting. "Hey, Laura," he said, "do you still hate me?"

"Of course I don't hate you." Laura's kindly tone gave Tony an inner stirring as she took a seat beside him. "But why do you have to read about that kind of man?"

"I want to be like him." Tony looked straight into Laura's eyes, enjoying the shock which he felt register in her face even though she didn't move a muscle. "I don't mean I want to do the things he did," he added quickly, "I just want to know more about the way guys in his kind of background live. In many ways, I wish I'd grown up in his background without doing the things he did."

"What do you think his background has to offer?"

"Well, guys like him are a lot less protected than I am, and they're tougher, and they get the finer things out of life much younger than I do."

"What specifically do they get?"

"Well, they're able to have intercourse." Tony spoke softly, seriously. It was pleasant to be able to talk in such a frank manner to Laura.

"Do you really think that at your age you're missing out on something?" Laura asked, and Tony told her in brief about his telephone conversation with Eddy, and about how his mother and grandmother thought Eddy was falling into bad habits. "Anyway," he concluded, "there are just whole areas of life about which I'm totally unsophisticated."

"So do you really need *that* kind of a book to teach you?" Laura jabbed with disgust at the paperback.

"There's just no room in your heart for it, is there?" Tony teased.

"There certainly is not."

"Hell, you're just plain over-protective."

"Well, that's my right." Laura spoke in a tone of assertive affection which Tony did not think he would ever forget. But despite her attitude, he worried on and off that she might tell Dr. V. about the book. Throughout supper, he was tense, but Dr. V. did not appear.

After supper, Tony got *The Lem Gitler Story* and settled on his bed. He concentrated less on his reading, however, than on Laura who glanced at him intermittently. For about an hour, he surreptitiously returned the same. He tried to tell himself that his real interest was in the book, but he knew he wanted to continue his argument with Laura. Finally, their eyes met.

"All right, Tony, enough is enough." Laura sounded weary as she turned toward Tony's bed. "You know, I almost feel you're using that book just to annoy me."

"What do you *mean?*" Tony became mockingly innocent.

"I don't have to tell you."

"Now you sound like Dar'dra," Tony teased and all but yielded to an impulse to take Laura's hand as he would have taken Deirdre's.

"Tony Hastings, whether you like it or not, I'm not Deirdre. I'm *Laura.*"

"Oh, I'm sorry, I didn't realize that," Tony smiled, and Laura turned abruptly away from him. "Hey, Laura, come back here." There was a hint of desperation in his voice.

"Is there any point in my talking to you?" Laura shrugged.

"Well, you shouldn't let me drive you away so easily. Look, I'm emotionally disturbed, and I'm supposed to need attention."

"Talk, talk, talk," Laura smiled as she returned to Tony's bed.

"Well, if you're gonna put up with it, you might as well sit down." Tony indicated a place beside him.

Laura complied, then her eyes fell on a Renaissance art book which Tony had gotten for his birthday. "Now *that's* very nice," she commented. "Do you ever look at it?"

"Well, hardly. You see, I just don't know much about that kind of stuff, and I'm just not a good appreciator. Hell, I shouldn't have even asked for it."

"Oh, Tony, must you always be a professor about everything you do?"

"A professor!" Tony's comeback was not entirely voluntary. "That's almost as bad as being a priest! Hell, I only want to be cultured. But I doubt I can even be that." He had concluded this after looking through his art book several times and finding himself unable to feel any emotion whatsoever.

"Tony, why don't we try looking at that book together?" Laura suggested.

"Sure, why not?" Tony rose from his bed, got the book, then sat down as close to Laura as he dared. "Here, let's just turn this to the middle." He flipped the book open, and for a moment he and Laura looked at a picture of the Virgin Mary holding a naked Christ child in her arms. "God, I hate that cherubic little bastard," Tony finally said.

"Why?"

"Because he takes up more pages in this book than all the other subjects put together, and there were so many interesting things that could have been painted back in the Renaissance."

"Oh, I see."

"You don't seem to really believe me."

"Might I suggest that you have some rather strong feelings about mothers holding their babies?"

"Frankly, I'm more interested in the kind of stuff I did out at Red Cloud."

"Like what?"

"Well, when the boss's fiancee wouldn't kiss him in public, he had all us young fellows get in line and kiss her on the lips. She was twenty-four and fairly pretty." Tony was glad to have Laura know he was accustomed to situations where girls of twenty-four were good for something more than tucking him into bed at night. What he did not tell her was how unsensational the experience had been, waiting in line, then taking his turn.

"So is what you did out there so completely removed from

this?" Laura failed to be impressed as she indicated the picture with her hand.

Tony smiled. "Can't we leave that kind of thing to Freud?"

"Tony Hastings," Laura snapped, "I don't think you know what you're talking about. And in any case, I've never known *you* to show any great respect for the genius of others."

"Can't there be a first time for everything?" Tony gave a slight snicker. He hoped his smart-aleck attitude would aggravate Laura to the point where she'd cease to argue with him and try instead to break his resistance to her through some demonstration of physical affection.

"Well, I guess you just want to give me the runaround," Laura sighed, and Tony was dismayed. Laura glanced down at the picture, then up at Mickey and Ralph who were firing their water pistols under the group table. She rose from the bed. "Haven't I told you two to keep those guns in your toy chests?"

"Why should we?" Ralph asked.

"Because lately there's just been a little too much emphasis around here on violence and murder."

"Murder?" Mickey became indignant. "Why, we're only playing that we're those guys who came around just before Christmas—you know, those bug and mouse men, like the one we saw squirting poison at a roach under the chair."

"All right, Mickey, that-is-still-enough. Now you two can either put those guns away or give them to me." After a minute's argument, Mickey and Ralph put their guns back in their toy chests, and Laura resumed her seat beside Tony.

"Hey, Laura," Tony looked down to hide his smile while he tried to sound thoughtful.

"What, Tony?"

"Do you think when I grow up I might make a good bug and mouse man?"

"Listen, I have to clear up around the table," Laura sighed. And she was impervious to his entreaty and apology as she rose from the bed. Tony stretched out and thumbed idly through his art book. He knew he had driven her away while all he wanted was to get closer to her, and closer, and closer. For a moment he rested his head on his pillow, wishing things had gone differently, wondering why they hadn't.

Suddenly Tony heard Dr. V. speaking to someone at the other end of the hall. And he acknowledged he was frightened as he listened to the slow, heavy footsteps that drew near the dormitory. You won't lose all courage, he told himself in anticipation of a Laura-inspired confrontation. But meanwhile, he saw no need to invite trouble, so he flipped *The Lem Gitler Story* onto its face. He hoped Laura would not say anything.

"Vell, how is everybody?" Dr. V. asked softly as he walked slowly into the dormitory.

"Fine." "All right." "O.K."

"Vell, good night." Dr. V. turned and walked out, his head down, his hands behind his back. As Dr. V. passed through the fire doors, Tony felt better. But at just that moment, Laura put down the broom and dustpan.

"I'll be right back," she announced. And while he wondered whether she was telling Dr. V. about his book, Tony noted he was less tense than he had been when Dr. V. was present. But as soon as he heard the fire doors reopen, his heart increased its tempo, only to calm when he saw that Laura was alone.

She approached his bed. "Tony," she said, "I just asked Dr. V. whether *The Lem Gitler Story* was the kind of book you should be reading, and he said you should give the book to me."

"Why?"

"You can talk to him about that if you want to. He says he will be in his office." It was then that Tony became almost certain he was going to get into trouble, but he wanted a moment to think and also to relieve himself.

Tony handed Laura the book as he rose from his bed. He felt her eyes on his back as he walked toward the bathroom, and this embarrassed him. He did not want her to think he had to relieve himself to prevent Dr. V. from making him wet his pants. He thought of home where privacy and freedom were taken for granted.

He stood in the toilet stall and tried to gather his thoughts. Since you know you'll get into trouble if you go down there, why bother to go, he questioned. The thing is you don't know, he continued; but there was something he sensed deeply about Dr. V., an angry righteousness he did not understand. Lem Gitler's sordid background, his rape and murder spree: Tony knew Dr. V. would not take kindly to his questioning the loss of a book that depicted these things.

But is there something indecent about your reading that book, he asked himself, realizing for the first time that he actually felt this to be the case. Then he decided it was probably the School, the pressure of Laura and Dr. V., that made him feel this way, since at home he would harbor no such view.

"If you thought you should be reading *The Lem Gitler Story,* why didn't you go talk to Dr. V.?" Tony articulated the question he thought Laura, or anyone, could pose to challenge both his courage and his convictions. No, he shook his head, there wasn't any honorable way to avoid confrontation. Immediately he went back into the dormitory and took a piece of candy. The candy was hard to chew because his mouth was very dry, but he hoped this interim action would conceal from Laura the connection between his urinating and his impending request to see Dr. V.

He went for a drink from the fountain, but he felt his mouth going dry again as he returned to the dormitory. Then he went over to Laura who was putting trash in the wastebasket. "Hey, Laura, I think I'd like to go see Dr. V." He tried to sound jaunty.

"Let me check to make sure he's free," Laura said, and announced her mission to the group. Tony felt himself the center of the group's silence during Laura's absence. He looked at Harry, shrugged helplessly, and was bolstered by sympathy from Harry's return gaze. He thought about the neighborhood just outside the School where people had not even heard of Dr. V. It was comforting to know that the outside world was nearby. He had an impulse to run off. "Dr. V.'s waiting for you. You can go down by yourself," Laura said as she re-entered the dormitory.

"Fine," Tony affected cheerfulness.

The door to the office was partially open. Tony could not see Dr. V. but knew he was at his desk. He knocked. "Yes, Tony, come in," then, "Sit down, Tony."

"What's this with the book?" Tony asked as he sat down on a

couch in front of Dr. V.'s desk. He raised his eyebrows and injected what he thought was just the right amount of concern into what was otherwise a manly, casual tone of voice.

"I sought you might have come to ask me vhy you have to alvays act so damn smart vis John in zhe classroom and to constantly bait at Laura who only tries to help you. I sought you might have come to explain vhy you must steep yourself in gore and murder razer zan somesing fit for a decent human being!" Dr. V.'s anger rose as he spoke. "Do I have to tell you how zis man you read about is vhat you might have been yourself? Must you try to be like him? And you know goddamn vell vhat I sink of such a book! Yet you vent and bought it!" Dr. V.'s hand slammed hard on his desk. "Now get zhe hell out of my office! I don't vant you in here!"

Tony rose quickly, made his way out through the partially open door, and sprinted up the stairs. Since Dr. V. had not slapped him, he felt he had gotten off lightly. Then suddenly, on nearing the linen closet, he heard the door to Dr. V.'s office slam, and he knew his troubles were only beginning. As he listened to the heavy footsteps on the stairs, Tony wondered whether he should wait in the hallway, then remembered he was not supposed to loiter in the front part of the building. He all but ran through the fire doors, and he thought of continuing to run, but instead he went into his dormitory.

Immediately he dropped down on his bed after an embarrassing exchange of glances with Laura who sat at the table where she was looking over the back cover of *The Lem Gitler Story.* How to occupy the next few seconds, avoid Laura's eyes, and watch the fire doors? Tony began to thumb through his art book, an acceptable activity good for all three. Then he heard the fast, heavy footsteps. Better to take it standing than sitting, he decided. The fire doors opened, and Tony rose to face Dr. V.

He was never quite sure how everything happened: Just total loss of bladder control, intermittent pissing in his pants while he was being roughly, clumsily hauled over to the group table. SMACK! SMACK! SMACK! SMACK! SMACK! SMACK! SMACK! SMACK! Dr. V.'s free hand kept traveling with fast, rhythmic precision back and forth from one cheek to the other. Somehow, Tony kept turning away from the blows, once or twice stepping on Dr. V.'s shoes, and somehow Dr. V. kept following him, never failing to connect with either cheek. "Vhere's zat book!" Dr. V. screamed as he pushed Tony against a couple of chairs.

"There." Breathless, Tony pointed to the book which lay beside Laura. There was a moment's silence while Dr. V. picked up the book and looked at it. Tony stood still, conscious of his damp underpants, of the fact that he was not crying even though he was shaking. He could feel the numbed tingling in both sides of his face.

"So, out of all zhe sings you should read, you pick zis to learn how ozers live!" Dr. V. punctuated his assertion by hitting Tony across the side of the head with the book. "Look who you pick to learn about! Just look who you pick! Look who you pick!" Back and forth, back and forth with the book, around the cheeks, around the ears, and around the temples. "Is zis zhe man you vant to imitate! Do you vant to be like him?" Dr. V. slammed the book hard on the table.

"No." Tony shook his head and tried to avoid Dr. V.'s eyes.

"Can you say zat to my face?" Tony made an effort to look up, then he looked down again while Dr. V. allowed a moment's silence to register Tony's inability to confront him. "You came to zis school vis zhe mind of a murderer!" Dr. V. shouted, "and I pulled you out of zhe gutter ven zhey vouldn't have you in Topeka! You know, I almost didn't take you!"

Tony looked up and nodded.

"So vhat is zhere to show for all zhese years!" Dr. V.'s eyes bore into Tony with a new intensity.

Tony stared ahead so that he vaguely saw Dr. V.'s right shoulder, and into his mind's eye flashed a picture of Granny standing bent before him, his hand raised to strike her. Are you a murderer, he wondered.

He refocused into Dr. V.'s eyes, no longer afraid of them. Rather, he wanted to drink in their power and imbibe a strength he did not understand, a strength to subjugate the things he feared in himself. "Just what can I *do*?" he challenged, "I want you to tell me just what I can do about all the cruel things inside me. And what can she do to help me?" Tony gently put his hand on

Laura's which rested on the arm of her chair. "You said she wants to help me. And remember when I came back from my Christmas visit, you said I was here to get help from others?" Tony felt Laura's hand squeeze his and a tremor ran through him, but it was almost erased by the intensity of his concentration on Dr. V.

"Zhere is very little anyvone can do to help you if you insist on dissipating yourself vis zhe kind of book you bought."

"The hell." Tony felt an unspoken rapport with Dr. V. which allowed him to speak roughly as he snatched up the book and ripped it apart at the binding. "I'm throwing this out." He turned toward the wastebasket, but moving suddenly, Dr. V. grabbed the two halves away from him.

"Zat vas a very pretty gesture," Dr. V. spoke dryly as he put the halves back on the table. "Now I don't vant zat book in here, not even in zhe basket, so you and Laura can go immediately and take it down to zhe garbage room." Dr. V. turned hesitantly and walked slowly toward the door. He paused in the doorway and looked searchingly at Tony. "Vell, Tony," he said softly, "I believe you vere sincere in vhat you asked me. And I can only tell you: try to be a decent human being and to do sings zat you can be proud of. If zat is vhat you really vant to do, zhen ve are all behind you." After that, he turned to leave and passed through the first-floor fire doors.

On the way down to the garbage room, Laura said, "Tony, I was really surprised at what you did to that book."

"Look," Tony answered, "I may not agree with most of the things Dr. V. said about the book or with most of the things he did. But I'd rather get rid of such a thing myself if you think my getting rid of it will help me become a decent human being." This was their only conversation as they descended the stairs, crossed the cloakroom, and went through the first-floor fire doors.

Laura unlocked the door to the garbage room, and Tony went in to dispose of his book. Now he felt there was something new between himself and Laura because he had grabbed her hand and asked how she could help him. And he sensed that whatever was new could assert itself at any minute. "Gee," he commented as he emerged, "it's dirty in there."

Laura put her hand on the back of his shoulder and drew him

toward her. "Listen," she suggested, "why don't you let me fix you a nice, warm bubble bath?" Tony stepped closer to her so that her arm extended further across his back. He wanted to fall into her arms, let her carry him upstairs, then undress him and bathe him. But all he did was take her free hand. Once again she squeezed it. Her expression was one of firm tenderness, and as Tony looked deeply into her eyes, he could feel tears begin to well.

He never knew how he would have answered Laura, though he doubted he would ever have let her give him a bath, but something else had begun to nag at him. "I believe zat you vere sincere," Dr. V. had said, and now Tony knew that he would have to see Dr. V. once again, or fall short of the compliment. "Listen, Laura," he said softly, "I need to talk to Dr. V. I've got some private stuff that we left unfinished."

"Again?" Laura's tone suggested she was apprehensive about another confrontation.

"It's just that I feel there are some important things that are private that need taking up. I need to talk to him."

"All right," Laura nodded. They went on through the basement and upstairs, and Tony waited while Laura knocked on the door to Dr. V.'s office.

"Yes, who is zat?" Dr. V. called out, and Laura entered. Then, after a few words with Dr. V., Laura emerged and told Tony he could go on in.

"Yes, come on in, Tony," Dr. V. said as Tony entered.

"Can I shut the door?" Tony asked.

"Yes," Dr. V. nodded, "close zhe door."

For the second time that night, Tony sat down on the couch that faced Dr. V.'s desk. "Well," he spoke immediately, "in some ways I really wasn't very sincere when I asked you how I could get rid of my cruelty because I knew of certain problems which I didn't tackle. Now what I'm going to tell you is really going to sound strange."

"So let's hear it."

"Well, sometimes I get these attacks inside me that make me suddenly feel as if I'm going to hit someone, or do something to somebody that can really be dangerous. I mean this isn't like the usual feeling I get. Often I want to hit somebody, and it's perfectly all right. I mean, I know I want to, but I'm going to resist it simply because it wouldn't be right to hit them. But this other thing I get makes me feel as if I'm going to do it when I don't want to. It makes me feel I'm going to hurt people who I really don't want to hurt, and often it happens just when I don't want to do anything harmful and it just wouldn't be moral." Tony sat back. There. It was out for the first time.

"I'm very glad you came down here," Dr. V. said after a moment.

"Well, this is what bugged me up in the dormitory when I asked you how I could get rid of my cruelty."

"So against whom do you have zhese impulses?"

"As I said, against people I don't want to hurt. Like on my last visit they came out against my grandmother. That was awful because I really didn't want to hurt her."

"No," Dr. V. smiled, "she's really a nice lady who has only your best interests at heart. So vhy do you sink you have zhese impulses?"

"I just don't know."

"Vell, you have many aggressions zat still need to be vorked out. I hope you can try to do zis in future sessions. You know, you're also quite sexually aggressive."

"Yes, I know," Tony nodded. "I had some quite strong sexual feelings when I saw this guide in Acapulco mangle a lizard." He was glad to finally tell this to someone. "It's often hard to discuss these things with Deirdre," he added.

"So maybe you feel you can no longer talk to Deirdre," Dr. V. suggested. "Maybe you need somebody else. But don't come to a quick decision."

"So what do you think of all that I've told you?"

"I can only emphasize vonce again zat I'm very glad you came down here. But I have no magic, and ve cannot settle anysing tonight."

"So do you think I'm dangerous?"

"Tony, I am sure zat you are zhe master of your fate. I am very certain zat you do not have to become explosively violent if you don't vant to."

Tony realized nothing in his external world had changed

because of what Dr. V. had just told him. He had wondered whether his will made him a menace to society and whether he should be locked up, but he had never really thought Dr. V. would consider such drastic measures necessary.

"Have a lot of other people had feelings like this?" Tony asked.

"Tony," Dr. V. smiled, "I sink you are quite an original person, but don't sink for a minute zat you are zhe only vone vis such problems."

"In a way, that's good to know."

"Good."

"Well," Tony sighed, "I guess that's it."

"Vone moment, Tony." Dr. V. raised his hand. "Does all zis have anysing to do vis zhe discussion you and your mozer had about zhe prison camps? She wrote me about zat."

"No," Tony shook his head, "that was something totally different."

"But Tony, vhy didn't you come to me if you vanted information about vhat it was like in zhe prison camps? You know I was in vone of zem."

"It all started when we were talking about this diary I'm keeping. From there, we went on to Anne Frank, and that led to talk about the prison camps. I asked Mother what she would do if one of the prison guards told her to work the gas chambers or get shot, and she said she would not work them. She thought it would be wrong."

"She's right."

"I'm afraid I disagree with her, and that's what we argued about." Tony conscientiously employed a tone of voice that made his opinion seem the burden it was.

"Vell, you can believe vhat you vant to believe."

Tony felt grateful that Dr. V. was not angry at what he thought. "But why do you agree with Mother?" he asked. "It seems wrong to sacrifice your own life when the other person's going to die anyway."

"But you vould lose your life. Zhey vould be sure to kill you in zhe end. People did not survive by such collaboration. Zheir chances vere in fact better if zhey refused."

"Yes," Tony nodded, "Mother told me that. You see, with that knowledge, I hope I would have the guts not to work the gas chambers. But what we were arguing about was that I might kill somebody to save my own skin, not how I'd act in a prison camp. After all, it's extremely unlikely I'll ever be in one. Now what I feel is that if a person's going to be murdered anyway and can't be saved, then you might as well kill him and save yourself. That would go for any situation."

"No, Tony," Dr. V. shook his head, "you should never lend yourself as a tool assassin. You are alvays responsible for zhe person you kill."

"Even if he's going to be killed anyway?"

"But you don't know zat. Zhe very fact zat zhey ask you to do zhe job indicates some ambivalence on zheir part. So maybe, if you don't lend your services, zhere vill be no murder at all."

"You mean then that your actions *are* an actual contribution to the killing. God, I hope I'd never do that. If Mother had argued from that angle, we'd have had no trouble."

"Vell, maybe your mozer vas more vorried about you zan zhe logic of your opinions."

"But what if the situation was one in which the person was positively going to be killed so that it really didn't make any difference whether or not you shot him, yet shooting him could save your own life?"

"But no such situation has ever existed."

"Well, let's imagine that it did."

"No! Tony Hastings, believe me, you vill have your hands full trying to solve real problems visout imagining zhose zat don't exist."

"I guess I do that because I feel what I'd do in certain situations, whether real or not, has a lot to do with what I am as I sit here on this couch."

"You vish to vork yourself like a puppet on strings vhere, if you pull vone string you are vone type of person, and if you pull anozer, you vill be still anozer type."

"*That's* one of the most important things about myself you've ever told me." Tony rose from the couch to emphasize what he was saying. "I actually wonder if that tendency isn't what keeps me at the School." Tony felt his second statement was somewhat antagonistic, but he also thought Dr. V. should know that his point merited further consideration.

"Vell, Tony," Dr. V. replied, "I can only tell you again and again: try in your daily life to act like a decent human being. Try not to act so smart. And do sings of vhich you can be proud. Zhen maybe you von't have to vorry so much. So, isn't it time for you to be getting ready for bed?"

"I guess so," Tony nodded. "Good night," he said as he turned toward the door.

"Just vone moment, Tony. I vant to tell you zat I truly admire zhe courage you showed in coming to my office. I know it vasn't easy for you. And also it pleases me to see zat you care so much about doing vhat you sink is truly right razer zan simply vhat your mozer or somebody else tells you. Vell, good night."

"Thank you," Tony smiled. "Good night," he said once again. Now he felt, in John's words, very good about himself, a little uncomfortably good. It was like when he had kissed the whore and aspired to a manhood that was not yet his. Now all the goodness he felt about himself was hard to contain because it was not entirely him.

Tony continued to feel good, uncomfortably good, on into the night after the lights were out and Laura had left the dormitory. Now he wanted neither to think about, discuss, nor read about Lem Gitler or any other aspect of violence. Constructive talks with Dr. V. always had this effect on him. Laura had once commented, "Dr. V. makes you feel all the good in yourself," and Tony felt this was true. He also felt incomplete. He nestled into his pillow. "Laura, people need each other," his whisper was a near whimper, "and there's a certain way they need to treat each other." He lay still, no longer feeling incomplete, no longer trying to work himself like a puppet on strings. As he grew more tired, he began to wonder about the similarity between his wanting Laura to give him a bath and what a man normally felt toward a woman.

Later he dreamed he was standing with his stepfather and one of his stepfather's professor friends in an art gallery. They were looking at a large, oblong painting with a mystical background of filmy clouds and jungle greenery.

The top part of the canvas showed a woman from the waist up, who cuddled a small, naked boy to her breast. Tony was touched with yearning by the woman's tender expression and the way she held the boy. She seemed to float within the background, and there was something intriguing about the way the density of the clouds seemed to vary from moment to moment. "The inconsistent texture of the clouds," the professor was explaining, "is an ingenious effect of lighting. Now you will have to step back to get the full import of this picture."

"Yeow!" Tony gasped involuntarily after stepping away. The upper part of the woman had disappeared in the cloudy haze, but in the lower half of the picture her naked loins were portrayed in coital union with the lower half of a man. Tony moved back to the picture, and the portrait of copulation seemed to fade in the haze. Once again he saw the fully clothed woman cuddling a small, naked boy.

"Some people," the professor continued, "believe this painting portrays more vividly than any other artistic work the hidden reality of man's love for woman." During this explanation, Tony did not take his eyes off the picture, but constantly scrutinized it from various distances.

"Or baby's love!" Tony's stepfather guffawed in his familiar tone of affectionate amusement. And Tony felt the two men smiling at him. Embarrassment shocked Tony out of his sleep. It was early morning.

He burrowed down under the covers, and for a while lay thinking about his dream. What an interesting picture, he thought, and wondered if it conveyed the real truth. In a wild moment's inspiration, Tony considered painting it, but he had never been able to transfer a mental image to paper. And he was sure there was no artist skillful enough to produce that picture in its entirety. Also, it had already faded from his mind. He tried to recall it, tried intensely, and at best was only able to glimpse it, the woman's tender expression always eluding him.

Then he realized he had actually been obsessed by a painting, even if only in a dream. And here you thought you could never be cultured, he chided himself blissfully. Certainly the gap in his life would not be so difficult to fill if he could latch onto a few things the way he had latched onto the picture. If only!

He looked at the early morning grey which shone through the dormitory curtains, and he lay still, pondering his dream. Then he picked up his watch; it read seven-thirty, a half hour until time to get up. Now it was pleasant to lie motionless and listen to the cold wind outside, and to the hum coming from the kitchen as the maids prepared breakfast. The School, its conflicts, its relationships, its struggles—Tony felt it all slumbering in an achingly beautiful unity.

But somehow this unity was dissatisfying. "Laura," Tony whispered his yearning.

"Is that you, Tony?" He was startled to hear Laura, and then he noticed her as she rose from several chairs where she had been resting by the group table. She wore a blue kimono, and her blond hair hung down over her shoulders. "So what's on your mind?" she asked as she approached his bed.

"I was surprised to see you," Tony answered.

"I see." Laura let Tony take her hand and pull her down beside his bed while she explained that Mickey had gotten her because he had a stomach ache. "Now maybe you can get a little more sleep," she said, and punctuated her suggestion with a gentle squeeze.

"I'll think about it." Tony returned the tender pressure and then let go of her hand.

"O.K." Laura patted his cheek, then returned to the table.

Tony remembered the night on the farm when he had almost concluded that life had nothing to offer him and that he might as well splatter his miserable brains against the fender of a speeding car. Now he was deeply and happily impressed by how absolutely wrong he had been.

16

Tony was annoyed at Igor and mad at Deirdre. He was annoyed at Igor whose idiosyncratic preferences made him want to shop in a hardware store where he could buy supplies for his electric panoply. He was angry at Deirdre who had decided that several stores were too much for a Friday excursion. From now on, the group was going to spend each shopping afternoon at just one or two stores. When Tony and a couple of the others had complained about this, Deirdre had said, "I know many of these things are just a nuisance, but this is the way it has to be because the School's the School. So I can only suggest that all of you do what you can to get out of here as soon as possible."

"But we're always being told not to rush things," Tony had shot back, and now, while he gazed at a gun rack in the Fifty-fifth Street hardware store, he found himself bitterly ruminating over Deirdre's carefree resignation to his circumstances. Little more than two weeks had passed since he and Igor had built their communications system, and Tony seriously wondered whether anything would carry over from that. But he was so angry that he almost hoped not, and he hoped the Eagles would run into the Hewds as they had the week before last. Then at least there would be a little spice to the dull, fruitless afternoon.

It was dark when the Eagles emerged from the hardware store. "I wonder where the Hewds are," Mickey said loudly as he looked around.

"Mickey!" Deirdre reprimanded in a tone which indicated he

should stop his line of talk. All the Eagles looked about expectantly, but they saw no sign of trouble as they crossed Fifty-fifth and started up Woodlawn, a quiet neighborhood street devoid of traffic.

They had no intimation of danger until they had gone a block and a half. Then Ronny looked back and said, "Hey, I think that's them." There was a group of boys less than a block away.

"Let's walk a little faster," Deirdre suggested, and the Eagles picked up their pace. But soon they heard the jeering voices of their antagonists who were gaining rapidly. "Listen," she stopped walking and spoke calmly to her group, "if we cross the street, we can go into that house with the lights on, and from there we can call the police." As the Eagles moved into the street, Tony noted that he was not at all frightened. He, Ronny and Harry formed what he thought was a tacit rear guard while Deirdre, Mickey and Ralph walked up front. Tony looked around and saw that his group was being followed by about seven boys, some as small as Mickey and Ralph, others about his size, and one a little bigger. We can probably handle them, he decided, and he almost hoped they would attack since it was embarrassing to be led to safety by a girl counselor. "Yaaay!" the boys suddenly screamed, and they charged the Eagles just as Tony, Ronny and Harry gained the other side of the street.

Tony braced defensively as the largest boy came at him. The shock of their contact forced him to give ground. Then they locked, arms gripping arms, in a wrestling hold, a safe but indecisive way to fight. In a glance, Tony could see Ronny and Harry also grappling. Igor shouted something in an angry tone. "Oh yeah?" somebody jeered.

Tony looked into the face of his grinning antagonist. Now he derived some satisfaction from the fact that there was nothing Deirdre could do to help him, but he also knew her presence gave him a sense of security.

Suddenly, Tony was pushed back toward a tree, and he was seized by the familiar feeling that he was struggling against someone stronger than himself. He gave ground but managed to avoid the tree by quick side steps. It's what you put into it, John had advised often enough, and Tony exerted extra strength for he did not want Deirdre or the group to see him give ground. Someone hit him on the back, and he noticed that Lewis and Igor were near him, both fending off attackers.

Suddenly his attacker lurched forward with an extra burst of strength, and Tony jumped, repeating quick, circular side steps, still trying not to give ground. Then he too applied more pressure, and the two continued rapidly in circles. Tony inclined his head, shut his eyes, bent his knees a little, and pushed with all the power he could muster. The wrestling hold was broken, and Tony brought his fist up as the boy staggered backward. It would have been easy to smash hard at the unprotected face in front of him, but Tony hesitated, afraid Dr. V. might think he had gone too far. Also, it was hard to be so vicious in such an innocuous fight. But anticipation of a blow made Tony's assailant trip back off the high curb and fall beneath the fender of a parked car. His expression darkened as he began to pick himself up. Braced again on the defensive, Tony tensed the way he did when he fought with Paul.

"Aaaay! Help! Let's get out of here!" Tony felt himself bumped by several boys as they ran past him. "C'mon!" One of the bigger boys grabbed at his assailant, and then Tony saw John bounding toward the group from across the street. Had John seen all this from his house? Tony remembered that John lived just a little way up the block.

"Anybody hurt?" John gasped. Nobody had been hurt. "Well, listen, why don't I walk with you and the boys back to the School?" he suggested to Deirdre.

"That *would* be nice of you." Deirdre was relieved. Now the Eagles saw no sign of their antagonists. At first there was rapid, excited discussion as the group started up the block toward John's house. Each had a different story to tell. Some of the boys commented on how Tony had toppled his opponent. And Tony was exhilarated as he corrected this version of his exploit by insisting that the guy had merely lost his balance and fallen off the curb.

The Eagles waited on the porch while John went into his house to telephone the police and to tell his wife where he was going.

Then, on the way to the School, Tony said, "Hey John, why don't you join us for supper?"

"Why I'd be delighted." He sounded pleased with the invitation, and his hand fell warmly on Tony's shoulder.

Suddenly Tony felt guilty. What was there between himself and John that he should act as though he enjoyed the idea of having John to supper? It was as though he were trying to show people that he was "in" with John. Still, he felt he wanted John with him, and he realized it might be nice to have him around inside the classroom.

Tony began an animated conversation with John and several of the others about the changing neighborhood, and this led to talk of changes that had been made over the years in the School buildings. There had been many changes which now brought back memories, and soon Tony and John were hashing over the good times they had had together. But his invitation to John, the talk they were having—all this was subordinate to the exhilaration derived from his successful fight, from the fact that Deirdre and the others had seen it. But what if that guy were to attack him again? Tony knew it would be tough for him. Yes, he would have to do something about himself, something to make himself a better fighter.

"It vill be safe to go shopping if John accompanies you and zhe boys," Dr. V. said to Deirdre at supper. "Zhen if zhose kids try somesing, John can grab vone of zem. Vould you like zat?" Dr. V. looked at the group.

"Yeeees!" His suggestion was hailed unanimously.

Dr. V. looked steadily at the Eagles, his expression not at all pleasant. "I sought so," he said quietly. "Zhey cry for revenge. Just don't take zem shopping in zat area, Deirdre." Then Dr. V. turned and went to sit down at the staff table.

"John, I just wanted to have you along. I wasn't even thinking of revenge." Tony turned to John in honest protest to what Dr. V. had said.

"That's right," Harry chimed in.

"It's the same with me." Lewis addressed Deirdre.

"So tell Dr. V.," John answered Tony.

Tony rose from his seat and started around the group table. At that moment, Dr. V. rose from his place. The two stopped and faced each other. "Vhat's zhe matter, Tony?" Dr. V. asked, and the whole dining room went quiet.

"It wasn't for revenge that I wanted to have John along," Tony answered. "I just thought it would be nice. Hell," he added, "we could get our own revenge if we wanted," and he instantly hated himself for the incomprehensible streak of machismo. Could Dr. V. still believe he wanted to be a decent human being? Tony avoided Dr. V.'s eyes.

Dr. V. regarded him with a closed-mouth stare that failed to betray his thoughts. The hope that he was not angry raced through Tony's mind. "Vell, I can believe zat you vant to have John along," Dr. V. finally spoke, his voice low. "Now go out and get your revenge, big shot." Tony stood rooted. "Vhat's zhe matter, Tony? Vhy don't you move?" Dr. V. asked curiously. He slowly approached the Eagles table. Then he stopped, never taking his eyes off Tony.

"I didn't say I could take the Hewds on alone without my group," Tony answered.

"I vant you to go," Dr. V. spoke, his tone ominous, and Tony's immediate fear was not the Hewds. "But just to see vhat happens," Dr. V. added with a hint of scorn—or was it curiosity—"let's find out who vill accompany you. Go on, ask zhe boys."

Tony turned toward his table. "Eagles," he said, and he paused a moment, feeling a tremor of defiant pride at the utterance of his group's name. Then he continued, "I need help. Am I going to have to go down to Fifty-fifth Street alone, or will some of you stand up from the table and come and help me so we can settle our shopping problem as a group?" Deirdre had always urged group unity and now Tony based his plea on it.

Quiet ensued. Soundlessness reverberated through the dining room, as everyone concentrated on Tony, Dr. V. and the Eagles. No one moved, and for a bitter instant Tony keenly felt the indifference with which he had always regarded his group. He was sure this indifference would always be his feeling even though he knew there was no reason for anyone to help him. The quiet became less and less bearable, and Tony shifted his eyes to Dr. V., who stood with his arms crossed, looking down, and obviously not inclined to turn the pressure of his eyes on anyone. But when Tony looked at him, he raised his head. Then Igor stood.

Slowly, shaking somewhat, pinching nervously at the skin around his jawbone, Igor stood opposite Tony at the other end of the group table. He had often echoed Deirdre's plea for group unity, and now he was practicing it. Harry hesitated but he rose just after Igor. Mickey and Ralph jumped up in order to be in the act, and Ronny and Lewis immediately followed suit so as not to be left behind.

All the Eagles were standing. John and Deirdre were the only ones still in their seats. Tony looked at his group in order to keep his eyes away from Dr. V. For an instant, he caught Harry's eyes. Then he tried to catch Igor's eyes for a beautiful moment of communication. But otherwise, neither he nor any of the other boys looked at one another. They all stared vacantly in any direction but Dr. V.'s. They stared and stood, confused in their new solidarity. Everybody was waiting for something to happen. Now it was Dr. V.'s turn to take the initiative. "So, Deirdre, vhy are you sitting?" he asked. "Don't you vant to be vis your boys?"

"I don't feel needed," Deirdre answered, and everyone knew she was happy. Now the Eagles were all smiling triumphantly: Tony at Igor, then at Harry and everybody else.

Tony turned from his group to Dr. V. "Do you still want us to go down to Fifty-fifth Street?" he asked, knowing Dr. V. had absolutely no plan to send them there.

"Vait a moment." Dr. V. strode over to the Eagles' table and picked up the empty hamburger platter. "Hester," he said to the cook who was standing by the door to the kitchen, "please take zis and put on a lot more hamburgers." Then he turned to the Eagles and said, "If you read zhe chronicles of all zhe famous varriors, you vill know zat zhey *never* vent off to fight until zhey had eaten vone hell of a big meal." He smiled at the Eagles, and the Eagles smiled back. "So I vant you to eat," he concluded. Then he returned to the staff table.

All of the Eagles ate vigorously, happily executing Dr. V.'s order. They ate and talked; tried to talk though they were not sure what to say. Tony was able to talk to Harry. It was harder with Igor, though he and Igor spoke, striving for a topic, for words. But there were no words, so they talked about what they ate, and they ate and ate. At the end of the meal Tony had consumed five hamburgers, Ronny six, Harry five, Ralph four, Mickey two, and Lewis and Igor had gorged themselves on three, much more than was their custom.

After a delicious dessert of chocolate eclairs, the Eagles rose as a group from the table and went upstairs. John accompanied them. "Could you wait with the boys for a few minutes while I go to my room?" Deirdre asked him.

"Sure," John nodded, and Deirdre left the dormitory. John glanced around at the Eagles who were slightly confused. They wanted to hold onto their new found unity, and they wondered what they were going to do now that their feast of togetherness had broken up. Tony stopped by his bed for a moment, then looked over at the table where Harry and Igor had gone to sit. They have the right idea, he thought. This was an evening that demanded a plan, something that would help continue whatever had been achieved at the table. He became aware that John was looking at him, and when he looked up, John flashed him his warm, familiar smile.

Tony smiled back and approached John. As on the first day of school after the vacation, he found himself quailing beneath John's warmth, but far less than before. "So," John said.

"So things went better than they looked like they'd be going at first."

"Yeah, you're really doing all right," John replied with calm satisfaction.

"But once again everything down at supper was all centered around fighting," Tony protested John's compliment even though he was happy.

"Oh, go along with you." John tousled Tony's hair. "You know, you *worry* too much."

"You know, that's one thing you're probably more right about than you've practically ever been about anything even though you may be right about one hell of a lot of things." For a triumphant moment Tony felt that even though he still had troubles in the classroom, even though he was not as close to John as he had been, he still had within him all the things they had achieved together. And this made him wonder if he really needed the School. He felt the stirring of a new power to grasp his life and make it happy.

Sometimes it seemed as if good things had a way of happening all at once. Deirdre came back to the dormitory and suggested that they see *Cyrano de Bergerac* which was playing at a nearby theater. This was certainly better fare than usual! And Tony wondered whether Deirdre had suddenly gained more confidence in the group. He hoped so. Shortly after the Eagles had unanimously hailed Deirdre's suggestion, John left for his home, and the group made ready to leave. Laura joined them. "I'd like to be with you all tonight," she explained, and her explanation was taken as a compliment.

On the way down the stairs, Tony and Ronny looked into each other's faces. "Oooh," their mouths formed long o's. "You deed purty well tonight," Ronny nodded a counselor-type expression of assurance.

"Ees zat vhat zhe Hounds Dog theenks?"

"Zat's right," Ronny nodded emphatically.

"Maybe tonight ve don't provoke zhe Hounds Dog," Tony suggested. He felt closer to Ronny than usual when they talked this way, and he thought Ronny felt the same.

"Slurp, slurp, he's leeking you," Ronny said.

"Vhat's zat?"

"He's leeking your cheek. You see, you can manage all right ven you vant to." Another counselor phrase.

"Oooooh," they nodded significantly, even warmly, into each other's faces.

It was mild for a March evening, so the Eagles walked to the theater while premonitions of spring wafted about them on soft, exciting winds.

"Hey, Deirdre, what if the Hewds come along?" Mickey's voice was like the wind, an excited whisper.

"Tony'll protect us," Deirdre answered.

"That ought to be easy as long as I have my comrades at my side." Tony's hand fell on Igor's shoulder.

"Th'that's right," Igor giggled happily. But there was little danger since the group was not in the Fifty-fifth Street area.

"You see, Harry, people *will* protect you," Tony said.

"Who's gonna protect who?" Harry grinned as he moved toward Tony, and they grappled playfully for a moment without either counselor protesting. Instead, it was Ralph who protested.

"Now break it up. You two can just protect me instead of each other." He thrust himself between Tony and Harry.

Moments later Tony found himself beside Laura. "How does it feel to be a leader?" she asked him.

"What?" He was surprised she would openly place him in such a perspective to his group.

"You heard," Laura answered, and Tony thrilled with pride as his hand slid into hers. He moved closer to her so that their shoulders touched. Now he felt as close or closer to his group than he had ever felt. "Hey, Laura," he said, "remember that night you stopped me and Harry from doing those push-ups when I thought it was so important for me to be stronger than everybody else? Well, now I wouldn't care if I was the weakest one in the group."

But this feeling remained something less than constant under the swashbuckling antics of Cyrano de Bergerac. After the movie, all the Eagles were talking about the exploits they had just witnessed. "Boy, wouldn't it be neat if the Hewds came to see this movie, too," Mickey suggested ecstatically.

"That's all we'd need." Deirdre's shudder broke into a laugh, and everybody laughed with her.

"Yeah, then we could get some swords. . . . " Mickey expounded, but Tony did not hear the rest. He and Harry had dropped behind the group.

"Boy, you'd never have believed earlier that we'd be leaving the School grounds again tonight," Tony was saying, "especially for such a movie."

"I really think Deirdre deserves an A," Harry smiled.

"You're right," Tony agreed, and they speculated on the possibility of more laxity on Deirdre's part about movies and television.

"Hey, what are you two doing back there?" Deirdre called.

"Oh, we were just having one of our staff meetings about you," Tony answered.

"Well, do you think you could come and join us? We want to pick a restaurant for snacks." This evening it seemed as though good things just kept coming. Good food was welcome anytime, and now the restaurant seemed to be an extension of the beautiful hamburger supper.

After a restaurant had been chosen, Tony once again found himself walking hand in hand with Laura. The spring winds continued to whisper in the darkness, and Tony felt the stirring of a thousand undefined anticipations. "Things are so wonderful," he whispered, and he felt a tremor as Laura freed her hand, put her arm around him and gave him a hug.

PART III

The Storm

17

"Hey," John glanced at his watch, "it's time." It was two-thirty on a late spring afternoon. His class started over to the playroom.

The rest of the School had already assembled when John's group arrived. Counselors and some members of the kitchen and maintenance staff stood along the wall at the near end of the playroom while another line ran from the door as far as the piano. The other class groups sat in semi-circular rows of chairs. The tables were decked with a large punch bowl and trays of fancy cookies. John led his group past the piano on top of which lay a large, square gift-wrapped package. When the class was seated, Tony looked over at the conspicuously vacant chair where the Blacksmiths were seated as a group. Then the stairway door clicked and there was absolute quiet.

Ted appeared, clad in a dark suit, followed by Dr. V. and Eunice. Tony was startled by Ted's handsomeness, for, dressed stylishly, his hair combed back into a perfect wave, he looked as if he had just played a leading movie role. His expression serious, Ted walked down past the piano and into the circle where he took his place with his group.

Dr. V. stopped by the piano, rested his foot on a chair, and cast a glance that took in the whole School. Then he looked down. "Vell," he began after a moment, "ve are gazared togezer for zhe sad occasion of saying good-bye to Ted who has been vis us now for ten good but very hard years. He has decided zhe time has come to take his struggle to zhe outside, vhere he is going to. . . ."

Dr. V. recapitulated what was virtually common knowledge: Ted was going to live at an agency home, work as a camp counselor in the summer, and begin the 9th grade at a public high school in the fall. Dr. V. went on to say he was not certain about Ted's readiness to leave, but that was what Ted wanted, and sometimes it was more important for a young man to make his own decision than to be right. However, he did not want to imply that Ted was wrong. Ted still had problems, particularly along academic lines, but perhaps it was now best for him to pursue his life away from the School.

Tony took a deep personal interest in what Dr. V. was saying. He felt that most of it could apply to himself, for recently something had made him question his need for the School with a new seriousness.

Granny had died. In April she had suffered a stroke and a sudden invasion of stomach cancer. She was taken to the hospital and kept alive by intravenous feeding. Near the end of April, Tony had had a week-long spring visit, most of it spent with Paul and his stepfather in Glenville. His mother had called from Kentucky, frankly telling him it was only a matter of time. Granny was too weak for an operation, and the doctors had concluded that she could die any day. In Glenville, Tony's bags had remained packed in readiness for immediate flight to Louisville if Granny's condition momentarily improved. There had been no improvement, but his stepfather put him on the plane to Kentucky at the end of his visit.

Now, sitting at Ted's good-bye party, Tony only half listened when Dr. V. launched into Ted's past and the progress he had made. Instead, his mind went back to the day he had last seen his grandmother (the last Sunday in April), a day on which something had happened to seriously alter his view about himself, his life.

* * *

Tony flew into Louisville on an early morning plane. A berth had already been reserved for him on the night train back to

Chicago. A close family friend met him at the airport and rushed him to the hospital, not even letting him stop to get his baggage. Granny had kept herself awake and refused to allow the doctors to give her morphine for the past twelve hours. She had insisted that she would not risk sleep until she had seen Tony once more.

At the hospital, Tony's mother told him Dr. Freeman wanted to give Granny a morphine shot immediately. "So you can only tell her good-bye for a minute," she broke into sobs. "And don't let her see you cry," she warned, though he was not at all tearful. Then she let him into the room.

"Oh my darling boy!" Granny held out her arms to Tony as he strode over and embraced her. They kissed each other on the cheek.

"How are you?" Tony asked as he eased her back onto her pillow.

"Fine, now that you're here." She smiled and for a moment looked almost like her usual self. Then suddenly, "Awwwww! Awwwww! Awwwww!" came her whispers of pain. With her chin drawn in to articulate the agony, her upper lip, withered and thin, imprinted itself against her teeth, reminding Tony of a decaying corpse he had seen in a picture. Then he noticed her bare arms, each a spindly blend of skin and bones as on mummies at the Oriental Institute. "I'm so glad I got another chance to see you," she said.

"I'm so glad to be here." Tony knew he was telling the truth, that he felt something, though not enough. They talked for a few moments with Tony conscious of the rapidly passing time, not knowing what to say.

"My, you look grand," Granny said more than once, for Tony had on his best suit. Her voice was a whisper and sometimes Tony had a hard time understanding her. She said something about being very sick, and Tony nodded, "I know."

"I love you, Granny." Tony looked into her half-shut eyes. A film had formed over them, but when the lids opened, Tony knew his grandmother could still see him.

"And I love you." They smiled gently.

The door to the room opened. "Dr. Freeman's here," Tony's

mother said quietly. Then she leaned over and said, "Tony's going back to Chicago tonight."

"Awwwww, I know." Granny had been told and had not forgotten. Then his mother stepped back. "Awwwww, awwwww," Granny's groan was a whisper as she struggled to raise her arms. "Come give me one last kiss." And Tony remembered that this was just how he had imagined her dying some four years before while playing jacks on the dormitory floor.

As he bent over, she put her arms around him, and he knew he would never forget the way she possessively clasped him, her hands pressing against his jacket. Her last kiss was full, and Tony returned it. "Awwwww," she sighed as she lay back. He took her hand as Dr. Freeman approached the other side of the bed.

"You can stay with her till this takes effect," Dr. Freeman said as he filled the syringe he was holding.

Tony looked down at his grandmother while the nurse pulled the covers back and helped Dr. Freeman with her nightgown. Granny's sigh was barely audible when the needle went into her thigh. "Say good-bye to my little fox for me." She meant the little glazed blue fox on the mantelpiece in the bedroom.

"Of course, Granny." Tony made himself smile. "Remember how we used to always play with him?"

"Tsssss." Granny gave what was almost a laugh. "Now you see that nothing happens to my little fox . . . awwwww!" Her effort to speak was checked as the nightgown was pulled into place and the covers put back over her. "Yes, he's your fox now—I remember how you used to play with him." Tony knew she was rapidly sinking from him. For an instant, he feared the tears behind his eyes might actually flow while he frantically searched for one last thing to say. "Oh my darling Tonikins with my little fox." Granny's mind seemed to be slipping into a happy past. "Good-bye, my darling Tonikins." She forced herself back into the present and looked up at Tony with her faded eyes.

"I'll always have you with me. I love you, Granny." Tony gently held his grandmother's shoulders and bent down and kissed her on the cheek, then kissed her again, closing his eyes to hide the tears. "Granny," he whispered, still holding her. Then he rose and turned away.

"She's asleep now." Dr. Freeman mercifully lifted the embargo on crying. Tony groped toward the corner near his grandmother's bed, and there he wept, at last letting the sobs break loose.

Before he left the room, Tony took one last look at his grandmother. Her breathing was barely audible, her face serene. But why had it always made her unhappy to see people cry? Didn't she expect them to love her? And how would she feel if she knew how little he reciprocated her love? But you do care, he tried to comfort himself.

Tony's mother had phoned for a taxi to take him back to the farm. As she walked with him to the elevator, he told her about the blue fox during their last moments together.

"Her mind goes back to the past a lot," his mother wiped her eyes. "And you know how you used to play with that fox."

"Yes, we still speak to him every now and then." Tony used the present tense as if to imply that their little game was not over. In fact, they had spoken to "Fox" in a sentimental, half-joking manner during Tony's last visit to the farm.

In the taxi, Tony reminded himself that he should make a point of saying good-bye to the fox for Granny since this was a last wish. Then he thought back to the day he had first noticed the deep blue glazed figurine on the mantelpiece in her bedroom.

Stretched out on all fours, the fox's head perked up in an alert attitude. Something appealing in its expression had drawn his attention one day when he glanced up at the various odds and ends on Granny's mantelpiece. He had stood on tiptoe and lifted the fox from its place. Its heavy weight startled him, and young as he was, he sensed it was fragile. "Oh, Tonikins," Granny called from her bed, "you must be very careful of that fox because I absolutely treasure it and would hate for anything to happen to it."

"I'll be very careful," Tony assured her as he settled with the fox on the blue rug that lay at the foot of his grandmother's bed.

"Did I ever tell you how I got that fox?"

"No."

"Well, when I was only six years old, my mother got very sick, and the doctor wouldn't let anybody except the nurse and my father go near her because she had dangerous germs. But one day when nobody was looking, I snuck into the room where she was lying in a big bed like this one. I climbed up on the bed, and when my mother saw me, she did a very noble thing. Do you know what 'noble' is, Tonikins?"

"No, Granny."

"Then I'll tell you. When a person is noble, he thinks of others instead of himself. Well, my mother was suffering a great deal, and she knew I was not supposed to get near her, but she didn't tell me any of this because she thought it might frighten me. Instead, she told me she would make me a present of anything I wanted in her room, but I had to choose my present very quickly."

"Are you crying, Granny?" Tony asked.

"A little bit. Now it wasn't very hard for me to make a choice because I'd been secretly wanting that little fox for a very long time. So I took the fox and left, not forgetting to say thank you, of course. Well, when I got out into the hall, I ran into my father who told me in a very stern voice to go and stay in my room until supper. But I didn't mind that because I had my fox to play with. So I played with the fox for a long time, but eventually I got tired of it. After all, I was only six. Now, what do you think I did?"

"I don't know." Tony shook his head, eager for the outcome.

"Well, I thought I might sneak back and see if my mother would give me another present. But a whole lot of people were out in the hall walking around and talking in low voices. So I had to make do with the fox. And then, a little later, while I was playing with the fox, my father came in and told me Mommy had died. So the fox was a good-bye present, even though I didn't know it when it was given to me. Now don't you think my mother was noble?"

"What do you mean?"

"Well, she didn't let me know how sick she was and how much she was suffering, and all she wanted was to see me happy. Now I have the little fox to remember her by, and that's why it's so precious to me. So I want you to be careful of it because it can break very easily."

During Tony's childhood, Granny had often repeated this story. Then Fox came to be included in fairy tales where he always appeared as Tony's companion.

When the cab pulled up to the turnaround, Tony paid the driver, then went to the kitchen to see if Julia had made him some lunch. He did not think he wanted anything, but Julia had some roast beef sandwiches ready. He took one and found to his surprise he was really hungry. As he rapidly consumed all the sandwiches and a coke, he felt as though he were imbibing new life.

Finished eating, Tony went around to the front yard where he planned to stroll a few seconds before going down to the cabin. There, in total privacy, he intended to give full rein to the sadness he had felt at the hospital. During the first part of the taxi trip, he had looked forward to this opportunity, but now he only wanted to walk around the yard.

It was a radiant day, warm for an early spring afternoon, and Tony found his senses soothed by the lush green of the thick grass. He inhaled the damp and pungent scent and could feel a luxuriant vitality seeping into his lungs. "Life can be good," Tony told himself with conviction. Birds chirped in relaxing harmony.

For a while he just walked, trying to gather strength out of the balmy afternoon to fortify himself for an expected onslaught of emotion. Then he went down to the cabin, took off his jacket and tie, and threw himself on his bed, but tears did not come easily. He realized he did not want to cry, and he felt a sense of loss as if his repression had killed his former sadness. Well, you probably just weren't sad enough, he reflected. He was tired, so he hugged his pillow and rested. Rest turned into a two-hour sleep. When he awoke, he stepped outside the cabin and noted that he now had the farm to himself because Julia's car was no longer on the turnaround. He went on up to his grandmother's room.

The blue fox looked out at him from its perch on the mantelpiece. "Hello, Fox," Tony said softly as he closed the door behind him. He looked into his old friend's eyes. "Good-bye, Fox," he said, and then as he turned away, "What do you mean—'good-bye, Fox'? You're supposed to be saying good-bye for Granny."

Tony took a quick look around the room: at the big bed on which Granny had told him so many stories about his adventures with the fox, at the little bedside table with the shoe box that housed an army of medicine jars. Then, over by the window next to the mantelpiece, he glanced at the delicate antique desk covered by a familiar clutter of correspondence. This was Tony's childhood setting undisturbed, but it would die with Granny, who had instructed that the house be redecorated and rented.

A black-capped chickadee perched on the bird feeder at the window. "Hello there," Tony said as if to an old acquaintance, but he thought it was probably the grandchild or great grandchild of one he had seen as a boy. Yes, every year he would see young chickadees, he thought, while he would never again be five, six, or seven. Never again would he listen in rapture to Granny's fairy tales about himself and the blue fox. Never would he love his grandmother as he once had. The only constant was this little world, Granny's room, where nothing had changed. "We will sing one song for my old Kentucky home." Tony hummed the final bars to his childhood tune as he cast another glance around the room. Are you trying to get sentimental, he jibed at himself. Was everything between himself and Granny, between himself and so many others, like the food he ate, which filled him one moment, but was soon no more part of him. "Granny, I wish I could keep you," he said.

In search of refuge from the future, and all it would not hold, Tony turned to the fox. "What a loving look you always give. And now Granny wants me to tell you good-bye for her," he said, aware that something deep within him sincerely believed he was not merely confronting an inanimate object. He lifted the fox from the mantelpiece and clutched it to his chest, still conscious of its weight, for it was heavier than it looked. You've got to be careful with it, he cautioned himself. And he began to wonder just where he would keep it.

First he thought of it on his and Ronny's dresser at the School. But their dresser top was very crowded. Suppose Ronny knocked it off by accident. Tony cringed to think of Deirdre and Laura hovering over him in anticipation of his feelings. Just how would you feel, Tony asked himself as he held the fox more closely. Don't you care about Fox? He looked down into the penetrating eyes and wished he could care more.

Then he decided it might be better to keep the fox safely

padded amidst the clothing in one of his drawers. But wouldn't people be bound to ask why he chose that manner to store such a beautiful object? Tony suddenly realized the fox was a very private thing and that he really did not want it at the School. Probably the best solution would be to have his mother keep it for him at home in Glenville.

"Oh honey, I'm sorry." Tony could hear in his mother's voice a new pain added to her deep grief for Granny as she apologized for having accidentally dropped and broken the fox.

"Mother, it's all right." Tony was emphatic as he continued to look at the fox and wonder just what he would do with it.

Suddenly he tossed the fox a few inches into the air and caught it. You're tempting fate, he warned himself. But after all, it really isn't very dangerous—just so long as you don't toss it very high. He felt an impulse in each forearm, urging him to toss with more force. He yielded a little. You'd really like to break it, wouldn't you, he observed as he caught the fox and held it tightly. Oh well, you won't, and he tossed it again, then again, just a little higher than before.

And then, as the fox fell tail first, Tony brought his hand up under it, and the tail jabbed his palm. He snatched frantically, but the fox eluded him, and shattered against the brick base beneath the mantelpiece. "NO!" Tony's hands flew to his face. Only a fragment of the head remained intact: a chip, consisting of one eye, the mouth, and an ear. In this, Tony felt there remained something of the familiar expression. Especially in the eye which looked straight up accusingly.

The ring of the telephone stabbed into his shock. He let it ring, not wanting to move, then finally picked up the receiver before the fifth ring ended.

"Tony, this is Mother." She was crying.

"Yes?"

"Granny died."

"Oh God no! I didn't think it would be now!"

"I'm terribly sorry. I'll call Dr. Vorlichten and tell him."

"I don't want to go back there tonight. I want to stay here for the funeral."

"I don't know if he'll want that."

"Tell him I want it."

"All right, I'll tell him. I'll call him, and then I'll be home very soon."

"I'm sorry, Mother. I hope you're all right. I'll see you soon."

"All right, honey, good-bye."

"Good-bye." Tony waited for the click at the other end of the line before he hung up.

"Oh Granny! No! I love you!" Tony gasped desperately and he sank down by the shattered remnants of something she had treasured in the last hours of her life. "I love you, Granny! I love you! I love you! I love you! I didn't mean to hurt poor Fox! I love him!" He looked down into the questioning eye. "Oh Granny, help me! What can I do? I love you, Granny. . . ."

". . . . What do you mean, you bastard. You know you don't love anyone but yourself," Tony suddenly cut himself short. Then slowly the familiar welling behind his eyes became very intense. "Good-bye, Granny, I'll always have you." He placed his forehead into his bent arm, lay over on his stomach, and cried long and hard in a way he never had, for the sadness newly erupted inside him, was a kind he had never known. It was not the agonized sadness he had once known so well, it was simply a sadness that was very, very sad, and he was sure now his grandmother would always be a part of him even if he could bear to lose her. Then, when his tears stopped, he said. "You're glad you broke the fox. You love the fox."

* * *

"You don't know a thing about love, Tony told himself with derisive triumph as he and the others rose from their seats and surged toward Ted. Dr. V. had concluded by saying that even if he had doubts as to the wisdom behind Ted's decision to leave, he was sure Ted could develop into a fine example of a man if he wanted to. Then everyone had clapped while Eunice placed the gift in Ted's lap.

Ted pulled the outer wrapping off a cardboard box which was bound by a thin rope. Grimacing slightly, he snapped the rope with strong hands. "Hey maaaan!" he exclaimed as he pulled out a knapsack. "Gee, that's neat!" "Isn't that nice!" the exclamations came from those surrounding Ted while he rummaged through various camping utensils packed inside.

"Vell, Ted," Dr. V. said, "ven you camp out on hard trails, you'll have zat to remember us by, because ve are going to alvays be vis you zhen."

Ted's eyes sparkled as he looked at Dr. V., but his smile seemed faintly bitter. This made Tony a bit sad, and he wondered how he would feel when it was his time to leave the school. Ted got up as Eunice brought him the first cup of punch and a couple of cookies. There followed a few minutes of chatter while everyone left the throng at some point to get refreshments. Standing at seeming ease, Ted responded casually to questions about his plans.

"I'm afraid, Ted, zhey are expecting you by four," Dr. V. called over from the punch table where he had been talking to Eunice.

"Well, I guess this is it." Ted flashed a smile.

"Good luck, Ted." Ronny's hand shot out enthusiastically. Then Ted found himself pressed by the younger children who vied with each other for a handshake.

Suddenly Ted looked out at Tony. "Hey, there's a man I want to say good-bye to." He reached over two smaller boys, and Tony shook his hand.

"You come back soon." Tony felt what was now a frequent welling behind his eyes.

"Don't push him, Tony. He vill come back ven he is ready." Tony chilled at Dr. V.'s reprimand, but he was almost certain Dr. V. only wanted to assure Ted of real freedom now that he was leaving.

"I couldn't push Ted," Tony answered, "*nobody* does that." He did not know whether Dr. V. grasped all that was behind his emphasis on the word, but Ted hadn't missed it.

"Good-bye, Ted! Good-bye! Good-bye. . . .!" the younger children shouted in chorus as Ted left the playroom with Eunice and Dr. V. It was too near three o'clock to return to the classrooms, but it was not yet time to go up to the dormitories, so the assembled School waited in the playroom, enjoying the refreshments. Tony ate a couple of cookies, then gulped down a fresh cup of punch.

After he threw away the cup, he found himself beside Deirdre. "Dar'dra," he said softly.

"What?" Deirdre asked as her arm went around Tony, and Tony caught her hand in his.

"Ted's not the only one leaving." Tony dropped what he considered a strong hint as he looked Deirdre in the eye. Before Christmas, after his grandmother's first stroke, he had felt he lacked Deirdre's ability to care about others. He had felt he needed to stay at the School until he could acquire her capacity to care. But he had broken the blue fox, and he was no longer so sure of his need.

"That's right, Ted's not the only one leaving," Deirdre said after a moment, and Tony's heart skipped a frightened, happy beat because he thought she was breaking some news to him. "This Saturday," Deirdre added, and Tony realized she was talking about someone else. Irma began calling the names of different groups, sending them up to their dormitories. As he started up with his group, Tony reflected that this Thursday would be Laura's last afternoon on duty.

Tony had not been surprised a few days before when Laura asked the Eagles to assemble at the table, and then told them she was leaving the School. She was perhaps the tenth counselor from whom he had heard this announcement. Since their conflict over *The Lem Gitler Story,* Tony felt his relationship with Laura had taken on a tender quality quite unlike anything else in his experience. But he also felt this relationship had not developed satisfactorily.

Often at night, Tony looked over at Laura while she sat at the group table. Hugging his pillow, he was able to embrace fleetingly the ecstasy of what he imagined it would be like to cuddle his head against her breasts. Occasionally, after she tucked him in, he would play on her counselor sensitivities by recapitulating experiences outside the School which were supposed to arouse scary feelings. In order to be honest, Tony never failed to emphasize that these experiences had not really terrified him, but he knew his honesty only served to make Laura think he was not up to facing their true effect. When he thought he had her sympathy at the right pitch, he took her hand and held onto it. Laura usually responded with a reassuring squeeze, and once Tony had cuddled his head on her forearm. But so far this was the extent of his accomplishment in what the boy at Red Cloud had called "messin' around." And now there was very little time left. Tony often wondered if Laura had begun to divine the real reason why he called her to his bed, if anybody knew how strongly he desired to have her hold him.

That evening, as he rested on his bed, his interest was gradually aroused by a conversation between Lewis and Laura. Leaning on the group table, his chin on his fist, Lewis looked with lively attention into Laura's face. Whereas Lewis was shy with his dorm-mates, he could be anything but shy with counselors when probing into their personal lives, and now he was interrogating Laura about her relationship with Dr. V. "So," his lips formed an O, and his eyebrows went up as he knitted his forehead, "at what times do you find it easiest to talk to your boss?"

"My boss?"

Using a form of address and tone employed, often reprimandingly, by Dr. V., Lewis said, "Yes Laura." He nodded significantly and added, "He is in a sense your boss."

"You're right, in a sense he's my boss," Laura conceded, "but that's not how we relate."

"Yes Laura," Lewis nodded, stressing the final vowel. "Now, let us discuss how you two do relate."

"In what way?"

"Well, when do you find it easiest to talk to him?"

"I guess at times when I'm sure of myself and know what I'm doing." Laura gave what Tony considered a typical counselor answer.

"Ummmmmm." Lewis' nose wrinkled as he pursed his lips thoughtfully. By means of persistent questioning, persistent guessing, Lewis had relentlessly probed the counselor policy of reticence on personal matters and had wheedled from Laura various trivia such as her age, her father's occupation, and the number of siblings she had.

"Tell me," he suddenly spoke in a clipped tone, "have you ever wanted to sit on Dr. V.'s lap?"

"What a question!" Laura blurted, obviously startled. "Why do you ask it?"

"You answer *me,*" Lewis' eyebrows went up for emphasis, "and I'll answer you."

"Well," Laura said, "don't you know it's only human and natural to want things like that sometimes?"

"Yes Laura, and you've sometimes wanted it."

"I've thought about it at times," Laura conceded. "Now why did you ask that question?"

"Because I wanted an answer." An impish grin curved upward on Lewis' face.

"Since you brought the matter up, I wonder if *you'd* like to sit on Dr. V.'s lap."

"No."

"But you raised the question."

"Not about myself." Lewis sounded peeved. "His is one lap I would not like to sit on."

"So, on whose lap would you like to sit?"

"Why don't you try to guess?"

"Well, maybe you'd like to sit on my lap." Laura smiled.

"Maybe." Lewis nodded curtly.

"Well, would you?"

"You've only one way to find out."

"All right, come here then," Laura said in a tone of having had enough as she moved her chair back from the table and opened her arms. "You know," she advised, "if you'd just ask for more things, you'd get more things."

"Yes Laura, that's true," Lewis nodded wisely as he rose from his chair. "But," he concluded as he settled into her lap, "this gives you a chance to use your psychology."

"Oh, c'mon," Laura pouted. Lewis was using one of his favorite phrases.

"Hey, Laura! Did you know they have more rodeos in the east

than in the west?" Ronny jumped from his bed with a magazine, his attitude one of concentrated inattention to what was happening at the table.

"Ronny, that-is-enough. Right now I'm with Lewis and if you have feelings about what's going on over here, why can't you say so?"

"I just said they have more rodeos in the east than in the west," Ronny protested.

"I sometimes think we have more rodeos in this dormitory." Tony had come over to the table.

"Ronny's not the only one with such feelings." Laura looked up at Tony as he took a piece of chocolate from the candy box. Then, to Lewis, "At least when *you* ask all those questions about me, *you're* able to get what you want."

"Ummmmm. So you've established a purpose for my questions." Lewis tried to shift for a more comfortable position, but he was a bit big for Laura, and he did not appear at ease. As he watched Lewis, Tony realized that he would be embarrassed to have the group see him in Laura's arms.

"Maybe you two would also like to sit on my lap," Laura said to Tony and Ronny.

"Maybe you'd like to sit on ours," Tony countered.

"Smart aleck to the end." Laura reminded Tony that she was leaving.

"Actually, I do have some feelings about all this," Tony quickly assented, "but I wouldn't want it out here with everybody watching."

"Nice of you to try and spoil it for Lewis," Laura said dryly even as Tony realized his tactlessness.

"Oh, I'm sorry, I didn't mean it that way." Tony turned helplessly to his bed. Lewis was so timid, so infinitely inoffensive, that Tony hated to hurt him, especially when he was in such a vulnerable position. He stood by his bed a moment and listened while Ronny began talking to Laura. Then, because he felt ashamed, he ducked out into the hall for the few moments' privacy afforded by the water fountain.

When he re-entered the dormitory, Tony saw that Ronny had

appropriated Laura's lap. As he dropped down onto his bed he noted that, like Lewis, Ronny also seemed uncomfortable. He was still talking a blue streak about cowboys and rodeos.

At snacks, Laura asked the Eagles if they would like her to join them for snacks on Friday evening. She was leaving Saturday afternoon. Friday would be her last night at the School, and Deirdre was on duty. After the Eagles readily extended the invitation, Harry asked about her plans for the future. Laura said she was going to live with a girl friend and take some graduate courses at the University. Several of the others asked questions about the kind of courses she planned to take. While he listened, Tony became conscious of a familiar sadness.

Often, around bedtime, the sadness was just there, elemental and undefined, until Tony realized he was missing Granny. It was not a deep sadness, not something that would get out of hand, but it was persistent. Ater smashing the blue fox and crying, "I love you, Granny!" there were times when Tony doubted his love, but this sadness helped efface that doubt.

After snacks, he opened his top drawer from which he took a small package, composed of five pieces of tissue folded several times over a tiny object. He unfolded the tissue and gazed down at the chip from the blue fox. The eye still seemed to look back at him.

The rest of the fox had been unsalvageable, and Tony had explained to his mother, "I broke it by accident, but the fox was as delicate as Granny, and I guess I just couldn't take that delicateness with me anymore." His mother seemed to understand perfectly, and Tony had been surprised at how easy it was to explain everything. After confiding to Dr. V. about his will against himself, Tony had for the most part ceased to be afraid of it. His explanation to his mother had been almost spontaneous, and it made him even more hopeful that this will had no real power over him anymore.

Now as he looked into the penetrating eye, he was glad to have only the little chip and not the whole fox. He felt almost comforted by the familiar expression from his childhood. "Good night, Fox." He kissed the chip and put it back into his drawer.

This was a game he often played now: that Fox was still with him, that he still had part of his life with Granny.

Minutes later, the lights were out, the Eagles in bed, and Laura was reading the night story. Tony lay hugging his pillow, feeling a sadness which made him yearn more than ever to hug Laura. The story finished, she made her usual rounds for a final good night.

"You all set?" she asked softly when she got to Tony.

"I guess so," Tony answered.

"Want me to tuck you in?"

"Listen, Laura," Tony said, "I really am sorry about what I said over at the table when you were with Lewis because I naturally have feelings for wanting that kind of thing too."

"Are you still thinking about that?" Laura smiled in surprise.

"Well, not all evening, just now," Tony whispered.

"Well, you should try to get some sleep. Do you want me to tuck you in?"

"I guess so."

"What's the matter?"

"Hell, you know me, I just think it's much too early to be getting to sleep." Tony spoke stupidly, unable to give an answer that would convey what was uppermost in his heart.

"Oh, what am I going to do with you?" Laura gave him a pat on the arm, tucked him in and left.

Come back! Come back! Come back, Tony pleaded silently and wondered why he had never told Laura what he felt about her. He quailed in embarrassment at the thought of telling, at the thought of having the staff know how much he wanted his counselor to hold him. Are you in LOVE? Tony shrank from the question. Best to leave it all unspoken. But unfulfilled?

He watched Laura as she rose from her chair and took the snack dishes out to the kitchenette. While he listened to her wash the dishes, he conceived an idea. It involved the chip from the blue fox. He had neither shown it to Laura, nor talked to her about it. In fact, there had been few words between them about his grandmother's death. Dr. V. had given Tony's mother permission to have him stay for the funeral and a couple of days afterward. On the day of his return, Laura had left town for a sister's wedding, so when Tony finally saw her, the immediacy of Granny's death had already faded. Nevertheless, he had told Deirdre everything about the fox, so Laura was bound to know about it.

Laura did not return to the dormitory right away. When she did come back, it was late, and Tony thought Dr. V. unlikely to make rounds that night. Though he felt he could act without interruption, he questioned the morality of what he planned. But Granny's death had made him more lonely at night, increasing his desire for Laura.

He got out of bed and went to his dresser, pulled open the drawer and took out the packet with the chip from the blue fox. He unwrapped it and stood looking at it a moment while he listened to Laura rise from her chair and approach him.

"What are you doing?" she asked.

"Oh, I'm just looking at this chip from the face of this fox my grandmother and I always used to play with. Sometimes, when I feel sad and alone, I want to look at it."

Laura showed that she cared by remaining silent in order to see if Tony had anything more to say. When she spoke, she only said, "Well, you should be getting some sleep now." Tony rewrapped the chip and put it back in his drawer.

"Must you be so proper?" he asked. Then, as he made his way back to his bed, "Sometimes I think you counselors have more counselor in you than heart." But he did not really sound angry.

"Tony, is there something you want from me?"

"I guess I do and that's why I got up," Tony said as he got down under the covers.

"So tell me what you want." Laura knelt by Tony. He was not sure what to say. "Can't you tell me?" Laura encouraged, and she gave him a gentle pat on the cheek.

"I wanta be patted," Tony's voice broke as he placed his hand over Laura's. And all in a moment, he moved her hand to his face, felt it softly rub his cheek as their fingers caught together in strands of hair on his temple. He felt his ear gently caressed, helped her caress it, and he could feel his penis throbbing violently.

"You know, you can be a very sweet boy." Laura's hand stopped moving. There was a certain strength in her voice which made Tony want to completely surrender to her. He increased the pressure on her hand against his cheek. "Do you mind being sweet?" Laura almost laughed.

"I wanta be sweet, and I wanta be in your arms just once before you leave."

He felt Laura's hands going around him as he rose and put his arms around her. Tears sprang to his eyes as he gently sank toward the rushing fulfillment of a ravenous, long tormenting hunger. But just as he was sinking into the softness of her breasts, the door opened.

Tony pushed himself away from Laura. "Vhat's going on here?" Dr. V. asked.

"Oh, we was jus' messin' around," Tony muttered, but so incoherently that Dr. V. could not possibly have understood him.

"Vell, it's getting late." There was a hint of reprimand in Dr. V.'s voice.

"You're right," Laura nodded, and she gave Tony a parting pat on the cheek.

When Laura went off duty, Tony burrowed down under the covers to do something about his throbbing erection. Moments later, he looked up at the night light which twinkled like a star before his misty eyes. "She's taught you a lot of tenderness you never knew before," Tony whispered. Then, "Laura," as his head sank into his pillow. But he found he no longer wanted to imagine himself in Laura's arms. Tomorrow was Friday, and Deirdre was on duty. Then on Saturday, Laura was leaving for good. He did not want to dream about something he could never have.

18

Shopping time had recently been changed to Saturday morning, so on Friday the Eagles had a free afternoon. "Let's go ride a horse!" Ronny made a suggestion he knew would be fruitless, and at just that moment Dr. V. walked into the dormitory.

Because her back was to the door, Deirdre did not see him. "How would you all like to go play kickball with the Blacksmiths?" She named one of the group's favorite activities.

As he watched Dr. V. slowly approach the chair in which Ronny was sitting, Tony felt it might in a sense be impolite, perhaps unsafe, to break the apprehensive silence that had settled upon the group. He knew that Dr. V. had no sympathy for Ronny's love of horses, that he wanted Ronny to concentrate on learning how to live with people. "So, don't you answer your counselor?" Dr. V. pushed Deirdre's question with an ominous calm as he stopped behind Ronny's chair.

"I'd like to go play with the Blacksmiths," Tony answered. "That would be nice," Harry agreed. "Sure, let's go," Lewis nodded, while Mickey and Ralph agreed with Harry that kickball was a nice idea. "I'd like to go," Igor said softly. "So would I," Ronny brought up the tail end of the consensus in a subdued voice.

"No!" Dr. V.'s hands clamped down hard on Ronny's shoulders and he hauled him out of his chair. "You go ride zat horse," he panted as he steered Ronny out into the hall. He made Ronny wait outside while the others got ready. Ronny rejoined the group as they started down to the locker room to get their spring jackets.

Deirdre got four bases and the kickball from the athletic cabinet. Then the Eagles went out in front of the School to the middle part of the Midway called the Dip, an oblong strip of lawn sunk into the ground. It ran several blocks and was bordered on its four sides by low hillocks. Near the School, the Dip was very crowded, so Deirdre said they would have to find a spot farther down. Staying above the Dip, the Eagles walked beneath trees planted at intervals on the rim.

"Hey, isn't that Laura!" Ralph exclaimed, pointing ahead. Tony noticed a sports car parked by the curb. In it a girl who looked like Laura was sitting close to a tall, brown-haired man. She gazed intently into his face. The man's right arm rested possessively around her shoulders. For a moment the Eagles just gaped. Tony was shocked that, contrary to counselor behavior, Laura would let herself be seen so near the School. But was she really so near? The car was parked well down the Midway. Still, Tony allowed himself to hope that some other girl was sitting by the tall, handsome man.

"O.K., let's go down into the dip," Deirdre spoke with crisp authority.

"Yes Lauraa!" Lewis' nose wrinkled as he suddenly called out in his nasal voice, "Are you enjoying your *romance*?" Deirdre turned on him, caught him by his jacket, and hurled him backward onto the brink of the hill. "Oof! You're not using your psychology," Lewis gasped huffily as his arms flailed to maintain balance. Lewis was startled by Deirdre's violence, but Tony could not help smiling at his aloof comeback. He felt he liked Lewis. Lewis did not even try to return Deirdre's gaze. Are you going to step out of line again? Cynically, angrily, Tony interpreted the question in Deirdre's expression. "Should try your psychology," Lewis muttered. He had dropped the personal "you," and Tony knew he was hurt.

As the group started down the hill, Tony could hear the smooth, powerful rev of the sports car motor. Obviously Laura and her handsome beau did not care to mix. "Hey, here come the Blacksmiths!" Mickey shouted, and Tony turned with the others to wave to them. Soon teams were picked, the bases spread, and

Tony found himself near the line between third and second base with Mickey carrying the outfield behind him.

The game began slowly and uneventfully so Tony had little more to do than stand at his place. He was rankled to the point where it hurt, for in his opinion Deirdre and Dr. V. had been too high-handed with Lewis and Ronny. But uppermost in his mind was Laura. Well, you knew she naturally went on dates, Tony argued, but last night he had muttered "We was jus' messin' around," and now it struck him with new force that, in Laura's eyes, he was nothing more than a little boy to be cuddled in his pajamas while she went out with a man who was probably bigger and handsomer than he would ever be.

Tony began to focus attention on the game. When Mike took his turn to kick, he took an extra step back because he thought Mike would kick hard—the way he had hit the guy in the bar on New Year's. Igor bent over with the kick ball and sent it at a slow roll to home plate. Mike took a step forward, kicked hard, and PNK! Tony leapt for the ball as it whizzed only a few inches beyond his reach. It sailed low over Mickey and rolled far down the Dip. Mickey started to trot after the ball while Mike began an easy sprint around the bases.

"Hey, c'mon!" "Can't you hurry!" Harry and Ronny shouted to Mickey. Then Ronny started to take after him.

"Stay in your place, Ronny!" Deirdre commanded.

"But he'll take all day," Ronny protested.

"Still, that's his field, and you can't expect a little boy to hurry all that distance."

"But look," Ronny gesticulated toward Mike who was passing third base at a walk.

"So the world won't come to an end," Deirdre shrugged. She did not approve of Ronny's competitive attitude, his driving effort to be best at everything. "Hey, you're holding things up!" "C'mon!" "Throw the ball!" Some of the others shouted angrily at Mickey as he started to walk back, holding the ball. Despite the chorus of rising voices, Mickey kept his pace. Back at his old position, he stopped and cocked his head defiantly.

"Mickey, why don't you throw the ball?" Harry was unable to hide irritation as he extended his hands diplomatically.

"If I have to go all the way out there to get it, then you all can just wait for it."

"Look, it was kicked out there." Harry's hands remained extended.

"You don't have to kick it out that far," Mickey reasoned. Tony thought Mickey's "you" applied to all the older boys, and he felt a spasm of outrage.

"Mickey, why don't you set up a boundary line?" Deirdre suddenly laughed. And Tony thought her amusement at Mickey greatly exceeded any concern about inconvenience to the older boys.

Well, if you don't like it, you can leave. Tony silently served himself Deirdre's ultimatum. Then, laughingly to Deirdre, as though he too thought Mickey was cute: "Deirdre, I guess Mickey would enjoy the game more if we'd all turn into babies like him."

"What did you call me!" Mickey bared his small teeth.

"A baby," Tony sneered.

"I'm not a baby!"

"Yes, you're a baby, a baby, a baby, a baby." Tony spat viciously.

"Boy, you're gonna get it later!" Mickey screamed helpless rage. Until recently Mickey had vented anger by threatening to complain to Dr. V., but he had been told he would have to carry out his threats if he continued to make them.

"Am I in trouble?" Tony shrilled as he clasped his hands in mock fear.

"You just wait! You're gonna get it!" Mickey hurled the ball for emphasis so that it bounced a few feet in front of Tony who caught it.

"Boy, I'm scared!" Tony made a pretense of crying.

"Tony, what-is-the-matter?" Deirdre emphasized her amazement at his attitude. Tony suddenly felt sheepish in the knowledge that he had put on quite an exhibition, and he shuddered at the possibility that it might be attributed to Laura.

"I was just being persuasive," he said as he held up the ball.

"You won't get that ball again!" Mickey threatened angrily as Tony casually flipped it to Igor. The rest of the game was played without incident. The afternoon was hot, the game long and hard. At the end, when the Eagles and Blacksmiths were on their way back to the School, Deirdre commented that everybody would need a bath.

That evening Tony landed in a bathing situation he disliked. It all started with Mickey and Ralph working together in rare, non-mischievous harmony on a Lincoln Log construction. Not wanting to interrupt them, Deirdre did not insist on early baths. Tony noted this with some frustration since it was now possible that Deirdre was going to be in the bathroom with one of them during the later part of the evening when the older boys usually bathed.

Deirdre had all but ceased to appear in the bathroom while Tony and Harry were in the tub. But recently brief appearances for trivial reasons had become more frequent. When Harry had asked her why, she had answered, "Laura and I aren't going to make any concessions to what you're trying to do and to the effect you're trying to have on others." Tony knew Harry had been the first to follow his ways and that Igor had recently followed suit. He was glad about Igor and Harry, but did not feel he had encouraged them, or that Harry had encouraged Igor.

Tony finished practicing his accordion a little after seven-fifteen, and Deirdre suggested that some of the older boys start their baths. Under the circumstances, an early bath was the safest course. But, unable to resist taking advantage of a newly liberalized TV policy, and having already had his privacy jeopardized on so many previous occasions, Tony decided to operate on the assumption that the bath situation would somehow right itself. At seven-thirty he went to watch a half-hour western in the playroom.

Shortly after eight, when he got back to the dormitory, Deirdre announced that Laura would be in at eight-thirty rather than a quarter to nine, the usual snack time. Tony decided to get bathed as fast as possible, but Mickey and Ralph were in the two tubs and he had to wait for one of them to finish. Ten minutes later, Ralph emerged with Deirdre following him, making a half playful, half serious effort to get behind his ears with a towel.

The rest of the boys had already bathed, so there was a free tub. Stripped to the waist and in his slippers, Tony took his pajamas and went into the bathroom where Mickey was still splashing around. Tony hung his pajamas over the door to one of the toilet stalls. Then he pulled his towel from its rack, went into the stall and shut the door. He threw the towel over his shoulders and slipped off his pants and underpants which he hung beside his pajamas. After that, he wrapped himself with the towel.

"Hey, Tony, I'm still mad at you for calling me a baby." Mickey spoke matter-of-factly as Tony quickly stepped across the bathroom and into the tub.

"That's your privilege," Tony remarked curtly as he undid the towel and hung it from a rack on the wall opposite the faucet.

"Why do you always wear that towel when you cross the bathroom?" Mickey asked.

"Because I like to," Tony answered in a manner he hoped would discourage further talk. He thought Mickey was looking at him with a new interest now that the towel was removed. He quickly sat down, turned on the faucet, and began to wash rapidly because he thought it likely that Deirdre would come into the bathroom to help Mickey.

Almost immediately he heard Deirdre's footsteps and the jingle of the bell on her key chain. Tony crossed his shins, making his legs form an upward V. Then he leaned forward, putting his forearms together, pressing his elbows against his stomach so that his hands cupped under the faucet. In this manner, he had his genitals hidden from view when Deirdre entered with a stack of plates and some spoons.

"Why're you bringing those in here?" Mickey asked.

"There's something wrong with the drainage in the kitchenette," Deirdre answered, "so I can't wash them out there."

"Hey, Tony, why're you sitting like that?" Mickey turned to Tony as Deirdre began to wash the plates.

"Because I like to." Tony felt a chill pass over his face and chest. Formerly, he had secured his privacy in a bathing suit. Deirdre had ruled that out, and he had covered himself with a rag until she had also prohibited that. Now he did not want Mickey calling attention to his final extremity.

"I think you sit that way because you don't want Deirdre to see your penis," Mickey remarked conversationally, and Tony felt another chill. He tried to tell himself he would like to bash Mickey's head in, but his only emotion was fear, fear and embarrassment. For a few seconds, Mickey continued to splash around happily, his lips vibrating as he made motor sounds for a toy boat which he ran through the water. "Boy," he commented, "you must hate taking baths."

"There're things I like better." Tony was casually evasive as he looked at the water bubbling from his cupped hands and flowing like a transparent coating down his forearms.

"You know, Mickey," Deirdre said, "there was a time when Tony used to have lots of fun playing with boats in the tub. But I haven't seen him do that in quite awhile." She dried one of the plates and laid it on the adjoining basin. Then she asked, "Do you think maybe you could get him interested again?"

"Does he have any boats?" Mickey became practical.

"Yes," Deirdre answered, "but he keeps them up in his closet."

"What kind does he have?"

"Oh, I think maybe you could get him to show you."

But Mickey suddenly became interested in something else. He had a birthday in the next few weeks, and a certain boat in a store window had caught his fancy. He began to expound its merits to Deirdre.

Tony just sat, watching sheets of water cascade down his forearms, and he wondered if he weren't numbed by the very intensity of his degradation. He was not surprised that Deirdre would compromise his privacy in order to be with Mickey, or to do the dishes. She had only gone too far in suggesting he play with toy boats like a seven-year-old. And he was frustrated by his inability to give a clear explanation of what he thought wrong with the way he was being treated. Then he remembered his mother often telling him how Dr. V.'s writing emphasized the importance of a child being relaxed about his body. And didn't his lack of feeling indicate he was in a sense relaxed? Had not Deirdre, with her totally casual attitude, put him at ease?

No use to pretend a modesty he no longer had, Tony decided, as he was gripped by an inspiration to lie back like Mickey. But his inspiration was accompanied by erotic premonition. Hardly what Deirdre wanted to arouse. Tony often worried that policies he despised were underwritten by a brilliance he could not understand. But in this case. . . .

Suddenly it occurred to him that the time was nearing eight-twenty. Laura might be a few minutes early for snacks. He knew he still cared about his privacy as he reached out and turned down the water, allowing the tub to fill more slowly. Water had already risen three-fourths of the way to the drain, and Tony wished Deirdre would finish the dishes and get out of the bathroom so he could wash.

Even though his sitting position hid his genitals, Tony knew he would hate to have Laura see him naked—naked like a little boy across from Mickey. Conscious of the fact that Mickey had ceased talking, Tony glanced across the bathroom. Mickey stood in his tub, massaging his erect penis with a wet soapy hand. "Hey, Tony, I wonder what penises have inside them that makes them get so stiff," Mickey remarked.

"Umph," Tony grunted, acknowledging that he had heard.

"Umph!" Deirdre echoed more loudly. "Is that all he has to say? Really, Tony, don't you think we know you have feelings about that too?" Then, laughingly, as Mickey dropped back down into the water and sent up a spray, "Hey! I'm trying to *dry* these dishes!" Mickey splashed around for a couple of seconds. Then he got out of the tub, took his towel, and went over to Deirdre.

"Dry me," he commanded.

"Just one minute until I finish here," Deirdre nodded.

Tony felt the anger subtly explode in his stomach. This is just too degrading, he told himself silently. There just has to be some difference between you and that seven-year-old baby. In a more conscientious effort to hide not only his genitals, but also his pubic hairs, Tony raised his knees so his forearms clamped more tightly together.

He looked around at Deirdre who had just begun to dry Mickey. "Here, do you want to dry between your legs?" Deirdre handed Mickey the towel. Tony flushed as he refocused his gaze into the trickling water. Anger began to throb in his chest. He felt it pushing into his throat, urging him to say something to degrade Deirdre, to keep his self respect . . . "Deirdre?"

"Yes, Tony?"

"You know, you're right in what you said. I do have feelings about the kind of stuff Mickey was talking about." Because of the way he was sitting, because he felt he was talking like a child, Tony began to feel silly. But he knew the thing he had to say was not going to be childish.

"Anything in particular you want to discuss?" Deirdre asked as she continued to dry Mickey.

"Well, I was thinking about how you were talking about my not playing with boats in the tub."

"Yes?"

Tony felt instinctively that it was dangerous to say what he had in mind, but he had to say it. "I was thinking," he said, "that it would be fun if we could take a bath together in the same tub. Then I could play with you instead of the boats."

A wide grin spread across Mickey's face. "Would you touch her vagina?" he giggled. Tony wished from the bottom of his heart that Mickey would shut the hell up.

Deirdre finished drying Mickey, then stood up. She looked straight at Tony while Mickey put on his pajamas. She did not say anything. Like Dr. V., Deirdre could stare silently at a person for moments on end. At first, Tony wanted to look back at her, but he thought it might make things worse. As the seconds went by, he noticed that the bath water was lapping up around the drain. He was afraid Deirdre's attention would be attracted to his sitting position because of the rising water. But, he did not want to move while she was looking at him. "Yes Tony," she finally said, "you say things like this and at the same time ask to be treated more like a man."

Tony felt shocked helplessness followed by the stir of deep rage. The very words he had used to strike back had now been turned on him to justify his degradion. But they're wrong! They're wrong! They're wrong! Tony screamed silently. And his "they" included not only Deirdre and Dr. V., but also his mother and stepfather in Acapulco, for contrary to his parents, he still did not think his fishing argument indicative of disturbance.

This inner turbulence was familiar; its source was a past in which *everybody* seemed to think he was wrong so often. And he now imagined he was running from a policeman who had been sent by everyone to lock him up. But he could resist them all! They were wrong! Wrong! Wrong! Well, anyway, they're wrong now, and you're going to resist them, Tony decided as he sat beneath Deirdre's merciless scrutiny.

"What are you going to do about that water?" Deirdre broke the silence.

"Mm," Tony muttered. A breath of fear moistened his face and chest. If she were going to insist he reach out and turn off the water, he would have to submit. Better that than a showdown with Dr. V.

"Hey Laura!" the cry went up in the dormitory, and Tony heard the Eagles greet Laura with a barrage of questions about herself and the man they had seen in the car. Deirdre turned away, and Tony reached out and flipped the drain lever. He thought of trying to turn off the water, but that was too risky. Then suddenly all was quiet.

"You mean to tell me," Dr. V. said, "zat none of you has ever seen a voman and a man togezer?" Nobody tried to answer Dr. V. "Since ven do ve mess into counselors' private affairs!"

"We shouldn't." "We don't." The response was humble.

"Zhen vhy can't you keep your goddam mouths shut!"

What about *our* privacy, Tony cried out silently, but there was no longer any room for bitterness in his heart, only fear.

"Vell, it really amazes me zat boys your age are so impressed by Laura sitting in a car vis a young man. You know zat in any ozer place but here you vould all get yourselves beat up for sticking your goddam noses into ozer people's business." A pause, then, "Vell, how are you, Igor? I'm glad to see zat at least you had some sense and vere not yaking vis zhe ozers. . . ." Light footsteps, the jingle of a keychain bell, and Tony ceased to listen to Dr. V. as Laura approached the bathroom.

Oh God, please help me! Tony's lips moved in desperate prayer. Deirdre picked up the plates and turned to the door.

"Do you need help with anything?" Laura stopped in the doorway. Tony could see the flap of her blue skirt, but that was all. He could not see her, and he was sure she could not see him.

"Do you want to get the spoons?" Deirdre indicated the basin with a backward movement of her head.

"Deirdre, I've got the spoons." Tony heard Mickey speak up from behind him.

"O.K.," Deirdre smiled. Tony watched the door as Mickey followed his two counselors pushing the door partway shut behind him.

Privacy at last! Tony turned off the water. He remembered reading about a man who was saved from burning at the stake by an unexpected rainfall. Although he kept marveling at his own narrow escape, he felt more anxious than relieved. Was Deirdre going to mention their exchange to Dr. V? Well, you're in danger now, but in five minutes you probably won't be, Tony tried to reassure himself as he began to wash.

"Ah, Tony." Tony felt a sharp breeze in his chest, and his calves weakened at the sound of Dr. V. calling from the dormitory.

"Yes, Dr. V.?"

"You finish vashing and come out here."

Instinctively, Tony decided to obey Dr. V. to the letter. He stood up in the tub and began to lather soap over his whole body, all the while keeping a watchful eye on the door to be ready to sit down at the first sound of a footstep, the jingle of a bell. So Deirdre had told Dr. V. about what he had just said. That probably meant a challenge to his privacy, a challenge on which he had staked his self-respect.

He turned on the shower, then lathered his face while he rinsed his body. His body rinsed, Tony momentarily abandoned caution and thrust his face into the rushing water. Light footsteps, the jingle of a key chain bell, and Tony's eyes snapped open. Laura! In one quick, horrified motion, he snatched his towel, slapped it around himself, then bent into the water to turn it off. Laura paid him no attention whatsoever as she calmly stepped over to the basin, took a sponge and wet it. Probably to clean the table, Tony thought as he brushed against her on his way to a toilet stall.

While he dried himself, he reflected that he had often wondered whether hate was an emotion with any constructive purpose. Now he knew. Hate was a killer of fear. He was still frightened, but he no longer feared that he might break under

Dr. V. No woman at the School was ever going to see him naked again, of that he was certain, and he had every intention of saying so to Dr. V. within the next few minutes.

Tony stood for a second in his pajamas, feeling his courage falter. Then he remembered that Laura was with the others, waiting for him to emerge for his confrontation. And she had just seen him naked like a little boy! Tony grabbed at the lock to the toilet stall, snatching the door open. So Laura had seen him naked; she wasn't going to see him frightened.

Dr. V. was smiling. Or, if he were not smiling, at least he wore a warm, friendly look which seemed to ask, "Vhy must you alvays come out vis your fists up?"

Tony found himself completely off guard. "You called for me." Dr. V. looked down at Mickey who was sitting in a chair by the table.

"Well," Mickey began, "after talking to some of the boys about the way they jumped on Laura, Dr. V. asked me how I was feeling, so I told him I didn't like the way you were calling me a baby."

"Vell, I vouldn't like it if somebody called me a baby izer." Dr. V. looked from Mickey to Tony.

"Well, I never do it unless he provokes it in some way by holding up a game or something which he just doesn't have to do."

"I know, I know," Dr. V. nodded, "but I sink, Tony, zat you should know how hard it is for a young boy to struggle vis growing up. Now I really don't need to tell you zhere are some sings you just should not call a boy of his age."

"Yes, I see."

"Very good," Dr. V. smiled at Tony. Then, to Mickey, "O.K., zat is settled?"

"Uh huh," Mickey agreed happily.

Dr. V. turned to leave the dorm. "Dr. V.?" Ronny spoke from his bed.

"Yes, Ronny?"

"This morning the dentist said I'm just getting my first wisdom tooth."

"I'm not interested." Dr. V. spoke unpleasantly. "Vhy don't you go tell zhe horse?"

That was wrong, wrong, wrong! Dr. V. could be right about some things, and plain wrong about others. Why does he have to fight Ronny's love for horses? Why did he have to do that to Ronny? Tony's eyes followed Dr. V. as he walked out of the dormitory.

You've gotta get outta here! You've gotta get out of here! It was a refrain in Tony's mind as he sat down with the others for snacks. The inspiration, comforting his deeply hurt pride, had begun to jell into conviction as he realized how deeply Dr. V. could sometimes be wrong.

He found snacks an ordeal. Though not about to cry, he did not want to talk, and he was afraid his reticence would stick out like a sore thumb. Nor did he think it advisable to attempt conversation since he felt unable to sound natural. Deirdre had put out cornflakes, and Tony, with a distaste for milk, could not even keep occupied by eating.

Conversation began with Ralph asking Laura why she wanted to leave. "Well," Laura answered, "I've learned a lot from working with you here, and now I feel I want to go out and try something else. But I'm really going to miss taking care of you boys an awful lot. I mean that." Tony thought bitterly of the tall, handsome man, then of himself and the others sitting around Laura in their pajamas like so many four-year-olds in an all-night nursery school.

"So Lauraaa," Lewis wrinkled his nose, "have you gotten around to reading all our histories yet?" The Eagles knew that the histories he referred to were filed in the front part of the building. When a child entered the School, a parent or guardian gave a thorough account of his life. These histories were augmented by the counselors who kept a continuous record of development.

At first Laura just smiled at Lewis, for he had asked her this question when she was very new and had not yet read them. Then, finally, she said, "Lewis, I've read them all twice."

"That's really quite a bit," Lewis acknowledged.

"Well, I wanted to learn all I could about you because I thought that would help me take good care of you."

Tony looked away from the table as he remembered that there had been one area of himself he had kept from her until the last half hour.

Some day, he thought, Laura would probably have a fifteen-year-old son. Certainly he would never have a twenty-four-year old woman, totally unrelated to him, come into the bathroom while he was taking a shower. Such things were reserved for boys at the School, the boys on whom the counselors learned how to bring up their own children.

Laura certainly knew, Tony thought bitterly, that he did not want her to see him naked. Did she have any inkling how much she had hurt him? Perhaps not. But if she did. . . . "Why Tony, we should really try to go into your feelings about this!"

You've gotta get out of here, was all Tony could say to himself. Then he noticed Deirdre looking at him.

"Tony, is something the matter?" she asked. The table went quiet as attention focused on Tony.

He forced a laugh, and refusing to lie by means of flat denial, he asked, "Why on earth should anything be the matter?"

"You should see your expression." Deirdre's words seared him. So his feelings were visible, when he so wanted to hide them under a crusty reserve because of what his counselors had done to him.

"What about my expression?"

"You should just see yourself," Deirdre said. "Are you unhappy about Laura's leaving?"

"Oh heavens no! Not a bit! Not a bit!" Tony ran his words together, and he hadn't finished before he realized how deeply he had stumbled into overstatement. "I mean, counselors come and go all the time, and I just don't think much about it either way," he went on quickly, forcing a laugh, and flushing beneath everybody's eyes. I hate this damn School! I hate it! *I hate it!* He might have screamed his release from a posture he could not maintain, but at just that moment, Ralph overturned the milk pitcher, and milk flowed over the table into the laps of Igor, Lewis, and Deirdre.

Never was Tony so glad to have attention turned from himself.

After the milk was cleaned up, Laura announced she had to leave and would come around five the following day to say good-bye. When she said good night to the group, Tony answered with the others, but it was an indifferent and barely audible good night.

Late that night, after Deirdre had gone off duty, Tony lay in bed feeling the tears behind his eyelids. "Why did she do that to you?" he grated silently. All for a sponge—but didn't she know how he felt?

Laura's seeing him naked had brought to irreparably degrading consummation what he most despised and feared in their relationship. He wanted to cry both about this and about a Laura whom he now decided had never existed. He could not quite define this Laura, but she was supposed to care about him as a person, about his dignity, and the fact that he was approaching manhood.

You've gotta get out of here! Only by total rejection of the School was Tony able to partially smother his outrage. You've gotta get out of here, he whispered desperately, half wishing somebody could hear him, while his fingers clawed at his seething stomach. And every now and then, he visualized himself and his group viciously tearing the clothes off their hurt, outraged counselors.

Over and over he thought of the man he had seen with Laura, and tried to visualize his face, to estimate his height. The subject became an obsession and Tony got up and went into the bathroom. The bright night light made his reflection perfectly clear in the mirror. He did not like what he saw, so he ran his comb and brush through his dry, disarrayed hair. But even after that, he was not happy with the young boy who stared back at him. He thought perhaps he should wet his hair and really comb it, but just as he was about to do that, he heard a sound. He turned around to see Harry enter the bathroom and close the door.

For a moment, they just faced each other. Harry's hand snaked out; his fingertip touched Tony's cheekbone just beneath the left eye. Harry brought his finger to his mouth and licked. "I taste salt," he said sympathetically, "and I don't think it comes from the sea."

Something in Harry's attitude almost made Tony burst into

tears, but he contained himself and stood silently, unable to speak. "Hey, Tony, I'm sorry that happened," Harry said, "And I don't blame you for being plenty mad, but really, the world hasn't come to an end."

"Did you see her go in?"

"Yes, and I saw you at snacks."

"Hell, as far as she's concerned, I'm no different from Mickey down here." Tony slapped himself on the groin.

"It's not that she doesn't think there's a difference. It's just that she doesn't care." Harry was bitter.

"I'm getting the hell out of this School," Tony continued in Harry's bitter vein. "Actually, this idea about leaving the School didn't start tonight. It started around when my grandmother died."

"Do you feel like talking about it?"

"Well," Tony began, thankful for Harry's interest, "when my grandmother was dying, I didn't think I had much feeling about her. Then by accident I broke this little fox she treasured, and I felt real bad and realized I really did feel deeply about her. I began to think about not being able to like people, but I found I really couldn't be so sure at all. And now I often feel a lot of my problems wouldn't bother me so much if I would just get the hell out into the world and live. You know what Dr. V. said about there being some things you just don't call a little boy?"

"Yes, I know," Harry nodded. "He was certainly right about that."

"I agree with you absolutely," Tony went on. "Well, Dr. V. mightn't think I'm ready to leave, but he sure doesn't know everything about me if he doesn't know that just as there's some things you don't call a seven-year-old, there's also some things you just don't do to a fifteen-year-old."

19

Saturday afternoon, shortly after three; the day was warm, grey, with exciting gusts of wind. "A lot of leaving, isn't there," Deirdre put an arm around Tony.

"Yes, Dar'dra, a lot." Leaving was really in the air what with Ted having just left, with Laura about to leave, and with Sam, a former Blacksmith, paying the School a visit shortly after having joined the Marines. All the Eagles, except Tony and Ronny, had gone to speak to Sam in the Blacksmiths' dormitory. Ronny was getting a box of books ready for storage in the school building, while Tony was making plans with Deirdre for some garden work he was going to do.

"Can you get the lawn mower when you finish taking the books over with Ronny?"

"Sure, I'll do that," Deirdre nodded.

"Well then, I'll get my hair combed so it won't fly in my face while I'm working, and then I'm going down to see Sam." Tony went into the bathroom and doused his hair with water. He wanted to be alone, and he was glad to be going out to mow the lawn in the Cloister.

The Cloister was a small, tree-shaded clearing, just off the corner of the side yard. Bounded on three sides by buildings, the Cloister was separated from the street by a high wooden fence. Vines grew thick on the walls of the buildings and over the steel net gate at the entrance. Named for its calm, secluded atmosphere, the Cloister had come to look rather wild because the grass had grown too high. When Dr. V. had mentioned this a few nights before at supper, Tony had volunteered to mow the lawn, and Dr. V. had complimented him on his initiative.

His hair slicked neatly back, Tony gazed in the mirror and liked what he saw. This startled him, for in the last eighteen hours, he had been so often disappointed by his boyish face. Now, resigned to his boyishness, he was able to note with pleasure that his features were almost handsome.

"Vell, Tony, are you beautifying yourself to go see Sam?"

Tony was surprised to hear Dr. V. who had been down with Sam and the Blacksmiths. "I'm just getting this hair plastered into place so it won't fly in my eyes when I go out to mow the lawn."

"So vhat are you packing?" Dr. V. addressed Ronny.

"Oh, I'm taking these books over to be stored," Ronny answered.

"You have some good books here, and zhey are not all about horses," Dr. V. commented. "Have you read zem?"

"Some of them."

"Vell, maybe now you begin to get down off zhe horse." Dr. V. put a hand on Ronny's shoulder as Tony emerged from the bathroom. Ronny looked uncomfortable, but happy. "So tell me how is zhe visdom toos?" Dr. V. asked.

"Oh, it's O.K.," Ronny smiled.

"Vell, I'm glad to hear zat. Now vhy don't you get zhose books stored so you can talk to Sam?" Dr. V. accompanied Tony toward the Blacksmiths' dormitory, and they encountered John at the stairway.

"Hi John, you going to see Sam?" Tony asked.

"You guessed it." When Sam first came to the School, John had been his counselor, then later his teacher. Tony and Dr. V. followed John into the Blacksmiths.

Sam lounged against the group table where he was surrounded by Blacksmiths and Eagles. He was a tall, muscular fellow, immaculate in pressed uniform. His large head had a sterile look with his scalp shining through the crew cut. When he saw John, he snapped to attention and saluted.

"Hi soldier," John greeted him.

While they talked, Eunice passed candy bars. Sam took his bar and looked at it. A second later he had removed the outer wrapping with his big hands. Then he peeled the inner wrapping halfway and took a hefty bite; his eyes registered the pleasure. "You know, you get to miss these things," he smiled. His eyes met Tony's. Tony grinned, took a bite from his candy bar and looked away.

"Yes, Tony, listen carefully. Enjoy zat vhile you can." Dr. V. gently gripped Tony's shoulder.

"They're not gonna always be passing these out to you," Sam remarked as he peeled the wrapping back further and took another bite.

"It's kind of sad," Tony spoke boldly, "but I just might learn to like this place better after I leave."

"Zhere, Tony, you may be right," Dr. V. laughed. "You may really come to miss us some day." Tony felt Dr. V's grip tighten. "You know, you join zhe Marines like Sam, and zhey vould have you in zhe brig zhe whole time because you vouldn't be able to keep your mous shut. You'd find somesing you didn't approve of zhe first day you got in, and you'd have to tell zem about it. So zhey vould lock you up, and ven zhey let you out, you'd tell zem zhey had no business to lock you up in zhe first place, and back to zhe brig you'd go."

Embarrassed by sporadic snickering and hoping to hear a tough soldier contradict Dr. V., Tony turned to Sam and asked, "Would they really lock you up just for saying something?"

"Well, they wouldn't lock you up for saying 'yes sir'."

Tony blushed as several people laughed outright. "Well, there really isn't that much to complain about, is there, I mean if you're not looking for it?" he asked quickly.

"Oh, I wouldn't say so." Sam was thoughtful as he looked at Tony. "Hell," he continued, "all they do is run you ragged from dawn to dusk and all you have to do is grin and like it. But don't let me scare you. After all, as a certain old man used to always tell me, you'll get out of it what you put into it, and that's life." Sam winked at John. "He still tell you that?" Sam looked back at Tony.

"He sure does."

"Well, that goes for the Marines too except there you've really gotta put, put, put!" Sam punched the air three times.

"I guess I just won't join the Marines."

"Maybe not, maybe not." Sam cocked his head pensively. "But I don't see why the Marines should give you such a hard time. Hell, they're a great outfit just so long as you're in the Army. And the Army's all right if you're in the Navy. So take your choice when you come of age."

"But really, if you have something to say," Tony floundered, "aren't there ways to express opinions? After all, the Constitution. . . ."

"To zhe brig! To zhe brig!" Dr. V. clamped his other hand on Tony's shoulder as though to steer him. "Tony, believe it or not," he laughed, "you may some day look back to zis present state of existence as a golden age."

"All right, Dr. V., but you. . . ."

"No 'buts', my dear boy. . . ."

". . . . but you have to admit there's a difference whether you like it or not!" Tony heaved against the lawn mower and billows of grass exploded over the whirring blades. "Look, Dr. V., with the military I'm in the service of my country, while at the School I'm only in the service of myself! So naturally I should expect to be treated a little better here." Then, switching to a new angle: You don't love your country, do you? Hell, why don't you just get rid of your damn citizenship and run off to the Amazon? After all, they say if you don't like it, leave. Well, why don't you just keep leaving until you find some place where they have the kind of freedom that's guaranteed you in the Constitution?

As he sadly exiled himself from School and country, Tony recalled the smile with which John had regarded him, a smile that seemed to say, "Did you think the School was the only place that wasn't going to be run to your liking?" John probably would have been happy at the School when he was fifteen, and he more than likely had enjoyed his military service no matter how bad the conditions.

Tony decided he could hardly hope to be like John, that he was not sure he even wanted to be. "Yes John, Yes Dr. V.," Tony hammered home, "the Army might be hell, but that doesn't mean there aren't some things you just don't do to a fifteen-year-old boy!"

Hey, just when are you going to go talk to Dr. V.? Tony stopped mowing as the question hit him. There was no reason not to simply leave the lawn mower and have it over within the next hour since Dr. V. was likely to be available in his office. But you don't feel ready to go, do you, Tony acknowledged. No, he wanted to tell Dr. V. something more than the simple fact that he would like to exercise his option to leave and that he did not see how he could help himself better at the School than on the outside.

He resumed his mowing and began to wonder if the anticipated confrontation would really culminate in his leaving. He thought not, but remembered that if he so desired, he could make it difficult for them to keep him against his will. So, when to announce his wish to leave? Now's as good a time as ever. You're waiting for the right moment, but it will never come. Then he issued the ultimatum: If you don't think of anything new to say by Sunday, then just go down Monday to whatever hell is waiting for you and show your guts. Tony pushed the lawn mower hard and the grass churned violently.

He had told Deirdre he would finish his job by four-thirty, perhaps earlier. This allowed him ample time to be on hand to say good-bye to Laura if she were coming around at five. And Deirdre had said she would come to get him if Laura showed up earlier. To attempt to avoid her in this situation would show his hurt, and Tony was not about to do that. He looked at his watch—already a bit after four! He marveled at how fast time could pass when he was angry. Then he began to anticipate the next hour.

He imagined Laura telling them all good-bye. She would be sad; she had become quite involved with the group, and it was not inconceivable that she would want to give each boy a hug. "I'm going to really miss every one of you," he could hear her say, and he could picture her open arms.

"Well, good-bye." Tony's hand extended politely from the lawn mower as he rehearsed casual detachment. Yes, he would just be one of the babies, and Laura would want to hug him along with the others. Tony rehearsed several times, striving for just the right demeanor; it was important that his manly attitude seem natural, that his detachment not appear put on. He recoiled at the thought of hurting his departing counselor, but she had hurt him, and he was not going to play the baby in her arms.

"Tony, have you been mad at me lately?" Tony imagined Laura was talking, that she was not leaving, and everything was as usual except her surprising him in the shower.

"Is there some reason why I should be mad at you?" he countered.

"I don't want to play games with you. You know your attitude as well as I do."

"Laura, I don't think I have to tell you why my attitude has been the way it has." Tony pictured himself turning away from her, but she followed him and took his arm. Then he realized where this was going to land him: In Laura's arms. He still wanted what he had wanted for so long.

He heard the door to the dormitory building open and shut. Perhaps that was Deirdre. He pushed the mower down the Cloister and peered through the densely tangled foliage. The person he saw was not Deirdre. It was Laura, and she was coming toward him. She wore a light suede jacket, and her blonde hair shone golden as it blew loosely in the soft breezes of the grey afternoon.

Tony drew back from the gate. So Laura had come around early to say good-bye. He was conscious of nothing except his pounding heart and a throbbing artery just above his temple. He heard Laura raise the latch and saw the gate open. She closed it behind her. Tony realized they were completely alone, more alone than they had ever been.

"Well, I've come to tell you good-bye," Laura said. She was smiling but her expression was sad.

"You're leaving early."

"I got everything packed, and I didn't want to just wait around." Tony was not sure, but he sensed adoration behind Laura's smile. They looked at each other. "You know, I'm going to miss you." She sounded as though she really meant it, and Tony realized he had no desire to hurt her.

The silence weighed. He felt he had to reciprocate her sentiment, but he neither wanted to miss—nor admit the possibility of missing—her. "It's funny how so much can develop in such a short time," he finally said.

"It is." Laura's smile widened for an instant. "Well, I don't want to keep you from your mowing." She glanced around. "Gee, you're doing a good job."

"Thank you."

"Well, Tony, I want you to know that I feel I've had some very deep experiences with you, and I'm always going to treasure them."

"I'm glad you feel that way."

"So I guess it's time to tell you good-bye." Laura's eyes glistened.

"Well, good-bye, Laura." Tony spoke with real feeling, but he only extended his hand. He would not be a baby in her arms.

Laura gave her hand to Tony. For a moment she hesitated. "Oh c'mon," she pouted in a tone of reprimanding tenderness, "don't act like such a big man."

"I *will* act like a man," Tony retorted defiantly as he stepped forward and threw his arms around her. He felt the softness of her breasts at his chest, while he let his head sink against the curve of her neck and shoulder. For a moment aching with wistful sweetness, he had all he had ever wanted from her, but now it could only hurt because he would never have it again.

They parted and Tony saw Laura out the gate. "Good-bye, Tony. I won't keep you from your work any longer," Laura said as they held hands for the final moment. Then, when he stepped back inside the Cloister, she shut the gate and put the latch into place. Immediately, Tony resumed his mowing, pushing the lawn mower back and forth, back and forth. He felt good about the way Laura had sent him back to work rather than allow him to watch her as she crossed the side yard to enter the dormitory building. But at least he could wave to her one last time, could see her once more! He heard her unlock the door.

He dashed to the gate, yanked it open, but could only see the door shut behind her. Sadness stabbed him. He felt the pain behind the ridge of his nose, just above his eyes. He shut the gate, then spread his arms and clutched at the tangled vines. He pulled himself to the thick foliage, caressed it with his stomach, his chest, his loins. He gritted his teeth and felt tears welling.

When he returned to the lawn mower, from somewhere in the depth of his being it started: "Big man kissed a whore; whaddaya know, big man kissed a whore; big man kissed a whore." Over and over his mind played it mockingly as on the night in Acapulco when he had kissed the whore and glimpsed a far off, dream-structured future. "So what you kissed a whore; big man kissed a whore." He remembered saying it all five months before, perhaps to the very day! And he felt a tantalizing proximity to the freedom he craved.

"Big man kissed a whore; whaddaya know, big man kissed a whore." He closed his mouth in an effort to quell the mockery. But it kept on, catching at his throat, pressuring him to speak; the old familiar will forcing him to do what he did not want to do. "Big man kissed a whore; big man kissed a whore." He succumbed to its pressure and wondered if his will were still a dangerous force. But much of the fear had been released by confession; he had broken the blue fox, and he had come to feel that this will functioned less out of harmony with and more in accordance to some of the deepest, most hidden urges of his nature. Now he thought it unlikely that the will would ever master him. "Big man kissed a whore. Big man kissed a whore." The mocking continued without mercy. Then suddenly it ceased.

"Dammit," he said softly as he stopped the mower. "God-dammit. You can just shut your trap." Then he looked out toward the gate, toward Laura's path beyond it. "You had something beautiful," he enunciated each word with conviction. "God-damn-sonova-bitch," he pushed the mower back and forth to emphasize each word, "you really did have something beautiful, real beautiful! John, you've been right all along. You sure do get out of life what you put into it."

What you put in, what you put in, what you put in: he thought fleetingly of how he had smashed the blue fox and found a dormant love, of Mark's coming to see "boy's bed," of Igor's standing up by him at the table and Deirdre's saying she didn't feel needed when Dr. V. asked her why she didn't join the others.

"Dar'dra." Tony clutched the handle of the mower. Yes, in a

sense there had been many nights like that over the years; he'd had a lot of beautiful things with Deirdre which had slowly changed him. "But now, Dar'dra," he said softly, "it's time to say good-bye."

"Yes." His eyes pierced the vines on the gate. "It's time to go out and get. . . ." He resumed his mowing as his monologue budded into a vision of Marta sitting beside him at the bar in Acapulco. Over the months, Marta had become only a shadow in his mind, but suddenly a vivid memory of the perfume on her ivory-smooth skin returned to him.

"Boy, John," he murmured, "there's a beautiful world out there waiting for me . . . and now I've had a lot of beautiful things at the School, but they'll all be nothing if I don't do as you say and put a hell of a lot into life by putting myself out into that world. After all, that's what the School's all about. It's not about itself, it's about the outside."

But aspiration was constantly plagued by reservation as he struggled hopelessly to integrate all he wanted to be with all he wanted to do. Maybe you're not ready to leave, he told himself, but it's just as likely that you are, so you might as well take the chance. He thought of the pelican, of the way it had cocked its eye at him on Chico's boat, and then again in his dream when he was in the carriage with Marta. "I wanta see the pelican. I wanta see the pelican. . . ." Tony yearned for the bird and the moment of communion that had lifted him out of himself to a deeply comforting but fleeting purity.

Now he realized all he would have to tell Dr. V. Yes, he had something beautiful, and that was what had to be communicated. Best, then, to go down Sunday. He would use the coming night to carefully plan what to say, and for the last time, entertain those nagging doubts against which it would be necessary to build arguments in preparation for whatever questions Dr. V. might ask. This was his plan when Deirdre came to get him at four-thirty.

While they put the lawn mower away, they talked about Laura, but neither had much to say. Tony groped for words the way he often did in session. He felt apprehension about his impending confrontation with Dr. V.

On the way up to the dormitory, Deirdre said she had made arrangements for the group to go get some supplies to prepare a picnic supper in the dormitory. “Hey, that’s a great idea!” Tony voiced his pleasure. Though he hadn’t realized it, he now knew he needed to have a simple good time.

While the group crossed the Midway, en route to the Fifty-seventh Street delicatessen, Tony noticed the sun, pale in a hazy sky. He became absorbed by the hot winds of late spring which blew with a strange, new intensity. Once again he thought of the pelican: “I’m closer to you now than when I first saw you,” he said softly.

When the Eagles got to the delicatessen, they heard a tornado warning and a thunder shower forecast over the radio. As they made their way back to the School, the winds grew wilder, and the sun slowly brightened the clouded skies so the whole atmosphere became radiant, darkly golden, unlike anything Tony had ever seen.

Deirdre had Tony and Harry shut the windows as soon as they got to the dormitory, but if the winds could no longer blow within, they were plainly audible without. They had a deep effect on Ronny. “Hey, Deirdre,” he said breathlessly, “guess what? This is the time of year when every true-blooded cowboy comes most alive because winds like these just get into his blood, and he just has to hit the trails.” Then, to everybody, “Gosh, I can hardly stand it. I know I should be out on the cattle drives in wide open spaces. I’m just not meant to be cooped up.”

At that point, Dr. V. put in an appearance, and Ronny abruptly ceased his line of talk. Dr. V. seemed to be in a good mood as he asked each boy in turn how he fared. “And how are you?” Tony reciprocated when Dr. V. got to him. “Oh, so so,” Dr. V. smiled.

“Like the rest of the world,” Tony laughed. After all, just what was so especially happy or exalted about Dr. V.’s life, about John’s or Deirdre’s?

Later, Tony, Igor, Ronny and Harry were all seated together at the table where they were fixing sandwiches. Across from them, Lewis was preparing a salad while out at the kitchenette Deirdre, Mickey, and Ralph were making fudge. “Gosh, the wind is something, isn’t it,” Igor said softly as he turned to Tony.

"Yes, I love it."

"Hey, y'you know, w'we have this blimp now, with a big window in it, and it can land right in front of the School just outside Dr. V.'s office. W'wouldn't it be neat to stuff it with blankets and take it out over the lake on a night like this?"

"Hmmmm," Tony grunted with interest. He liked the idea, but he did not want to encourage Igor's fantasies.

"Hey, m'maybe we could get Dr. V. to come along," Igor persisted.

"He's been pretty nice today, hasn't he?" Ronny broke in.

"Y'yes, he has," Igor agreed.

"You two seemed to be making up this afternoon," Tony commented to Ronny.

"Yes, I guess we were, sort of," Ronny smiled. "Oh! Let me tell you guys something—I had a neat dream last night! You want to hear about it?"

"Sounds like it ought to be interesting," Harry said.

"Well," Ronny began, "I dreamed that I had my ranch and there were always tourists coming from the crowded cities who wanted a vacation away from their scrunched-up sitting-down jobs. Anyway, one of the hands came along and told me there was this tourist up in the main house. So I went up to say hello, and there was Dr. V.!"

"Boy, Ronny, some dreams aren't hard to interpret." Tony spoke with exuberant happiness. "What happened then?"

"Oh, the dream ended."

"Hey, Ronny," Igor became inspired, "m'maybe when you have your ranch, I can fly Dr. V. out there in that blimp I was telling you about."

"Put it there, man!" Ronny thrust out his hand, imitating one of Ted's gestures. "I'll set up a special landing place just for blimps!" While Igor and Ronny shook hands, Tony and Harry smiled at each other.

Forty-five minutes later, everyone had eaten his fill. The wind was wilder than ever, and flashes of lightning cast fantastic hues in the turbulent skies. Deirdre asked Tony if he would check to make sure all the windows were locked. The last window was the one that faced the Midway. He paused by it, then settled himself on the shelf which jutted out beneath the sill. The golden twilight was a little frightening, but it also beckoned.

Suddenly the wind ceased and all was quiet. The whole world outside turned a dark yellowish tropical green, but green most of all, humid and luminous. This is how it must look when there's a storm over the Amazon, Tony decided, and he thought of the pelican flying in ominous skies over a lush expansive jungle. Thunder cracked violently directly overhead, and a torrential sea of rain exploded, rain wrenched viciously by new winds that swirled it in savage eddies.

Tony sprang to his knees, his elation exploding with the storm. "Ronny," he said softly, "get up on your horse, and go riding into the West. Only, when you get there, ask Dr. V. out to join you, and then break his sitting-down-job-ass into the saddle. It'll do him good.

"Igor, go up in your blimp, but don't forget to take us all along, and perhaps Dr. V. too so you can drop him at Ronny's ranch.

"And, as for you, Tony, you've had something beautiful which means that whole world out there is yours for the taking. You don't need to dream up any arguments. Just go down and claim it."

Tony heaved himself off the shelf and practically bumped into Harry. "Hey, what did I hear you say?" Harry asked.

"Look, Harry!" Tony pointed to the stormy outdoors.

"It's really something, isn't it?"

"Yes, and I want you to remember for the rest of your life that out in that world there are a thousand miserable situations in which a couple of bastards like us can make friends. Deirdre," Tony turned from Harry, "I want to see Dr. V."

Minutes later, Tony walked with Deirdre through the fire doors, on through the second floor hallway with its pungent mothball smell. At the top of the stairway leading down to Dr. V.'s office, they met Sam.

"Hey, Tony, you two spare me a minute?" Sam flashed his ready grin. "Something I wanta tell you."

"Sure, go on," Tony nodded.

"O.K., what I want to tell you is that stuff I said about the Marines back in the dormitory's all true as far as it goes, but there's more to it. See, we were just sort of ribbing you this afternoon. You know, about the brig. Now, like I said, the Marines are a tough outfit. We're so tough that the whole world feels it. And to be that way, life in the Marines has gotta be tough, tough, tough." Sam jabbed for emphasis. "But you know something? No place is as tough as this school. Are you going down to see the old man now?"

"Yeah, that's where I'm going."

"Hm, just where I was," Sam laughed. "Well, let me tell you. If you can buck that old man, then you've got the rest of the world at your feet."

As he followed Deirdre down the stairs, Tony's transport was such that in retrospect he was not going to remember his feet touching the steps. Rather it was going to seem as if he'd been floating, then sitting across from Dr. V., waiting as Deirdre went out, feeling perfectly sure of himself, though not at all sure what he was going to say. Then there was a knock on the office door.

"Come in," Dr. V. called out.

The door opened. "Dr. V., can I see you?" It was one of the newer counselors from the girls' floor. Dr. V. stepped out into the hall, and they spoke for a moment.

"Tony, I'll be gone a few minutes. Can you wait for me?" Dr. V. looked back in at Tony.

"Sure," Tony nodded, "I'll wait right here." Then he was alone. He looked out the front window. The storm had ceased almost as swiftly as it had begun.

Dr. V.'s absence began to weigh heavily. Tony tensed at the thought that Dr. V. might be slapping somebody. Then, once again, the ever-plaguing doubt. He remembered the genital pleasure he had derived from the guide's mutilation of the lizard. The potential for that pleasure had not been extinguished by his experience with Laura. Despite his dream about the picture, the gap in his life yawned as wide as ever, and even though Igor had stood by him at the supper table, he still needed to be tough. Had he changed at all since last summer at Red Cloud when he had felt himself an outsider with other boys his age? Probably not.

Just what does the School have to offer that you can't get anywhere else? The old argument was useless as he faced up to the fallibility of the conviction that had impelled him to come down to Dr. V.

Dr. V. returned, and Tony began to talk. "I've been thinking about what I have to talk to you about for a long time. Really, it all started on the day my grandmother died," and he told Dr. V. what he'd recounted to Harry the previous night about the blue fox. He proceeded to other things: Igor's standing up by him at supper, Mark coming to see "boy's bed," and all that John had given him, his relationship with Deirdre, and even his private "staff meetings" with Harry, carefully omitting any explicit mention of what their talks were about. He also talked about his need to be tough, the gap in his life, his reaction to the guide and the lizard, and how he felt that his relationship with Deirdre and Laura had helped him to develop a different, non-aggressive sexual outlook. But that was all he said since he did not really want to discuss what he had experienced with Laura.

He talked feverishly, and soon he noticed he had begun to repeat himself. Also, it seemed to him that his presentation was disorganized. He paused for breath.

"Now take your time, Tony." Dr. V.'s reassurance had a calming effect.

"Well, I guess it all gets down to this," and Tony made an effort to summarize his case. "I feel I still have a lot of problems, but I also feel it's time to take all the beautiful things I've told you about out into the world where I can make best use of them. My feelings are very mixed, but I feel them very strongly, so I had to talk to you. It's almost as though those beautiful things will stop helping me if I just stay here."

"No, zat you don't have to vorry about," Dr. V. shook his head. Then he was silent for a very long moment. "Tony," he finally said, "at your present stage of development, I do not sink you could have told me anysing I vould like better to have heard from you, but, my dear boy, you are not ready to leave zis school."

"Well, what is it you think I can do here that I can't do elsewhere?" Tony shot back.

"You've just finished telling me many of zhe sings you have done here. Do you sink zhere is not more for you to do?"

"I feel I could do the same elsewhere."

"Tony, take my advice and stay."

"I'm sorry, but I just can't understand that advice."

"Don't apologize. Now vhy not accept zhe advice on credit? After all, I have often been right about you in zhe past vhen nobody else sought you could be helped. And if I am wrong, it only affects a few years, vhile if you are wrong, it can affect your whole life."

Tony was stumped. Then he looked up into Dr. V.'s eyes as he had during the confrontation over *The Lem Gitler Story*. "Dammit," he said, "I'm sorry, but I have a deep conviction which I just can't get rid of. I feel I'm ready to leave and even if I have my doubts about it, I want you to back my leaving unless you can ruin my conviction."

"I have no desire to ruin zis conviction, but let it stand zhe test of a little time. Zhere is no need here for a quick decision. And ve can talk about zis again over zhe next few months."

Moments later, Tony was standing before the fire doors in the front hallway. So, he thought, you haven't changed a damn thing, and he wondered how much he had seriously expected to change. But the storm in its stirring aftermath was still around him. He could feel it in the moist air with its damp smell of mothballs, and with a surge of joy he realized that his dream had not died. "Over the next few months, you'll just have to buck the old man. That's all there is to it." He spoke to himself with quiet courage.